LONG ROAD
TO MERCY

ALSO BY DAVID BALDACCI

ATLEE PINE SERIES
Long Road to Mercy

MEMORY MAN SERIES
Memory Man
The Last Mile
The Fix
The Fallen

WILL ROBIE SERIES
The Innocent
The Hit
The Target
The Guilty
End Game

JOHN PULLER SERIES
Zero Day
The Forgotten
The Escape
No Man's Land

KING & MAXWELL SERIES
Split Second
Hour Game
Simple Genius
First Family
The Sixth Man
King and Maxwell

THE CAMEL CLUB SERIES
The Camel Club
The Collectors
Stone Cold
Divine Justice
Hell's Corner

SHAW SERIES
The Whole Truth
Deliver Us from Evil

STANDALONES
Absolute Power
Total Control
The Winner
The Simple Truth
Saving Faith
Wish You Well
Last Man Standing
The Christmas Train
True Blue
One Summer

SHORT STORIES
Waiting for Santa
No Time Left
Bullseye

DAVID BALDACCI

LONG ROAD TO MERCY

GRAND CENTRAL
PUBLISHING

NEW YORK   BOSTON

Copyright © 2018 by Columbus Rose, Ltd.

Cover design by David Litman. Cover photo by Eduardo Garcia/Getty Images. Cover copyright © 2018 by Hachette Book Group, Inc.

Grand Central Publishing

Hachette Book Group

1290 Avenue of the Americas, New York, NY 10104

grandcentralpublishing.com

twitter.com/grandcentralpub

First Edition: November 2018

Grand Central Publishing is a division of Hachette Book Group, Inc. The Grand Central Publishing name and logo is a trademark of Hachette Book Group, Inc.

The publisher is not responsible for websites (or their content) that are not owned by the publisher.

The Hachette Speakers Bureau provides a wide range of authors for speaking events. To find out more, go to www.hachettespeakersbureau.com or call (866) 376-6591.

Library of Congress Cataloging-in-Publication Data has been applied for.

ISBNs: 978-1-5387-6157-1 (hardcover), 978-1-5387-1470-6 (large print), 978-1-5387-6453-4 (signed edition), 978-1-5387-6454-1 (B&N.com signed edition), 978-1-5387-6452-7 (B&N Black Friday signed edition), 978-1-5387-1436-2 (international trade), 978-1-5387-6155-7 (ebook)

Printed in the United States of America

LSC-H

10 9 8 7 6 5 4 3 2 1

To Kristen White, our right arm and left leg:
I don't know what we'd do without you,
and I hope we never find out.
To a wonderful colleague and friend.

LONG ROAD
TO MERCY

I

EENY, MEENY, MINY, MOE.

FBI Special Agent Atlee Pine stared up at the grim facade of the prison complex that housed some of the most dangerous human predators on earth.

She had come to see one of them tonight.

ADX Florence, about a hundred miles south of Denver, was the only supermax prison in the federal system. The supermax component was one of four separate encampments that made up the Federal Correctional Complex located here. In total, more than nine hundred inmates were incarcerated on this parcel of dirt.

From the sky, with the prison lights on, Florence might resemble a set of diamonds on black felt. The men here, guards and inmates, were as hardened as precious stone. It was not a place for the faint-hearted, or the easily intimidated, though the deeply demented were obviously welcome.

The supermax currently held, among others, the Unabomber, the Boston Marathon bomber, 9/11 terrorists, serial killers, an Oklahoma City bombing conspirator, spies, white supremacist leaders, and assorted cartel and mafia bosses. Many of the inmates here would die in federal prison under the official weight of multiple life sentences.

The prison was in the middle of nowhere. No one had ever

escaped, but if anyone did, there would be no place to hide. The topography around the prison was flat and open. Not a blade of grass, or a single tree or bush, grew around the complex. The prison was encircled by twelve-foot-high perimeter walls topped with razor wire and interlaced with pressure pads. These spaces were patrolled 24/7 by armed guards and attack dogs. Any prisoner reaching this spot would almost certainly be killed by either fangs or bullets. And few would care about a serial murderer, terrorist, or spy face-planting in the Colorado soil for the final time.

Inside, the cell windows were four inches wide and four feet long, cut in thick concrete, through which only the sky and roof of the facility could be seen. Florence had been designed so that no prisoner could even tell where in the structure he was located. The cells were seven-by-twelve and virtually everything in them, other than each inmate, was made from poured concrete. The showers automatically cut off, the toilets could not be stopped up, the walls were insulated so no inmate could communicate with another, the double steel doors slid open and closed on powered hydraulics, and meals came through a slot in the metal. Outside communication was forbidden except in the visiting room. For unruly prisoners, or in the case of a crisis, there was the Z-Unit, also known as the Black Hole. Its cells were kept completely dark, and restraints were built into each concrete bed.

Solitary confinement was the rule rather than the exception here. The supermax was not designed for prisoners to make new friends.

Atlee Pine's truck had been scoped and searched, and her name and ID checked against the visitors list. After that she was escorted to the front entrance and showed the guards stationed there her FBI special agent credentials. She was thirty-five, and the last twelve years of her life had been spent with a shiny badge riding on her hip. The gold shield was topped by an open-winged eagle, and below that was Justitia, holding her scales and sword. It was fitting, Pine thought, that a female was depicted on the badge of the preeminent law enforcement agency in the world.

She had relinquished her Glock 23 pistol to the guards. Pine had left in her truck the Beretta Nano that normally rode in an ankle holster. This was the only time she could remember voluntarily handing over her weapon. But America's only federal supermax had its own set of rules by which she had to abide if she wanted to get inside, and she very much did.

She was tall; over five eleven in her bare feet. Her height had come from her mother, who was an even six feet. Despite her stature, Pine was hardly lithe or willowy. She would never grace a runway or magazine cover as a stick-thin model. She was solid and muscular, which had come from pumping iron religiously. Her thighs, calves, and glutes were rocks, her shoulders and delts sculpted, her arms ropy with long cords of muscle, and her core was iron. She also had competed in MMA and kickboxing and had learned pretty much every way that a smaller person could take on and subdue a larger one.

All of these skills had been learned and enhanced with one aim in mind: survival, while toiling in what was largely a man's world. And physical strength, and the toughness and confidence that came with it, was a necessity. Her features were angular and came together in a particularly attractive, almost bewitching, manner. She had dark hair that fell to shoulder length and murky blue eyes that gave the impression of great depth.

She had never been to Florence before, and as she was escorted down the hall by two burly guards who hadn't uttered a word to her, the first thing that struck Pine was the almost eerie calm and quiet. As a federal agent, she had visited many prisons before. They were normally a cacophony of noise, screams, catcalls, curses, trash talk, insults and threats, with fingers curled around bars, and menacing looks coming out of the cells' darkness. If you weren't an animal before you went to a max prison, you would be one by the time you got out. Or else, you'd be dead.

It was *Lord of the Flies*.

With steel doors and flush toilets.

Yet here, it was as if she was in a library. Pine was impressed. It was no small feat for a facility housing men who, collectively, had slaughtered thousands of their fellow humans using bombs, guns, knives, poisons, or simply their fists. Or, in the case of the spies, with their treasonous acts.

Catch a tiger by its toe.

Pine had driven over from St. George, Utah, where she used to live and work. In doing so she'd motored across the entire state of Utah and half of Colorado. Her navigation device had told her it would take a little more than eleven hours to traverse the 650 miles. She had done it in under ten, having the benefit of a lead foot, a big-ass engine in her SUV, and a radar detector to get through the inevitable speed traps.

She'd stopped once to use a restroom and to grab something to eat for the road. Other than that, it had been pedal to the floor mat.

She could have flown into Denver and driven down from there, but she had some time off and she wanted to think about what she would do when she got to her destination. And a long drive through vast and empty stretches of America allowed her to do just that.

Having grown up in the East, she'd spent the majority of her professional life in the open plains of the American Southwest. She hoped to spend the rest of it there because she loved the outdoor lifestyle and the wide-open spaces.

After a few years at the Bureau, Pine had had her pick of assignments. This had been the case for only one reason: She was willing to go where no other agent wanted to. Most agents were desperate to be assigned to one of the FBI's fifty-six field offices. Some liked it hot, so they aimed for Miami, Houston, or Phoenix. Some aimed for higher office in the FBI bureaucracy, so they fought to get to New York or DC. Los Angeles was popular for myriad reasons, Boston the same. Yet Pine had no interest in any of those places. She liked the relative isolation of the RA, or resident agency, in the middle of nothing. And so long as she got results and was willing to pull the duty, people left her alone.

. And in the wide-open spaces, she was often the only federal law enforcement for hundreds of miles. She liked that, too. Some would call her aloof, a control freak, or antisocial, but she wasn't. She actually got along well with people. Indeed, you couldn't be an effective FBI agent without having strong people skills. But she did like her privacy.

Pine had taken a position at the RA in St. George, Utah. It was a two-person outfit and Pine had been there for two years. When the opportunity arose, she had transferred to a one-agent office in a tiny town called Shattered Rock. It was a recently established RA due west of Tuba City, and about as close to Grand Canyon National Park as it was possible to be without actually being in the park. There, she enjoyed the support of one secretary, Carol Blum. She was around sixty and had been at the Bureau for decades. Blum claimed former FBI director J. Edgar Hoover as her hero, though he'd died long before she joined up.

Pine didn't know whether to believe the woman or not.

Visiting hours were long since over at Florence, but the Bureau of Prisons had accommodated a request from a fellow fed. It was actually twelve a.m. on the dot, a fitting time, Pine felt, because didn't monsters come out only at the stroke of midnight?

She was escorted into the visiting room and sat on a metal stool on one side of a sheet of thick polycarbonate glass. In lieu of a phone, a round metal conduit built into the glass provided the only means to verbally communicate. On the other side of the glass, the inmate would sit on a similar metal stool bolted into the floor. The seat was uncomfortable; it was meant to be.

If he hollers let him go.

She sat awaiting him, her hands clasped and resting on the flat, laminated surface in front of her. She had pinned her FBI shield to her lapel, because she wanted him to see it. She kept her gaze on the door through which he would be led. He knew she was coming. He had approved her visit, one of the few rights he possessed in here.

Pine tensed slightly when she heard multiple footsteps approaching. The door was buzzed open, and the first person she saw was a beefy guard with no neck and wide shoulders that nearly spanned the door opening. Behind him came another guard, and then a third; both were equally large and imposing.

She briefly wondered if there was a minimum heft requirement for a guard here. There probably should be. Along with a tetanus shot.

She dropped this thought as quickly as she had acquired it, because behind them appeared a shackled Daniel James Tor, all six feet four inches of him. He was followed in by a trio of other guards. They effectively filled the small enclosure. The rule of thumb here, Pine had learned, was that no prisoner was moved from one place to another with fewer than three guards.

Apparently, Tor warranted double that number. She could understand why.

Tor had not a hair on his head. His eyes stared blankly forward as the guards seated him on his stool and locked his chains into a steel ring set into the floor. This was also not typical of the visiting policy here, Pine knew.

But it was obviously typical for fifty-seven-year-old Tor. He had on a white jumpsuit with black rubber-soled shoes with no laces. Black-framed glasses covered his eyes. They were one piece and made of soft rubber with no metal pins at juncture points. The lenses were flimsy plastic. It would be difficult to turn them into a weapon.

In prisons, one had to sweat the small details, because inmates had all day and night to think of ways to harm themselves and others.

She knew Tor's entire body under the jumpsuit was virtually covered in largely self-inked tats. The ones that he hadn't done himself had been inked on by some of his victims, forced into becoming tattoo artists before Tor had dispatched them into the hereafter. It was said that each tat told a story about a victim.

Tor weighed about 280 pounds, and Pine calculated that only about 10 percent of that would qualify as fat. The veins rippled in his forearms and neck. There wasn't much to do in here except work out and sleep, she assumed. And he had been an athlete in high school, a sports star, really, born with a genetically gifted physique. It was unfortunate that the superb body had been paired with a deranged, though brilliant, mind.

The guards, satisfied that Tor was securely restrained, left the way they had come. But Pine could hear them right outside the door. She was sure Tor could as well.

She imagined him somehow breaking through the glass. Could she hold her own against him? It was an intriguing hypothetical. And part of her wanted him to try.

His gaze finally fell upon her and held.

Atlee Pine had stared through the width of glass or in between cell bars at many monsters, a number of whom she had brought to justice.

Yet Daniel James Tor was different. He was perhaps the most sadistic and prolific serial murderer of his, or perhaps any, generation.

He rested his shackled hands on the laminated surface, and tilted his thick neck to the right until a kink popped. Then he resettled his gaze on her after flicking a glance at the badge.

His lips curled momentarily at the symbol for law and order.

"Well?" he asked, his voice low and monotone. "You called this meeting."

The moment, an eternity in the making, had finally come.

Atlee Pine leaned forward, her lips an inch from the thick glass.

"Where's my sister?"

Eeny, meeny, miny, moe.

2

THE DEAD-EYE STARE from Tor didn't change in the face of Pine's question. On the other side of the door where the guards lurked, Pine could hear murmurings, the shuffling of feet, the occasional smack of palm against a metal baton. Just for practice in case it needed to be wrapped around Tor's head at a moment's notice.

From Tor's expression, she knew he could hear it, too. He apparently missed nothing here, though he had eventually been caught because he had missed *something*.

Pine leaned slightly back on her stool, folded her arms across her chest, and waited for his answer. He could go nowhere, and she had nowhere to go that was more important than this.

Tor looked her up and down in a way that perhaps he had used in sizing up all his victims. There were thirty-four of them confirmed. *Confirmed*, not total. The actual number was feared to be triple the official count. She was here about an unconfirmed one. She was here about a single victim not even in the running to be added to the tally of this man's zealous depravity.

Tor had escaped a death sentence due solely to his cooperating with authorities, revealing the locations of three victims' remains. This revelation had provided a trio of families some closure. And it had allowed Tor to live, albeit in a cage, for the rest of his life. In her mind, Pine could see him easily, perhaps smugly, striking that bargain, knowing that he had gotten the better end of the deal.

His victims were dead. He wasn't. And this man was all about the death of others.

He'd been arrested, convicted, and sentenced in the midnineties. He'd killed two guards and another inmate at a prison in 1998. The state where this occurred did not have the death penalty, otherwise Tor would have been on death row or already executed. That had led to his being transferred to ADX Florence. He was currently serving nearly forty consecutive life terms. Unless he pulled a Methuselah, he would die right here.

None of this seemed to faze the man.

"Name?" he asked, as though he were a clerk at a counter checking on an order.

"Mercy Pine."

"Place and time?"

He was screwing with her now, but she needed to play along.

"Andersonville, Georgia, June 7, 1989."

He popped his neck once more, this time to the other side. He stretched out his long fingers, cracking the joints. The huge man seemed one enormous jumble of pressure points.

"Andersonville, Georgia," he mused. "Lots of deaths there. Confederate prison during the Civil War. The commandant, Henry Wirz, was executed for war crimes. Did you know that? Executed for doing his job." He smiled. "He was Swiss. Totally neutral. And they hanged him. Some weird justice."

The smile disappeared as quickly as it had emerged, like a spent match.

She said, "Mercy Pine. Six years old. She disappeared on June 7, 1989. Andersonville, southwestern Macon County, Georgia. Do you need me to describe the house? I heard your memory for your victims is photographic, but maybe you need some help. It's been a while."

"What color was her hair?" asked Tor, his lips parted, revealing wide, straight teeth.

In answer, Pine pointed to her own. "Same as mine. We were twins."

This statement seemed to spark an interest in Tor that had not been present before. She had expected this. She knew everything about this man except for one thing.

That one thing was why she was here tonight.

He sat forward, his shackles clinking in his excitement.

He glanced at her badge once more.

He said eagerly, "Twins. FBI. It's starting to make sense. Go on."

"You were known to be operating in the area in 1989. Atlanta, Columbus, Albany, downtown Macon." Using a tube of ruby red lipstick taken from her pocket, she drew a dot on the glass representing each of the aforementioned localities. Then, she connected these dots, and formed a familiar figure.

"You were a math prodigy. You like geometric shapes." She pointed to what she had drawn. "Here, a diamond shape. That's how they eventually caught you."

This was the *something* Tor had missed. A pattern of his own creation.

His lips pressed together. She knew that no serial murderer would ever admit to being outwitted. The man was clearly a sociopath *and* a narcissist. People often discounted narcissism as relatively harmless because the term sometimes conjured the clichéd image of a vain man staring longingly at his reflection in a pool of water or a mirror.

However, Pine knew that narcissism was probably one of the most dangerous traits someone could possess for one critical reason: The narcissist could not feel empathy toward others. Which meant that the lives of others held no value to a narcissist. Killing could even be like a hit of fentanyl: instant euphoria from the domination and destruction of another.

That was why virtually every serial murderer was also a narcissist. She said, "But Andersonville was not part of that pattern. Was it a one-off? Were you freelancing? What made you come to my house?"

"It was a *rhombus*, not a diamond," replied Tor.

Pine didn't respond to this.

He continued, as though lecturing to a class. "My pattern was a rhombus, a lozenge, if you prefer, a quadrilateral, a four-sided figure with four equal-length sides, and unequal-length diagonals. For example, a kite is a parallelogram only when it's a rhombus." He gave a patronizing glance at what she had drawn. "A diamond is not a true or precise mathematical term. So don't make that mistake again. It's embarrassing. And unprofessional. Did you even prepare for this meeting?" With his manacled hands, he gave a dismissive wave and disgusted look to the figure she'd drawn on the glass, as though she had imprinted something foul there.

"Thank you, that makes it perfectly clear," said Pine, who couldn't give a shit about parallelograms specifically, or math in general. "So why the one-off? You'd never broken a pattern before."

"You presume my pattern was broken. You presume I was in Andersonville on the night of June 7, 1989."

"I never said it was at night."

The smile flickered back. "Doesn't the boogeyman only come out at night?"

Pine reflected for a moment on her earlier thought about monsters only striking at midnight. To catch these killers, she had to think like them. It was and always had been a profoundly disturbing thought to her.

Before she could respond, he said, "Six years old? A twin? Where exactly did it take place?"

"In our bedroom. You came in through the window. You taped our mouths shut so we couldn't call out. You held us down with your hands."

She took out a piece of paper from her pocket and held it up to the glass, so he could see the writing on that side.

His gaze drifted down the page, his features unreadable, even to an experienced agent like Pine.

"A four-line nursery rhyme?" he said, tacking on a yawn. "What next? Will you break into song?"

"You thumped our foreheads as you recited it," noted Pine, who leaned forward a notch. "Each word, a different forehead. You started with me and ended on Mercy. Then you took her, and you did this to me."

She swept back her hair to reveal a scar behind her left temple. "Not sure what you used. It was a blur. Maybe just your fist. You cracked my skull." She added, "But you're a big man and I was just a little kid." She paused. "I'm not a little kid anymore."

"No, you're not. What, about five eleven?"

"My sister was tall, too, at age six, but skinny. Big guy like you, you could have carried her easily. Where did you take her?"

"Presumption again. As you said, I'd never broken a pattern before. Why would you think that I had then?"

Pine leaned even closer to the glass. "Thing is, I remember seeing you." She looked him over. "You're pretty unforgettable."

The lip curled again, like the string on a bow being pulled back. About to let loose a fatal arrow. "You remember seeing me? And you only show up now? Twenty-nine years later?"

"I knew you weren't going anywhere."

"A weak quip, and hardly an answer." He glanced at her badge again. "FBI. Where are you assigned? Somewhere near here?" he added a bit eagerly.

"Where did you take her? How did my sister die? Where are her remains?"

These queries were rapidly fired off, because Pine had practiced them on the long drive here.

Tor simply continued his line of thought. "I assume not a field office. You don't strike me as a main-office type. Your dress is casual and you're here outside visiting hours, hardly by the Bureau book. And there's only one of you. Your kind likes to travel in pairs if it's official business. Add to that the personal equation."

"What do you mean?" she asked, meeting his gaze.

"You lose a twin, you become a loner, like you lost half of yourself. You can't rely on or trust anyone else once that emotional cord is broken. You're not married," he added, glancing at her bare ring finger. "So you have no one to interrupt your lifelong sense of loss until one day you kick off, alone, frustrated, unhappy." He paused, looking mildly interested. "Yet something happened to lead you here after nearly three decades. Did it take you that long to work up the *courage* to face me? An FBI agent? It does give one pause."

"You have no reason not to tell me. They can take off another life sentence, it won't matter. Florence is it for you."

His next response was surprising, but perhaps it shouldn't have been.

"You've tracked down and arrested at least a half-dozen people like me. The least talented among them had killed four, the most talented had disposed of ten."

"Talented? Not the way I would describe it."

"But surely talent *does* come into play. It's not an easy business, regardless of what society thinks about it. The ones you arrested weren't in my league, of course, but you have to start somewhere. Now, you seem to have made a specialty of it. Of going toe-to-toe with the likes of me. It's nice to aim high, but one can grow too ambitious, or become overconfident. Flying too close to the sun with the wax betwixt the wings, that sort of thing. Death so often results. Now, it *can* be a divine look, but not, I think, on you. However, I'd love to try."

Pine shrugged off this deranged soliloquy ending with the threat against her. If he was thinking of killing her, that meant she had his attention.

She said, "They were all operating in the West. Here, you have wide-open spaces without a policeman on every block. People coming and going, lots of runaways, folks looking for something new, long strips of isolated highways. A billion places to toss the remains. It encourages... *talent* like yours."

He spread his hands as wide as he could with the restraints. "Now see, that's better."

"It would be far better if you answered my question."

"I also understand that you came within one pound of making the U.S. Olympic team as a weightlifter when you were in college." When she didn't respond he said, "Google has even reached Florence, Special Agent Atlee Pine from Andersonville, Georgia. I requested some background information on you as a condition for this meeting. You've also earned your own Wikipedia page. It's not nearly as long as mine, but then again, it's early days for you. But long careers are not guaranteed."

"It was one *kilo*, not one pound. The snatch did me in, never my best pull. I'm more of a clean-and-jerk girl."

"Kilos, yes. My mistake. So actually, you're a bit weaker than I thought. And, of course, a failure."

"You have no reason not to tell me," she repeated. "None."

"You want *closure*, like the rest of them?" he said in a bored tone.

Pine nodded, but only because she was afraid of the words that might come out of her mouth at that moment. Contrary to Tor's assertions, she had prepared for this meeting. Only, one could never fully prepare for a confrontation with this man.

"You know what I really, really like?" said Tor.

Pine kept staring at him but didn't react.

"I really, really like that I have defined your entire, pathetic life."

Tor suddenly leaned forward. His wide shoulders and massive bald head seemed to fill the glass, like a man coming in through a little girl's bedroom window. For one terrifying moment, Pine was six again and this demon was thumping her forehead with each word of the rhyme, with death to the one last touched.

Mercy. Not her.

MERCY.

Not her.

Then she let out a barely audible breath and involuntarily touched the badge on her jacket.

Her touchstone. Her lodestone. No, her rosary.

The movement did not go unnoticed by Tor. He didn't smile in triumph; his look was not one of anger but of disappointment. And then, a moment later, disinterest. His eyes hollowed out and his features relaxed as he sat back. He slumped down, his energy, and with it his animation, gone.

Pine felt every cell in her body start to shut down. She'd totally just screwed this up. He'd tested her, and Pine had not risen to the challenge. The boogeyman had come at midnight and found her lacking.

"Guards," he bellowed. "I'm ready. We're done here." As soon as he finished speaking, his lips spread into a malicious grin and Pine knew precisely why.

This was the only time he could order *them* around.

As they came in, unhooked him from the ring, and began to lead him away, Pine rose.

"You have no reason not to tell me."

He didn't deign to look at her.

"The meek shall never inherit the earth, Atlee Pine of Anderson-ville, twin of Mercy. Get used to it. But if you want to vent again, you know where to find me. And now that I've met you—" he suddenly looked back at her, a surge of ferocious desire flashing across his features, probably the last thing his victims ever saw "—I will *never* forget you."

The metal portal shut and locked behind him. She listened to the march of feet taking Tor back to his seven-by-twelve poured-concrete cage.

Pine stared at the door a moment longer, then wiped the lipstick off the glass, the color of blood transferred to her palm, retraced her footsteps, retrieved her gun, and left ADX Florence, breathing in crisp air at exactly one mile above sea level.

She would not cry. She hadn't shed a tear since Mercy had vanished. Yet she wanted to feel *something*. But it just wasn't there. She was weightless, like being on the moon, nothing, empty. He had drained whatever she had left right out of her. No, not drained.

Sucked.

And, worst of all, what had happened to her sister was still unknown.

She drove a hundred miles west to Salida and found the cheapest motel she could, since this trip was all on her dime.

Right before she fell asleep, she thought back to the question Tor had asked.

And you only show up now? Twenty-nine years later?

There was a good reason for this, at least in Pine's mind. But maybe it was also a flawed one.

She didn't dream about Tor that night. She didn't dream of her sister, gone nearly three decades now. The only visual her subconscious held up was herself at six years old trudging to school for the first time without Mercy's hand inside hers. A bereaved little girl in pigtails who had lost her other half, as Tor himself had intimated.

The better half of her, thought Pine, because she had been the one constantly in trouble, while her ten-minute-older "big" sister had habitually stood up for her, or covered for her, in equal measure. Unfailing loyalty and love.

Pine had never felt that again, not in her entire life.

Maybe Tor was right about her future.

Maybe.

And then his other jab, the one that had gotten through her defenses, and nailed her right in the gut.

You define me?

When she felt her lips begin to tremble, she rose, stumbled to the bathroom, and stuck her head under the shower. She left it there until the cold was so unbearable she nearly screamed out in pain. Yet not a single tear mingled with the freezing tap water.

She rose at the crack of dawn, showered, dressed, and headed home. Halfway there she stopped to get something to eat. As she got back into her SUV the text landed in her phone.

She sent off a reply, closed the truck door, fired up the engine, and floored it.

3

THE GRAND CANYON was one of the seven natural wonders of the world, and the only one located in America. It was the second largest canyon on earth, behind Tsangpo Canyon in Tibet, which was a bit longer but much deeper. The Grand Canyon was visited by five million people from around the globe every year. However, no more than 1 percent of those folks would ever reach the spot where Atlee Pine was currently: the banks of the Colorado River right on the floor of the canyon.

Phantom Ranch, located at the bottom of the Canyon, was not only the most popular under-roof accommodation down here, it was the *only* one. Those who trekked down here could do so in one of three ways: by water, on a mule, or courtesy of their own two feet.

Pine had driven to the Grand Canyon National Park Airport. There, she had climbed inside a waiting National Park Service chopper and made the vertical descent to the canyon bottom. After landing, Pine and her companion, Park Service Ranger Colson Lambert, had immediately set off on foot.

She strode along, eating up ground with her long legs, her gaze looking and her ears listening for rattlers. That was one reason nature had given them a rattle—to make people leave them alone.

Where's my rattle? thought Pine.

"When was it found?" she asked.

"This morning," replied Lambert.

They passed a slight curve in the rock, and Pine eyed a blue tarp that had been erected around the remains of their victim. Pine counted two men there. One was dressed as a wrangler. The other, like Lambert, was in the uniform of the National Park Service: gray shirt, light-colored, flat-brimmed hat with a black band on which were printed the letters USNPS. Pine knew him. His name was Harry Rice. In physique, he was a carbon copy of Lambert.

The other man was long and lean, and his face had been viciously carved by the outdoor life he led in an unforgiving environment. He had thick, graying hair that had been shaped by the wide-brimmed hat he held in one hand.

Pine flashed her badge and said, "What's your name?"

"Mark Brennan. I'm one of the mule wranglers."

"Did you discover it?"

Brennan nodded. "Before breakfast. Saw the buzzards circling."

"Be more precise about the time."

"Um, seven thirty."

Pine passed by the privacy tarp, squatted down, and looked over the carcass as the others gathered around her.

The mule weighed more than a half ton, she figured, and would stand about sixteen hands high. A mare bred with a donkey produced a mule. They pulled more slowly than horses, but were surer footed, lived longer, and pound for pound were about as strong as anything on four legs and possessed enormous endurance.

Pine slapped on a pair of latex gloves she had pulled from her fanny pack. She picked up a whip lying next to the unfortunate animal. Called a *motivator* by the mule wranglers, it was used by the riders to convince the mules to ignore the pleasures of grass sticking out of the rock on the trail, or the advantages of simply taking a nap standing up.

She touched the severely stiffened foreleg of the beast.

"It's in rigor. Definitely been here a while." Pine said to the wrangler, "You found it at seven thirty. Was it stiff like now?"

Brennan shook his head. "No. Had to chase some critters away, though. They were already starting to get into it. You can see that there and there," he added, pointing to various places where flesh had been ripped away.

Pine checked her watch. It was six thirty p.m. Eleven hours had passed since the mule had been found. Now she needed to establish a parameter at the other end.

She shifted her position and looked at the belly of the beast.

"Gutted," she noted. "Upward stroke and then a slit along the belly." Pine looked up at Brennan. "I take it this is one of yours?"

Brennan nodded and squatted on his haunches. He looked sadly at the dead animal. "Sallie Belle. Steady as a rock. Damn shame."

Pine looked at the dried blood. "Her death wouldn't have been painless. No one heard anything? Mules can make a lot of noise, and this canyon is one big subwoofer."

"It's miles from the ranch," suggested Rice.

"There's a park ranger station down here," noted Pine.

"It's still a long way away, and the ranger on duty didn't hear or see anything."

"Okay, but there had to be plenty of hikers and boaters at the Bright Angel Campground next to Phantom Ranch. The Ranch can't accommodate all of them, and the rest go to Bright Angel for the most part. And while I know it's 'a long way away,' the mule had to get from the Ranch corral to here."

Lambert said, "There *were* lots of people there. But no one we talked to saw or heard anything."

She said, "More to the point, who has the balls to lean under a mule and start slicing into its belly?"

Brennan said, "Right. And my two cents? You gut a mule you're going to hear it in the next county."

Pine eyed the saddle. "Okay, so who and where is the rider?"

"Benjamin Priest," said Rice. "No sign of him."

Brennan took up the thread. "He came down yesterday. Part of a crew of ten."

"That's your limit, right?" said Pine.

"Yeah. We bring two groups each day. We were in the first group."

"So, he rode down here and then what?"

"We stopped overnight at Phantom. We were going to head out this morning after breakfast. Over the Black Bridge and back up to the South Rim. Just like normal."

"It's about five and a half hours down and close to the same back up?" said Pine.

"Just about, yeah," agreed Brennan.

Pine surveyed the area. It was over eighty degrees on the canyon floor and twenty degrees cooler on the South Rim. She could feel the sweat collecting on her face and armpits and around the small of her back.

"When was it noticed that Priest was missing?"

Rice said, "This morning when folks came to the dining hall for breakfast."

"Where was Priest staying? In one of the dorms or a cabin?"

Brennan said, "One of the cabins."

"Tell me about last night."

Brennan said, "They all had dinner in the dining hall. Some folks played cards, wrote postcards. Some sat on boulders and cooled their feet in the creek. Typical stuff. Then everyone went off to their sleeping quarters, including Priest."

"When was the last time anyone saw him?"

Rice answered, "Best as we can tell, around nine last night."

"But no one actually saw him get in his bunk or leave the cabin later?"

"No."

"So how did Sallie Belle get here?" she asked, looking at Brennan.

"At first I just thought she had gotten out somehow. Then I

noticed her saddle and bridle were missing. Someone had to put them on her."

She continued to watch Brennan. "What were you thinking when the mule was missing?"

"Well, I thought maybe somebody had decided to go off on a joyride before breakfast." He shook his head. "I've seen folks do some crazy shit down here."

"Describe Priest."

"Late forties, early fifties. About five feet eight. Around one eighty."

"White? Black?"

"White. Dark hair."

"Good shape?"

"He was thick. But not really overweight. No marathon runner, though."

"You have a two-hundred-pound limit for mule riders?"

Brennan nodded. "That's right."

"Did you ever talk to him?"

"Some, coming down."

"Seem nervous?"

"He looked a little green a few times. Mules have fused spines and they walk along the outside of the trail. So their torsos and, along with them, the riders, are sometimes going to be over the edge. It can be unnerving at first. But he soldiered on."

She looked at Lambert. "What do you have on him?"

Lambert took out a notebook and unclipped the cover. "He's from DC. Works at one of those Beltway government contractors. Capricorn Consultants."

"Family?"

"Not married, no children. Has a brother who lives in Maryland. Parents are deceased."

"So you've notified him?"

"He was listed as the emergency contact on Priest's paperwork. We let him know that his brother is missing."

"I'll need his contact info."

"I'll email it to you."

"How did his brother sound?"

Rice answered. "Worried. He wanted to know if he should fly out. I told him to sit tight. Most people who go missing do turn up okay."

"But some don't," replied Pine. "Where's his stuff?"

Lambert said, "Gone. Must've taken it with him."

Rice said, "His brother phoned Priest after I talked to him. Also tried his email. He called me back and told me there was nothing. No response."

"Social media activity?"

"I didn't think to ask about that," said Rice. "I can follow up."

"How'd he get here? Car? Bus?"

"I heard him say he came by the train," volunteered Brennan.

"Where was he staying?"

Rice said, "We checked at El Tovar, Bright Angel, Thunderbird, and the rest of the possible places. He wasn't booked at any of them."

"He had to stay somewhere."

"It could have been at one of the campgrounds, either inside the park or nearby," noted Lambert.

"Okay, he took the train up here. But if he came from DC he probably first flew into Sky Harbor. He might have stayed somewhere there until he went to Williams, Arizona. That's where the train leaves from, right?"

Lambert nodded. "There's a hotel at the train depot. He might have stayed there."

"Have you made a search down here?"

"We covered as much ground as we could. No trace so far. And we're losing the light."

Pine took all this in. In the distance came the sharp bark of a coyote followed by the echoing rattle of a snake. There might be a standoff going on out there between predators as the lights of nature grew dim, thought Pine. The muscular walls of the canyon held a complex series of fragile ecosystems. It was the human factor that had intruded here. Nature always seemed to get on all right until people showed up.

She turned her head to the left, where a long way away lay Lake Mead near Arizona's border with Nevada. To the right, and also a great distance away, was Lake Powell in Utah. In between these two bodies of water sat the gargantuan Canyon, a deep gash on the surface of Arizona, visible not only from an airliner at thirty-five thousand feet, but also from outer space.

"We'll need to bring in an organized search team tomorrow and go grid by grid," said Pine. "As far as possible. What about the other mule riders with Priest? And the campers?"

Lambert said, "They all headed out. Some before we even knew Priest was missing."

"I'll still need all their names and contact info," said Pine. "And let's hope if something *did* happen to Priest that we didn't let whoever did it hike or ride a mule or raft it out of here."

Lambert looked uncomfortable with this and quickly glanced at his fellow ranger.

"Anybody keep watch over the mules during the night?" Pine asked.

Brennan shook his head. "I checked on them around eleven last night. Everything was fine. We got some coyotes and mountain lions down here, but they're not going after a pack of mules in an enclosure. They'd get the shit stomped out of them."

"Right, like someone would have when they gutted her," said Pine pointedly, looking at the dead Sallie Belle. "So at least at eleven, Sallie Belle was alive. The ranger on duty didn't hear anything. What's his name?"

"Sam Kettler."

"How long's he been with NPS?"

"Five years. Two here at the Canyon. He's a good guy. Ex-military."

"I'll need to talk to him," said Pine as she mentally catalogued all she had to do. Then her gaze ran over the dead animal. Something was not making sense.

"Why is the bleed-out above the mule's withers? It should be below the belly."

She looked up at the men, who stared blankly back at her.

"The mule's been moved," Pine said. "Help me turn her."

They each grabbed a leg and maneuvered the dead animal onto her other side.

There, carved on the mule's hide, were two letters: *j* and *k*.

"What the hell does that mean?" said Lambert.

What the hell does *that mean?* thought Pine.

CHAPTER

4

THIS IS SAM KETTLER," said Colson Lambert.

Pine had been standing on the front porch of the Phantom Ranch dining hall when Lambert had approached with another man dressed in a ranger uniform.

"He was on duty when Priest and the mule went missing," Lambert added.

Pine took Kettler in with one efficient sweep.

He was nearly six two, his forearms tanned and heavily muscled. He took off his hat to wipe sweat from his forehead, revealing close-cropped, light blond hair. He looked about her age. His eyes were light gray. He was an attractive man, she thought, the muscles of his lean jaw clenching and unclenching as he stood there.

"Colson said you didn't hear anything?"

Kettler shook his head. "It was a pretty quiet night after the campers went to bed. I made rounds, did some paperwork, checked on a trash can that someone didn't secure properly. Critters got inside and made a mess. Shooed them away. Other than that it was pretty routine."

"Colson's filled you in?"

Kettler shifted his feet. "A rider missing and a mule cut up." He grimaced. "Sick stuff."

Pine said, "My basic questions are, why take out the mule, and why kill it? Now, we don't know for sure that Priest did any of that. Someone else could have done it, and maybe Priest stumbled onto it and the person had to shut him up."

"That's true," conceded Lambert.

Pine shook her head. Her gut was telling her that this theory was not true. Too many coincidences. Too many things that had to go both right and wrong for it to happen.

Life was not the movies, or books. Sometimes the simplest answer was the right one.

She flicked a glance at Kettler. "Think again. You see anything out of the ordinary?"

He shook his head. "If I had, I would have reported it."

"No sounds of a mule being ridden away?"

"I'm pretty sure I would have heard that. What time do you think it happened?"

"Not sure. After eleven, certainly."

"My rounds carried me pretty far from the corral. If the mule was taken out then, I wouldn't have heard it necessarily."

"Okay, you think of anything else, let me know."

"Will do. Good luck."

He walked off at a good pace, covering the ground easily and quickly. She noted the bulge of his shoulders as his shirt pulled tight against them.

"What now?" asked Colson, drawing her attention away from the departing Kettler.

"Considering we're going to be searching the Canyon starting early tomorrow morning, I'm going to have some dinner and go to bed."

Hours later Pine was staring up at the ceiling of a ten-by-ten spare room at Phantom Ranch. The staff had found a mattress for her and a sheet and a lumpy pillow. This was her home for the night. There was no hardship in this: She had spent much of her life staring up at ceilings in places that did not belong to her.

Phantom Ranch was located in an area that had originally been called Roosevelt Camp, after President Theodore Roosevelt. He'd stayed there in 1913, after declaring the Grand Canyon a national monument. Pine had also learned that it had been Roosevelt who'd ordered the Havasupai Indian tribe to leave the area so that the park could be constructed, essentially evicting them from their home. The defiant Havasupai had taken twenty-five years to do so, long after Roosevelt's death.

Pine didn't blame them.

The current Phantom Ranch had been designed and named by Mary Elizabeth Jane Colter, the famed Canyon architect. It had been built in 1922 and was shaded by yellow cottonwood trees and sycamore trees, and had dirt paths crisscrossing throughout. It was a little oasis down at the inner gorge of the Canyon. In the little canteen was a mail pouch for visitors to put their postcards in. The mule train would take it up the following day. The postcards were all stamped with: "Mailed by Mule from the bottom of the Grand Canyon." What could be cooler than that in a world of smartphones and devices named Alexa that ruled your life?

She had some changes of clothes and other necessities that she always kept in her truck, along with her investigative duffel. These she had transferred onto the chopper that had carried her down to the Canyon floor. Out here, there weren't FBI forensics teams just waiting to go in and "CSI" any crime scene that needed parsing. FBI special agents stationed at small RAs pretty much did it all.

And she was the FBI's point person for the Grand Canyon. So, right now, Pine was a cavalry of one. And that was just fine with her.

The current hikers and mule riders were all in their beds in either the dorms or the slant-roofed rustic cabins. Pine had eaten with them in the large dining hall at a long table with wooden-back chairs on the floor and old, dark ceiling beams above. No one knew who she was, and she volunteered no information about herself or why she was there.

Pine wasn't into small talk; she much preferred to listen to other people. You learned something that way.

At dinner, she'd opted for the stew and cornbread and three glasses of water. Hydration was important down here. She'd spoken again with Lambert and Brennan before hitting the sack. Now it was nearly one a.m., and outside the thermometer still hovered near eighty, making the room close and warm. She'd opened the window to let some air in and had stripped down to her underwear, her two pistols within easy reach.

She had no idea where Benjamin Priest might be. He could have hiked out of the canyon by now, but surely someone would have seen him. His description had been given out to everyone by the rangers. It had been posted on NPS's website. And if he had killed and carved those letters on Sallie Belle for some inexplicable reason, he would be held accountable.

She had written up her case notes and emailed her superiors the details, sending along the list and contact information of the hikers, rafters, and mule riders that she had gotten from the Park Police. These would be fanned out to agency offices across the country, so that follow-up could be done. The Flagstaff office had also been notified and had advised her to keep them abreast of developments.

There was nothing more to do, really, until morning.

She listened to the sharp wind outside, and the sounds of flowing water from nearby Bright Angel Creek.

They had posted two sentries by the carcass. Otherwise, poor Sallie Belle would probably be picked clean by nocturnal predators. Pine opened her eyes as the Grand Canyon and the dead mule were pushed aside for the time being in her thoughts.

In their place emerged Daniel James Tor.

In some ways Pine had waited nearly her entire life to confront the man she believed was responsible for her sister's disappearance.

Why twenty-nine years?

Six months ago, Pine had only a vague memory of the man who had entered their bedroom nearly thirty years before. Doctors had called it many things, but it boiled down to amnesia brought on by her youth and the traumatic circumstances of the event. For Pine's own well-being, her mind wouldn't let her remember. Not as a child, and apparently not as an adult, either.

Her mother had found her unconscious and bleeding in her bed early the next morning, the tape still over her mouth. An ambulance had been called. She had been taken to the hospital. They feared for her life numerous times during a series of major operations. Eventually, her skull had healed; there had been no permanent damage done to her brain. Thus, she had eventually gone home from the hospital, the only child now left in the Pine household.

She had been of little help to the police. And by the time she arrived home, the case had grown cold.

Pine had gone on with her life. Her parents had divorced, principally because of what had happened that night. Both only in their midtwenties, they had been drunk and high and had never heard an intruder come into their home, eventually falling asleep while one daughter lay grievously injured and the other was spirited away by the nighttime invader. They each blamed the other for that.

And, in addition to that, the primary suspects had been her parents. One cop in particular thought that Pine's father, drugged out and stoned, had gone into his daughters' room and taken Mercy, killing her and disposing of her body somewhere.

And though both her mother and father had passed a polygraph and Pine had said that her father wasn't the man who had come into the room that night, the police really hadn't believed her. The town quickly turned against the Pines and they'd had to move.

After the divorce, Pine had lived with her mother, enduring an existence forever changed by Mercy's disappearance.

As Pine had grown older, her life had seemed aimless, her ambitions nonexistent. She felt no purpose in anything. It seemed her only goal was to simply underachieve at everything. She had already started drinking and smoking weed. Her grades were for shit. She got into fights, suffered detentions, and got busted by the cops for underage drinking. On numerous occasions, she'd even shoplifted stuff. She didn't care about anyone or anything, including herself.

Then she had gone to a county fair and, on a whim, had decided to have her fortune told. The woman in the little tent had been dressed up with a turban and veils and colorful robes. Pine had remembered smirking at all this, certain it was a sham.

Then the woman had taken hold of her hand and looked down at her palm. But her gaze had almost immediately returned to Pine's face.

The woman's features exhibited confusion.

"What?" Pine had asked in a disinterested tone.

"I feel two pulses. Two hearts."

Pine had stiffened. She hadn't told the woman she was a twin. She hadn't told the woman anything.

The woman looked at Pine's palm more closely, feeling along a line on the hand.

Her brows knitted.

"What?" Pine asked again, this time totally focused.

"Two heartbeats, certainly." She paused. "But only one soul."

Pine had stared at the woman, and the woman had stared back at her.

"Two heartbeats and one soul?" said Pine. When the woman nodded, she'd asked, "How can that be possible?"

The woman had said, "I think you know that it is more than possible. You know that it is *true*."

From that moment on, Pine had pushed herself relentlessly at everything she had attempted. It was as though she were trying to live two lives instead of simply one. To achieve for her sister, to accomplish what Mercy never had the chance to do on her own.

Her physical size, natural strength, and athleticism had led her to be a star sportswoman in high school. She played basketball, ran track, and was the pitcher on the state championship softball team.

Then on a dare she had joined the boys' football team in the weightlifting room and discovered that she could lift more than many of them. That was when her passion and drive and ferocious ambition had been focused on the barbells. She had risen like a rocket onto the national scene, winning trophies and acclaim wherever she went.

Some billed her as the strongest woman, pound for pound, in America.

And then she had gone on to college, where she had tried, and failed, to make the Olympic squad.

By a single kilo, about 2.2 pounds.

The feeling of failure, not really for herself but actually for her twin, had been paralyzing. But there was nothing she could do about it except move on.

Next up was the world of the FBI, her career, the only one Pine believed she would ever have.

And in that career, she had always consciously steered herself west, because out here, in the great open spaces, some of the worst predators on earth hunted for their victims. She had read about them all, researched them all. She had grown so good at profiling, in fact, that she had been offered a slot at the Behavioral Analysis Unit 3 at the Bureau. That unit investigated crimes against children.

She had declined. She did not want to profile monsters, though technically there was no such position as a *profiler* at the FBI. That was a myth perpetuated by popular culture.

Instead, Pine wanted to put her handcuffs on these offenders, read them their rights, and watch as the justice system put them in a place where they could never hurt anyone again.

This future for her had been ordained the moment Mercy's

forehead had been last thumped by the finger, and by the man saying, with chilling finality, "moe."

And that was where her life stood, until six months ago.

Then, a friend who knew something of Pine's history suggested that she try memory reconstruction through hypnosis.

She had heard of the process, because the Bureau had undertaken it with some of their cases with mixed results. It was a controversial subject, its supporters and critics equally vocal. And Pine knew that the procedure had led to false memories conjured and innocent people harmed as a result.

Yet she had nothing to lose by trying it.

After Pine's multiple sessions with the hypnotherapist, Daniel James Tor had finally emerged from deep within her subconscious, like a sadistic beast climbing from its hellish hole into the blast of daylight.

The problem was that prior to being hypnotized, Pine had known all about Tor for a long time. Anyone who studied serial murders would know the name of Daniel James Tor. He made the likes of Ted Bundy seem inefficient and inept. She had studied his career, the arc of his active periods, the backgrounds of his victims.

Thus, the obvious questions had to be asked: Did she pull Tor out of her subconscious because he really did come through that window on the night of June 7, 1989? Or did he fall out of her mind because she wanted him to? Because he had been in the area during that time? Would the man lead to closure for her, whether he actually did it or not?

Pine's father was long dead: He had swallowed a round of double-aught buckshot after drinking and drugging in a craphole motel in Louisiana for a week, ending his life on his daughters' birthday. Pine did not consider that to be a coincidence. Her father had perhaps been trying to show her he felt guilty for what had happened. Instead, he ensured that every one of her birthdays would share the memory of her father's having blown his head off.

Her mother was still alive. Pine knew where she was, but the two had grown apart. Adulthood had not drawn daughter closer to mother; if anything, it had increased the distance, maybe rivaling that of the Grand Canyon's massive width.

Perhaps it was even wider, because, as Pine had found, the mind could really accomplish anything, particularly when it was playing games with you. It could make you see things that weren't there, or not see things that were staring you right in the face.

So was it Tor, or had the hypnosis been a complete bust?

The truth was, she didn't know.

She closed her eyes again, but they almost immediately fluttered open. It wasn't because she couldn't sleep. It was because there was someone moving outside.

It took Pine twenty seconds to pull on her clothes and shoes and place her backup Beretta in the ankle holster and grip the Glock 23 in her right hand.

And then she did what she always did.

Atlee Pine charged straight toward the unknown.

CHAPTER

5

IN THE WIDE-OPEN SPACES of northern Arizona, with little competition from ambient light, the sky was littered with stars.

Yet in the depths of the Grand Canyon, while the sky was clearly visible, the stars seemed to have lost a bit of their luster when their light had to travel all the way down to the floor of the canyon. And that was when you realized how steep the walls were. They seemed to absorb every bit of light before it could get to the bottom.

Pine crouched in the darkness and performed a 360-degree sight line, pivoting on her heels as she did so.

No one was out that she could see. The darkness was not broken by someone sneaking a smoke, which was illegal in the canyon due to fire danger. There was no light from a phone. Depending on one's phone carrier, you either had spotty reception or none at all. There was no Wi-Fi. The Ranch had a pay phone that accepted credit cards. That was it in the technology department. Facebook, Instagram, and Twitter addicts would have to wait until they returned rimside to indulge their habit.

Her gaze kept arching out farther and farther, taking in more darkened ground.

There it was again.

Stealth. Not casual. She had experienced both and instinctively knew what separated one from the other.

She made her way forward in a half crouch, one hand firmly on her Glock.

In her other hand was a Maglite. Its beam would catch on a scorpion here and there, outlining the venomous creatures in a burst of startling white.

Then came the whinny of a mule. There were two mule corrals down here, a commercial one for Phantom Ranch and one farther away that was used by the Park Service. But that corral was on the other side of Bright Angel Creek and near the banks of the Colorado. This whinny had to come from the nearer one, Pine knew.

So maybe whoever was out there was looking to take out another mule and dispose of it, and maybe add more alphabet letters to its hide. Was it the AWOL Benjamin Priest in some fit of insanity against large animals?

She made her way quickly and as quietly as possible to the corral.

Pine continued to shine the light over the ground as she walked along. There were six species of rattlesnakes down here, and they all came out at night. She wasn't all that worried about stepping on a rattler. They could feel the vibrations of her feet against the dirt and would move away.

The corral was a hundred feet ahead. The steps she had been hearing had stopped.

A moment later she heard another whinny followed by a snort.

And then on her left, she saw movement. The man came out of the darkness and showed himself to Pine.

It was Sam Kettler. He put a finger to his lips and pointed in the direction of the mule corral. Pine nodded.

Kettler skittered over to her.

"Someone's down there," Pine said.

"I know. I've been following both of you, I guess."

"See who it was?"

"No."

"Well, let's go find out. You armed?"

Kettler patted his holster. "Hope I won't need it. I didn't join the Park Service to shoot people. Had enough of that in the Army."

They moved forward together, with the least noise possible.

Pine noted approvingly how Kettler moved, his silhouette kept to a minimum, each step carefully chosen. He seemed to glide, not walk, over the uneven ground.

The corral was now in her sight line.

She inserted her Maglite on the rail on top of her Glock right as she reached the corral.

Kettler took out his pistol and thumbed off the safety.

The disturbance was coming from the far side.

Kettler pointed to himself and then motioned to the left. Pine nodded and headed right.

A few moments later she started to sprint, turned the corner, and stopped, her light and gun muzzle on the person in front of her.

Kettler was already there, his weapon trained on the same target.

The person screamed and jumped back.

"FBI! Hands up where I can see them, or I will fire," Pine commanded.

She relaxed just a tiny bit because the person looked to be a teenage girl.

"Oh, shit," exclaimed the girl. She was dressed in shorts, with crew socks and flip-flops and a short-sleeved T-shirt. She started to cry. "Please don't hurt me. God, please don't shoot."

Pine dropped her muzzle to forty-five degrees. Her gaze was on the long object in the girl's right hand. She took a step closer and then pointed her muzzle to the dirt.

It wasn't a knife. It was a carrot.

Kettler stepped forward, but lowered his gun as well.

"What the hell are you doing out here?" demanded Pine.

The girl held up the carrot. "I came to feed Jasmine. She's the mule I rode down."

"Do you know a mule was found dead yesterday morning?"

The girl nodded. "I guess that's why I came down here, too. I wanted to check on them."

Pine holstered her gun. "What's your name?"

"Shelby Foster."

"Okay, Shelby. Are you here with your family?"

"My dad and brother."

"Where are you from?"

"Wisconsin. There's nothing like this place there. It's so beautiful here."

"Yeah, it is. Okay, Shelby, feed Jasmine her carrot, and then we're going to walk you back to where you're bunking."

Kettler put his gun away, too, and looked down at the flimsy flip-flops. "There are rattlers and scorpions around here, ma'am. That's hardly appropriate footwear."

"I have boots back at the cabin. I just didn't want to put them back on. My feet are all swollen from the ride down."

Kettler smiled kindly. "Yeah, that happens. But next time, think before you walk, okay?"

Later, as they walked back to one of the cabins, Shelby said to Pine, "So you're an FBI agent?"

"Yes, I am."

"I thought they were mostly guys."

"They are. But I'm not."

"That's cool, actually."

"Yeah, it is," Kettler agreed, drawing a glance from Pine.

"Did you find out who killed the mule?" Shelby asked.

"Not yet, but we will."

"Who could have done such a horrible thing?"

"Unfortunately, there are horrible people out there, Shelby. So always be aware of your surroundings. Don't watch your phone screen 24/7. And don't have earbuds in all the time. That makes you an easy target. Be aware. Okay?" When the teenager looked crushed, Pine tacked on a smile and added, "Girls have to look out for each other. Right?"

Shelby returned the smile and nodded, and Pine watched as she hurried into her cabin.

Kettler said, "Well, I better get back."

"Thanks for the assist, Mr. Kettler."

"My old man is Mr. Kettler. I'm just Sam."

"I'm Atlee."

Kettler looked around. "You know, I came down here for some peace and quiet. Never expected anything like this to happen. Everybody's on edge."

"You've had missing persons down here before."

"Yeah, but we've never had a mule killed. For some reason, that's upset me more than the missing person." He nodded at her. "Let me know if I can do anything to help."

Pine took out a business card and handed it to him. "Cell phone's on the back of the card. You think of something, or just want to talk, give me a ring."

He tipped his hat. "Maybe we can catch a beer sometime. Colson said you live up at Shattered Rock."

"Yeah. Been there about a year."

"I'm in Tusayan, not that far away."

"No, it's not."

He slipped the card into his shirt pocket. "Well, see you around."

He smiled and walked off. She watched him go, her thoughts settling on something she had just learned.

If the teen had been able to leave her cabin and get to the corral pretty much undetected that meant Benjamin Priest could have, too. The mule was dead. And maybe Priest was, too.

The Canyon was big, but it would be hard for a body to go undetected for long. At the very least the carnivores flying overhead or lurking on the ground would signal where it was located. But Pine was more interested in finding Priest alive. She had questions for him. She hoped he'd have answers. She didn't like people who killed animals, especially because they sometimes moved on to killing people.

She checked her watch. In about six hours they would start looking in earnest for Mr. Priest. And whether they found him dead or alive, Pine had a feeling that she was going to have a lot more questions. And that maybe, just maybe, this would only be the tip of the proverbial iceberg.

CHAPTER

6

P INE WIPED A BIT of sweat from her forehead before it leached into her eyes. She was sitting on a boulder and looking out toward the Colorado River. They had been at it for nearly eight hours, starting right after breakfast.

Seven rangers and her. To cover a land mass that, with the park above, was larger than the state of Rhode Island. Even using a chopper, the odds were not in their favor. And there were no circling buzzards to help them out.

So, they had found exactly nothing. No sign of Benjamin Priest. No sign of where or how he might have gotten out of the Canyon.

Pine gave another searching look around. If he had tried to climb out yesterday morning, it would have taken him hours. In fact, the rule of thumb was, it would take twice as long to hike out as it took to hike down.

Pine shook her head in confusion. But if the guy was going to hike out, why take a mule out of the corral? She knew from Brennan that Priest was not going to ride a mule up by himself in the dark. The guy had had a tough time coming down in the *daylight* with an experienced wrangler next to him.

Sallie Belle's corpse had been helicoptered out earlier using a winch and a harness designed for large animals. A postmortem would be performed on her body. Pine had a hunch about something, and the post might be able to determine if she was right or not. She had used as many of the tools in her investigative duffel as seemed reasonable under the circumstances, and none of them had led to any clues, much less answers.

Lambert came up to her. "When I texted you about this, you said you were out of town on personal business. Everything okay?"

She glanced at him. "Just getting some R and R. The Bureau allows you to do that every once in a while."

"So were you on vacation? I wouldn't have called you in if I'd known that."

"Relax, Colson, I was on vacation and now I'm not." She studied the ground in front of her.

"You hear anything back from Flagstaff yet?" Lambert asked.

"Not yet. And I'm not sure how high we are on the priority list."

Lambert looked out over the ground. "I don't think we're going to find him down here."

"Maybe not alive. So we need to bring in the cadaver dogs."

"Will do."

"A teenager went out to the mule pen last night with a carrot for Jasmine, the mule she'd ridden down."

"To the mule pen? What happened?"

"We escorted her back to her cabin and I told her to be more careful in the future."

"We?"

"Kettler was there, too. He'd heard her as well."

"I'm not surprised. Sam doesn't miss much."

"He said he was in the Army. And you mentioned that, too."

Lambert nodded. "Special Forces. Someone he served with told me Kettler got a slew of medals, including the Purple Heart. But he never talks about it."

"The soldiers who did the most talk the least," said Pine.

"That's what I think, too. He's an amazing athlete. He's done the twenty-four-hour ultramarathon. And the rim-to-rim-to-rim run down here. He wasn't that far off the record."

Pine knew that the record was held by a man who had done that run in under six hours. That was a forty-two-mile trek that involved twenty-two thousand feet of vertical change.

"That's impressive." She paused. "He said you told him I lived in Shattered Rock."

"Well, he asked me after you two met earlier."

"Did he say *why* he asked?"

Lambert looked at her in surprise. "Maybe he likes you, Atlee."

"I guess in my line of work, I don't think about things like that."

"Well, we all have a private life. But then again, I've got three teenagers at home. So, I don't know how much *private* I can have in my life right now."

"Uh, that would be none."

Lambert grinned and looked around. "So, what do we do now?"

"Before it gets too dark, I'm going to fly out of here on your chopper."

"What will you do up there?"

"Investigate the hell out of this."

"I hope I didn't call you in just for a dead mule. I know you have other cases to cover."

"No problem. I'm at a one-agent RA *and* a woman. So I can multitask with the best of them."

7

PINE THREW HER DUFFEL down on the floor and looked around her tiny, Spartan one-bedroom apartment on the edge of Shattered Rock, a town so small that the outskirts and the minuscule downtown area were kissing cousins. The apartment building was three stories tall and fully rented out by a variety of tenants. There was only one other three-story "high-rise" in town—a hotel that catered to those visiting the Grand Canyon.

She had never lived in anything larger than a one-bedroom place since leaving home. And her childhood home was a two-bedroom ranch in rural Georgia.

She'd heard that the author Margaret Mitchell had never lived in a place with more than one bedroom for a simple reason: She had never wanted houseguests. Pine didn't know if that was true or merely anecdotal, but she could relate to the feeling. She was a no-visitors, one-bedroom kind of gal, too.

She had no flowers in pots, no pets in crates, no hobbies waiting for her to pick them back up when she returned from working on a case. She had heard that your work should not be your life. Yet without it she would have no life. And she was perfectly fine with that.

After losing Mercy, she had been put into counseling. As a bereaved six-year-old, she had found it confusing, scary, and, ultimately, unhelpful.

Four years ago, she had tried it again. With the exact same result. She had sat in a group counseling session and had listened as the attendees went around the room discussing their most personal issues. When her turn had come, Pine, who had been shot, stabbed, and attacked multiple times in the line of duty, had started to sweat and taken the coward's way out—she had passed on her turn and never gone back.

For some reason, all of this had made her averse to possessions. She wanted to go through life with as few as possible. These included people as well. Some shrinks might interpret that as her being fearful of another significant loss. And they might not be far off the mark. But Pine had never allowed herself the time or opportunity to dig deep enough into her psyche to prove that theory true or false.

She showered to take off the dirt and sweat of the Grand Canyon. She dressed in fresh clothes, sat down at her knotty pine kitchen table, which had come with the apartment and which also doubled as her home office, and checked her emails, phone messages, and texts.

There was one from her direct superior out of Flagstaff. He wanted to know what progress she'd made on the case thus far. As Pine scanned the email, she noted about a dozen people who'd been copied on it. Two on the cc list were far higher up the food chain than her immediate superior, and the others she didn't even recognize.

The only reason she was involved was that the Grand Canyon was federal property and carried a special cachet in the eyes of the U.S. government. And the Shattered Rock RA really was there for all things Grand Canyon. She had hit the ground running after being assigned to this job. And she had worked hard to build a good relationship with the National Park Service office, local police, and Indian tribes in the area. It could be a tricky endeavor, but Pine had kept at it, and her sincerity and hard work had finally won the locals over.

Pine made herself a cup of coffee, sat back down in front of her laptop, and typed in a search for Capricorn Consultants. Lots of things popped up, but none of them had anything to do with defense contracting.

She texted Colson Lambert to confirm that was the name of the firm and where he had gotten that information.

Lambert texted back a few minutes later telling her that Priest's brother had volunteered that business name and the field it was in.

Pine looked at her watch. It would be after eleven p.m. on the East Coast. Probably too late to call the brother.

She looked back at the email trail and had a sudden inspiration. She went on an FBI personnel database and looked up all the names on the cc list whom she didn't know.

She blinked when the man's picture and background came up.

This was a name buried in the cc list. But he shouldn't have been.

Peter Steuben. He was the executive assistant director of the FBI's National Security Branch, which meant he was the top guy there. The NSB was one of the six FBI branches. It had been created in 2005 in the wake of 9/11 and the suddenly critical fight against terrorism. It was a vastly important branch, in some ways the most important branch of the FBI right now, as it took on myriad global threats against the United States.

And here was its head guy dumped in a cc list on a case involving a dead mule.

And maybe a missing person connected to a company that didn't seem to exist, although she supposed that some defense contractors didn't exactly want a public footprint or a fancy website.

Pine had worked at the East Coast FBI before. She felt that the Bureau personnel on the other side of the Mississippi were buttoned-down, uptight, by-the-book types who did not understand why the same rules and procedures could not simply be lifted from New York or DC and plopped on top of the Southwest like a giant template of law enforcement cookie-cutter protocols.

Pine clearly understood why those rules didn't necessarily apply, principally because there was a slew of different elements out here, all wanting and some certainly deserving of a voice and respect.

Out here pretty much everybody had multiple guns, along with a healthy skepticism of the federal government. And here you could drive all day without seeing another human being across terrain that sometimes resembled that of an uninhabited planet.

Yet she had long since given up fighting that battle with the East Coast boys. She kept her head down, did her job, and never asked for help unless she really, really needed it.

But if the NSB was interested in her case, she didn't know how successful that strategy would be. She could imagine a chopper full of ramrod-straight FBI agents with Jersey accents landing right in the middle of her case and politely but firmly telling her to back the hell off.

Fueled by this thought, she looked at her watch again and decided to take a chance.

She punched in the number Lambert had given her and waited while it rang on the other end.

On the second ring an anxious voice said, "Yes?"

"Mr. Priest?"

"Yes?"

"Edward Priest?"

"Yes, who is this?"

"I'm Special Agent Atlee Pine with the FBI in Arizona."

"Oh my God. It's Ben, isn't it? He's dead. Oh shit. Oh, sweet Jesus!"

Pine could hear the man start to sob.

She said firmly, "No, Mr. Priest. No, that's not why I'm calling. I'm investigating your brother's disappearance, but we haven't found him yet. For all we know he's still very much alive."

She listened as his breaths slowed.

He barked, "You scared the holy crap out of me. Why are you calling this late?"

"I apologize for that, but in a situation like this time can be of the essence. You told one of my colleagues that your brother worked at Capricorn Consultants?"

"That's right. He does."

"They're a Beltway firm?"

"Yes!"

"Do you have an address and contact info for them?"

Now Priest hesitated. "Contact info?"

"Or an address."

"I...I don't have that information. I just recall my brother telling me that's where he worked."

"When was that?"

The tone turned from gruff to suspicious. "Why is this so important? He went missing at the Grand Canyon, not on the DC Beltway."

"The thing is, I looked them up, but I can't find a firm by that name located in the DC area."

Silence. Then: "I...I think it was about six months ago when he told me."

"So, he never took you to his office?"

"No."

"Did he ever talk to you about his work?"

"He...he would make that joke, you know, the usual one when dealing with...stuff around DC."

"You mean, 'he could tell you, but then he'd have to kill you'?"

"Exactly."

"Okay."

"Agent Pine, what is going on?"

"I'm not sure right now. Could you fill me in on your brother's background? Education, early life, family, that sort of thing."

"I already told the other guy."

"It would really help if you told me, too."

A long sigh was followed by, "We were mostly raised on the East Coast, but we moved around a lot. Our father was in the Navy. Retired as an 0-7."

"Rear admiral, lower half."

"Yes, that's right. Were you a Navy brat?"

"No, but I have friends who were. What else?"

"Ben was, I mean, *is*, my younger brother. We have two older sisters. Ben lives in Old Town Alexandria, Virginia. One sister lives in Florida, and the other near Syracuse."

"I understand your brother isn't married."

"No, he never took the plunge. His work was his life."

"Education?"

"Georgetown. Undergrad and grad."

"Political science?"

"Yeah, how'd you know?"

"Lucky guess. Can you give me his home address?"

"Look, I want to cooperate, but it just occurred to me that I don't actually know if you are who you say you are."

"Colson Lambert from the U.S. Park Service contacted you before. I can give you my badge number and a phone number to call at the Bureau to confirm I'm an agent with them. You can call me back on this number tomorrow, if you like."

Priest didn't say anything right away. "No, I guess it's okay. I mean, why would you be calling me if you weren't with the FBI, right?"

I can think of a few reasons, Pine thought to herself. But she told Priest none of them.

He gave her his brother's home address.

"So, no word from Ben?"

"No. Look, I asked this Lambert guy if I should fly out."

"I think you need to stay where you are. Anything develops

I'll call you immediately. And feel free to call me with any questions or concerns. Or if you think of anything that might be helpful."

"Do you think this has to do with Ben's work?"

"I can't say that it doesn't. At least not right now."

"Do you think he's dead?"

"I don't think anything. We don't know enough. But just to cover the obvious angle, did your brother have any enemies?"

"Not that I know of."

"Okay. Have you talked to your sisters?"

"No, should I?"

"Yes. Just in case he might have contacted them."

"Oh, right. I hadn't thought of that. But I think he would contact me before them. We don't live very far away from each other."

"Still, just in case. You don't have to alert them to anything being wrong. Just casually ask if they've heard from their brother."

"Okay, I'll do that. And let you know if they have."

"Thanks, Mr. Priest. I appreciate it."

"Do you think you'll find Ben?"

"I'm going to give it my best shot. One more thing. Do you have a recent photo of your brother you can send me?"

"I do. My wife's birthday party last month. It's me, my wife, and Ben. I'll email it."

"Great." She gave him her email and then clicked off.

A minute went by and then the photo dropped into her inbox.

She opened it up and looked at the picture of three people standing side by side. One was a tall man about six three, and lean. This was obviously Edward Priest. In the middle was his wife. On the other end was a shorter, thickset man wearing glasses who could only be Ben Priest.

She thought of a few more questions and decided to call Edward Priest back.

"I got the picture, thanks. Couple of quick questions. In the picture, your brother is wearing glasses. Does he also wear contact lenses?"

His reply made Pine's eyes widen and her thoughts swirl in completely new directions.

"No, Agent Pine, you've got it backwards. *I'm* the one wearing the glasses, not Ben. He's the tall one on the left."

8

GOOD MORNING, Special Agent Pine."

Pine had just unlocked the door of the FBI's office in Shattered Rock. It was a hardened portal with a pickproof lock and an intercom-and-video system. It might seem like overkill in a place like this, but there was a good reason for such enhanced security protocols. In the late seventies two FBI agents in El Centro, California, had been shotgunned to death in their unsecure office by a social worker under investigation for misuse of funds. Ever since then the Bureau had hardened pretty much all their offices in the field, from the largest to the smallest.

Carol Blum had greeted Pine from her desk in the front room of the two-room office. The other building tenants included a law firm, a dentist, a home contractor, and a title insurance company.

And another federal law enforcement agency.

Pine shut the door behind her.

"You know, Carol, we've been working together for a while now. You can just call me Atlee."

"I like to keep things professional. I understand that was the way Mr. Hoover preferred it."

"Well, the offer remains open. And *Mr.* Hoover was a long time ago."

Pine had on jeans held up by a wide leather belt with a large square brass buckle, dusty boots, and a white shirt with a windbreaker over it. By contrast, Blum was dressed in a navy blue jacket and white pleated skirt. Low heels, nylons, and her thick, auburn hair carefully done up in a bun. Her makeup was minimal, and Pine actually thought she needed none. She was a striking woman who had kept herself fit, possessing enormous emerald green eyes that contrasted vividly with the reddish hair, an angular chin, elevated knuckles of cheekbones, and an air about her that seemed exotic, as silly and dated as that term seemed now. But the other term someone would unfailingly apply to her would be: professional.

"I put your recent case files on your desk. Flagstaff will be calling in this afternoon for a routine update. It's on your calendar."

"Thank you."

"You know, I like it that you never post and coast."

Pine lifted her gaze to the woman's.

Blum said, "I've worked in other offices where right before the supervisor sit-down comes, agents rush around to drop in a new page and a fresh serial number."

"I know what the term means, Carol."

"But you never do that."

"Never saw the point. I work cases to solve them, not play paperwork tricks."

"How was your time off?"

"It was just fine."

"What did you do?"

"I went on a trip."

"Somewhere fun?"

"Not particularly, no."

The enormous eyes widened a bit more. "Would you like to talk about it?"

"Not really, no."

The eyes dimmed. "Would you like some coffee? I just purchased a Keurig for the office."

"That must have cost you a ton of paperwork."

"It would have except I bought it with my own money."

"You're brave. Coffee would be great, thanks."

"Black?"

"Just like always."

Pine went into her office and closed the door.

She found it puzzling and more than a bit hypocritical that Blum wanted to keep things strictly professional and was still eager to learn every facet of her boss's personal life. But then again, maybe she was just being friendly. Despite being together for about a year, Pine didn't think she knew Blum very well.

She probably thinks the same thing about me. And maybe that's just fine.

She hung up her windbreaker in a small closet, sat down behind the battered, standard issue gunmetal-gray desk, the kind that the FBI seemed to own by the boatload, and turned on her desktop computer.

The Bureau was still behind the times on technology, and her computer was about eight years old. When she really needed to crank out something she just used her laptop or her phone. Some days she was surprised she didn't still have a dial-up internet browser.

Blum knocked and came in carrying a steaming cup of coffee with a saucer.

"Did you eat breakfast?" she asked.

"No."

"Are you hungry? I can run to the bagel shop. It's no trouble."

"I'm good, thanks."

"Breakfast is the most important meal of the day. I have six kids. I know that for a fact."

Pine glanced up from a file she had just opened. "I'll keep that in mind."

"Anything else?"

Pine knew that Blum just wanted to keep busy, but the fact was Pine could pretty much do everything by herself. It was only a matter of time before the Bureau figured that out, too, and made her secretary expendable. But then again, the wheels of the FBI's bureaucracy could turn very slowly. Blum might actually retire before they caught on.

"No, I'm—" She paused as Blum looked at her expectantly. "There is one thing. Can you find out if the letters *j* and *k* hold any significance? And not just as alphabet letters."

"In relation to what?"

"They were carved on the hide of a dead mule at the bottom of the Grand Canyon. I know it's not much to go on, and I don't expect you'll find anything."

However, Blum was looking pensive. "Well, one thing *does* come to mind. But let me research it for a bit."

She walked out. Pine stared after her in surprise for a moment before spending the next hour going over her other case files in preparation for her monthly phone call with her supervisor. She had spent her time here getting to know all the law enforcement in the area. Pine had also visited the local Indian tribes, who, collectively, had an enormous footprint here. They were not the sort you won over in a matter of weeks. It was baby steps, a little at a time. But during her time here Pine had already captured a bank robber, broken up an opioid ring, and nailed a serial rapist preying on those living on tribal lands, and that had helped her gain the trust of those she needed to do her job.

She moved her case files to the side and finished her coffee, which tasted strong and acidic going down. She glanced over at the far wall that still bore the indentation of a fist.

It had not been thrown by Pine, but *at* Pine by a suspect who had decided to turn violent.

The second indentation in the wall below the first was larger.

It marked where the suspect had been thrown headfirst into the wall after his fist had missed its mark and Pine had brought the dispute to a swift resolution.

She was cuffing the man with her knee firmly planted into the lower back of the nearly unconscious man when Blum, who had certainly heard the scuffle, had calmly opened the door and asked Pine whether she needed the police to take the "moron" away.

It had been her suggestion that Pine leave the marks on the wall.

"Some people are visually stimulated," Blum had said. "And a picture *is* worth a thousand words."

It had been a brilliant suggestion, Pine had thought, and the marks had remained. The guy had filed a complaint against her. Said that Pine had attacked him without cause. Ever since then, Pine had kept a hidden video camera in her office with audio capability. The button to activate it was in the knee well of her desk. It wasn't for her protection, at least not her physical protection. It was in case another "moron" tried to lie about who attacked whom.

Her cell phone buzzed. She looked at the number and frowned. She took another sip of her coffee.

Flagstaff was calling. Early. That was never a good thing.

"Pine," she said.

"Hold for Roger Avery, please," said a woman's voice.

Roger Avery?

He was not Pine's immediate supervisor, and thus she had not been expecting a call from him. He was two levels above her immediate boss. He'd been with the Bureau for only six years, less than half her time on the clock, but now agents were making supervisor in as little as three or four years. Pine had never filed the necessary paperwork to make supervisor and indeed had fought against every effort to take her from the field and plop her permanently in an office. She had a distinct opinion of an FBI supervisor: They sat at desks all day and told other agents how to run their cases, playing Monday morning quarterback at every opportunity, while others did the heavy lifting.

Pine could stomach her direct contact, but she never liked to talk to Avery. She'd rather undergo a colonoscopy without the propofol.

The voice came on a moment later. "Pine?"

"Yes, sir," said Pine.

"Surprised to hear from me?"

"Well, I was expecting the call to go over my cases. But not from you, sir."

"I like to keep my finger on the pulse, so I'm making the calls this week."

Finger on the pulse. The man would have failed every polygraph given to him.

"The call's on my calendar for this afternoon."

"I just thought I'd get it done earlier. I know you don't like to sit behind your desk. But if you're busy?"

Like any other supervisor, he didn't mean that. If she told him to take a flying leap, her ass was done. She said, "No, absolutely works for me." She reached for her case files, but his next words made her stop.

"I'm sure you're doing just fine on your regular caseload. I've never had to ding you on anything in *that* regard."

His words were clear enough. He *had* had to ding her on sometimes too zealously pursuing her cases. Yet she had never felt that hurt feelings or a broken limb should ever be cause for not discovering the truth. The "moron" she'd launched into the drywall had not just filed a complaint against her, he'd also filed a lawsuit. Both had been dismissed after it was learned that the man had attacked cops and ordinary citizens with regularity.

"Okay," said Pine. "Is there something else you need then, because I was actually just about to head out?"

"Let's talk about the Canyon."

Now Pine eased forward in her cheap desk chair. It was a ratty piece of crap from a going-out-of-business office store and had no lumbar or any other sort of support. It was like sitting on Jell-O in the middle of an earthquake. She was pretty sure she'd end up just buying a new chair using Agency funds and take the heat for not filing the necessary forms. If the Bureau's admin folks wanted to travel to Shattered Rock and smack her hand for buying something decent to sit on, so be it.

"The Canyon?" she said.

"The dead mule?"

"Right."

"How's it progressing?" asked Avery.

"I'm working it. Early days."

"Right. I just wanted some more details."

"I did forward my prelim report to you."

"I read it. I was wondering how things are going since then."

Pine said, "I don't know who did it, why they did it, how they did it, or where they are now. Other than that, things are going pretty good."

He ignored this sarcasm, which surprised her. "Benjamin Priest?"

Pine had, as yet, told no one that the man calling himself Benjamin Priest was not in fact Benjamin Priest.

"I talked to his brother late last night."

"And what were the results of that conversation?" said Avery patiently.

I think he knows the answer and he wants me to confirm it. Or not.

"His brother knew nothing about Capricorn Consultants. No address, no contact info. His brother had never really spoken about it to him. And I can find no evidence the place even exists." Before he could respond to this Pine decided to turn the tables. "Have you been able to confirm otherwise, sir?"

"*I'm* not working the case, Pine. You are."

"Yes, sir."

"What else?"

Pine decided to drop an H-bomb. "It seems that the National Security Branch is interested in this case. Maybe you've heard something?"

Avery didn't say anything for a few seconds, which felt infinitely longer to Pine. All she could hear was her supervisor's breathing. It seemed to have quickened a bit.

Did I just piss my whole career away?

"Keep working the case, Pine," he finally said. "And if you need help, ask for it."

"Yes, sir."

"And...Atlee?"

"Atlee" now? Curiouser and curiouser.

"Yes?"

"Make sure you have eyes in the back of your head."

The line went dead.

Pine had been given that advice exactly one other time in her career.

And it had come during a case when it turned out the Bureau had been watching *her*.

A moment later Blum opened the door. She must have heard the phone ring and at least the distant murmurings of her conversation.

"Is everything all right, Agent Pine?"

Pine looked up at her.

"Everything's just fine, Ms. Blum."

9

THE CHOO-CHOO TRAIN. Or the Hooterville Express. Pick your poison.

Pine was staring at the front of the train depot in Williams, Arizona. It was from here that the Grand Canyon train made the trek up and back each day. The trip to the Canyon's South Rim covered sixty-five miles each way and took a leisurely two hours and fifteen minutes. She could have flown from Phoenix to Seattle in less time.

Pine had just spoken to various train personnel, showing them a picture of the real Benjamin Priest. No one remembered seeing him on the train. She then gave a description of the fake Priest but was told that quite a few gentlemen fit that description.

A round-trip train ticket had been issued to a Benjamin Priest, and that ticket had been used on the way up to the South Rim. So one of the men had to have been on the train. The return ticket to Williams had not been used, though. The ticket had been bought with cash, so there was no credit card record. That was interesting, thought Pine, because the ticket hadn't been cheap. Had it been done to hide someone's identity? Probably.

Next, Pine trudged over to the Railway Hotel and went inside. There was a fireplace with a stone surround, carpet your feet sank into, polished wood balconies and columns, and a general air of upscale hospitality. Its livelihood depended on the folks who took the train, Pine imagined. And they had apparently done all they could to present an appealing look to encourage folks to stay here before heading out.

She checked in at the front desk and showed the young woman there the picture of the real Priest and told her when the man had likely stayed there. Then she gave the description of the imposter as well. The woman shook her head.

"I don't recognize either of them."

"Were you on duty at that time?"

"I was, actually. I do the day shift."

"Anyone else working the front desk then?"

"No, just me."

"Okay, did you have a guest named Benjamin Priest check in on the day I gave you?"

She clicked some computer keys and shook her head. "No, no one by that name. So, I guess he didn't stay here."

That was not necessarily true, Pine knew. He could have used an alias, had a fake ID, and worn a disguise. She thanked the woman, walked outside, and concluded that her trip here had been largely worthless.

She got back into her truck and started it up.

Then her phone buzzed. It was Carol Blum.

"I'm sending you a news article I found from the *Arizona Gazette*," said Blum.

"What about?"

"An exploration that allegedly took place in the Grand Canyon."

"When did it *allegedly* take place?"

"In 1909."

"And why does that have relevance to my case over a century later?"

"Just read the article. And I'm also sending you a more recent article that sort of dissects the 1909 one. Together they will show you the relevance."

"Okay. But can you give me a hint?"

"The letters *j* and *k* have apparently been carved in the Grand Canyon before."

"What?"

"Just read the articles and then we can talk."

Pine sat there for a few moments with the AC blowing directly on her because it was nearly ninety outside. And though the heat was mostly a dry one, ninety degrees was still hot, dry or not.

Her phone dinged and she opened the email. Blum had apparently enlarged the article so that it could be easily read. It took Pine a few minutes to go through it.

Back in 1909, two Smithsonian Institution–backed explorers named Jordan and Kinkaid had supposedly stumbled upon a remote cave high up on a sheer cliff in the Canyon.

Jordan and Kinkaid? *J* and *K*.

She read on.

On entering the cave, they had found evidence of an ancient civilization that might be, as the article said, using a long-discarded derogatory term, "Oriental" in origin, or even Egyptian. Supposedly, the pair found everything from urns to mummies and a Buddha-like statue in what was described as an underground multiroom citadel.

The second article was from only a few years ago, and it had gone into great detail. It took Pine about ten minutes to read through it. The author of this article was clearly as skeptical as Pine was about the supposed expedition. The Smithsonian had no record of any explorers named Jordan and Kinkaid. And Kinkaid, who the old article had said possessed a camera of the first order, hadn't managed to take a single picture of any of his supposed discovery of the century. The author did go on to try to pinpoint the location of the cave. He thought a likely possibility was around Ninety-Four Mile Creek and Trinity Creek.

Pine knew that there were sites along there with Egyptian names:

Tower of Set, Isis Temple, and Osiris Temple. According to the more recent article, around the time these areas were named, there were major expeditions going on in Egypt, and such names were often in the news back then. In the so-called Haunted Canyon area were Asian-inspired names such as the Cheops Pyramid and Buddha Cloister and the Shiva Temple. The Canyon was also filled with spots named after ancient mythological gods and goddesses from Egyptian, Greek, Hindu, Chinese, and Nordic legends.

The writer concluded that the Canyon indeed had many caves and that many of them had been discovered over the years by hikers and explorers. It seemed that he thought the cave claimed to have been found by Jordan and Kinkaid might have actually been inhabited by the Anasazis, the first people to occupy the valley. They were the originators of the pueblo style of dwelling and built caves in the cliffs, as did many ancient cultures.

The Navajos were descendants of the Anasazis, whose name meant "ancient one" in the Navajo language. There was even a so-called Mummy's Cave in the Canyon de Chelly where the Anasazis had lived. It was about three hundred feet above the Canyon floor and comprised of two adjacent caves housing a dwelling space consisting of more than fifty rooms and circular ceremonial structures dating back more than a thousand years.

And then she read the last paragraph of the later article. Apparently, the author speculated, Jordan and Kinkaid had carved the letters *j* and *k* into the rock above the entrance to the cave. What he was basing this on Pine didn't know, because the writer never gave a reason.

She called Blum. "How did you come up with all this stuff so fast?"

"I grew up in Arizona, so I knew about the 1909 *Gazette* article. It's part of the local folklore. When I was a teenager my father and I hiked to the bottom of the Canyon. He was an amateur local historian. He'd told me about the legend when he was pointing out all the Egyptian-named sites down there. I thought it was all hogwash, really, though I could tell my dad thought there was something to it. But I mean, Egyptians in Arizona? Please. But the letters *j* and *k*? Jordan and Kinkaid. That's what I remembered when you asked me to research it this morning. It may have nothing to do with your case, but it was the only thing I could find even remotely on point."

"Well, it was good work, thanks. So you've hiked down there?"

"Oh, many times when I was younger. And I've done the mule ride, too. But that was years ago."

"Good to know."

"Are you coming back to the office?"

"I might." Pine checked her watch. "I know you get off in an hour."

"I'll stay and work on this. I have nothing else to do today."

"I'll request some overtime for you then."

"Don't worry about it, Agent Pine. It's nice to feel useful."

"Thanks. Maybe I'll see you later then."

Pine drove off wondering what an expedition that might have never happened more than a century ago had to do with a dead mule and national security.

Maybe I don't want to know.

10

Pɪɴᴇ ᴘᴀssᴇᴅ ᴛʜᴇ sɪᴛᴇ of the eponymous Shattered Rock on her way home.

It was only a mile outside of town; in fact it was really the only reason there *was* a town.

Local legend, later backed up by some actual facts provided by NASA and other federal scientists over the years, claimed that a meteor about the size of a Volkswagen Beetle had struck this spot about a zillion years ago. There once had been a small, rocky outcrop here, but the plummeting meteor had pulverized it, leaving a crater and large chunks of rock lying everywhere over the otherwise pretty flat landscape.

And voilà, the name Shattered Rock had come into the local lexicon. The town had only been incorporated about a hundred years ago under that name, when an enterprising young man by the name of Elmer Lancaster had left his small town in Pennsylvania to make his fortune out west. He had apparently stumbled upon the rocky debris, coughed up a local fable, and decided to put down roots. He had begun selling meteorites from a stand on the side of the only road running through the place and had even hired some Native Americans to help him. Dressed in full tribal wear they had danced across the road holding the "rocks from the heavens" as they termed them, and the tidy sum of five dollars would allow you to own one.

It had actually been a profitable business, since there were literally millions of chunks of rock, and even if they ran out, they could always make more.

Lancaster used some of his money to start laying out streets and subdivisions and constructing buildings and necessary infrastructure. He also put out the call that his now-named town of Shattered Rock was the most important geological location on planet Earth and open to families and businesses to move to. People from other places, who perhaps had more gullibility than good sense, bought into this, and Shattered Rock was properly born. It had not, however, experienced enormous growth over the century, but still had a population of roughly a thousand souls, who did a variety of things to make a living, as folks did in every other small town. That included exactly one person with a gun who carried an FBI shield.

Meteorites were still sold from a large plywood building to tourists passing through, though inflation had kicked in and the price was now fifty dollars per chunk. But the Native Americans had wised up and were no longer working for others. An enterprising Hopi and his Navajo partner had bought the meteorite franchise and were, by all accounts, doing fine. They also served coffee, cold beer, and wickedly delicious scones. And Pine had bought one of the rocks, but only to support the local economy.

She pulled into the parking lot of her apartment building. It was stucco sided with a red tile roof, very southwestern in style. The railings were wrought iron, and the stucco was painted a muted yellow. The flora and fauna planted around it were indigenous to the area, which meant they could survive without much water. The Southwest had many good things, but reliable rainfall was not one of them.

When Pine's boots hit the asphalt, she could feel the heat from the tar wicking through her soles and into her socks and from there into her feet. The sun was intense at this elevation, which was about the same as Denver's. And it was now beating down on Pine.

She had run into some traffic because of an accident and gotten back too late to return to the office. But Blum had emailed her on the way with some more information. She was going to go over it while sipping a beer in her apartment. That was her idea of a night out without actually going out.

On the way to the stairwell leading to her digs, Pine approached two men in their twenties in the parking lot. They were lounging against a cherry red Ford F150 with a jacked-up frame and double-wide rear tires. It looked ready for a duel at a Monster Truck smashup. They were smoking weed and drinking beer. One was indigenous, with his long, dark hair clipped at the back with a leather thong. He had on dirty jeans, a colorful short-sleeved shirt, and a stained, wide-brimmed hat. A knife in a leather sheaf rode on his belt. The other guy was white, with skin that was peeling from sunburn, a fact readily apparent since he was wearing a tank top.

He also had a Sig Sauer in a hip holster.

Arizona was open carry, concealed carry, any carry you wanted, no permit, training, or brain required.

Pine glanced at the rifle rack in the cab of the Ford. Suspended there were a sleek Browning over/under twelve-gauge shotgun, and an AR-15 that could kill a whole lot of people in a very short amount of time.

Pine recognized one of the men but not the other. She nodded to them as she was passing by.

"I hear you're a fed?"

This came from Sunburn.

"Who wants to know?"

Sunburn threw his empty beer can into the truck bed. "I was a fed once. Army. They screwed me over," he said quietly, his menacing gaze boring into her.

Pine couldn't tell if he was stoned or just creepy. Or both.

"Sorry to hear that."

"So are you a fed or not?" he said, drawing closer.

"Yeah, I'm a federal agent."

"They'll screw you over, too."

"Not so far."

He took a puff on his joint.

She watched him and said, "And maybe you need to knock that off and clear your head. Especially if you're driving. You don't want any more trouble with the authorities, right?"

"This is a free country, right? I *fought* for that shit."

"You got your medical marijuana card? Otherwise, it's illegal to possess or use it in Arizona. And under federal law you shouldn't be carrying a gun if you're using weed, though the state of Arizona sees it differently."

"Got PTSD. Left my card at home. You can arrest me if you want."

"If you don't have a card, I could arrest you. It's a felony."

"Like I said, I *got* a card. Just forgot it. I was in Iraq, lady. You go to Iraq, you'll want to smoke weed too."

Pine eyed his buddy, who seemed disinterested in the whole interaction.

"How about you?"

"I left my card home too."

Pine shook her head. She was not arresting these guys for that. But still.

She eyed the AR-15 and said to Sunburn. "I'm assuming you passed a background check for the AR."

"Not my gun," replied Sunburn.

Pine, who was done with this exchange, said tersely, "Right. Okay, you guys have a good evening. Just don't drug, drink, and drive, okay? And be careful with your weapons."

She started to walk past him when Sunburn moved in front of her.

"I ain't done talking to you."

"Yeah, well, I'm done talking to you."

As she moved past him, he roughly grabbed her arm.

Pine gripped his wrist, bent it backward, drove it behind his back, and launched him headfirst into the side of the truck. His forehead punched into the sheet metal and he slowly slid to the ground.

With her free hand Pine whipped out her Glock and pointed it in the direction of the other guy, whose hand had drifted to his knife.

"Don't do it unless you want to die right here," barked Pine. "Put it on the ground and kick it away. Now."

The man quickly did as she ordered, laying the weapon in the dirt and then propelling it about two feet away with his boot.

Sunburn slowly groaned and turned over on his back. She reached down and jerked his Sig from the holster.

"Hey, you can't take my gun!" he protested.

She pointed her gun at his head. "You ever lay a hand on me again, you won't be waking up. You got that?"

When he didn't answer she nudged him with her boot. "I said, you got that?"

"Yeah, I get it, okay. Shit!"

"And be thankful I don't want to waste another minute of my life dealing with you idiots. Now clear out of here."

He struggled up and, with his buddy's help, climbed into the passenger seat of the Ford.

When his friend went to get his knife, Pine placed her boot over it.

"Don't think so." She paused and studied him. "I know you. Your old man is Joe Yazzie, isn't he? You're his oldest, Joe Jr. Does he know you're hanging out with dicks like that?"

"I'm twenty-four, I can hang out with anybody I want," retorted Yazzie.

In her periphery, Pine kept a visual on Sunburn, just in case he went for the Browning or AR.

She said to Yazzie, "Then exercise better judgment. What are you doing here anyway?"

"Our buddy lives here. Kyle Chavez."

Pine nodded. She knew the Chavez family. The parents were illegals, hardworking, never in any trouble, and went to Mass every Sunday at the only Catholic church in town. But their son, Kyle, was a piece of work, and giving them endless trouble. He had nearly come Pine's way a couple of times.

"Like I said, exercise better judgment."

"You think you're a badass?" screamed Sunburn from the truck.

"Get him out of here before I change my mind about arresting you both," Pine said.

Yazzie quickly climbed into the truck, started it up, put it in gear, and drove off.

Pine watched them go until they were out of sight.

Then she picked up the knife, shoved Sunburn's Sig into her pocket, and walked up the stairs to her apartment.

Now she really, really wanted that beer.

11

BLUM'S EMAIL had contained more information about the website where she had originally found the two articles.

If the letters carved on the mule were referring to Jordan and Kinkaid, then the person who had carved them might have accessed this website. And whenever you accessed a digital space, you left behind your electronic prints in the form of an IP address. The Bureau had busted many a crook who didn't understand this. It was a long shot, Pine knew, but Blum had also told her that there weren't very many websites dealing with this subject, so they might just get lucky. Ordinarily, Pine would have forwarded this information to IT specialists at the Bureau who could check out web traffic to a site.

Yet she hesitated to do that now.

Eyes in the back of my head.

Avery had told her that, and yet he was no particular ally of hers. But she was under his chain of command and maybe he was giving her some subtle assistance for some reason as yet unknown. Or maybe he was setting her up to swing in the wind. She supposed only time would tell which possibility was correct.

She finished her beer and took two pork sausages out of the fridge. She had already fired up her little hibachi that was out on the balcony. It had come with the apartment, having been left behind by the last renter. She only had to add a fresh bag of charcoal. Pine wasn't much of a cook, but eating out every night was not in her budget, or good for her physical well-being.

She plopped the fat sausages on the hot grill, and her nostrils were instantly assailed with the smell of cooking spiced meat.

She grabbed a bottle of water from her fridge, uncapped it, and took a long drink. Dehydration was a real problem here. People trying to hike the Canyon failed all the time to take this into account, despite all the warning signs posted everywhere about how much water and salty foods to carry with you, and how much to consume during your trek. Becoming dehydrated was potentially deadly. Blood pressure dropped to dangerously low levels, the heart slowed, the organs could begin shutting down. And then you were gone. All from not imbibing enough H_2O.

She mixed a small salad, cutting up tomatoes, cucumbers, snap peas, and beets. She sprinkled a homemade lemon vinaigrette over it and set it on the kitchen table. A few minutes later she checked on the sausages. They were plump and bursting and marked with the tines of the grill.

Just how she liked them.

She sat at her table and ate, while she used her laptop to look through the website Blum had found. It was quite conspiratorial in tone. The whole country, maybe the whole world, was wallowing in paranoia. She thought it was still anyone's bet as to whether the internet would turn out to be more good or evil.

She texted a friend of hers who worked for a satellite office of Google in Salt Lake City and gave him the information on the site, with a request that he track the IP addresses that had accessed the site within the last several weeks. Pine had no idea what sort of traffic this site experienced, so she felt it was practical to put in a time parameter, if just to see what sort of volume she'd be looking at.

She finished her dinner and put her plate and utensils in the dishwasher.

It was nearly nine o'clock now, but she wasn't really tired.

She received an answering text from her friend in Salt Lake. He had gotten the information and would try to have something for her tomorrow.

Pine sat back and thought things through. It was quite a mish-mash in her head. How did a carved-up mule that might be tied to an old legend square with a defense contractor gone missing, along with the man impersonating him?

No, she was wrong about that. It was still unproven that Benjamin Priest *was* a defense contractor. He could be something else entirely. And Benjamin Priest wasn't even technically missing— the man pretending to be him was.

And why the Bureau's national security interest?

Pine couldn't even prove that the real Benjamin Priest had ever visited the Grand Canyon. The only concrete evidence she had was that someone calling himself Benjamin Priest had ridden Sallie Belle down to the Canyon floor and then vanished, leaving a mutilated mule in his wake.

Had the impersonator hiked out at night? Hikers did make the trek from rim to rim at night, to avoid the heat of the day, which could feel like a sauna from May to September.

Pine had made the nighttime journey numerous times, taking a quick nap on the banks of the Colorado at midnight before hiking up to the opposite rim to see the sunrise. But she was in excellent physical shape, knew the trails, and had the right equipment, including headlamps. Walking along rocky, uneven narrow trails with sheer drops without lights was a suicidal endeavor.

So, a guy who was nervous coming down on a mule would have had to hike up alone in the dark. Pine had no way to explain this seemingly incongruous possibility.

And she certainly wouldn't figure it out tonight.

She stripped off her clothes and took a shower, and put on a pair of gym shorts and a white tank top.

She sat on the bed and looked at her heavily callused hands. She had had to scrub hard to get out the fine bits of weightlifting chalk embedded in her fingers.

When she wasn't traveling for a case, she lifted three times a week at a gym in downtown Shattered Rock. It used to house a Chinese restaurant, but apparently the denizens of the Rock would rather push iron than eat kung pao. Next door to that was an MMA studio, where she practiced her kickboxing three days a week. On the seventh day, unlike God, she didn't rest. Instead, she put on her Nikes and ran along the flat, dry plains, with an unforgiving sun beating down on her.

The unincorporated town of Tuba City was to the east of Shattered Rock and hugged the westernmost edge of the Navajo Nation like a parenthesis. Shattered Rock lay just outside the boundaries of the Navajo's territory, sitting within the Painted Desert. The summers were hot and dry and the winters cold and equally dry because of the barrier mountains to the south.

Her first winter here, Pine thought her skin was literally going to break off. She had gone through a ton of moisturizers and kept a humidifier in her apartment and office running from November to April. Even then, she'd had to buy lip balm and Aveeno by the crate.

She lay back on her bed, one arm across her forehead as she stared up at the dark ceiling. It was a little after ten, and even with her window shut she could hear the baleful howl of a coyote coming from somewhere.

They'd had coyotes back in rural Georgia. While she had watched, her father had shot one that had gone after their chickens. Her father wasn't the best shot, and the animal hadn't died right away. Pine could recall her eyes filling with tears as the poor beast writhed in pain. The bullet must have hit its spine and paralyzed its rear legs. Her father had walked over and calmly shot the coyote in the head, ending its misery.

He had turned to his remaining daughter, taken the smoldering cigarette from his lips, and stuffed the still-smoking pistol inside his belt.

"You don't let things be in pain, Lee, you hear me. That's one'a God's creatures, so you got to put them out of their misery, okay? You hear me, girl? Pain ain't no good that way. Ain't right. You hear me now?"

This had occurred after Mercy had been taken from them. They were all changed, all on edge, all different from what they had once been. Pain, yes, they were all certain that Mercy had been in pain.

She had wiped her eyes and nodded at her father, but her gaze had remained on the dead animal, its lifeless eye seemed to be trained solely on her, as the blood pooled around its destroyed head. She would never forget the howl the beast had made when it had first been shot. Shot for simply hunting for something to eat. She would never forget its piteous writhing on the ground, its spine crushed by a bullet, unsure of what had just happened, but instinctively knowing that its life was just about over, even as it desperately tried to rise and flee.

And survive.

On this thought Pine's memory lurched to her sister.

And how Mercy must have felt something similar to this, as she was taken from the only home she had ever known. Her life forfeited by an unknown force. For no reason at all other than a violent lunatic's whim.

Did someone put you out of your misery?

Did someone take the pain away, Mercy?

I hope he did. I pray he did.

At that exact moment Pine wanted to finally let something out of her that had been inside far too long. She was a dammed-up river desperately needing a release.

But it wouldn't come. The tears would not come.

The imposing image of Daniel James Tor briefly flitted across her mind.

If he had taken Mercy, she prayed that the end had come quickly. But knowing Tor's history, she very much doubted that was the case.

With her sister's features firmly in her mind, Pine fell into a troubled sleep.

As she usually did.

12

GRAND CANYON, ONE.

Cadaver dogs, zip.

And why should that be a surprise? thought Pine.

The Canyon was nearly 280 miles long and up to eighteen miles wide, with more nooks and crannies than you could count in a lifetime. It was no wonder that a body had not been found. But it could be that no body had been found because no corpse was there *to* be found.

Lambert had texted her early that morning with the results, or the lack thereof.

Pine didn't have the resources to check every pocket of the Canyon, not that anyone did. And then there was the mighty Colorado River that had served as both jackhammer and scalpel to the hard and soft rock constituting the Canyon. It was the only reason there *was* a Canyon. If Mr. Imposter had fallen into the icy and swift-running Colorado, his body might be in Mexico by now.

Pine changed into her workout gear and grabbed a duffel with clean clothes, which she had packed the night before. She climbed into her truck and drove off.

It was a ten-minute trip to her gym. It was pretty much a ten-minute drive to everywhere in Shattered Rock. You knew you were in rush hour if you saw more than one car at the same time. She parked on the empty street.

It was early and the heat had not yet built. But the sun had already started its rise and the warmth would follow with it, until sweat would sprout on anyone who happened to be outside moving at anything faster than a slow walk.

It would be two more months before the weather would approach anything that could be called cool or refreshing.

And right now, Pine was going to sweat *inside*.

She nodded to the owner of the place as she walked in.

His name was Kenny Kuni, a transplant from Maui. He was about five eight and a massively ripped 240 pounds.

He was on the squat rack with enough stacked plates to make the barbell bend at the ends. Kuni nodded back and then did another set. His shirt was soaked through from his battle with the barbells, and his shorts were stretched tight over his monster-veined and tanned thighs.

His gym was old-school, hard-core with no fancy bells and whistles, just the basic tools for the seriously inclined pusher of iron.

And another thing: Kenny didn't believe in AC when one was working out. The only thing you got were two floor fans moving warm air from the left to the right and back again with every feeble oscillation. If you didn't sweat in here, you needed to have your glands and pores checked.

There were two other people in the gym. Both were regulars. One was a tall black guy in his fifties who had washboard abs, the other a stocky white guy in his forties working hard to come back from a scoped knee. Pine didn't know their names and in fact had never asked. She just knew them by their routines. The same was probably true of them toward her. The regulars didn't come here to chat. They came here to push as much weight as they could. They saved their breath to do just that, because if you did it correctly, you wouldn't have any wind left over to talk.

She took off her sweatshirt, revealing the tank top underneath. This also showed off four tats Pine had. On one delt was the symbol for Gemini, the astrological mark of the twin. It was simply the Roman numeral two, which looked like the symbol for Pi, but with another line added at the bottom. On the other delt was the astrological symbol for the planet Mercury, which ruled the world of the Geminis. It was comprised of a cross on the bottom, a circle on top of the cross, and an upward crescent on top of the circle.

Along both of Pine's long arms, starting at the forearms and working their way up toward each delt, were the words "No Mercy."

Gemini, community, sisters. Pine had had the tats put on in college. During her weightlifting career, many had remarked on the images since they had been clearly visible while she competed. Pine had never answered any queries about them. The tats were for her and her sister, and no one else.

She warmed up and hit the weights with a ferocity that was clearly channeling the frustration she was feeling with her investigation.

Multiple sets of flat and then incline bench press, military and swimmer's press, the squat rack, deadlift, calf raises, depth charges, push-ups on one leg, regular pull-ups and then round-the-world reps that had her take her chin from hand to hand, dips, pounding the core with medicine balls, pendulum lifts with a thirty-pound kettle ball, and then a forty-pound one. Then came isometrics that had the sweat pouring off her from standing in one spot, followed by endless deep lunges with the kettles being passed under each hammy, decline push-ups, crunches, sumo squats with ass-busting dumbbells, and then she jumped rope for ten minutes, doing crossovers every fifth rep.

Then it was time for the pièce de résistance. Everything else had simply been a warm-up. A rehearsal for the real show. She wanted to do it while she was tired, otherwise, what was the point?

She loaded the plates on a bar, chalked her hands, and bent over the bar.

Pine was tall for a female weightlifter. This was an advantage and a disadvantage. From simply a physics point of view, shorter people had shorter distances to heft the weight. And shorter muscles tended to be more explosive in nature, because of the very same rule of science. But Pine's longer muscles gave her tremendous leverage that shorter muscles simply could not muster.

She closed her eyes and focused everything she had in a way that only a trained athlete needed to. The mind ready, she needed to execute what was called the "dynamic start." This would separate the weights from the floor. With a sudden, explosive movement, Pine performed the clean part of the lift, curling the loaded bar under her chin while simultaneously nailing the squat perfectly. She then performed the bounce, rose up with the barbell, completing the concentric phase, and, with a whoosh of released air, jerked it cleanly overhead as she split her legs performing the drive position. Then, legs parallel, she held the weights steadily aloft.

Clean and jerk. Done.

There was a lot more to the Olympic lifts than people probably thought. It wasn't merely about brute strength. Pine had seen enormous men, far stronger than she, fail to clean and jerk or snatch as much weight as she could. You needed to be strong, for sure, but your technique needed to be flawless. That was why terms like *the bounce, the concentric, the double-knee bend* or *scoop, the drive, the dynamic start,* and *the second pull* were all things that had been beaten into her mind and her muscle memory. You needed to do all these things at the exact right moment and with the requisite forward and upward momentum to have a chance of moving twin columns of massive plates stacked on a bar where you wanted them to go.

She dropped the barbell, stopping it with her hand as it bounced back up, and then the weights fell back to the floor and stayed there. It was a practiced motion, one she had done thousands of times before.

She unloaded some weights, spun on the collars, readied her-self, measuring her breaths, squaring her feet, chalking her hands once more. For this one she put leather lifting straps on her wrists, because the torque on those joints was going to be a bitch. This ensured that her hands and the metal would not go their separate ways.

Okay, this is for the gold. Or at least a spot on the damn team. In my dreams.

She bent down, set the wraps, and gripped the barbell with her hands spread wide, nearly touching each inside plate. She got her mind straight, because it was just as much mental as physical. Maybe more mental. She imagined the burst of force and the precise move-ment required to take this weight from the floor to over her head in one nearly seamless motion. The bar would initially come up to about her waist for less than a beat, and then with a powerful flick, be cast over her head, her arms straight, her butt a few inches from the floor. It was not a natural movement, and it required immense core strength and concentration. There was no margin for error.

That was the essence of the snatch.

Whoever had devised this lift, Pine thought, was one sick bastard.

This lift was, and always had been, her nemesis, her Waterloo, the reason she had not gone to the Athens Olympics in '04. Athens, where it had all started, way back in 1896. How special would that have been? Well, she'd never found out.

Pine steadied her breathing, going longer and longer on the inhales and exhales. She was building up to the exact right timing of her last inhalation and exhalation where the snatch phase would come. It was all timing, technique, and a level of explosive strength most people couldn't comprehend, male or female.

She performed the first part flawlessly, squatting there with her arms in the shape of a V and the weight directly above her head, her butt nearly touching the rubberized floor. Her pull, power, scoop, and second pull execution had been one of her best ever.

Only she wasn't done.

Okay, Atlee, this is for the money. Just stand up. Couldn't be simpler. Just stand up. One...two...three...

But when she tried to rise, things started to unravel—a tremble of thigh, a twitch of hamstring, the slightest giving way of her left triceps—and she had to drop the bar, falling back on her ass in the process.

She sat there, breathing hard, the sweat dripping down her face and onto her chest, her gaze pointed at the floor.

Defeated.

Six-pack and Knee Rehab had long since gone.

But Kenny Kuni was still there.

"You good?" he called out in a casual tone as he did some paper-work at the front counter.

She nodded and gave him a thumbs-up.

Not the first time this had happened.

He went back to his paperwork.

"Shit," she muttered. She was *not* good. Despite her excellence in the first half of the lift, her form had sucked in the final stage, which was all that mattered. Her mental mechanics had completely broken down. She had been intimidated. Afraid.

Shit.

She finally rose and performed the Yoga and Pilates regimen that constituted her cooldown. Her muscles felt good stretching out, the tendons, ligaments, and cartilage all thanking her for the relief after the merciless pounding of iron.

She hit the shower, changed into her work clothes, and walked out, hair still wet.

This had been her time. Now the FBI owned her for the rest of the day.

13

Pᴉɴᴇ ᴅʀᴏᴠᴇ ᴛᴏ ʜᴇʀ ᴏꜰꜰɪᴄᴇ and entered the underground parking garage. There was a guy on duty there, and after hours the overhead door would come down, requiring key card access.

This level of security was not because of Pine's presence.

It was because of the other law enforcement agency located here.

ICE. Immigration and Customs Enforcement.

Today, it was more known for immigration enforcement. And they were very active in Arizona, rounding up and deporting masses of people. It had become a political football, really.

Because of that there had been threats made. And the building might be a target. Hence the security guy and the overhead door with key card access.

Pine routinely saw some of the ICE guys in and around the building. She knew all the agents there, but didn't really hang with them very often, because they kept to themselves. She was FBI, under the Justice Department. ICE was under the Department of Homeland Security. There was a bit of a federal rivalry there, but their work almost never overlapped. But they were fellow feds and she would always have their backs if they needed it.

The underground garage kept the sun off the cars during the day. It was actually a necessity here, especially during the summer. Otherwise, she would have let her truck run without her in it for a few minutes with the AC cranked to max. And she'd still sweat when she got in.

She parked next to a vehicle with a cover over it.

This car had once belonged to a veteran FBI agent named Frank Stark, who had been a mentor of hers during Pine's second field assignment. Every FBI agent got their creds, badge, and *first* assignment upon graduating from Quantico. The first-year assignment was done as a probationary agent, to see if you could cut it in the field. After a year's time, you were no longer a probie and were transferred to your next assignment.

Pine's had been Cleveland, sometimes referred to in FBI circles as the "mistake on the lake."

It was there that she had met Stark.

She lifted the cover off and stared down at the 1967 Ford Mustang convertible, with parchment interior and matching top, and an iconic frost turquoise exterior. It had been meticulously restored by Stark, with the aid of the junior fibbie Pine.

The car restoration had been a project conducted in Stark's workshop/garage behind his 1950s-era house set in a neighborhood of homes that looked identical to each other running as far as the eye could see.

When Stark had asked if she wanted to help, Pine's first inclination was to say no. This was Stark's last posting, everyone knew that. He was biding his time to collect his pension. And he had this hobby of restoring old cars. But something in the man's request struck a chord in Pine, and she volunteered to help. At least for a bit.

They had started out disassembling the car fore to aft, keeping a record of all parts and putting them in labeled boxes. Some they had reused, others they had discarded. They had taken a lot of photos of the process to refer back to. Stripping the car down to its metal bones, they'd used walnut shell and glass beads media blasting to remove all the paint, because those materials wouldn't peen the metal. There were special tools you needed to strip the car, although they had improvised some, even using a bottle opener to remove the drip-rail molding. They'd done a rear floor pan reinforcement, so they could convert the single exhaust to a dual output.

The chassis had been fully refinished and painted with a specialized silver undercoating. The exterior had been reinstalled after having been sanded down and repaired, or, where restoration was impossible, new metal panels had been precisely tooled to the car's original specs by a local company that Stark had found. Then the exterior had been painted the exact same shade of frost turquoise as the original. They'd also reworked all the electrical, and either purchased new screws and bolts or restored what they had.

After all the painting was complete they'd installed Dynamat, which kept the noise and exhaust heat under the car, where it should remain. The original engine had been the 289 V-8, of which only a few hundred were put in this model. But 1967 also had brought the first major redesign of the Mustang and had offered a larger engine option. So they'd dropped in a big block 390, which had been in the vast majority of the Mustangs built that year. That had necessitated the dual exhaust, since the 390 couldn't efficiently run off the single pipe. The 390 V-8 mustered 320 horsepower, plenty of muscle for a car that size.

The convertible top was beyond repair, but Stark had located a company that did replacements, and Pine had worked side by side with Stark to install it. Then there were new tires and rims, chrome front and back bumpers, new lights all around, refurbished grille and dashboard, parchment leather seats back and front, and a ton of elbow grease and more money than Stark really wanted to spend. However, Pine felt that the vet agent, a widower and childless, just wanted to do something to fill in a life that had become permanently lonely and would become infinitely more so once he handed in his badge. Since Pine had been equally lonely, it had been a good match. They could work together for hours and even days without saying much more than, "Will you pass me that wrench?" or "Grab me a cold beer."

The initial bit of volunteerism had stretched into nearly two years. Stark had retired a month after they completed the project, and Pine was being reassigned at the same time. But before she left they had taken a long ride in the fully restored Mustang. Stark had let her take the wheel on the way back and she had opened it up on the highway, letting the four carbs of the big block ooze power all over the asphalt as they shot like a rocket down the road.

They had already decided that if they were stopped by the cops, they would use their FBI badges to get off. The federal agents decided they were entitled to one get-out-of-jail-free card.

With the top down and the wind ripping through her hair and the speedometer at nearly 120, it had been the best feeling Pine had had in years. She'd truly felt wonderful. If Stark hadn't been thirty years her senior and crotchety as hell, she might have, in her euphoria, planted a kiss on him.

Unfortunately, a month after Pine had left for her new assignment Stark had died from a heart attack. He'd been found in his garage, slumped over in a chair, a socket wrench on the floor, apparently where it had dropped from his hand when he died.

Pine had been stunned to learn that in his will Stark had left her the title to the car. She had gone to retrieve it, and the Mustang had traveled with her to every assignment thereafter.

When she'd relocated, she'd driven it out west. Rather than keep it at her apartment when she was transferred to Shattered Rock, she'd kept it here, where it was protected from the sun and certain predators on two legs. She still had nightmares about somebody carjacking the vintage ride and then rolling it.

It was the only thing really that she had ever owned. Every time she drove it, she realized how much work had gone into restoring it. This represented two years of her life. It was the longest personal commitment she had ever made. Far longer than she had ever committed to a personal relationship.

She ran her hand along one fender and thought back to Stark, who was wise beyond his years, no doubt yearning for a daughter he would never have, until Pine had shown up for work one day only a year removed from busting her butt at Quantico.

He'd been a good friend, maybe the only true one she'd made at the Bureau, or maybe anywhere else.

He'd told her once, as they were installing the single Holley four-barrel carburetor, that the Bureau had really been his life. Except for restoring old cars.

He'd wiped his hands on an old rag, taken a sip of beer from a plastic cup, and eyed her from under tufted white brows. "Don't make that mistake, Pine," he'd growled. "Don't let this be it for you."

She'd ratcheted down the last bolt on the carb and glanced up at him.

"How do you know it was a mistake?" she'd asked.

"If you have to ask, you haven't learned shit from this whole thing."

As if restoring the Mustang was a *whole thing* other than simply putting an old car back together.

And maybe it was. And maybe Pine *had* gotten it. But that didn't mean she would ever do anything about it.

She put the cover back on the car and was heading up the stairs to her office when her phone buzzed.

It was her IT buddy in Salt Lake City.

"You got anything?" she asked as she emerged in the hallway leading to her office.

"I do, but it's strange."

"This whole case is strange. What do you have?"

"There have been lots of people who accessed that website over the last few months. I couldn't track them all down, but there was one that stood out."

"Which one?"

"I recognized one of the IP addresses" was his surprising reply.

"How could you have done that?" she asked.

"Because it was *yours*, Atlee."

"I know that," she said impatiently. "I went on the site recently to check it out. So did my assistant. She's the one who told me about it."

"I knew that was your address from when you contacted me. But when I checked out things further, I noticed some funny lines of code in the mix, so you might want to have the FBI geek squad check your computers."

"Why?"

"Because I think you might have been hacked."

14

"COFFEE, AGENT PINE?"

Pine had just entered her office when Blum greeted her.

The older woman was dressed, as always, in a highly professional manner. Skirt, jacket, pumps, hose, minimal jewelry, and a bit less makeup than normal.

Pine absentmindedly nodded and walked on to her office.

She closed the door, sat at her desk, and stared at her computer.

Hacked?

By who and why?

Her friend had told her something else. That whoever had done this could have easily done it remotely. In essence, taking control of her computer and making it do things the hacker wanted without ever entering the premises.

"If he's infiltrated your computer, he can see every keystroke you perform," her friend had told her.

Pine yanked the power cord off the computer at the same moment Blum opened the door with her cup of coffee.

"Problem?" asked Blum.

"I've been hacked."

Blum raised an eyebrow and then set the coffee down in front of Pine.

"Should I pull my cord, too?"

"Probably."

"I'll call the support services folks in Flagstaff straightaway. They'll send somebody up."

"Thanks."

"Does this have to do with the website I showed you?"

"I don't know. Maybe."

Blum closed the door behind her as she left.

Pine took out her phone and studied it. Was this compromised, too?

She looked at the landline on her desk. To bug that they would have had to break into her office, or at least the telecommunications box. But that was in the underground garage in a locked room with video surveillance, courtesy of ICE's presence here. She doubted they had accomplished that.

When the IT people came from Flagstaff she would have them check everything. Until then, Pine decided to just not call or email or text anybody from her office or her personal phone.

She left her coffee sitting on her desk and exited her office, rushing past Blum so fast the woman could only say, "Agent Pi—" before she was out the door.

She took the steps two at a time to the garage, got into her truck, and sped out into the sunshine.

There was a convenience store about three blocks away. It had something she really needed, something that was almost impossible to find anymore.

Pine pulled into a free space in front, hopped out, and made a beeline for the pay phone hanging on the outside wall next to the machine containing bags of ice. Shattered Rock actually had several public pay phones for two reasons: As hard as it was to believe, not everyone here had a mobile phone. And cell reception here could be really crappy.

She dropped in some coins and made the call.

Park Ranger Lambert picked up on the second ring.

"Hello?"

"Colson, it's Atlee."

"What number are you calling from?"

"Never mind. Look, has anything weird been happening on your end with respect to the Priest disappearance?"

Pine had still not told Lambert, or anyone else, that the man calling himself Benjamin Priest was not, in fact, Benjamin Priest.

"What do you mean 'weird'?"

"Out of the ordinary. Like have you gotten any inquiries from further up the food chain?"

"No, nothing like that."

"So, any progress on the case?"

"Cadavers turned up nothing, like I already reported. We've searched everywhere we can think to."

"Will agents from your Investigative Services Branch become involved now?"

"Above my pay grade."

Pine frowned into the phone receiver. This did not sound like the Colson Lambert she knew.

"Did Edward Priest ever send you a picture of his brother?"

"Look, Atlee, I don't mean to be rude, but I gotta go. Stuff at the office. Talk soon."

And he clicked off.

Pine slowly hung up the receiver. Well, he had indirectly answered her question. There *was* weird stuff going on, on his end.

She stuffed more change into the machine and punched in the numbers.

The phone rang and rang and then Edward Priest's voice mail came on. The mailbox was full, so she was unable to leave a message.

Frustrated, she hung up the phone, got back into her truck, and drove off. She checked her rear and side mirrors to see if any stealth vehicle was taking an overt interest in her SUV.

On the way back to the office, she pondered what to do.

Lambert was obviously stonewalling her. Edward Priest's mailbox was full. Her computer and possibly her phone had been compromised. The Bureau's National Security Branch was in the loop. Her supervisor's boss had called her, made inquiries about only this case, and then gave her a not-so-subtle warning to watch her back.

And on top of that she had a missing man who was supposed to be someone else, only wasn't. And where was he? And where was Benjamin Priest?

And who had killed and mutilated the damn mule and why? And what did an over-a-century-old, probably bogus story of Egyptians in the Grand Canyon have to do with any of it?

She ran a hand through her still-damp hair and decided now would be a good time to return to the scene of the crime.

She turned in the opposite direction, heading west.

Thirty-five minutes later she was at the South Rim of the Canyon. Her federal badge gained her free admission to the park. She slid into an empty space near Park Headquarters in a section reserved for the Park Police. Her ride had federal plates, so she didn't expect that to be a problem.

She got out and looked around. The place was filled with tourists. Most would simply walk along the South Rim path admiring the views and taking pictures. Some would stay overnight at the various lodgings. Others would head back to wherever they had come from. Still others had taken mules down or would hike down into the Canyon.

Though a popular tourist destination, the Canyon was an extreme environment. People died here every year. The causes were many and included heart attacks, falls, animal encounters, dehydration, and hyponatremia, an electrolyte disorder where your brain swelled with an excess of fluids. In addition, some rafters drowned in the punishing rapids of the Colorado River.

As she was standing there, Pine saw a man dressed in athletic shorts, a tank top, and running shoes jogging down the pavement toward the parking lot. He stopped, stretched, and then headed toward a muddy Jeep with its canvas top down. It also had a power winch on the front bumper.

An ARMY STRONG sticker was on the rear fender.

"Hey, Sam."

Sam Kettler turned around as Pine called out.

She walked over to him. "Don't you work nights here?"

"Usually, but not last night."

She looked him over. The tank top and shorts revealed what his uniform had not. The man was ripped. Each muscle melded perfectly into its neighbor. And unlike some guys who had inflated chests and swollen arms, matched with an underdeveloped lower body, his thighs, hammies, and calves were the most defined part of his musculature.

"So what are you doing here now?"

"Running the trails. Just finished."

Pine looked over his shoulder. "Which one did you do? It's already pretty hot."

"South to North and then back."

"You did rim-to-rim-to-rim?"

He nodded, reached inside his Jeep, and grabbed a towel to wipe down.

"How long did it take you?" she asked.

"Six hours and fifty-eight minutes. I started really early."

Her jaw slackened. "To run forty-two miles with twenty-two thousand feet of vertical change including five thousand feet on the run back up to the South Rim?"

He finished wiping off and took a bottle of water out of the fanny pack around his waist. "I guess that sounds right, yeah. It's still way off the record. I'll never beat it."

"But there isn't one person in a million who could run it as fast as you did."

He finished the bottle of water. "What are you doing up here?" he asked.

"Came to check in."

"Find out what happened to the mule?"

"Not yet, working on it."

"I'm sure you'll get there." He looked away and seemed to tense, his gaze averted.

She waited a few moments, but when he didn't say anything, she said, "Well, see you around."

She started to walk away.

"Hey, Atlee?"

She turned. "Yeah?"

"You got time for a beer and maybe some dinner tonight?"

"You're not working tonight either?"

"Other reason I ran today." He grinned impishly. "I'm not twenty anymore. I need some time to recover."

She considered his offer. "Sounds good."

"There's a place in Shattered Rock."

She smiled. "Let me guess—Tony's Pizza."

"How'd you know?"

"It's pretty much the *only* place in Shattered Rock to get a beer."

"Seven o'clock work?"

"See you then."

Pine walked into the headquarters and asked for not Colson Lambert but the other park ranger, Harry Rice.

Rice, as it turned out, was over at the mule barn, she was told, so Pine headed there. She found Rice with the mules and also the mule wrangler, Mark Brennan.

"You're not wrangling a group today?" said Pine to Brennan, while Rice watched her with a look that Pine thought was unnecessarily wary.

But maybe not, considering what he might have been told by his superiors.

Brennan was rubbing salve on a mule's forelegs. "We got a shipment of supplies coming in today. I'm handling it. Two other wranglers are leading the group down."

Pine nodded and looked at Rice. "I spoke to your buddy, Colson. Doesn't look like the investigation is getting much traction."

"We looked everywhere for the guy," said Rice, keeping his attention on a point to the left of Pine's shoulder. "Never found anything."

They all fell silent for about a half minute.

"Colson didn't seem very interested in doing any more work on the case. That your position too, Harry?"

Rice again wouldn't meet her eye. "I'm a Park Ranger, not a cop."

"But what about ISB? Are they taking up the case? I asked Colson, but he blew me off."

Rice shrugged. "Above my pay grade."

"Seems to be the standard response these days," replied Pine, wondering if he and Lambert had been scripted.

Brennan looked from one to the other. "Something going on here I don't know about?"

"Probably," said Pine. "Mark, you saw this guy Priest. I want you to talk to a sketch artist I use and give that description to her."

Rice said, "Why? You use a sketch artist if you're trying to ID somebody. We already know who the missing guy is."

"Do we?" asked Pine.

Rice looked taken aback. "His brother told us. He's Benjamin Priest."

"I asked Colson if he got a photo of Priest from his brother. He wouldn't answer me."

Brennan said, "Wait a minute, are you saying this guy *wasn't* Ben Priest?"

"I like to confirm everything. Not just assume." Pine glanced at Rice. "Did you guys just assume, or did you confirm?"

"I don't like your tone, Atlee," replied Rice.

"And I don't like getting played, *Harry*."

Brennan kept looking between the two feds, the confusion on his features growing.

"So, Mark, I need you to come with me for the sketch artist."

"But I got stuff to do here."

"Find somebody else to do it."

As they walked out into the daylight, Brennan said quietly, "What's going on here, Agent Pine. I mean, you guys are both with the federal government, right?"

"Right. But the federal government is a big, unwieldy beast at times. And I go my own way." She pulled out her phone and brought up the photo that Edward Priest had sent of his brother. "See the tall guy in this photo? You recognize him? Could he have also been in the group of ten with Priest?"

"No, no way. Nobody that tall was in the group. And nobody who looked close to that guy."

"Did you take a group photo? Did anyone take photos of each other?"

"People could have taken shots of each other. But there wasn't any group photo that I know of."

Pine put her phone away. "Okay, let's go see that sketch artist."

CHAPTER

15

Jennifer Yazzie was married to Joe Yazzie Sr., who was an officer with the Navajo Nation Police. He was one of about two hundred sworn cops and pulled patrol duty working out of the Tuba City Police District on the western side of the Navajo reservation. Riding in his department-issued Chevy Blazer, Yazzie alone was responsible for about seventy square miles of territory. Pine knew he performed his duties with a Glock 22 sidearm, pepper spray, an AR-15, a shotgun, body armor, an expandable baton, and his most important tools: a calm demeanor and an understanding of the area and the people that inhabited it that came only from having grown up there.

Jennifer Yazzie worked as one of about three hundred support staff at the Nation Police. Although her main duties were in the IT department, she was an accomplished artist, having sold her pieces throughout the Southwest and having her works shown in numerous regional exhibitions. She was the police force's unofficial sketch artist in residence.

Yazzie also worked in the Tuba City Police District, and that was where Pine drove to with Brennan.

Though she had a child who was twenty-four, Yazzie was only forty-five. She was a lean five five with long, dark hair and finely etched lines around her eyes and mouth. She possessed an easy smile, as though whatever she was doing brought her great joy.

Pine had met her within a month of moving to the Shattered

Rock RA. Along with working hard to meet with all the local law enforcement agencies, she had provided them resources and assistance over many cases. Pine also had sat on her share of bar stools drinking with them, getting to know them and the policing realities here. The Bureau actually graded an agent on her ability to strike up good relationships with the locals, and would even speak directly to these other agencies, to find out whether the FBI agent in question was doing a good job at that or not.

During one of those times, Yazzie had joked with Pine that women in law enforcement were still rare enough that they all needed to keep up the professional sisterhood. Pine had agreed. The representation of women in law enforcement was still appallingly low in most parts of the country. Here, in the wild and wooly Southwest, Pine thought it was negligible.

After Pine had introduced Brennan and discussed what she needed, Yazzie led them to a small conference room, where she had not paper and brushes or pens but a laptop computer.

Yazzie smiled and said, "Like just about everything else, sketch art has gone digital."

Pine and Brennan sat down across from her while Yazzie punched in some keys and brought up a computer program. She looked over at Brennan.

"You ready?"

He nodded. To Pine, the man looked nervous and uncertain, as though he were about to undergo a painful medical exam or polygraph instead of feeding a memory of a certain person to Yazzie, so she could recreate the image on the computer screen.

Yazzie asked a series of questions, each one a little more detailed than the last. From the basic, male or female, to the shape of a nose, the curve of a chin, the wrinkles on a neck and around the eyes, to the texture of the person's hair, along with the color.

After about an hour of this back and forth, Yazzie swung the computer around so they could see the finished results.

"How'd I do?" she asked.

Pine watched as Brennan's jaw dropped. "Damn, ma'am, that's him."

"Nice to get positive feedback," said a smiling Yazzie.

"Jen, can you print that image out for me and also email it to me?" said Pine.

"You got it."

As they were leaving, Pine drew Yazzie aside after telling Brennan she would meet him at the truck.

"Ran into your son the other night outside my apartment building."

Yazzie's easy smile devolved to a frown. "Joe Jr.?"

Pine nodded. "He was with some sunburned jerk who has a beef with the feds. I had to take him down a peg."

"Tim Mallory. He got kicked out of the Army for drinking and drugs. He moved here last year from Philadelphia. Joe's been hanging out with him."

"He's not a good influence. And Joe said he was there to meet up with Kyle Chavez. Also not a good influence."

Yazzie said, "I didn't know he'd been messing around with Kyle."

"They were also smoking weed and drinking. Look, I know that's not unusual with young guys, but I don't want to see Joe get into trouble that he can't get out of."

"His father's been trying to get him to try out for the police, but he has no interest."

"What is he doing?"

"Not much. He works odd jobs. He comes home sometimes. I cook him meals, try to get him motivated about his future. But not much seems to work with him."

"His brothers?"

"Thomas is in college in Portland, Oregon. Matt's a senior. He's going to West Point."

"That's great, very impressive."

"But not Joe. His father isn't happy. It's all he thinks about. His namesake. You know."

"I don't know because I've never had kids. But I imagine it can really mess with you."

"Joe's at his wit's end. Nothing he says seems to get through." She shrugged and smiled sadly. "My son's Navajo name is Ahiga. Do you know what that means?"

Pine shook her head.

Yazzie sighed resignedly and said, "It translates to 'he fights.' And Joe Jr. has lived up to that name. At least when it comes to his parents."

"I just wanted to give you a heads-up."

"Thanks, Atlee. I'll let my husband know too. And good luck with your missing person case."

Pine walked out into the heat and sun thinking that she would need something a lot stronger than luck. And she was also thinking that motherhood was not for her.

She dropped Brennan off at the park, turned around, and drove straight back to Shattered Rock.

Carol Blum rose from her desk when Pine entered the office.

"The IT folks have been over our computers. They actually did it remotely. They found some things on there that shouldn't have been and removed them."

"So the computers had been compromised?"

"Yes. They're checking to see where it might have come from. I'm thinking it might have happened when I went on that website. If so, I'm very sorry, Agent Pine."

"Don't worry about it," said Pine. "I think it might have happened regardless."

"They also checked out our phones. Both our cell and landlines. They're fine."

"Good. Because I'm out of quarters."

"You did have a message from the forensics lab at Flagstaff. They wanted you to call. I have the number."

Pine took this information into her office and closed the door.

She called the number. On the second ring a person picked up.

She was Marjorie Parks, an assistant medical examiner with the FBI. Pine had worked with her before.

"Well, Atlee, I have to admit, I've never done a postmortem on a mule before. Well, technically with an animal it's referred to as a necropsy. I guess I have you to thank for that."

"Yeah, it was a first for me, too. What'd you find out?"

"The death wound was performed with a long-bladed knife with an upward angle, not quite a scythe shape, but something along those lines."

"The letters on the hide?"

"They were done with a knife as well. Any idea what *j* and *k* refer to?"

"We did some research on our own and might have pulled up a lead."

"Good luck on that."

"So what drug was used on Sallie Belle?"

"Who told you about that?" said Parks in surprise. "I was saving that for last."

"You're not going to start cutting a half-ton mule without knocking it out first."

"I'm sure. Okay, the tests show that the drug used was romifidine. It's a sedative typically used in veterinary medicine with large animals, like horses and mules."

"Okay, we know the how. Now the only questions are who and why."

"And those are usually the toughest of all to answer."

"It's why I get paid the big bucks."

16

FOR SOME STRANGE REASON, Pine had a hard time deciding what to wear to meet Kettler for dinner and a beer.

"It's not like you've never been on a date, Pine," she said to herself, as she held up one outfit after another in front of the mirror tacked to the back of her closet door. "Though it has been a while."

In the end, she settled on a sundress with a sweater on over it, and sandals. She'd carry her Glock in her purse and leave the Beretta home. She hoped the date wouldn't warrant a backup weapon.

The drive there took only a few minutes. She saw the Jeep parked at the curb and looked at her watch. One minute to seven. Mr. Kettler apparently liked to be early.

She parked and went inside, immediately seeing him near the rear, because the place was so small. He rose and waved.

He was wearing jeans and an untucked white shirt that made his tan seem even deeper. The top button was undone, revealing smooth, bronzed skin. His short hair was a bit messy, like he'd just let the air dry it on the ride over. It only served to enhance his attractiveness, Pine thought.

In lieu of a formal handshake, they exchanged a brief hug.

As they sat down, he said, "You look different out of uniform. I mean a really nice different." He lapsed into an embarrassed silence.

She let him linger there for just a few seconds before rescuing him. "Thanks. I'm not sure whether I like you better in the shorts and tank top or what you're wearing now."

They both laughed, and the ice was officially broken.

They ordered beers and then salad and pizza.

They clinked bottles, and each took a long sip.

He looked out the window. "You like living here?"

She shrugged. "It's close to work. My office is right down the street."

"Same building as ICE, right?"

"How'd you know?"

"They've been coming around the park a lot more. Rounding up illegals. I had to go over to their office a couple times to provide some information. And a bunch of us rangers have had to attend some conferences there."

"Conferences? What about?"

"The best way I can say it is recognizing our duty as federal officers to notify them about illegals so they can come get them."

"You don't have any illegals working for the Park Service. They couldn't pass the background check."

"No, but we have contractors, landscapers, people working in the gift shops and restaurants, driving delivery trucks, that sort of thing."

"Do you turn in many?"

"None so far. Hey, if they do something criminal, I'd be all over them. But if they work hard and keep their noses clean, I'm not getting in their business."

"Sounds like a good philosophy to me. So, how long did you sleep after your run today?" She tacked on an impish grin.

"About as long as it took me to run the trails. I'm not getting any younger."

"Special Forces to Park Service. Quite a segue."

"Who told you about Special Forces?"

"Colson. He said someone you served with told him. Chest full of medals including the Purple Heart. Impressive."

"It sounds a lot more impressive than it is."

"How so? You were serving your country fighting in a war."

Kettler finished his beer and waved at the waitress for another. After she brought it, he took a swig and said, "It wasn't a war, Atlee."

"What was it then?"

"I didn't sign up to shoot..." He abruptly stopped and looked away.

"Shoot what, Sam?"

"Nothing." He was silent for a few moments. "Hey, let's change the subject. I didn't ask you out to talk about a stupid war."

She studied him for a few moments. "You did your job, Sam. You did what you were supposed to. No more, no less. That's all we can do."

He looked up. "To answer your question, I joined the Park Service because it was all about protecting something worth protecting right here, in this country. I don't pull my gun. I help people enjoy the Canyon. I wake up every day with that one purpose in mind. And it's a great place. Puts a smile on my face every day."

"And in your free time, you play Superman and run the trails," she said, smiling.

He grinned back. "I'm sure you've done it, too."

"I've hiked a lot of the trails. Never ran them, at least not like you."

"It's pretty damn exhilarating. Makes you feel great to be alive to experience it. I'd love to share that feeling with you."

"Well, you might get what you wish for," she replied warmly.

Their pizza and salad came, and they took a few minutes to eat while they chatted on topics ranging from local politics and relations with the Indian tribes to how a big hole in the ground was among the most dazzling sites on earth.

Finished with their meal, they drained their second beers and then went for a walk.

An ice cream truck rambled by with its bell tinkling, and on impulse Pine bought them both vanilla cones.

They strolled along, licking at their dessert while the night's heat enveloped them.

It was hot enough, in fact, for Pine to take off her sweater and wrap it around her waist.

"Didn't figure you for tats," said Kettler, looking over her arms and delts.

"I like to surprise."

"Gemini and Mercury," he said.

"You know astrology?"

"Just when I read my horoscope. What do the 'No Mercy' ones mean?"

"Just something personal," she said tersely.

"Oh, okay," he said quickly, noting her uncomfortable look.

"Sorry, I get funny about stuff like that."

"No worries. I get funny about stuff, too."

She said, "I didn't see any tats on you the other day."

"I've got one, but not in a place you could see."

"Where would that be, I wonder?" she said playfully.

In response, he edged down the waistband of his jeans, exposing the top of his hip. She bent down to look because the tat was small.

"Wait a minute, is that Hobbes?"

"Yeah, from *Calvin and Hobbes.*"

"Okay, ex–Special Forces with a cartoon tiger on his hip. Count me officially stunned."

"What can I say? It was my favorite comic strip when I was a kid."

He edged his trousers back up, then motioned to her muscular arms. "Olympic-caliber lifter, right?"

"Okay, for the record, I had nothing to do with that Wikipedia page," replied Pine. She shot him a curious glance. "So you checked me out before tonight?"

The question was asked in a mildly flirtatious way.

"I actually checked you out from the moment I saw you."

She laughed.

"I guess your career doesn't lend itself to much free time," he said.

"Not usually, no."

"Well, I'm glad you made time tonight."

She touched his shoulder. "Yeah, me too. It was fun."

He glanced down at her exposed calf. "What were you shot with?"

"Most people think it's a mole."

Kettler shrugged. "I'm not most people. I've seen enough entry wounds to last a lifetime."

"Luckily, just a twenty-two-caliber. Round stayed in, otherwise the exit wound would've been really ugly."

"How'd it happen?"

"Arrest gone wrong. I made a mistake. Learned my lesson. Never to be repeated." She paused. "Okay, that's my story. Where were you wounded to earn the medal?"

He shook his head, smiled, and finished his ice cream. "Not in a place I can show on the first, or second, or maybe the tenth date. I'm sort of old-fashioned."

She hooked him by the arm. "Good, because I'm sort of old-fashioned, too."

17

Pᴵɴᴇ sᴛᴵʀʀᴇᴅ, ᴍᴏᴠᴵɴɢ to the right in her bed and then back to the left. She was coming out of some vague dream and something was flitting in her ear, like a bothersome gnat.

She finally opened her eyes and looked at her buzzing phone on her nightstand.

The electronic gnat to which the entire world was now enslaved.

She picked it up and said groggily, "Pine."

"Agent Pine. It's Ed Priest."

Pine sat bolt upright, fully awake now like she'd downed a pot of coffee and poured a second one over her head. "I tried calling you, but your voice mailbox was full. I couldn't leave a message."

"Something weird is going on," said Priest.

"Give me every detail."

"I don't know if I want to do this over the phone."

"I can come to see you. I can get a flight out in the morning."

"You won't have to do that. I'm in Arizona."

Pine checked the clock on her phone. It was nearly eleven.

"Are you at Sky Harbor?"

"No. I flew into Phoenix from the East Coast but took a puddle jumper to Flagstaff. I just landed."

"Stay there. I'll come to get you. Give me a couple of hours."

"The place is closing down. I think mine was the last flight in."

"There's an IHOP in Flagstaff." She gave him the address. "It's open 24/7. Do you have a rental?"

"No, but there's a cabstand."

"It's only about four miles into town. I'll meet you there."

Pine swiftly dressed, grabbed both her guns, and headed out.

It was a lonely drive at this time of night under a sky thick with stars and the occasional whizzing-by satellite. That was one of the main differences for Pine between the ambient-light-filled eastern U.S. and here.

The sky.

You could see every millimeter of it, the vastness, the im-penetrability. It was a part of your daily life, that upward glance into the cosmos. Every night it seemed to try to show how truly insignificant you were. And eventually, you started to believe it. And a daily dose of humility wasn't so bad.

As she roared south, Pine's mind was going in several different directions at once. Before she had been awoken by Priest's phone call she'd been ruminating over how to get to Ed Priest, since he was the only way she could see to get to his brother. Well, she'd gotten her wish hand-delivered to her.

She pulled into the parking lot of the IHOP and jumped out of her SUV, reaching the front entrance in two long strides. She opened the door and looked around. There were about fifteen customers seated at a variety of tables and booths, but it didn't take her long to spot Ed Priest. He looked just like he did in the picture he'd sent her. He was all the way in the back at a booth, trying to be inconspicuous behind a large menu while at the same time looking nervously around. A rolling suitcase with straps and stickers sat next to him on the floor.

She hurried over to him, glanced at his suitcase, and slid into the seat across from him.

"Agent Pine?"

She took out her creds and shield and showed them to him.

He sat back, looking relieved.

"Call me paranoid, but can I see some ID from you?"

He took out his Maryland driver's license and showed it to her.

"Now why did you decide to come out here?" she asked.

"Because I don't know where Ben is. I haven't heard from him. No one has. It's like he's disappeared."

"I want to show you something," said Pine.

She took out her phone and brought up an attachment to an email she had received earlier from Jennifer Yazzie.

She held the picture in front of Priest.

"You recognize this guy?"

"No. Should I?"

"This is a digital sketch of the man calling himself Benjamin Priest, who rode a mule to the bottom of the Canyon and then disappeared. As you can see, he doesn't look anything like your brother. He looks a lot more like you, which is why I thought Ben was you in the picture you sent."

Ed Priest laid down his menu and continued to stare with greater intensity at the image on the phone screen.

"I...I don't understand. Why would this man be calling himself Benjamin Priest? And then where the hell is my brother?"

"When was the last time you actually saw your brother?"

The waitress came by and Pine ordered a coffee, while Priest ordered a full breakfast.

"I haven't eaten all day," he explained to Pine as the waitress walked away. "Nervous flyer. I can't eat on planes."

"Probably better for you. Plane food sucks. So, your brother?"

"It was maybe two weeks ago or so. He came by our house."

"Did he have a reason?"

"Not really. He called and asked if he could come over for dinner. He said he had some free time and just wanted to see the family."

"How did he seem?"

Priest sat back and played with the edges of his paper napkin.

"You have to understand that my younger brother was the star in the family. High school valedictorian, quarterback on the football team, and he was the star shooting forward of the basketball team, even though he hated basketball. But he knew he was good at it. He graduated top of his class at Georgetown while I went to the University of Maryland."

"Both good schools."

"Yeah, well, Ben was on another level. I'm just glad I was older. He would've been a damn tough act to follow. He was successful at everything he touched. And he was tall and good-looking. You saw his picture. I missed out on all that."

"But never married? No kids?"

"No. He dated in high school and college, but once he got out, he was fully focused on his career."

"Which was what?"

They paused as their coffees were delivered.

Pine took a sip of hers. "Your brother's career?"

"Right now, your guess is as good as mine. All I know is he traveled the world. Hell, I took the kids to Disney World two years ago and he called up to wish me a happy birthday. I asked where he was, and he said, 'Oh, somewhere in the Middle East.' Another time he was in freaking Kazakhstan. My kids would get holiday gifts from him, and the boxes would have all these foreign stickers and labels and stuff on them. I'd have to pay customs on some of it just to get them released."

"And you never asked him what he did for a living?"

"Like I said, I did, and he made that joke. I didn't want to push it. I just thought he had to keep it secret. He wouldn't be the only one like that in the DC area."

"Capricorn Consultants?"

"He brought it up one time when I asked him how things were going. He said he'd started his own company. I asked him what it was that he did, and he said he helped people who needed it."

"I could find no record of any Beltway company called Capricorn Consultants."

"I know. I looked, too. I'm an accountant. I work at a CPA firm in Maryland. I checked the government records. There was nothing."

"You didn't tell me how he seemed when he came over for dinner two weeks ago."

"Understand, my brother can be really intense, and he's super smart. He knows everything about everything. I used to joke with him that he'd kill it on *Jeopardy*. But that night he seemed relaxed and more open to talking than I'd ever seen him."

"What did he talk about?"

"Politics. World events. Baseball. He's a Nats fan."

"Did he ask you for anything? Did he give you anything? Did he request that you do anything for him?"

"No, nothing like that."

Priest's food came, and he took a few moments to pepper and salt his eggs and douse his pancakes in syrup.

He looked up at Pine watching him. "You don't look like you eat stuff like this," he said.

"You might be surprised." She took another sip of her coffee. "So, you came out here with what expectation?"

"I'm not sure I have one. But I'm really worried about my brother. Whenever I contacted him before he'd always get back to me. It might take a few hours or even a day, but he always got back to me. Not this time. I really think something's happened to him. And now you tell me it wasn't even him in the Grand Canyon. But this other guy was using my brother's name. Do you think he did something to my brother? And stole his identity?"

"I don't know," said Pine. "But did anything specifically cause you to come out here?"

Now Priest looked uncomfortable.

"Your voice mail was full," she said. "You're an accountant. You strike me as a by-the-book kind of person. You don't return phone calls, clients get pissed." She paused. "So who was calling you so much that you didn't want to answer?"

Priest laid down his fork and fingered his coffee cup. "I'm just a normal guy. I've got a wife and kids. Like I said, I go to Disney World on vacation. I coach my son's Little League baseball team. I'm not equipped to be involved in some crazy international conspiracy thing."

"International conspiracy thing? Care to explain?"

"It's just a feeling."

"You think your brother is, what, a spy?"

"Middle East, Kazakhstan? A company that doesn't exist? And now this? It's hard for me to admit, but I don't really know my brother at all. At least not his professional side."

"But you said you knew your brother was going to go to the Grand Canyon."

"Yeah. He phoned and told me about the trip. He'd never done the mule ride. Said it was on his bucket list. He was excited. He'd scheduled it a long time ago. I guess you have to."

"You do. And you have no idea how the guy I showed you on my phone ended up going in his place?"

"No. Are you sure that my brother *wasn't* part of the group that went into the Canyon?"

"I showed the picture you sent me of your brother to the mule wrangler who traveled down to the floor of the Canyon that day. He said your brother was definitely not part of the group. He said there was no one even close to looking like him, even if maybe he was in disguise. Your brother looks to be, what, six three and about one eighty?"

"That's right. He got all the height in the family, too," he added nervously, glancing at Pine's FBI shield. "But my brother is a good guy. He wouldn't be involved in anything bad, that I know."

"You just told me you didn't really know your brother at all, at least his professional side."

Priest slumped back. "Yeah, I guess I did say that."

"So, what were all the voice mails on your phone?"

"Hang-ups. I finally checked them. They were all from the same number. When I called the number back no one answered."

"Can you give me the number? I can check it out."

Priest took out his phone and read out the number, and Pine added it to her phone contacts.

"What are your plans while you're out here?" she asked.

"I don't have any. I flew out here really in a panic. Then I decided to call you. To see what you might suggest."

"I'm not sure I have a good answer for you. But you have to understand, Mr. Priest, that if your brother is involved in something serious, *you* could be in some danger."

"Me! Why?"

"Certain people may assume your brother told you something important. Or by your coming out here they may think your brother communicated with you, and that you flew out here to meet with him."

"But no one knows I'm here except you."

"Did you book your flight with a credit card?"

"Well, yes. Of course, I did."

"Then you're in the system. And people who can access the system could know your movements. They could be watching us right now."

Priest looked around the restaurant before staring back at her. "Shit, are you serious?"

"Very serious."

"I feel like I'm in a freaking movie. So what do I do now? Should I get a hotel somewhere? Or maybe I can stay with you?"

Pine pondered this for a few moments. "You can stay at my place at least for tonight, or what's left of it, until we think of other arrangements."

"Are you sure? I don't want to be an imposition. And if you're right and people are watching me, then you could be in danger, too."

"I signed on for that when I took the job, Mr. Priest."

"Please, just call me Ed. Can I hit the restroom before we leave? With everything going on my stomach's giving me fits."

"Sure thing. I'll get the check."

Pine kept Priest in her periphery as he headed to the restroom, while she went to the woman at the cash register and paid the bill. Later, she led him to her truck and loaded his bag into the back.

They got on the road and headed back north.

She checked her watch. It was going on two in the morning. One thing Pine was certain of: She wasn't going to get a lot of sleep this night.

18

Pine gave Priest her bedroom and she took the couch in the front room. She had insisted on this. She lay down on the couch and closed her eyes. The dawn was not that far off.

She estimated it was about thirty minutes later when she heard the noise for the first time. A bump, a footstep, a squeak of door or window. Or something else.

Her fingers closed around her pistol as she blinked rapidly to adjust her eyes to the low levels of light.

The *tick-tock* of the kitchen clock echoed in her head as she listened for the sounds to resume. When they did, she rolled quietly off the couch and laid the two pillows out lengthwise, covering them with the blanket she'd had over her. She next slid along the hardwood floor to a far corner of the room, crouched there, and took aim with her pistol. With her free hand, she reached to her left.

Tick-tock, tick-tock.

Then squeak, then steps.

She kept her gun trained on a certain spot across the room.

The figure appeared in the doorway and then hurried over to the couch.

The silhouette of a gun was pointed at the couch. It remained there for a few seconds, the hand holding it shaking precipitously.

Then the gun was lowered, and the figure stepped back and started to turn away.

With her free hand, Pine hit the light switch.

The figure jumped back.

"Put the gun down and lie on the floor facedown with your hands over your head, fingers interlaced, and your feet spread. Do it now or I will shoot you."

Ed Priest did exactly as Pine had ordered.

His every limb quaking, he set the pistol down, got on the floor, and put his hands behind his head, his legs spread-eagled. He started to quietly sob.

Pine rose and walked over to him, picked up the pistol and set it down on the coffee table.

She sat on the couch and looked down at the man.

"How...how did you know?" asked Priest, his cheeks wet with tears.

"You made it easy. One, you're a really bad liar. I had training on that at the FBI. But I didn't really need it. When I asked who had called you all those times and you said you had called them back but no one answered, you showed every sign of lying. And I called the number you gave me. It's not in service. And then there were all the furtive glances you gave me at the IHOP. *And* your suitcase. That was the real giveaway."

"My suitcase!"

"It has a CAGPT sticker on it. That stands for 'check and give protection to.' It's what they do with valuable or fragile instruments. And also, it's what they sticker a case with that has a gun inside. But I knew for certain you had a gun in there, because the airline had zip-tied it, probably at the point of destination. It's a procedure they started to use after the Fort Lauderdale shooting. One zip tie for a pistol, two for a rifle. Yours has one, hence, a pistol. And in addition to that, your suitcase is easily small enough to be a carry-on. But you had to check it, as evidenced by the baggage claim sticker on the handle. Again, because you can't carry a gun on a plane. So why would a seemingly mild-mannered CPA be carrying a gun with him? Except maybe to use on the first person he called when he landed in Arizona? When you quickly suggested that you might stay with me, that sort of sealed it."

"If you knew all that, why didn't you just arrest me?"

"Simple. You hadn't done anything illegal. You can carry a gun in a suitcase. You can carry a concealed weapon in Arizona. I needed to see what you were going to do with it. When you made your intentions clear, so did I." She paused. "The question is why. You *are* Ed Priest with the accounting practice and family and Disney World vacations and all that. You're not some government assassin or mafia hit man."

"So you checked on me?"

"Of course I checked on you. I don't believe anyone unless I can verify it. Now do you want to get off the floor, sit in that chair, and tell me why you just tried to kill me?"

Priest gingerly got to his feet and plopped heavily into the chair across from her. He was still dressed in his traveling clothes.

"I was telling you the truth when I said I called the number back. But I was lying when I said no one had answered. They must have taken it out of service after they talked to me last."

"What did they tell you?"

"That if I didn't fly out here and kill you, my wife and my kids were dead."

"And you believed them?"

"They also sent me photos of my wife out shopping, my kids at school. They were obviously watching them."

Pine thought about this. *Why send this guy to do the dirty deed? Whoever was behind this couldn't come up with a pro to do the hit on me?* "Why did they say I had to die?"

"Because you were investigating my brother's disappearance."

"And did they say why your brother had disappeared?"

Priest hesitated. "No, not really, but I knew it was serious."

"As serious as murdering a federal agent? That can get you the death penalty."

"My family means more to me than my own life," barked Priest. He slowly calmed. "But I couldn't pull the trigger. I...I guess I'm not a killer."

"Clearly not. I was watching you."

"So what happens to me now? Am I going to prison?"

"I saw you weren't going to actually kill me. But when they find out you didn't pull the trigger, they're not going to be happy with you."

Priest buried his face in his hands and started sobbing heavily. "Oh my God, my family. I've killed my family."

"That we can take care of. I'll have them placed in protective custody until we figure out what the hell is going on."

Priest stopped crying and looked up at her. "You...you can do that?"

"But in return you need to help me."

"But how? I don't know anything."

"You may know more than you think. And right now, you're the best lead I have."

"So how do we proceed?"

"I make the call to take care of your family. And though it's nearly morning, I suggest we get some sleep. We've got a lot of work ahead of us."

"I'm really sorry about all this, Agent Pine."

"It wouldn't be the first time someone wanted to murder me."

He let out a sharp breath. "Jesus, I don't know how you do a job like that."

"Funny, it's the only job I've ever wanted *to* do."

19

Your family is in an FBI safe house back in Maryland," Pine told Priest over coffee in her kitchen later that morning.

"How did you explain that to them?"

"You mean how did I explain *your* involvement in all this?"

"Yes, I guess I do."

"I know how to word these things, Ed. You can breathe a little easier, at least for right now."

"So, what do we do?"

"We need to find your brother, for starters."

"But how?"

"You have his contact info?"

"Of course. And I've left dozens of messages. He hasn't returned any of them."

"Maybe we need to rephrase your messages."

Priest's jaw slid lower. "What do you mean?"

"Call him and leave a message that says your family has been threatened and that you're being blackmailed into attempting to murder a federal agent. You desperately need his help because you don't know what to do, but you're seriously thinking of pulling the trigger. Tell him he has a half hour to get back to you before you do the deed."

Priest simply stared at Pine for a few moments. "You can't be serious."

"I'm so serious that if you don't do it right now while I'm sitting here, I'm going to arrest you for the attempted murder of me."

"I thought you were trying to help me."

Pine shook her head. "I never said that. My job is to find the truth. I will go over and through anybody to get there, including you and your brother."

Priest closed his eyes and rubbed his brow with a shaky hand, covering his face.

Pine pulled his hand away. "You've got to step up now, Ed. No time to hide. Take out your phone and make the call."

Priest punched in the number.

"Put it on speakerphone."

"You don't trust me?"

"Do I really need to answer that question? You came here to put a bullet in my head."

Priest put the phone on speaker.

A voice came on. "This is Ben. Leave me a message. I'll do my best to get back to you."

Pine nodded at Priest, who left his message, following her instructions to the letter. Then she hit the End button and looked across at him.

"And now?" he said.

"And now we wait for thirty minutes."

"And if he doesn't call back?"

"Then you cross the Rubicon. I'll have to take you in."

Priest frowned. "Look, it's just my word against yours that I came here to kill you."

Pine took out her phone and hit some keys.

Priest's voice came on, explaining why he had come there to kill Pine.

"You recorded it all?" said Priest.

"Of course I did. This is the big leagues, Ed. You want to survive this, you need to up your game."

"I didn't ask for any of this shit to be dropped in my lap," he replied testily.

"Don't blame me, blame your brother. If he calls back in thirty minutes, you're going to arrange to meet him. And I'll be going along for the ride."

"But we have no idea where he is."

"Which is why we're waiting for him to tell us."

Pine fell silent and sat back. Priest looked immensely anxious. But he, too, didn't speak.

Until twenty-eight minutes later when his phone rang.

Priest glanced at Pine, who nodded.

She said, "Don't put it on speaker—he might get suspicious."

"What do I say?"

"Act natural. You're pissed, confused, and you want to hear the truth."

Priest answered the phone and held it to his ear while Pine leaned in close to listen.

"Hello?"

"Eddie?"

Priest blurted out, "Ben, where the hell have you been? What is going on? My whole life just came crashing down around me."

"Just calm down, big brother. It'll be okay. But please tell me you haven't killed a federal agent."

"Not yet. But Mary and the kids."

"They'll be okay."

"You don't know that!"

Pine tapped Priest on the arm and put a finger to her lips. She mouthed the words *Let him talk.*

Priest fell silent. A moment later his brother started speaking. "You were never supposed to be involved in any of this, Eddie, I'm sorry. It got out of hand."

"What did?"

"I can't talk about it, not over the phone."

Pine touched Priest on the shoulder again, pointed at him and then at the phone.

Priest said, "Then we have to meet. You can tell it to me face-to-face."

"Where are you now?"

"Arizona. Near the Grand Canyon where you were supposed to have disappeared. That's why I flew out. Where are you?"

"Not that far away, actually."

"Where do you want to meet?"

"There's a hotel at the Grand Canyon, on the South Rim. El Tovar."

Pine looked at Priest and nodded.

"Okay, I'm sure I can find it."

"We can meet there tonight, for dinner. You can make the reservation under your name. Make it for later. Nine o'clock. Just so you know, I...I won't look like myself."

"Have you been hurt?"

"No, I mean I'll be in disguise."

"Oh, okay."

"Does anyone know you're here?"

"No, I told no one."

"Nine o'clock then at El Tovar. I'll explain what I can then."

Before Priest could say anything, the line went dead.

He clicked off the phone and set it down. As though he'd been holding his breath, Priest blew air out of his mouth and slumped back in the chair.

Pine rose from her chair and poured another cup of coffee.

"So, we do nothing until tonight?" he said.

"*You* do nothing until tonight. I have things to accomplish."

"Do I just stay here then?"

"You do, but not by yourself. I'm having a local buddy of mine come over to look after you."

"You mean to make sure I don't hightail it out of here."

"That's one way of looking at it. He's a retired cop. A Hopi police ranger. The Hopis are traditionally known as respectful of the Earth and peace-loving. But you try anything with my friend and he'll lay your ass out so fast, you won't know what hit you."

"Thanks a lot," snarled Priest.

"You're welcome, a lot."

20

THE EL TOVAR HOTEL had opened in 1905 and was located at the Grand Canyon's South Rim. Named after an early Spanish explorer, it was one of a chain of hotels originally owned and operated by the Fred Harvey Company. It was only twenty feet from the rim of the Canyon and constructed in a rustic style using Oregon pine and local limestone. There was a pyramidal roof, turrets, verandas, dorms, and gables. The interior was a mash-up of the arts and crafts movement, southwestern Indian design, and Swiss-inspired woodwork. The rear dining room had sweeping views of the canyon beyond.

Ed Priest walked up the broad front steps into the hotel. It was a minute after nine o'clock, but it was still quite warm outside, even though the sun had long since melted into the west.

He walked swiftly through the lobby and to the dining room at the rear.

He gave his name to the maître d' and was escorted to a table far in the back. The hour was late for dinner, and the room was nearly empty.

There was no one at the table, which was set for two people.

Priest sat down and looked around.

He checked his watch and fiddled with his napkin.

The waitress came over to take his drink order, but he deferred until his guest arrived.

Another ten minutes went by, and Priest's anxiety grew. He bit his nails, constantly surveyed the dining area, and absentmindedly clinked his fork against his knife.

"Eddie?"

Priest looked up to see the tall woman staring down at him.

At first, he looked confused, but when he gazed more closely at the woman, his jaw slackened.

"Ben?"

"Keep it down, Eddie, I have excellent hearing."

Benjamin Priest was dressed in blue slacks, a long-sleeved white blouse, a beige linen jacket, and low pumps. A dark wig covered his head, and his face was modestly covered with makeup. Tinted glasses covered his eyes.

He sat down and placed his purse in the seat next to him.

"When you said a disguise, I didn't know you meant this," hissed Ed.

"That's the point. To be unpredictable."

"I was hoping you'd say that," said Pine as she slid into a seat across from Ben.

He jerked and started to rise until Pine set her FBI shield on the table and slid open her jacket, revealing her holstered pistol.

"Let's not create a scene, Ben," said Pine, and he slowly resumed his seat.

"Who the hell are you?"

"Your friendly neighborhood FBI agent. So now that we're past that, you need to tell me what the hell is going on."

"I can't. You're not cleared for it."

"If I'm not cleared for it, then I doubt your brother is. So if you can't tell him, why are you here?"

"It's complicated."

"I never doubted that."

"Look, I can't get into all this here."

"Then where? You were the one who arranged to meet here."

Ben looked around nervously. "Outside. I have a truck. But you need to understand that you don't know what you're involved in."

"I completely agree. That's why I'm here. To understand."

"You're really with the FBI?"

She held up her badge with one hand and slipped her ID pack out with the other.

Ben scrutinized both and said, "Outside."

As they headed toward the front entrance, Ben's and Pine's gazes were constantly swiveling. Pine was looking for anyone who seemed to be paying them even a bit of attention. But there were only a few guests coming and going, and a handful of hotel workers. Ed Priest, by contrast, kept his gaze straight ahead.

They reached the front doors and Pine took the lead. She opened the door, stepped out, took a sweep of the area, and nodded to the two men.

"Where's your ride?" she asked Ben Priest.

"In the parking lot over there. The light green Explorer."

"We'll take your truck and come back later for mine. Give me the keys, I'll drive."

"Where are we going?" asked Ben.

"For a little ride and a lot of talk. From you."

Ben rode shotgun and Ed was in the back.

"Start from the beginning," said Pine as she steered them out of the parking lot and onto the road heading out of the park. "Capricorn Consultants?"

"It doesn't exist."

Ed said, "But you told me that's where you worked, Ben."

Ben swiveled around to look at his older brother. "I'm sorry, Eddie. It comes with the territory."

"Which is what, exactly?" said Pine. "Are you in the intelligence field?"

"I used to be," replied Ben.

"For our side?"

"It's not that simple."

Pine said, "It is for me. If you're a spy for another country, we're going to have a big problem."

"Shit, Ben, please tell me that's not true," exclaimed Ed.

"I can work for interests outside this country without working *against* this country. But allies are allies until they become enemies. And sometimes our enemies can be allies. It's a fluid situation."

"So, do you work for one of our allies or one of our enemies?"

"I work for myself after working for Uncle Sam and others. And doing it well and honorably."

"Okay, go on," prompted Pine.

"I put out my own shingle."

"Doing what?"

"I help arrange things."

"Like what? The guy on the mule pretending to be you?"

"You've no doubt heard of money laundering?"

Pine said, "Not only have I heard of it, I've investigated cases dealing with it."

"Well, money is not the only thing that can be laundered. You can launder *people*, too."

"You mean switching their identities? Making them disappear?"

"Something like that," answered Priest.

Pine could sense he was lying but decided to move on. She said, "Talk about the guy on the mule. He disappeared and left behind a dead animal with the letters *j* and *k* carved on it."

Ben let out a long breath. "I don't know what that means."

Pine thought he might be telling the truth on that one. "Was it part of the plan that the guy would head out at night on a mule?"

"Yes."

"Okay, what was the plan?"

Ben shook his head. "I can't get into that."

"Do you know where he is now?"

Ben shook his head again. "I haven't heard from him."

"Does our government know about whatever he's doing?"

No answer.

Pine said, "The FBI's National Security Division *is* very interested in all this. Did you know that?"

Ben took off his glasses and wiped at his eyes. "I'm not *unaware* of it."

"Spoken in true doublespeak," said Pine sharply. "You've told me basically zip, and I'm rapidly losing my patience."

"Ben, you need to work with Agent Pine," implored Ed. "She has my family in a safe place. We were threatened."

"I know, Eddie. You told me, but there's nothing I can do."

"Bullshit! You were the one who got us into this."

Ben snapped, "No, you got yourself into it. You should have stayed out of it. Then they never would have come after you."

"All I did was try to contact you when you disappeared. What did you expect me to do?"

Ben pointed at Pine. "You spoke with her. You talked to the FBI. They know that."

"Who does?" said Pine quickly.

Again, Ben would not answer.

"She called me," said Ed. "What was I supposed to do?"

"Look, this is getting us nowhere," said Ben. "I need to get back."

"You're not going anywhere," said Pine. "You either work with me, or I'm going to arrest you."

"On what charge?"

"Obstruction of justice and wasting police time. The search for you cost thousands of dollars and wasted the time of a lot of first responders who could have been helping other people."

"That's bullshit and you know it!"

"We can let a judge sort that out. But I'd prefer that you answer my questions so we can get to the bottom of this."

"Who said I wanted to get to the bottom of it?" replied Ben coolly. "Or that I wanted you to?"

"You've put your brother and his family in danger. You need to help fix that."

"No, I really don't."

"Ben!" exclaimed Ed. "We're your family."

His brother turned to look at him. "On this, my family comes second. It's just too big. I'm sorry, Eddie, but that's how it has to be."

"You son of a bitch!" screamed Ed. "And everybody thinks you're the golden boy! You're nothing but a selfish bastard."

Pine wasn't paying attention to either of them. They were on a lonely stretch of road. It was completely dark, and she could see no lights behind her.

But still. Her professional antennae were going crazy.

"Hold on," she called out.

A moment later something hit them from behind with such force that the rear wheels of the Explorer were lifted off the pavement. The truck came back down so hard that they were propelled toward the ceiling, only kept in check by their harnesses engaging. With the impact, all the air bags deployed.

The truck swerved off the road and onto the dirt shoulder. Just beyond the shoulder was a six-foot strip of grass, and then a wall of thick trees.

Pine did not fight the wheel. Peering around the air bag, she calmly steered into the direction the truck was moving so she could regain control of it.

They cleared the shoulder, and then the six feet of grass.

"Brace," she called out.

A moment later the truck slammed into the wall of trees. But Pine had maneuvered the truck just enough to prevent it from broadsiding the trees, which would have crushed the side of the truck she was on. Instead, the truck impacted the trees at the corner of the left front fender.

With the air bags already deployed, Pine's head hit the window.

And then the already damaged gas tank fully cracked and the leaked fuel caught a spark. A trickle of flames headed up the side of the SUV.

Inside the truck, Pine let out a groan and then lapsed into unconsciousness.

21

A LITTLE GIRL. Beckoning to her.

A small hand held out to provide assistance.

A whisper of urgency.

Hurry, Lee. Come on. You're in trouble. Come on. Quick now, Lee.

Pine came to as quickly as she had fallen unconscious. She pushed the deflated air bag and side curtains out of the way and saw in the rearview mirror flames creeping her way.

The commingled scents of burning plastic and upholstery were nauseating.

She could smell escaped fuel and knew that the impact had cracked the gas tank.

The image of her sister calling to her slowly faded.

Lee, instead of *Atlee*. That was what Mercy had always called her. The truncated name had stuck growing up. She was Lee Pine until she went to college.

For some reason, she had not minded the change back to Atlee. The name Lee represented her past. And right now Pine wasn't sure she had much of a future.

She undid her harness and looked across at the passenger seat.

Ben Priest was slumped against the door, a thin trickle of blood running down his forehead.

In the backseat, Ed Priest was moaning and holding his shoulder.

Pine tried to open the door, but it wouldn't budge. The impact had jammed it. She slid into the backseat, reached across Ed, and opened the door. She unharnessed him and pushed the injured man out of the truck, as the flames crept closer.

She could feel the heat over every inch of her. It was fierce and made her skin tingle. Any second and the fumes in the cracked gas tank could ignite. And then in a flash of flames and vapor ignition it would all be over. They would collect her scattered remains in a trash bag.

Her boots hit the dirt and she pulled Ed away from the truck.

Ignoring the danger, she ran back to the flaming truck, yanked open the passenger seat door, unharnessed Ben, and pulled him free. She lifted the tall man over her shoulder and fast-walked him away from the truck before laying him next to his brother.

Next, she crouched, pulled her gun, and looked around. Whatever had hit them must still be out there. She wiped away blood from the side of her face and with her free hand she called 911 and requested assistance, giving her location as specifically as she could.

She looked at her watch. It was nearly ten o'clock. She had no idea how long it would take for the local cops to show.

The explosion lit the night, and Pine ducked down as debris from the Ford sailed through the air. Parts of the truck crashed down all around them.

Ed Priest suddenly cried out.

She scuttled over to him and saw a piece of metal sticking out of his upper arm.

It was a part of the trim from the Explorer. It had pierced his skin like a fired arrow and the wound was bleeding heavily.

She took off her jacket and wrapped it tightly around the wound. She didn't attempt to take out the piece of metal. That might cause a gusher of blood if it had grazed an artery.

"Help's coming," she said.

He nodded and lay back on the ground, groaning.

And then Pine saw the headlights.

Not from the ground.

But in the air.

The chopper swiftly shed altitude, its searchlight delicately probing the ground like a snake's tongue before coming to rest first on Pine and Ed. Then it found the still unconscious Ben Priest and held there.

It landed barely fifty feet away, its prop wash pummeling them and providing more oxygen to the burning truck, fanning the flames and smoke all over the road.

Another mini explosion occurred, causing Pine to momentarily duck before returning her attention to the chopper. She studied its silhouette and its blade configuration.

"What's happening?" groaned Ed.

"Just keep still and quiet," she whispered back, her gaze steady on the chopper.

Pine reached into a small compartment attached to her shoulder holster and pulled out her laser sight. She clipped it to the top of her gun's Pic rail and lined up her shot on the aircraft's main prop assembly.

And then her target changed as the chopper doors on the left opened and two figures in body armor and combat helmets climbed out. Both carried M16s, with laser sights. These guys were ready for war.

Seeing this, Pine lowered herself to the ground, spread-eagled, making her target silhouette as small as possible. But she knew this was no longer a fight on equal terms, if it ever was.

Her Glock and backup Beretta had no chance against a weapon that was designed for max firepower and resulting death on a battlefield. A torso or head shot from a combat weapon was pretty much not survivable. It didn't wound; it made organs disappear.

She decided she might as well give it a shot. She called out, "FBI. Identify yourselves or I will open fire."

Neither of them made any indication that identification would be forthcoming.

Instead, one of them threw something toward her.

She put her head down and told herself it would be over in a second. No pain. Just...nothing.

Another part of Pine kissed her ass good-bye.

Still another part of her cursed that she was going to die without even knowing why.

The thrown object hit the ground. There was a flash of light and an explosion.

And once more Atlee Pine's world went dark.

22

Special Agent Pine?"

Pine drew in a long breath and an antiseptic odor filled her nostrils.

She wondered if Heaven was super clean.

She doubted Hell would bother.

"Special Agent Pine?"

Her eyelids fluttered open and then closed.

Then they opened again and remained that way.

Carol Blum was staring anxiously down at her.

The older woman breathed a sigh of relief as her boss's gaze fixed and then held on her.

Pine rocked her head from side to side and saw that she was lying on a gurney.

"Where am I?"

"Emergency room."

Pine touched her forehead. There was a gauze bandage wrapped around her head. "How did I get here?"

"Ambulance."

"What about the others?"

"Others?"

Pine tried to sit up, but Blum put a hand on her shoulder and gently nudged her back down.

"I was with two men," said Pine.

"I don't know anything about that. I got a call that you had been in an accident and had been brought here."

"Who called you?"

"The hospital."

"Why would they call you?"

"They actually called the office. They must have seen your badge. I got the message from there. I called them back and then drove straight here."

"I phoned the cops about a situation. We were hit from behind. Someone tried to kill us."

Blum shook her head. "Again, no one told me anything about that."

At that moment, a doctor in a white coat and light blue scrubs came in with an iPad in hand. He was in his late forties with thinning hair and a calm, almost bored look.

"How are we doing, ma'am?" he asked in a cheery tone.

"I'm fine," said Pine. "What about the two people with me? They were injured, too. One of them badly."

The doctor's casual demeanor evaporated. "Other people? There were no other people. You've had a concussion. I don't believe you're thinking clearly."

"I'm thinking *very* clearly," said Pine. "There were two men in the vehicle with me."

He shook his head. "Look, I'm the only doctor on duty in the emergency room. One ambulance came in last night. With you. Automobile accident. You ran off the road and were injured."

"And who told you that?"

"The ambulance crew."

"How about the cops?"

"I haven't seen any cops."

"Shit." Pine sat up and pushed off efforts by the doctor to stop her. "Where are my clothes. And my guns?"

"In a secure locker," said the doctor.

"Get them. I need to get out of here."

"We're keeping you for observation."

"No, you're not."

"I'm the doctor here and I'm telling you—"

Pine swung her legs off the bed, her bare feet hit the floor, and she pulled off whatever medical devices were attached to her.

"I'm an FBI agent. And I'm telling you to get my stuff, or I'm going to arrest you for interfering with a federal officer."

The doctor looked at Blum as Pine stood there in a flimsy hospital gown. Even in her bare feet she towered over him. And the look on her face, with the bloody bandage wrapped around her head, was of a woman who was not to be denied.

The doctor said to Blum, "Is she serious?"

"Well, I've never known her not to be. So, it's a safe bet that you're going to jail if you don't do as she says, which I highly recommend that you do."

Twenty minutes later, Pine, fully clothed and gunned up, was striding out of the hospital with Blum next to her.

The sun was just starting to rise.

"How did you get the message from the office?" asked Pine.

"I didn't until I checked the line early this morning."

"How early do you check it?"

"Four o'clock every morning. Just in case. I wish I had checked it before."

"There were two men," said Pine as she took off the head bandage and dropped it into a trash can. "We were intentionally run off the road, and then a chopper landed. There were two guys in body armor with combat weapons. One of them threw a flashbang or concussion grenade and knocked me out. I'd already been hurt in the crash, so that accounts for what happened." She looked at the sky, checking the status of the rising sun. Her watch had been damaged in the crash and her phone had run out of juice. "I must've been out for about eight hours."

She looked over at Blum. "Do you believe me?"

"I would hope you wouldn't have to ask that, Special Agent Pine. Of course I believe you. So the people in the chopper must have taken the two men."

"Or else the car that hit us came back for them. But yes, they were taken."

"Does this involve the dead mule case and the missing person, Ben Priest?"

Pine nodded as they reached Blum's light green Prius in the parking lot.

"Only the Ben Priest that went missing wasn't the real Ben Priest."

They climbed into the car and Blum started it up.

"So where is the real Ben Priest?" Blum asked.

"He was one of the men with me last night. He and his brother, Ed. Ed flew in from the East Coast and called me. I picked him up at an IHOP in Flagstaff and took him to my place. He tried to kill me while he thought I was sleeping."

Blum took this startling information in stride. "Did he indeed? How badly did you beat him up?"

"I didn't have to. He chickened out. He's actually not a bad guy. His family was threatened. It was them or me. So he came out here to do the deed, then got cold feet. But through him I was able to connect with the real Ben Priest. We met last night at El Tovar. Then we got in Ben Priest's Explorer and drove off heading south. That's when we were attacked."

"That qualifies as a busy night."

"We need to go to the site of the crash. I need to check some things."

She gave Blum the directions, and about an hour later they arrived at the spot.

There was nothing there.

The burned-out carcass of the Explorer was gone. The tire marks on the shoulder had been tidied up and the debris field policed.

Blum pulled off to the side of the road and they got out.

They walked the site together.

"They did a good job cleansing the site," said Pine. "But not good enough."

She pointed to a felled tree.

"Somebody cut this tree down last night with a chainsaw. You can see the teeth marks on the wood. Then they used the chainsaw to tear up the spot where the Explorer hit the trunk. But if you dig in there, you're going to find the green paint and other residue from the truck." Next, she pointed to patches of dirt along the grass shoulder. "They had to cut those out because the grass there was burned. And I'm betting that if you brought a metal detector out here, you'd find a shitload of tiny pieces from the Explorer. And when it blew up, I'm certain there are parts of it that ended up far away, and in the woods over there."

"Still, someone went to a lot of trouble to clean this up," said Blum.

"I pulled both guys from the truck. When it blew Ed got hit with a piece of shrapnel in the arm. That's why my jacket is missing. I used it to wrap his wound." She pointed at her shirtsleeve, where there were traces of blood. "And they missed this. It's *his* blood. Some got on me when I was tending his injury."

"You said you called the police?"

Pine nodded. "And I imagine they would have gotten here at some point. But there was no way they could have gotten rid of all the evidence before then."

"I can check on that," said Blum. "And see what happened." She paused as she stared around at where the attack had taken place. "You didn't tell anyone about the imposter Ben Priest?"

Pine glanced at her. "No, I didn't."

"Because you felt something was out of sorts?"

"Yes."

"Well, with choppers, body armor, and soldiers carrying assault weapons and throwing flashbangs at you I can see why."

"This is getting weirder by the minute."

"Oh, I always thought it was a little weird to begin with. I mean, you don't see a dead mule with letters carved on it every day of the week."

They had just arrived at the office and gone inside when Pine's phone buzzed. She had charged it using Blum's car charger. She did not look pleased at the name on the caller ID.

Blum glanced at her. "Let me guess. The chain of command is calling?"

Pine grimaced. "Yep."

"The only question is, how high up?" said Blum.

"Looks to be pretty damn high," said Pine grimly.

CHAPTER

23

CLINT DOBBS was the special agent in charge at the Phoenix Field Office. He was ultimately in charge of every FBI office in the state of Arizona and had a legion of agents under his command. But right now, it seemed, all his attention was focused on one, who held down the newest and only one-agent office in the entire state.

Atlee Pine.

"Your job as a solo agent in an RA is to do everything, Pine," said Dobbs, his tone strident as Pine sat behind her desk listening. "But to also do everything by the book. There is no margin for error."

"Yes, sir. I'm aware of that, sir, and I've done that."

"Oh, so you've done that in this case?" he said skeptically.

"Yes, sir."

"Then why do I have a family in Maryland in protective custody at your request, calling up the Bureau and demanding to know where their husband and father is? And that person just happens to be the brother of the man who recently went missing in the Grand Canyon? A case that you're investigating? Now, I have talked to your direct superiors, and they have no record of being in the loop on any of that, Pine. So, would you like to reconsider your answer that you've done everything by the book on this sucker?"

"The situation demanded immediate action, sir. I didn't have time to fill everyone in. But it was going in my next report."

"Don't bullshit with me. I've got better things to do with my time than be on a phone call with the eighth and smallest RA under my command. I expected better from you, Pine. You've done great things at the Agency, but crap like this can ruin a good career."

"Yes, sir."

"I'm trying to give you a friendly warning here, Pine."

"Yes, sir. I appreciate that, sir."

"I'm not sure you do. See, whatever you do wrong comes back to reflect negatively on me. That's the price you pay for being an SAIC."

"Fully understand, sir."

"No, again, I don't think you do, or you wouldn't have done what you did. Do you think I'm calling you for the hell of it? I've actually got more important things to do. But my cell phone was ringing off the hook at five a.m. It was Washington calling. The DD himself. Hell, I guess I was surprised the director didn't call."

"And how is the deputy director?"

"Don't be insubordinate, Pine. I won't stand for that."

"Not my intention, sir."

"Anyway, the DD called me in a lather. I'm not sure I have hearing left in my right ear. I can't have this, Pine. I really can't. You get that?"

"Got it, sir."

"And now I understand that you were involved in a car accident?"

"I *was* in an accident, sir. But I'm okay. Just shaken up. They released me from the hospital and I'm back at work."

"Did you smash up your Bureau-issued vehicle?"

"No, I was in another SUV, sir."

"And what is the status of this other vehicle?"

"It's no longer drivable. But that's on my dime. I have insurance. Nothing for the Bureau to worry about, sir. I was off duty."

"Pray that I don't find out differently."

"Yes, sir."

"And, Pine, take some time off. From what I understand, the missing person case is going nowhere. And you know as well as anyone that people go missing from the Grand Canyon all the time. Some get found, and sometimes their bodies get found. But I don't believe it's good use of your time or taxpayer dollars to be on this case. So far, all we really have is a dead mule. The locals can sort that out. So, take some time off, get your head straight, file your insurance paperwork, and stay the hell out of trouble. Am I clear?"

"Could not be clearer, sir."

But Dobbs had already clicked off.

Pine put down the phone and looked up when someone knocked on her door.

Blum poked her head in. "Is the coast clear?"

Pine nodded. "My ass was just officially kicked all the way from Phoenix."

"Let me guess: Clint Dobbs?" said Blum.

Pine nodded. "The one and only."

"I worked for him once, way back, when he was fighting his way up the ladder. It was clear he wanted to be an SAIC, even back then. Some agents want to work the field. Others want to work from behind a desk. Dobbs was the latter."

Pine remained silent.

"He was a real jerk back then. They say he's mellowed." Blum paused and studied Pine.

"He basically ordered me to take time off."

"Are you?"

Pine looked at Blum. "I'm an FBI agent. I'm not supposed to work outside the lines."

"But you're not satisfied?"

"I was almost killed by what appeared to be my own government. The guy in charge of the National Security Branch is on the case's email thread. My über boss just told me the DD called up and chewed him out, with the result that I've been told to go take a vacation."

"So, the question is, do you work outside the lines or follow lockstep?"

Pine didn't answer right away. When she started speaking, her words came out slowly.

"They could have easily killed me last night. I was incapacitated. But they took Ben and Ed Priest. They could have taken me, too."

"Why do you think they didn't?"

"You kill an FBI agent, you poke a hole in a hornet's nest."

Blum nodded. "I found some things out while you were on the phone with Dobbs. First, the local police received your phone call but had been called off before they got to the scene. They said it was you calling back and saying it was all a mistake."

"What else?"

"The stretch of road you said you were on?"

"What about it?"

"I called a friend of mine who's a state trooper. Part of his beat is that area. A buddy of his was on duty last night. He saw a road crew blocking off a section of that highway."

"A road crew?" repeated Pine.

"Yeah. But I know for a fact they just finished repaving that road. So what would they have been working on?"

"They were working on getting Ben Priest away from me. And that would account for why I didn't see any other cars."

She had screwed up. Meeting Priest in public had seemed the safest route. But she had underestimated whomever they were up against. Her mistake might have cost both men their lives.

Blum interrupted her thoughts. "It takes some juice to get a road shut down, Agent Pine."

"Yes it does."

"Are you thinking that the FBI knows what's going on? I mean that they know what happened last night, and they're calling you off the case before you get hurt?"

"Or before I discover the truth."

Blum shook her head, her features angry. "I've always been able to rely on the Bureau, even if I didn't agree with everything it did. I mean, we're the good guys."

"I joined the FBI to do two things: protect good people and punish bad people. Pretty simple. But that makes things black and white."

"And this situation is obviously *not* black and white," said Blum. "So where does that leave us?"

"I can't work this case within normal parameters."

"Options are limited, then. What are we going to do?"

"*We?*" Pine shot her a glance. "No, that won't be happening. If I do this and get canned and they find out you helped me, it's over for you, too."

"But I'm your secretary. It's my job to assist you."

"Carol, this is not in the normal course of your job. I'm talking about going off the grid. I can't let you go down that road with me."

"Why not? I'm certainly old enough to make my own decisions."

"But it could be career suicide for you."

"Well, I've actually been thinking about a job change. My husband divorced me so he could be with some floozy. My kids are all grown and living all over the place, except near me. I'm not really sure what to think about that, but I guess I'm at the age where I don't let it bother me too much."

"What were you thinking about doing?"

"Well, becoming a private detective. I mean, after all these decades at the Bureau, I've seen it all, from case files to post-mortem and forensic reports. I've observed cases investigated well, and cases investigated deplorably. And hell, I've written enough reports that agents were supposed to write, to understand how things are put together. And held enough newbie agents' hands while they tried to understand the Bureau's eccentricities. And I listened to everything and remembered everything. And physically

I'm perfect for the role. I mean look at me. No one would see me as threatening. And I can just listen and observe all I want."

"I'm seeing a side of you I didn't know existed, Ms. Blum."

Blum gave her an incredulous look. "Well, it's about time, Special Agent Pine. Frankly, I expected you to be a little faster on the uptake."

24

Pᴉɴᴇ ᴡᴀs ᴄᴏᴍʙɪɴɢ out her hair and staring in the mirror of her bathroom.

She had showered and washed the blood off the wound near her temple. Her head still throbbed from the impact with the truck window and the effects of the concussive device.

She had covered the wound with a Band-Aid, and then let her dark hair cover it, and the bruising there.

But on the other side, she lifted her hair and stared at the scar from her other wound.

The one from long ago.

The permanent one. Courtesy of the man who had taken her sister.

It was dark outside now. Blum had driven Pine up to the Grand Canyon to pick up her truck, and both women had returned to the office and worked there for the rest of the day.

Pine glanced away from the reflection of the scar on her temple, took out her phone, and studied the image on the small screen. This was the digital sketch that Jennifer Yazzie had done for her. This was the image of the missing man, the imposter Ben Priest, at least according to the recollection of Mark Brennan.

There were facial recognition databases that the image could be run through, but if Pine accessed those platforms using her FBI passwords, they would know what she was doing.

And if Clint Dobbs was true to his word, she might no longer be an FBI agent. So, right now, this image, this lead, was no use to her, until she found a workaround. Which she intended to do as soon as possible.

She put her phone down and traced the scar with her finger.

A cracked skull had once lurked under this fissure.

A six-year-old with a cracked skull. That was a serious thing indeed, more so since she had lain all night, bloodied, battered, and unconscious with the cracked bone and bruised brain.

Yet Pine had never once complained about that. She had been the lucky one.

Mercy had not.

She wanted to know, for absolute certain, that Daniel James Tor had been the one who had taken her sister. Pine needed to know this, because it was apt to be the only closure on her sister's disappearance that she would ever receive.

She had just undressed to get into bed when her phone rang.

It was Sam Kettler.

"Sorry to call so late," he said.

"No, it's fine. What's up?"

"Just wondering if you had time for a beer?"

"I don't think Tony's is open now," she said.

"I know. But I'm only about twenty minutes from your place and, well, I thought you might like to hang out for a bit. It's a nice night."

Pine didn't answer. She was about to embark on a journey that might possibly be the beginning of the end of her career at the FBI.

Talk about lousy timing.

He said, "Hey, Atlee, it's okay. Look, I was a knucklehead for calling out of the blue and so late, too. Don't know what I was thinking. I'll just—"

"No, it's okay. Come on over. A beer sounds good right now."

It actually does. And who knows when I'm going to get another chance?

"Hey, are you sure? I don't want to pressure you into anything, and I sort of feel that I am."

"You'll come to find out that I'm sort of immune to pressure like that. But let's drink in your Jeep. My place is sort of messy."

"Oh, absolutely. I wasn't thinking of inviting myself over like that. I thought we could just sit on the steps or something."

She smiled. "Old-fashioned, I know."

She gave him her address and put on shorts and a T-shirt. She kept watch out her window, and when she saw him drive in, she went downstairs without bothering to put shoes on. That turned out to have been a bad choice, since she had to hop across the asphalt because of the day's heat retained there.

They sat in his open Jeep and cracked open two cold beers. The temperature was still around eighty at nearly eleven p.m.

"Damn, that is good," she said, draining about half of her bottle.

He grinned and stared out the windshield. "Simple things in life, right?" Then he looked at her and frowned. "What happened there?"

He was pointing to the side of her face, near her temple, where her hair had fallen away when she turned.

She touched the Band-Aid there. "Just me being clumsy."

"You don't strike me as the clumsy type."

"Yeah, well, you might be surprised. But, really, it's nothing, Sam."

He nodded and fidgeted.

She noted this and said, "What?"

His gaze on the steering wheel, he said, "There's a…a concert tomorrow night in Phoenix. I switched to the day shift for it. It's Santana. You interested?"

He looked over at her.

Pine felt very uncomfortable. "Um, thanks for the invitation. But I can't make it. I'm sorry."

He quickly looked away. "Hey, no sweat. Short notice. Don't

know what I was thinking." He chuckled. "Always wanted to play guitar like Carlos. Me and a million other guys. Only problem is I can't even hum without being off-key."

"Rain check?"

"Sure, you bet."

They were both silent for a few moments, staring off through the windshield.

Pine was feeling awkward and off-kilter. Part of her was thinking about the man next to her. And the other half was going through all the details of her upcoming journey.

For his part, Kettler seemed to have withdrawn into a shell after she had turned down his invitation.

Pine cleared her throat and said, "So, what made you come to work at the Grand Canyon?"

He perked up at the question. "Hell, it's a fascinating place. It's not just the geological formations and the terrain and the hiking and all that. It's got this unbelievable history. So much started right here."

"Like what?"

"Ever heard of Maasaw?"

"No."

"He's the Hopi god of death. He's said to actually live in the Canyon. And you have the ancestral Puebloan granaries at Nankoweap Creek. And Eagle Rock at Eagle Point on the West Rim. It's considered sacred by the Hualapai. And some in the Hopi tribe believe the Canyon is the site of the *sipapu*, the portal through which they climbed a reed cast into the sky and used it to reach the Fourth World."

"You believe all that?" asked Pine, hiking her eyebrows.

He looked sheepish. "Well, I'd like to believe some of it. For me, the Canyon isn't just a tourist destination. It's a living, breathing place. It has a dozen plants that live nowhere else. And the place is constantly evolving. The algae in the river brought in crustaceans, which brought in trout, which brought in the bald eagle. It's one of the only bird species that uses the river corridor as its winter habitat." Kettler tapped his temple. "You see, it's smart. It's a living thing. How cool is that?"

Pine smiled. "The way you explained it, pretty cool, actually. I'm seeing another side of you, Mr. Kettler."

"I keep a go pack at work. Sometimes when I'm off duty I go hiking or running. Or even do some climbing."

"Climbing?"

"Yeah, I was an Army Ranger. To qualify for that status, you had to do a lot of mountain climbing. You do that down in Georgia. It's sort of a hobby of mine now. I keep climbing ropes and D-links and other equipment in my go pack. And I've climbed mountains all over." He glanced at her. "You might like it."

"I might. With the right company." She smiled and punched him lightly on the arm.

Kettler's brow furrowed.

"Something wrong?"

"Look, full disclosure. There was another reason I came over tonight."

Pine sat up straighter. "What?"

"Colson Lambert and Harry Rice?"

"What about them?"

"They've been reassigned."

"What! Where?"

"Zion National Park in Utah. Effective immediately. Pretty damn inconvenient, since both of them have families with kids in the local schools. Harry and Colson are going up and leaving their families behind until things can get straightened out." He glanced at her. "I take it from your reaction that you didn't know."

"I had no idea at all."

"Does this have something to do with the mule? I mean, how could it? But that's the only thing out of the ordinary. I mean…" His voice trailed off.

"It might, Sam. It probably does, in fact."

"Okay. I guess you can't tell me about it?"

"No, I really can't."

"Good enough for me. But I thought you needed to know about Lambert and Rice."

"I did, and I appreciate the heads-up. I really do."

They remained silent until Pine said, "If you ever want to talk about stuff…"

"Like what?"

"Your time in the Army?"

"Well, I'm not in the Army anymore. That's in my past. I want to look ahead."

Pine thought about her own personal situation. "Sometimes you can't move ahead until you deal with stuff in your past."

"That's true, I guess. But I was a soldier, just like a lot of guys. I'm good. I really am. No problems."

"Okay."

They said their good-byes, which included a hug that lasted a bit longer than the one at Tony's Pizza.

Pine could feel the strength of Kettler's fingers as they gently sank into her skin through the flimsy fabric of her T-shirt. She fully took in his scent, sweat mingling with soap and shampoo. She felt herself a little light-headed. But then what she was going to do the next day came crashing down on her like a chunk of concrete.

She pulled back and then gave him a quick kiss on the cheek.

"Thanks for the beer. And the Santana invite. It meant a lot."

"Anytime," he replied, his hand grazing her bare arm. "Look forward to hanging out some more."

She headed back to her apartment, having once more to hop on the asphalt until she got to the cooler pavement. She turned around to find Kettler grinning at her.

She looked down at her bare feet. "I know, goofy, right?"

"Nothing wrong with goofy from where I'm standing. Looks pretty damn beautiful, in fact."

Two minutes later, after she had watched Kettler drive off in his Jeep, Pine collapsed on her bed.

Pretty damn beautiful, huh?

She kept catching herself smiling as she relived the time spent with Kettler. But then the reality of what lay ahead took over, and her smile faded.

What were the odds that she would finally find someone she enjoyed being with, only to have her job pop up between them like, well, like the Grand Canyon?

And that's what you signed up for, Atlee, when you put on the badge.

She got up the next morning at seven a.m., picked up the phone, and called Carol Blum.

"I'll meet you at the office in an hour."

"I'll be there. You're right—before you start your vacation, we might as well take some time to get all your old case files in order."

"Roger that."

"Where are you going?"

"I'm going to hike and camp at Mount Nebo in Utah. Need to clear my head. I've got all my stuff. I'm leaving from the office to drive there. Be gone a couple weeks. Flagstaff is covering for me. I've fixed it all up. The office is officially closed while I'm out. So you're getting some time off, too."

"Well, then I'm going to see my daughter in Los Angeles. I've got a new grandbaby I haven't spoiled yet."

Pine put on her sunglasses, drove to her office, parked in the underground garage, and took the stairs to the elevator.

Blum was there ahead of her. With coffee.

At eight that night, the garage door went up and Pine's black SUV pulled out, turned right, and headed to the highway north.

Blum's Prius was right behind her. It drove off in the opposite direction.

Two SUVs started up. One followed Pine's truck, and the other tailed Blum's Prius.

At midnight, the garage door opened once more.

The 1967 Mustang drove out, its top and windows up.

Pine was at the wheel. Blum rode shotgun. Pine was dressed in jeans, a long-sleeved cotton shirt, and a windbreaker. Blum had changed from her skirt, jacket, and pumps into slacks, flats, and a light blue sweater.

They'd each drawn a bunch of cash out of their bank accounts, because credit and debit cards would not be an option now.

Another car was back in the garage with the custom cover for the Mustang over it.

Pine turned left and headed to State Route 89, taking it south.

The pair had "officially" just gone rogue.

25

YOU'RE SURE they can't trace the car?" asked Blum as they got on Interstate 40 heading east.

"I brought it here in the middle of the night when I moved to Shattered Rock. I put it in the office garage and I only drive it at night, and even then it's been a handful of times since I've been here. That's why I kept the trickle charger on it, otherwise the battery would be dead."

"But they could trace the tags."

"If they do, it won't come back showing me as the owner, because I never had it retitled in my name."

"Why?"

"Because the man who owned it should *still* own it, except he happened to die. As far as the law is concerned, he still owns it."

"How long will it take us?"

"It's about twenty-two hundred miles. Thirty-three hours if we don't stop."

"I'm no spring chicken. We have to stop or else you'll need to reupholster."

"My bladder's not that big, either. But it's Interstate 40 pretty much the whole way, and west of the Mississippi we can really fly. I figure two days. That is, if you drive, too."

"That's ambitious. But I'm game. Talking about flying, I suppose a plane was out of the question?"

"Credit cards, IDs. In the system. Yep, out of the question. That's why we shouldn't use anything other than cash. I have a debit card for emergencies, but it's tied to a friend's account, not mine. I'll just pay my friend back if I have to use it. And to the extent we can, we don't use our real names. Anything like that can trip us up. And we never unpack our stuff in case we have to leave some place in a hurry."

"Understood. Where is your friend taking my Prius?"

"Far enough so that anyone trailing you will believe you're going to LA. Don't worry, he'll take good care of it."

"And your truck?"

"I picked Mount Nebo for a reason. My friend who drove out in it is actually going to hike and camp there for the next two weeks. I doubt whoever's following her will stick for the whole trip once they see where she's going."

"And your phone?"

"In the truck. In case they're tracking it, I'm in Utah for the foreseeable future. I put yours in the Prius. I have a bunch of burner phones for us to use. They're in my bag behind your seat. And I loaded my contact list on each one, along with the digital sketch of the fake Ben Priest."

"Can't they trace the purchase of burner phones and then track the SIM card?"

"They could if I had bought them. I didn't. Someone did it for me, as a favor. And this was about six months ago."

"Before you even knew we would be doing this?"

"I like to prepare for pretty much anything, and being able to go off grid at any time but still communicate is a necessity." Pine glanced over at her companion. "We need to be on our A game, okay? We're playing in the big leagues."

"I knew that as soon as I joined the FBI." Blum checked her watch. "It's nearly one in the morning. Are you good to drive?"

"I slept on the floor in my office for eight hours. I'm good until at least Oklahoma City."

"Isn't that far away?"

"About thirteen hours pedal to the metal. We can stop for a late lunch."

"I'm impressed with your stamina."

"I drove from the East Coast in this car to Utah in two and a half days. I only stopped to use the bathroom, catnap in parking lots, and I ate on the road." Pine patted the car's dash. "There's just something about this ride. You want to keep driving."

As they drove along Pine said, "You don't believe that this Jordan and Kinkaid found a secret cave in the Canyon full of Egyptian artifacts?"

"No."

"Did your father?"

Blum took her time answering. "I think my father *wanted* to believe it. He went down there enough times looking for it. Never found it, of course."

"Even with a helpful *j* and *k* carved over the front door?"

Blum smiled. "My father spent his whole life working a job he hated. What he really wanted to be was an adventurer, you know, sort of like Indiana Jones."

"Is he still alive?"

"No, neither of my parents are. How about you?"

"My mother's still around."

"Where does she live?"

"You better get some sleep so you're ready to take over when I'm burned out."

Pine drove on.

They ate barbeque for lunch in Oklahoma City. Then Blum, who had slept most of the way and was perfectly fresh, took over the wheel, while Pine put the passenger seat back as far as it would go, stretched out her long legs, and immediately fell asleep.

Blum drove with only brief stops to use the restroom and to stretch her legs, and once to doze in a parking lot for an hour.

As they neared Nashville, she pulled off at another rest stop and nudged Pine awake.

"Bathroom break," said Blum. "And tag you're it on the driving. I'm beat."

Pine nodded. It was pitch-black now, though the crack of dawn was only a few hours away. The rest area only had one operating light, and it was a feeble one at that. At this hour, there were no other vehicles here.

Pine yawned, stretched, and popped her neck as she followed Blum into the ladies' room.

As soon as the door closed behind them it was pushed open again. Three men came in.

They were all tall and lean and good-looking and appeared to be in their very early twenties. They were all fashionably dressed in clothes that were expensive but made to look like they weren't. Two wore khaki shorts, revealing tanned, muscular legs, and colorful Robert Graham short-sleeved shirts and docksiders. The third wore soft, baggy, faded jeans, a white long-sleeved shirt untucked, and Gucci loafers.

One of them crumpled up a beer and threw it into an empty stall. Then they stood there staring at the two women.

Blum turned around and eyed them. "You have the wrong restroom. Men's is the other door."

The man in the jeans stepped forward. He glanced at his friends and grinned, flashing perfect white teeth. "No, *this* is definitely the place we want because *you're* here."

"You have got to be shitting me," said an incredulous Pine. "Did you guys just come from a frat party, or what?"

The man smiled at her and produced a bottle of Maker's Mark from his back pocket. "Operative word being *party*, ladies."

Blum eyed Pine, who was gazing at the half-empty bottle. "That is not happening," Blum said to him.

"Come on, we've been looking for someone just like you two," said the man. "Mature women, what could be better? And trust me, you'll like what you're going to get."

He unscrewed the cap on the Maker's and took a swig before passing it to his friends, who each took a drink.

Pine studied each of them. "Is this really the only way you can get laid?"

"Hell, we can have anyone we want. I can lay on the charm like nobody's business. And my family's rich." He hooked a finger at his two companions. "These guys too."

"So why lie in wait outside a ladies' bathroom waiting for a target?"

The man grinned. "Because we *can* and we *want* to."

"Not with us, you can't," retorted Blum.

The man's grin slowly faded. "I don't think you have much choice."

Pine said, "Then I don't think you've thought this through."

The man pulled a small knife from his pocket and opened it.

"I don't like to do it this way, but whatever works. Now, you just do what we say and nobody gets hurt."

"Oh, somebody's definitely going to get hurt," replied Pine.

She marched forward and disarmed the man by breaking his wrist. When he howled in pain and doubled over, she grabbed the back of his neck, jerked him downward, and knocked out his two perfect front teeth with a vicious uppercut delivered with her knee. Then, using his bulk against him, Pine flipped him into the mirrored wall over the sinks, shattering it. He fell onto the porcelain, caught his face on a faucet, rolled off, and hit the floor. He lay there bloody and stunned, groaning in pain.

"Hey, hey!" yelled one of the other men. He launched himself at Pine before reeling backward after Pine planted the bottom of her boot into his throat. He slammed against the wall and fell to his butt, gagging for breath.

She walked over and finished him off by bouncing his head

off the tiled wall with a forearm strike. He slumped to the floor unconscious.

The last man snarled, "You're dead, bitch. I've got a black belt."

He stopped snarling and leapt back when Pine pulled out her gun and pointed it at him.

With her other hand, she took out her FBI shield. "And I've got this, Mister Moron."

"Aw, shit!" exclaimed the man. "Son of a bitch!"

"Get on the floor facedown," ordered Pine. "Do it!"

The man did as he was told and then blurted out, "Hey, if you had a damn gun why didn't you just pull it? Why'd you have to kick their asses?"

Blum said, "Because she *can* and she *wanted* to."

Pine took out zip ties from her jacket pocket and bound all three men together, legs and hands, back to back, so they were totally immobile. After Pine and Blum used the restroom and finished washing up at the sinks, Pine dialed 911, told the dispatcher what had happened, gave her location and added, "I can't stay to press charges, but just hold them for a few years on account of being stupid."

When Pine slid behind the wheel of the Mustang, Blum said, "You were quite impressive back there."

"I was incentivized."

"Well, I get that. We were being threatened."

"No, I mean I had to use the bathroom really bad."

Later on, Pine turned onto Interstate 81 North and punched the gas.

This stretch of asphalt was known as the Trucker's Highway as it wove through the mountains, and they passed many a big rig along the way. They stopped for takeout at a twenty-four-hour diner near Roanoke, Virginia. As they drove on, Pine cradled greasy fries in her lap and munched on a double cheeseburger, while Blum nibbled on hers and only occasionally ventured to pick up a fry.

"You don't like burgers and fries?" asked Pine.

"Oh, I do. But at my age, they don't like me like they used to. In that regard, they're sort of like men." A few minutes later she lay back against the seat and fell asleep.

Hours later Pine reached Interstate 66 and took it due east toward Washington.

It was right about then that Blum woke up. Stretching, she said, "Where are we?"

"About two hours outside of DC."

"I've never been to DC."

"With all your rah-rah talk about Mr. Hoover, that surprises me."

"Well, he was already dead when I joined up, so…"

"But there is the Hoover *Building*, which is falling apart, by the way."

"You never worked there. You were at the WFO," she added, referring to the Washington Field Office.

Pine shot her a glance. "You checked up on me?"

"Well, of course I did. Did you want an idiot for a secretary?"

"I visited Hoover quite frequently. They were looking for another home, but apparently Congress won't give them the money."

"Well, it's about time someone stopped wasting taxpayer dollars."

"Right, so the Pentagon can spend it on more ten-thousand-dollar toilets."

"Where are we staying once we get there?"

"I've got a buddy. He's on overseas assignment. We're staying at his place in northern Virginia."

"For a loner, you certainly have a lot of buddies."

"So long as they keep their distance, I'm good."

They drove on, the ride nearing its end.

26

THE "BUDDY'S" CONDO was in Arlington, Virginia, in an area known as Ballston. Kurt Ferris was a CID investigator in the Army and had been recently deployed overseas for six months to investigate crimes involving those who wore Army green in other countries. Pine had met him when they'd done a joint case together involving a smuggling ring operating out of Fort Belvoir that had international implications.

They'd solved the case and ended on good terms, which had prompted her to contact him about a place to stay in Virginia. Instead, he had offered his apartment up to her, since he wasn't using it. He swore he would not mention the arrangement to anyone after Pine told him she was working undercover on a Bureau case.

The condo was near the Ballston Mall. The area had been widely renovated and was one of the most popular residential areas for well-educated and well-heeled millennials, who had come here to work and play. Initially, Pine had been surprised that Ferris could afford a place here on his Army pay, but then remembered that his parents had left their only child a fairly substantial inheritance when they'd died in a car accident.

The condos were new, and all doors were operated not by keys but by passcodes. Ferris had given the necessary ones to Pine. That was good, because she didn't want to have to give her name or show ID to the building personnel.

Blum stowed her bag in her room, keeping everything in the bag in case they had to get away fast, as Pine had advised.

She took a stroll around the three-bedroom condo. It had high ceilings and a small balcony overlooking a rectangle of park. The furnishings were tasteful and plush, and the kitchen was well stocked and equipped with Wolf and Sub-Zero appliances.

After Blum checked out this and the pantry and the various cooking utensils, Pine emerged from her bedroom. Blum said, "Beautiful place. Is your friend single?"

"Yeah, he is."

Blum picked up a picture from a credenza. It showed a tall, handsome man in his Army dress blues with two older people. "This him?"

"Yeah, that's Kurt, and his mom and dad."

"Quite the looker, and definitely a good friend to let you stay here. You two must have a *close* relationship."

She looked at Pine expectantly.

"I'm not into girl talk," said Pine.

"Neither am I, considering neither one of us are *girls*."

Pine sighed. "I think Kurt wants to be more than friends. No, he *does* want to be more than friends. But I don't think he and I being together would be a good idea."

"Career in the way. He's in the east, you're in the west?"

"That's partly it, yes."

"What's the other part?"

"Maybe I haven't figured that out yet."

"Fair enough. Men can be simple, but relationships are not, at least from the woman's perspective."

"I did meet, I mean, I...there's this park ranger."

"Really, what's his name?"

"Why, you know a lot of park rangers?"

"Actually, I do."

"Sam Kettler."

"Don't know him."

"He's only been at the Canyon a couple years. He was on duty at Phantom when the guy went missing."

"So that's how you met and then started dating? Pretty quick."

"I wouldn't exactly call it dating. We went out for pizza and beer one time. And then he brought some beers over to my place the night before we left town. We sat out in his Jeep and drank them."

"You must be intrigued with him."

"Why do you say that?"

"You just said you went down to his Jeep and drank beer with him right before you were leaving on this trip. You had a lot on your mind. You could have easily declined the offer. Only you didn't. Pretty simple deduction."

"Well, I guess I *am* intrigued with him."

"Nice guy?"

"Yeah."

"Where'd you leave it with him?"

"Nowhere, really. I think he'd like to see me again."

"And you?"

Pine took a breath and rubbed at her mouth. "It's complicated."

"And you might be more complicated than most."

"Why do you say that?" Pine said sharply.

"I know about your past, Agent Pine. When you were a child?"

"That has nothing to do with anything."

"Are you sure about that? It would have traumatized anyone."

"I'm *not* traumatized. I wouldn't be in the FBI if I were. I would have punted on the psychological testing."

Blum nodded. "Okay. In the interests of getting it all out there, I also know that you went to ADX Florence to find out some things."

Pine gazed stonily at the woman. "I told no one about my trip."

"But you had to get special permission to visit after hours. That request came through the FBI bureaucracy. I saw the trail. Did you find what you needed to?"

"No, I didn't," Pine said in a tone that clearly indicated this conversation was over.

Blum put the picture down. "Now what?" she said.

"I'm taking a shower. I still have residue of the three creeps in a women's toilet on me. I suggest you do the same."

Pine undressed in the bedroom and caught her image in the vertical mirror hanging from the wall.

She looked first at the scars from her various encounters at the FBI. The bullet wound on the back of her calf that Kettler had noticed. An arrest gone to shit. She'd been lucky to survive it. The wound was small, and ugly. As she had explained to Kettler, the round had never come out of her. A surgeon's scalpel had later done the trick. That was good, because the exit wound might have blown out an artery. Now, it just looked like a small, blistery melanoma.

The knife slice on her left triceps had been a mistake on the part of an agent she'd been working with when handling a suspect. Fortunately, she'd been able to recover and take him out before she or her partner had paid the ultimate price. The scar looked like a centipede.

She turned around and looked at her lower back. That hadn't been the Bureau. That had been the weights. Lower back surgery was pretty typical for Olympic-caliber power lifters.

She could not bring herself to look at the delt tats: Gemini and Mercury.

She did lift her arms to show the words "No Mercy" on each.

No, not the words. The name.

She took a shower, letting the hot water and soap wash away the remnants of their encounter at the rest stop. She toweled off, put on fresh clothes, and then finger-dried her hair.

She walked into the kitchen to see Blum sautéing some vegetables on the cooktop.

"What are you doing?"

"We both need a home-cooked meal. And your buddy left a well-stocked fridge. I'm assuming it's okay if we use it?"

"He said it was. I'll leave him a check for the food we use. So, you cook?"

"I had six kids to feed. What do you think? Although, actually, when they were growing up, it was more Hamburger Helper and mac and cheese. Six kids meant I didn't have time to spend hours on cooking a meal. And I worked too, outside the house. Did your mother cook?"

Pine didn't answer the question. She sat down at the kitchen table and took out her laptop.

"Still working?" said Blum as she peppered the vegetables. "We just drove across the country. You could take a break for an hour."

Pine typed in some information and waited for the search results to come back. "Actually, best sleep I've had in a long time, snoozing while you drove," she said.

"It *is* a beautiful car. My ex had one sort of like it. It wasn't nearly as nice. He knew nothing about cars, unfortunately. It finally had to be junked."

"The guy who owned it was pretty special. He helped me out a lot in my early days at the Bureau. I wouldn't be nearly so *outgoing* but for him."

Pine tacked on a very brief smile to this statement, as though trying to make fact what was really nothing more than speculation for most people who knew her.

"Hallelujah for friends," said Blum.

"What are you making?" Pine asked.

"Chicken Milanese. I do it pretty well, if I do say so myself. He's got some ciabatta dinner rolls I'm going to warm in the oven, too. You want to do a salad? The fixings are in the fridge. Don't use the arugula, that's for the chicken."

Pine rose, washed her hands, and dried them off on a dish towel. She grabbed a large bowl from one of the cabinets, then opened the fridge and pulled out the necessary ingredients.

Blum said, "I have to say, I never imagined us preparing a meal together on the East Coast, or anywhere, actually."

"Life is unpredictable," said Pine as she sliced up a tomato and then a cucumber on a cutting board she'd taken from a drawer.

Blum prepped the chicken breast cutlets, dredging them in plain Greek yogurt and then dressing the meat in bread crumbs together with oregano, basil, and thyme. She coated a pan with extra virgin olive oil and cooked the cutlets for three minutes on each side.

After finishing the salad, Pine set the dining room table, then put the bowl of greens on the table.

Blum squeezed a sliced lemon over the cooked chicken cutlets and plated them over beds of arugula. She took the rolls out of the oven and put them in a basket that she had lined with a cloth napkin.

"I see your friend has a wine chiller," said Blum, pointing to the appliance under the kitchen counter. "I'm more of a red person, but a Chardonnay or even better a Pinot Grigio would go well with the chicken. You want to check while I carry the plates and rolls in?"

A minute later Pine came in carrying an uncorked bottle of Pinot and a wineglass in one hand, and a Fat Tire Belgian ale in the other.

"My idea of a nice white," said Pine, holding up the beer.

She poured the wine into the glass and set it in front of Blum before taking her seat.

Blum clinked her wineglass against Pine's bottle of beer.

They ate in silence until Pine said, "This is really good."

"I can show you how to make it."

Pine didn't respond to this at first. "You know, that might be nice. I'm, uh, I'm not that much of a cook."

"Simple is best. And fresh ingredients."

"Right. So, um, maybe you can teach me a few dishes." She glanced away and took a quick swig of her beer.

Blum looked at Pine closely. "For Sam Kettler?"

"What are you talking about?"

"Oh, come on, Agent Pine. I'm too old to be manipulated."

Pine smiled. "Okay, I *do* like him. We seemed to connect."

"Well, thank God, there's no law against that. You said he likes you, and after what you told me, I agree. And whether you think it's complicated or not, I think you should see him when we get back."

"*If* we get back," said Pine, turning serious once more.

"I stand corrected. So what's our next step?"

Pine put her fork and knife down and picked up her beer. "His brother gave me Ben Priest's home address. It's in Old Town Alexandria. I would expect the place is being watched, so we're going to watch the watchers and do some recon at the same time."

"Okay."

"Then there's Ed Priest's family. I need to contact them without anyone knowing."

"Aren't they still in protective custody?"

"I don't know. I couldn't get them into an actual safe house. But I had uniformed FBI looking after them. That might have been pulled after the call Dobbs got from the DD."

"And then we have the men in the chopper who took away the Priest brothers. Any idea who they might be?"

"I can make some deductions."

Blum took a sip of her wine and looked across the table thoughtfully at her boss. "What are they? And, more importantly, what are they based on?"

"I recognized the type of chopper."

"What was it?"

"A UH-72A Lakota. I've actually ridden on them."

"Who uses it?"

"Mostly, the United States Army."

27

KURT FERRIS had also left his two-year-old Kia Soul for Pine to use. She knew he'd owned a decked-out Dodge Ram pickup with double rear wheels before coming to DC from the wilds of Fort Bragg, Texas. However, he'd found the Ram was too big to drive and park in the traffic- and space-challenged Ballston area, so he'd traded it in for the Kia. Pine knew the man wasn't happy about it, because he'd told her he wasn't. He said he felt like a wimp on wheels.

She was parked at the curb about five townhomes down from Ben Priest's nineteenth-century row house on Lee Street in Old Town Alexandria, Virginia. It was an upscale, historic area located along the Potomac River.

She'd Googled real estate in the area and had calculated that Priest's home was worth north of two million.

She wondered what sort of work he had done to afford that sort of residence.

Like allowing a man to take his place on a mule ride down to the floor of the Grand Canyon and then disappear? Priest had mentioned "laundering" people, but she hadn't believed him. Yet maybe she needed to think about that some more.

Priest had told her that he'd worked for American intelligence before hanging out his own shingle. If Pine could have used normal Bureau resources, she might have been able to do a far deeper dig on the man, finding out perhaps what agency he worked at, and what sort of work he did there. Yet Pine was doing something she should not be doing, so those official resources were not available.

She had watched the home for a while, and was convinced that Priest's home was not under surveillance by anyone else.

This gave Pine an opening.

She had seen the woman before when she had gone out earlier. She lived in the row house next to Priest. In fact, the homes were attached. Pine had checked the backs of the houses. The backyards were separated only by a low-level fence. There might have been some interaction there.

The woman looked to be in her sixties, with thinning white hair styled in a way that indicated she had money and wasn't adverse to pampering herself. This was also shown by her designer clothes and shoes and sunglasses. She was also tanned and fit, and she carried herself with the air of someone who had had the pleasure of giving orders rather than following them. This had been confirmed by what Pine assumed was the woman's uniformed maid or house-keeper, who had been handed a cluster of bags from a late model burgundy Jag convertible parked in front of the woman's house. The woman had then carried them inside.

From her perch and using binoculars, Pine had seen the names on the shopping bags: Gucci, Dior, Louis Vuitton, and Hermes. The hall of fame of fashion.

Pine had never owned a single thing from those brands. She was more of an Under Armour girl. Yet even if she had wanted to, she doubted she could afford anything they sold. She doubted she could afford the *bags* the stuff came in. And her physical dimensions did not meet high-fashion standards. She was big where societal norms told women to be small, and small where the ladies were supposed to be big.

As the woman turned and walked down the street, carefully navigating the lumpy laid brick pavers in her stilettos as she checked her phone, Pine got out of the Kia and strode down the street, paralleling the woman. She timed it so that they would intersect at the next block.

"Excuse me, ma'am?" said Pine.

The woman, jolted from her digital bubble, looked askance at Pine in her jeans and windbreaker and boots.

"Whatever you're selling I don't need," she said immediately, in a deep, well-cultured voice.

"It's not that."

"And I don't have any cash if you need a handout. Bye-bye."

The woman proceeded on her way. Pine followed.

The woman stopped and held up her phone, which had a gold cover. "I will call the police if you don't leave me alone."

"I *am* the police," said Pine, holding up her FBI shield.

The woman slowly lowered her phone. "*You're* with the FBI? No way."

"I really am."

The woman ran her severe gaze over Pine and said, "You don't look like you are."

"That's sort of the point when you're on a stakeout."

"You're watching someone?" The woman looked horrified and then blurted out, "What's Jeffrey done?"

"Jeffrey?"

"My husband. He's a *money manager*. They're always doing something illegal. He's my *second* husband," she added, as though that exonerated her from any associated liability she might have. A hand fluttered to her bosom. "Thank *God* I kept my assets separate. The little sneak."

"I'm not here about Jeffrey. I'm here about your neighbor."

"My neighbor? Which one?"

"Ben Priest."

The woman gazed at Pine in a new light and then gave her a knowing look. "He's an interesting fellow, that one."

"What's your name?"

"Melanie Renfro."

"Have you lived in your house a long time?"

"Yes. Twenty years. Jeffrey moved in with me after we got married. He lived in DC. Capitol Hill. You couldn't pay me to live there. Taxes are twice Virginia's. It was either he moved here or there wasn't going to be a marriage."

"You want to grab some coffee?"

"That's where I was going, actually."

Pine followed Renfro into a coffee shop on King Street, the main avenue that bisected Old Town and ended at the Potomac River. They ordered, got their coffees, and headed back outside to sit in an enclosed area of tables. They were the only ones there, though people were passing them on the street. Mostly moms with strollers and some men and women in suits and carrying briefcases.

Renfro took a sip of her coffee and patted her lips with a paper napkin. "What has Ben done?"

"You said he was an interesting fellow?"

Renfro nodded and looked around as though they were in a movie and she was checking on eavesdroppers. When she caught Pine staring, she grinned and said, "This is so thrilling. The most exciting part of my day today was supposed to be a hair coloring and a waxing. This is so much better. And far less painful than a waxing."

"Glad I could do that for you. So, Priest?"

"Right. He moved in about, oh, seven years ago. I was still married to Parker, he was my first husband. He died of a heart attack four years ago. I married Jeffrey two years later. Some of my friends thought it was too soon. But at my age, hey, you don't know how much time you have left. Burn the candle to the end, right?"

"Right. So you knew Priest?"

"Oh, yes. I've had him over for dinners, cocktail parties, barbeques, that sort of thing. I have a wonderful caterer, if you ever need someone."

"What was your impression of him?"

"Oh, that he'd been everywhere, done everything. Could talk eloquently about any number of subjects. He knew several languages. And he was tall and very handsome. I used to invite him because I knew he would be fascinating for the other guests and eye candy for some of my girlfriends. He would flirt with them, nothing serious, but they loved it. He seemed to know how to play a role, work a room."

"Did he tell you what he did for a living?"

"He told me he'd taught over in England, Cambridge or Oxford, anyway, one of them. Then he'd made money in investments and traveled the world. I thought he was independently wealthy. He kept odd hours. Gone for long periods of time and then I'd see a cab dropping him off at two in the morning."

"He never mentioned working for the government?"

"Look, if you are with the FBI, I want to help you. But, I really don't know you at all. And these days fake badges and stuff can look really genuine."

"Okay, I understand that. I'm looking for Ben Priest because he disappeared when he was in Arizona. That's where I'm assigned."

"Oh my God. Do you have any idea what happened to him?"

Pine pulled back her hair to reveal the wound she'd suffered when the Explorer had hit the tree.

"I was with him when he was abducted. I was almost killed, too. I don't like it when people abduct other people. I like it even less when people try to kill me."

The blood drained from Renfro's face. "Oh my God, you poor thing."

"So any help you can give me would be much appreciated."

"Absolutely. With Ben my thought was, is he some sort of spy? I mean he's obviously brilliant and knows all these languages. And he looks sort of like James Bond, right? I've seen him in a tux. God, if I were twenty years younger, I might make a run at him. Hell, ten years younger. Jeffery's brilliant and makes a ton of money, but he's the spitting image of Don Rickles."

"Okay. Did he ever invite you to his place?"

Renfro looked puzzled. "Now that you mention it, no. Wait, I take that back. I've had drinks in his backyard."

"But never in the house?"

"No. I guess I never thought about that. I mean, he was a guy. And I always liked to do the parties at my place. And maybe his house was a mess. He was a bachelor, after all." She paused. "He was, wasn't he? I never saw any women over there. Wait, is he gay? That would really depress four of my girlfriends. And me too, quite frankly."

"Not that we know of. Anything he ever said that struck you as odd?"

Renfro drank her coffee and mulled over this query. "Odd how?"

"No particular way. Just your impression."

"Well, there *was* something. I was having a dinner party outside. This was not that long ago."

"Okay, what happened?"

"Well, Ben was his charming self, regaling the guests with some story about traveling overseas."

"Did you catch where?"

"Not exactly. Let me think. He said something about inadvertently crossing a border and that he was lucky to get back unscathed."

"Go on."

"Now I remember. He said one of the *Stans*. I wasn't sure what he was talking about. Stan who?"

"One of the Stans. Uzbekistan, Kazakhstan. Used to be part of the Soviet Union. Central Asia."

"Oh, right. I guess that does make sense. Hey, what can I say? I went to college to find a husband. Well, he said that the world really was unpredictable and you just never knew what was going to happen. I asked him if he was talking about anything specifically."

"What did he say?"

"He said, 'I would have to wait and see.'"

"How did you take that?"

"Well, then he laughed and drank down his wine, pinched my arm in a playful way, and told me not to listen to him. That he was just kidding around. Too much booze. But the thing was the party hadn't been going on that long. That was only his second glass."

"Did you ever know him to do that before?"

"No, not really. I mean not in that way. He seemed, well, anxious. I remember catching a glimpse of him just staring off into space. He never did that before at my parties. He was always right in the center of things regaling people. It was odd."

Pine next took out her phone and showed her the digital sketch that Jennifer Yazzie had done.

"Have you seen this man around before? With Priest?"

Renfro studied the picture. "You know, he does looks familiar."

"How?"

Renfro leaned back in her chair and let the sunlight hit her face. "I'm not a good sleeper, never have been. My mother was an insomniac, and I'm convinced I got that from her." She leaned forward and cupped her hands around her coffee.

"It was, oh, maybe one in the morning. I was upstairs. I'd just gotten back from the kitchen with a cup of tea. I was looking out the window onto the street. The moon was out and it was really as clear as day. A car pulled down the street and stopped in front of Ben's house."

"What kind of car? A cab?"

"No. It was a regular car. I guess these days it could have been an Uber or something like that. Anyway, a guy gets out. He goes around to the rear of the car. The driver had popped the trunk. He pulled out his bag. And when he did that, he sort of reflexively gazed up, and I got a real good look at him." She tapped Pine's phone. "And he looked a lot like that guy."

"Did he go into Priest's home?"

"The door opened. Someone was there. The man passed through and the door closed."

"You think it was Priest?"

"I couldn't see the person, really. But who else would it have been?"

"Did you ever see the man again?"

"No."

"And when was this?"

"I can tell you exactly, because Jeffery was gone on a business trip. It was ten days ago."

The woman glanced up at Pine, who was staring off.

"Does that help you?" asked Renfro.

"Yeah, it does."

"If he is a spy, maybe, I don't know, our enemies have him," she said breathlessly.

Or we *might have him*, thought Pine.

28

Carol Blum adjusted the mirror on Pine's Mustang so she could see better.

It appeared to her that Ed Priest had done well for himself. He and his family lived in an upscale community in Bethesda, Maryland. Their home was a two-story brick painted white, with a three-car side-load garage. The landscape was nicely done, all water-loving flowers and sweeping lawns, which was quite foreign to Blum.

And all that mulch! She shuddered.

She stiffened a bit when the car pulled out of the garage and headed down to the street.

Mary Priest was driving, and two young boys were in the backseat.

As the Lexus SUV passed by, Blum caught a glance at Priest's profile through the open car window.

The face was pale, the features pinched, the cheeks reddened.

The woman had obviously experienced a hellish time and was probably continuing to do so, although it appeared that Mary Priest and her sons had been released from the protective custody that Pine had arranged.

Blum fell in behind Priest, and the two cars made their way out to one of the main arteries leading into downtown Bethesda. The children were clearly school-age, but it was possible that after what had happened Mary had decided to keep them home from classes.

She followed at a discreet distance in light traffic. The Mustang did tend to stand out.

The Lexus pulled to a stop in front of a building on a side street in Bethesda. The sign out front proclaimed it to be one of those educational centers where kids went to bone up on math and English and other subjects. Priest got out and led her sons into the building, while Blum found an open space across the street.

Five minutes later Priest came back out, but she didn't get into her car. She started walking down the street. Blum got out of her car and followed.

It was nearly noon, and Blum wondered if the woman was going to do some shopping while waiting for her kids. And then Priest swerved into a building.

Blum quickly followed.

It was a movie theater.

Priest bought a ticket and Blum purchased one for the same movie.

She trailed Priest down the hall and into the theater.

It was empty.

Priest took a seat in the middle, while Blum took the same seat several rows behind.

She settled down and waited. Her first thought was that Priest was waiting for someone, but the woman was not checking her phone or watch or looking toward the entrance. She just stared down at her hands.

As the previews came on, Blum decided to risk it.

She got up from her seat and moved to Priest's row, taking the chair one over from the woman.

Priest didn't even look up. She seemed lost in thought.

This gave Blum a chance to study the woman. She looked to be no more than forty, petite with dirty-blond hair that fell to her shoulders. Trim and fit looking, she was dressed in cream-colored slacks, flat shoes, and a light blue short-sleeved shirt that showed off defined, tanned arms. Her Kate Spade handbag sat in the chair next to her.

She dabbed at her eyes with her hand. Then the tears came more fiercely and she put her head in her hands.

Blum opened her purse, took out a packet of tissues, and handed them across.

Priest saw them, jerked up, and looked over at Blum. But when she focused on the older woman next to her, she instantly relaxed, smiled briefly, and thanked her. She took out a few tissues and handed the packet back. She wiped her eyes clear and then blew her nose.

"I...I think it's allergies," said Priest, not meeting Blum's eye.

"I think it might just be life," said Blum. "I've sat in my share of theaters with 'allergy' problems."

Priest laughed lightly and looked embarrassed. "I didn't even want to see this movie. I just picked it because it was playing now."

"I did the same thing," said Blum. "Just wanted to get out and about."

"I'm Mary."

"Carol," said Blum. They shook hands. "It's nearly lunchtime, if you'd prefer that. At my age, I look forward to meals. And you look like you could use something to eat."

"I can't remember the last time I ate. Do you...live around here?"

"No, I'm visiting from another part of the country. I have friends here, but they're working today. Do you know a good place to eat?"

"I do."

"Shall we?"

Priest laughed. "I've got some time to kill, so what the hell?"

They walked outside, and Priest led Blum over to another street.

"It's a French-style café. The menu's good, though a little rich, and I could use some wine, actually."

Blum nodded appreciatively. "Sounds fine to me. I long ago stopped counting calories and restricting my alcohol consumption."

"I really look forward to those days," said Priest wistfully.

They were led to a table in the back by the greeter.

As they settled in and looked over their menus, Blum said, "I know this sounds like a cliché, but I'm a good listener. I have six kids and I'm divorced, and no, it wasn't amicable. I've got lots of grandkids, some I still haven't seen. I've traveled widely and experienced pretty much everything, so if you want to talk, I can give you an excellent armchair quarterback analysis."

Priest smiled and rubbed at her eyes. "God, it was like you were dropped from Heaven right when I needed you."

"Sometimes the world works in mysterious ways."

They ordered two glasses of merlot, and each took a sip before Priest plunged in.

"This is going to sound crazy, even to someone like you."

"Okay."

"It's my husband."

"That doesn't sound crazy at all."

"No, no, you don't understand. He's not cheating on me or anything. Ed's a good guy."

"So what's the issue, Mary?"

Priest shook her head. "You're not going to believe me."

"I assure you that I will."

"My husband. Well, it started with his brother."

"What did?"

"His brother is into something, I'm not sure what. And now we're sucked into it too."

"Into something? Do you mean criminal?"

"That's just it, I don't know. What I can tell you is that my husband left on a trip without telling me where he was going. He's never done that. He's as vanilla as they come. He's a CPA, for God's sake."

"Is he back yet?"

"No, and here's the other thing. The frigging FBI came to our house and said they were there to protect us."

"Good Lord! And you think it was connected to your brother-in-law?"

"It has to be. I mean none of this stuff ever happened before."

"Have you spoken to your husband?"

"Not since he left. I'm terrified. I have no idea if he's okay or not."

"But you're no longer being guarded? I mean here you are out and about without armed guards."

"That's the other strange thing. They just upped and left. They said everything was fine. False alarm."

"What did you do?"

"I did what any wife would do. I blew a fucking gasket, pardon my language."

"I would have, too."

"I was screaming at these guys. 'Where's my husband? What's going on? Why are you involved?'"

"And what did they tell you?"

"Absolutely nothing. They just left. I got on my phone and started calling around to all of Ed's friends and business associates. But none of them had heard a thing."

"And his brother?"

"I called him too, but he didn't answer. I left a bunch of messages. Nothing. The jerk. He has little enough to do with us, really. And now this!"

"But you don't know for sure that he is involved in all this."

"Then why hasn't he called me back?"

"Does he live nearby?"

"In Old Town. Old Town Alexandria. It's in northern Virginia, just across the river."

"Have you been to see him?"

"I drove over there the same day the FBI left. I knocked and knocked. No answer."

"I suppose you don't have a key? You could have checked to see if he was all right. He might be injured or something."

In answer Mary rummaged through her purse and took out a key. "I do. Ed had one from a while back. His brother probably forgot all about it. It was when he was out of town for an extended period and he needed Ed to go over and check on things."

"So, did you go in?"

"I was afraid to. Besides, there's an alarm system and I don't know the code, only Ed did. And we never go there."

"That is a remarkable story. I wish I had some advice to offer, but I truly wasn't expecting something like that. I was just assuming it was some sort of domestic issue, or something with work or extended family."

"I know, but it was just a relief to tell someone. I felt like I was going nuts. I really did. And then you showed up like an angel."

Blum felt a pang of guilt at the woman's words, but her loyalty was not to this woman. There were bigger issues at stake.

"I'm just glad our paths crossed," said Blum with all sincerity.

They ordered their food and talked while they ate.

Blum said, "I think you should keep trying to call your husband, but don't go back over to your brother-in-law's house. If the FBI is involved, there might be something dangerous going on. You need to think about your own safety and that of your kids. At this point, I think you just do nothing. If your brother-in-law is into something criminal, you don't want to get in the middle of that."

"But should I report Ed missing? I mean, he *is* missing. My God, I can't even believe I'm saying this. My poor husband."

Blum looked at her thoughtfully. "Give it a day. Then you can think seriously of doing that. I'm very sorry this has happened to you. You strike me as a good and caring person. And obviously none of this is your doing."

Priest's face crinkled up and tears slid from her eyes.

"I know. I mean life is complicated enough without this crap. I've got two sons to raise. And Ed provides a great living, but he has to work crazy hours. For most of the time it's just me and the kids. Until now that was fine. But now, I mean, I have no idea where Ed is."

They started chatting about their respective families, and after their meal was done Blum said, "Why don't you go to the bathroom and wash your face? Your makeup's not running, so there's no worries there, but your eyes are awfully puffy and red. Here." She pulled a bottle of Visine from her purse and handed it to Priest. "I'll watch your things. And I insist on paying for lunch."

"Oh, no, you really don't have to do that."

"It's the least I can do after all you've suffered."

Later, the two women walked to the education center, where they parted company.

"Thank you so much, Carol."

"I didn't really do anything."

"Yes, you did. You listened, and you believed me. That's enough."

The women shook hands and Blum walked back to her car.

Inside, she opened her purse and took out the key to Ben Priest's home, which she'd slipped from Mary's purse while she'd been in the restroom.

The price of lunch had been well worth it.

And maybe she and Pine could find Mary Priest's husband. Preferably alive.

29

Two A.M. was a good time to commit a breaking and entering.

Pine thought this as she squatted in Ben Priest's backyard disabling the electronic pipe to Priest's home security system and phone line. A few snips, a reroute of a circuit, and she could walk right in and the security system would have no clue about the breach.

This trick of the trade had not been in the official training at the FBI, but Pine had supplemented her skill set with an abundance of self-learning. This particular technique had been taught to Pine by the owner of a home security company. People and organizations with deep pockets could effectively protect against what Pine was doing by hardening the pipe and security measures that powered the alarm system. Most homeowners, even ones like Ben Priest, typically could not, or at least couldn't do it well enough.

Pine rose, did a 360-degree check, and then hurried up to the back door. She kept to the shadows because she knew that Melanie Renfro suffered from insomnia, and a window in her home looked out over Priest's rear yard.

She inserted the key Blum had given her in the lock and turned it, and a few moments later she was inside the house and closing the door behind her right as the wind picked up and the first few sprinkles of rain landed on the rear brick stoop.

Pine listened but heard no beeping, showing that her security workaround had been effective. She took out her Maglite and shone it around. The house had a bit of a musty smell to it, not unexpected in a place this old, no matter how well it had been maintained.

The back door opened onto a mudroom with built-in shelves and rain boots standing up in one corner. She moved past this and into the adjacent kitchen.

It was small and not particularly well laid out. As she viewed it under the beam of her light, she could see that the appliances were old, the cabinetry was several decades old, and the flooring looked and felt like linoleum. She opened the fridge. It was empty and not particularly clean.

She checked each of the drawers and cabinets. They were mostly empty. A few plates, a few utensils. Pine got the feeling they were either just for show or had come with the place when Priest purchased it.

The rain was really pouring down now. She could hear it smacking the roof and pelting the windows. Then a gash of lightning illuminated the interior of the house and was followed almost immediately by a loud crack of thunder.

She left the kitchen and entered the small dining room. It was a dining room in name only, since it was unfurnished. The elaborate chair rail and moldings on the walls were dusty, and in desperate need of fresh paint. An old-fashioned chandelier hung from a ceiling medallion shaped like a pineapple.

She'd hoped that Priest would have an office in his home, and that wish was granted when she opened the door to the room opposite the dining room and on the other side of the front foyer.

Inside, she shone her light around to reveal a large, square partner's desk with a leather chair, a wall of books, a desktop computer, and a small wooden file cabinet. This place definitely looked to have been used.

She searched everything. The file cabinet was empty.

The desk drawers the same.

She opened each book and shook it to see if anything fluttered out. Nothing.

She sat down at the computer, certain that it would be password-protected.

A black screen confronted her. There was no prompt even to enter a password. The computer had been wiped clean. Its hard drive had been probably taken or destroyed.

Shit.

The question was: Had Priest done it, or had someone else?

She left the office and ventured up the narrow staircase to the second floor.

There were three bedrooms and adjoining baths up here.

Pine checked each one, ending with Priest's bedroom. She could tell it was his because it was the only one that was furnished. The man apparently, like Margaret Mitchell, did not want to encourage visitors.

There was a bed with an ornately carved headboard, an old armoire that held a few clothes, and that was it.

Ben Priest was definitely into minimalism. The bathroom was small, and the medicine cabinet was as empty as the fridge downstairs.

Pine was starting to wonder if the man even lived here.

Or else he had emptied the place before he'd headed west.

Or someone else had.

Melanie Renfro hadn't mentioned any moving vans, and the furniture was still here, what little there was.

She stared at the bed and then performed the obvious: She looked under it.

Her Maglite hit on something. The bed was high off the floor so there was room. She stretched out a long arm and snagged it, pulling it toward her.

She sat on her haunches and examined the contents of the old cardboard box.

A ratty basketball jersey, a tarnished trophy. She checked the date. It was from more than twenty years ago. She read the inscription.

"Most Valuable Player—Football, Ben Priest."

It was from the high school Priest had attended.

There was a pair of tube socks with blue stripes at the top.

And an old basketball, partially deflated.

Why keep this? Did he forget it was even under there?

She sat on the bed and examined the items again.

Jersey, socks, trophy, basketball.

Basketball?

What had Ed Priest said?

His brother hadn't even liked basketball, but he knew he was good at it.

So why keep a basketball here? And a partially deflated one at that.

She scanned the ball with her light, inch by inch.

Then she probed with her fingers.

Because of her height Pine had been recruited to play basketball in high school and had also competed in the AAU program. She had held thousands of basketballs. Her fingers instinctively knew what the surface felt like, though each ball was slightly different.

Then she found it.

There was a faint short seam, one that did not really line up with the others.

She hit this spot with her Maglite. It ran along one of the black stripes on the ball, barely perceptible. She wouldn't have even seen it, if she hadn't felt the anomaly. It was only about two inches long. She felt with her fingers along this line and sensed a bit of a bump.

Hardened glue. The manufacturer hadn't done that; it was an add-on.

Pine pulled out the Swiss knife she always carried with her and made the cut right along the seam. The leather opened up easily under her blade, and the remaining air quickly escaped as she cut the ball open and separated the two halves.

There was no interior bladder, just a black lining under the leather exterior.

She wasn't focused on that. She was riveted on the flash drive that was glued to the interior liner. Glued, not just pushed through the hole. Because otherwise it would rattle around if someone picked it up, giving the secret away.

She used her knife to gently free the device from the liner.

She put it in her pocket, put the cut-up basketball back in the box, and slid it under the bed.

She had risen to her feet when she heard a door downstairs open.

30

PINE SLIPPED OUT HER PISTOL.

She knew if she moved, the old plank floor was going to creak, alerting whoever was down there to her presence.

She looked at the window, a foot away. Could she make it without treading on the floor?

She didn't think so; consequently, she didn't move at all.

But that status was going to quickly become unsustainable.

Normally, in this situation she would announce herself and tell whoever it was to identify themselves. But she had broken into the house, and she was acting outside her duties as a federal agent. If it were the police down there, she was potentially in a world of trouble.

If it weren't the police, she was potentially still in a world of trouble.

So she stood there, not moving and waiting.

If they were cops, they should call out a warning to anyone in here to show themselves.

She pivoted her head to the side of the house facing the street. Through the window she didn't see any lights shining through it, so there was no cop car out there with its rack lights ablaze.

She heard footsteps move across the planks downstairs and then stop.

She could imagine the thought process.

Move, stop, process. Move again. Stop. Process.

The footsteps reached the stairs and she heard them coming up.

Okay, this was going to get very dicey, because the spot where she was standing would leave her totally exposed as soon as they opened the door to the bedroom.

Suddenly, outside a slash of lightning lit the sky.

Wait for it, wait for it.

The resulting pop of thunder was so loud, it shook the house.

Pine took advantage of this to slide across the floor and behind the door.

The footsteps started up again. Then she thought she caught words spoken back and forth. She couldn't hear what, but that meant there was definitely more than one person down there.

She still liked the odds so long as she could take them by surprise. If not, then the odds would quickly turn against her.

The sounds of the footsteps mingled with hushed voices reached the top landing. They moved, as she had, from one bedroom to another, until there was only this one left.

She followed their progress by listening to the creaks and squeaks of the planks.

Pine didn't move as the sound of the steps came toward the door.

She saw the door move an inch. And then it was pushed open until the bottom of the door caught on the uneven floor and halted before it hit her.

Two figures came in.

Pine cautiously peered around the door. They weren't cops, unless the police had started wearing black ski masks.

Both men were armed. Both men were in a crouch and looking around the space.

Pine was hoping that they would not turn her way.

Her hope turned out to be a false one.

As soon as the man saw her, Pine kicked the door, and the edge caught the guy smack in the face. He grunted, fell backward, and slammed into the other man as he went down. As he fell, his gun arced upward. A single shot blasted into the ceiling as his finger reflexively pulled the trigger. The impact of the round into the ceiling sent plaster chips and dust down on them.

The first guy landed on his butt, and before he could fully right himself, Pine put him down for good with a roundhouse kick to his head, putting all her weight and substantial leg strength behind it. He slumped back down without making a sound.

The second man scrambled to his feet, but before he could line up a shot, Pine's fist crushed his jaw with an overhand left that she delivered from a semisquat position, maxing her kinetic leverage. She heard the bone crack on impact. As he dropped his gun and slumped over in pain, she followed that blow with a sweep kick, cutting out his legs and sending him back to the floor. Hovering over him, she performed an eye strike with her index finger. When he howled in pain and grabbed his face with both hands, she bounced his head off the floor with the heel of her boot.

He groaned once and then joined his buddy in unconsciousness.

Pine quickly searched them, but they were carrying no IDs. She stripped off their masks and took pictures of them both with her phone. She took a moment to examine their weapons and took photos of them, too.

The next moment she was hurtling down the stairs.

She left the way she had come.

Pine cleared the brick wall at the back of the rear garden area and dropped onto the street on the next block over. She walked swiftly to the next intersection, then turned left and made her way over to Priest's street. She peered cautiously down it to see if there was anyone else lurking around the man's house.

There was no one she could see. They might be in one of the cars parked on both sides of the street, but it was far too dark to make out anyone inside any of the vehicles.

She rubbed her knuckles where she had clocked the guy.

She would have to ice that later.

They weren't cops. They weren't federal agents. They were two guys in ski masks with guns. Who were they? More to the point, who were they working for? And why was Priest a subject of interest for them?

She had to assume that they weren't there because of her. If they'd seen her break into the house they would have been far more cautious about entering the only room where she could have been hiding. One guy would have gone in and flushed her, and the second guy would have taken her out.

At least that was how she would have played it.

Her mind was working so rapidly that she had barely registered the fact that it was raining hard. That is until another streak of lightning made her realize she was standing under one of the many very large trees that dotted the streets of Old Town, their aged roots laying havoc to the laid brick sidewalks.

She turned in the direction opposite from Priest's and made her way back to the Kia.

It was after three, and in another few hours the dawn would be breaking.

She wanted to get back to her place and see what was on the flash drive.

As she was approaching her car, Pine noticed a movement to her left.

It wasn't stealth. The person wasn't intending to sneak up on her.

"Can we speak?"

She turned to face the person. He was a small, trim man of Asian descent, maybe in his early forties. He was wearing a raincoat, spectacles, and a slouch hat. He had an umbrella in one hand, but curiously was holding it by the wrong end.

Pine answered his request by pointing her gun at him.

He didn't flinch at the sight of the weapon.

He said, "I sincerely believe you are an intelligent person. I think a meeting might be in both of our best interests."

His speech was slightly accented, but his English was perfect, if a bit awkwardly formal.

"Who are you?"

"Perhaps a person who can at least partially explain the, um, delicate situation you presently find yourself in."

"I'm listening."

"Not here. We shall be more comfortable somewhere else."

"I'm not going anywhere with you."

"I really must insist upon this."

Pine indicated her weapon. "I think I have the upper hand."

He moved so fast, she never really saw his umbrella hook her gun and rip it out of her hand. Pine simply realized she was suddenly weaponless, something she never liked to be.

Pine squatted down and feigned assuming a fighting stance. Then she lifted her pants leg and grabbed her Beretta. Before she could bring it up, he leapt forward and neatly kicked it out of her hand.

She stood and faced him. "Who are you?"

The man set his umbrella on the hood of a car parked on the street. "I must insist upon your accompanying me. I have a vehicle at hand."

"I'm not going."

Again, he moved so fast, Pine barely had time to attempt to block his kick. She was knocked backward and flipped over the car hood. She landed on the sidewalk on the other side.

She rose quickly, but not quickly enough. The next blow lifted her off her feet, and she slammed back into a tree growing through the brick sidewalk.

She rose, wiped the blood from her mouth, and set her hands and feet in a defensive posture.

"You are quite stubborn," said the man.

Pine said nothing. She was conserving her breath. She'd never battled anyone as quick as this guy, not even her MMA instructors. He was five inches shorter and thirty pounds lighter than she was, and yet his blows were about the hardest she'd ever felt.

She kicked out with a feinting roundhouse, which he easily blocked. Her momentum had carried her into a crouch, which was intentional. She exploded out of this position with an elbow strike aimed at his throat. It was a clever move, yet he simply edged away, and kicked her in the backside, sending her sprawling into the wet street.

Pine slowly rose and brushed off her pants and blew on her scraped palms.

The man said, "I think we can agree that this situation is becoming a trifle ridiculous."

Pine could see only one way out of this.

She launched herself forward and took a vicious kick to the head, followed by one to her oblique.

Both blows were staggering, but Pine's skull was pretty damn hard, and a lifetime of lifting phenomenally heavy weights had made her core iron.

She started to stumble, as though she was going down.

At the last moment she lunged forward, wrapped her legs around the man's torso and left arm, ripped his right limb straight up, and locked it down in an arm bar.

The momentum of her charge and their comingled weights caused them to topple into the middle of the street. The man's hat fell off.

Pine squeezed her muscular legs around his torso, even as she levered his right arm over his head, trying her best to rip it from its socket.

She could hear him breathing heavily. She locked down on his torso even more, her goal to stop his diaphragm from moving up and down. Without that mobility, one could not remain conscious or alive.

She thought she could feel him weakening.

She was wrong.

With the index finger of his pinned left hand he jabbed hard into Pine's inner thigh. As he dug into it, applying an immense amount of pressure, Pine lost all feeling in her leg, and then a jolt of pain shot through her muscle and joints and rocketed up her entire side.

She cried out, helpless, as he forced her useless left leg off him.

An instant later his elbow smashed against the side of her jaw with such force that her leg lock was completely broken. Another elbow strike and her arm bar also fell away, allowing him to roll to his left, get to his feet, crouch, and deliver a crushing stomp kick to her belly.

She threw up what little was in her stomach.

She lay on the street, so dazed that she could barely see the little man rise above her.

"I misjudged you," he said. He balled up his fist. "You are not quite so intelligent as I first believed."

The siren cut through the silence of the night. The sound seemed to be heading toward them at speed.

The man looked toward the sound, which gave Pine the only opening she needed.

Though he'd outmaneuvered her at every junction and was by far the better fighter, the man had made one mistake: He'd misjudged the length of her legs.

She shot her right leg straight up and kicked him hard in the balls with the toe of her boot.

He cried out, bent over, and staggered back.

Pine watched from street level as, still hunched over, he snatched up his hat and moved haltingly into the darkness as the sound of the siren headed for them.

Pine slowly stood and, dragging her still-numb left leg behind her, recovered both her guns, unlocked the Kia, collapsed inside, and then slouched down in her seat a few seconds before the police car turned onto the street and sped past her.

Someone must have heard the fight and called the cops.

Pine rolled down the window, spit blood along with part of a tooth out of her mouth, started the car, put it in gear, and slowly drove off.

The fucking flash drive better be worth it.

31

Do you need any more ice, Agent Pine?"

Blum was at the door to the bathroom.

Inside, Pine was sitting naked in the bathtub, which she had partially filled with ice from the under-the-counter icemaker as well as the fridge's icemaker.

"No, I'm good," Pine called out.

"You still didn't tell me what happened."

Pine moved her arms and legs gingerly in the ice bath. "I will. Just give me a little time."

The feeling had come back to her left leg, but it still throbbed like hell.

"Can I get you something to eat or drink?"

"I'll take a beer."

"It's seven in the morning."

"Make it two beers then. Thanks."

Pine heard Blum walk away, and she slumped back into the ice.

She could sit in here for only a few minutes more. She'd been in and out of the ice several times for the better part of three hours. While she needed the ice to take the pain and swelling away, any person's tolerance for this was limited.

By the time Blum came back and knocked on the door, Pine was slowly lifting herself out of the ice bed. She wrapped a towel around herself, opened the door, and accepted one of the beers from Blum.

"You look like hell," said Blum. "Your jaw is swollen, your lip is cracked, and your left eye is puffy. And you're moving like you're a hundred years old. Were you in a fight or did you fall off a building?"

"Sort of feels like both," mumbled Pine as she sat down on the toilet lid and took a long drink of the beer. Then she wrapped some of the ice from the tub into a washcloth and held it against her face.

"I'll trade the second beer for the whole story," said Blum, holding up the can.

Pine glanced up at her and finally nodded. "Sit down, it might take a while."

Blum sat primly on the edge of the tub and looked at her expectantly.

Pine laid out for her what had taken place, from the moment she'd stepped inside Priest's home to getting the crap kicked out of her and driving away afterward.

"He was the best I've ever seen," said Pine. "Fought some pretty good ones. This guy was way out of my league."

"But in the end, you bested him," pointed out Blum.

Pine coughed, winced, put her beer down, and clutched at her side. "Doesn't really feel like victory."

She got up, opened the medicine cabinet, took out a bottle of Advil, downed four with a swallow of sink water, and resumed her seat.

Blum said, "This flash drive, have you opened it yet?"

Pine shook her head. "I'm just hoping there's something in there that will help us."

"Priest must have thought it pretty important, if he hid it away like that."

"That's what I'm counting on. Otherwise, there was zip at his house."

"Can I make you something to eat?"

"I'm good. I just need to check the flash drive, and then I

need some sleep. The ice is working. I can feel the swelling going down."

Pine rose and gingerly walked into her bedroom after running hot water in the tub to empty out the ice. She dressed in sweats and ankle socks, and walked into the kitchen carrying her laptop and the flash drive. She still held the ice pack against her face.

Blum put a cup of hot tea down in front of her. "Peppermint. It's good for anything that ails you."

"You don't get a buzz from peppermint."

"It's a different kind of buzz. Drink."

Pine set down the ice pack, took a few sips from the cup, then opened her laptop and inserted the flash drive into the USB port.

She hit the requisite keys, and what was on the USB started to load on the screen. They both stared at the writing and blank box there.

"Shit," exclaimed Pine. "Of course, it's password protected." She shook her head. "I got my ass kicked for this?"

"Can you figure out the password?"

"Maybe. If it's something personal to Priest. But if it's a random computer-generated password, you need a lot of computing power to break it."

"Well, something will occur to us. Now, any idea who the two men at the house were?"

"No, but I have a way of checking."

She took out her phone and dialed up the pictures she had taken of their weapons. "They don't look like any pistols I've seen before. Hang on. I'm going to check this out online."

Blum said warningly, "They already hacked us once. Can't they track us through your computer?"

"They could if I weren't using a variation of a VPN."

"VPN?"

"Virtual Privacy Network. It's like allowing your online

footprint to be hidden in secure tunnels. The one I'm using is really top-grade. It allows me to use the Web virtually anonymously."

Pine brought up a database of pistols. She scrolled down page by page, all the time glancing at the photos she'd taken. She stopped on one. "Damn."

"What?"

"Hold on."

Pine kept scrolling, and then stopped when she got to a photo that matched the other pistol. She looked up at Blum. "It's no wonder I didn't recognize them."

"What do you mean?"

"One's an MP-443 Grach. And the other's a GSh-18."

"Those surely aren't American pistols. I've never heard of them."

"No. They're *Russian*. The Grach's carried by the police, and the GSh by the military."

Both women stared at each other for an uncomfortably long moment until Blum said matter-of-factly, "Well, of course the Russians are involved. They're always the bad guys."

"But why? And what does Moscow have to do with a dead mule in the Canyon?"

Neither one had an answer to that.

"You need to get some sleep, Agent Pine. You need to heal and rest. I have a strong feeling that you'll need to be at your best."

"I think we both will."

Pine went to her bedroom and stripped off her clothes, because even the light, floppy sweats against her battered body hurt. She looked down at her oblique. There was a massive yellow-purplish bruise where the guy had walloped her. She felt along her leg to where he had applied the pressure with his finger to break her leg lock. Her limb was still tingling. He must have found a nerve there she didn't even know she had.

She gingerly lay back in the bed with the ice pack still cemented to her face. In her other hand, she clutched her Glock.

She took several deep breaths, and the result was bruised ribs carping at her.

Pine closed her eyes and let her thoughts wander back to the two men in the house.

The two *Russians*.

And then there was the umbrella-wielding ass kicker.

He wanted her to go with him somewhere. He said he would explain things to her, the predicament she found herself in.

She wanted to know how he had come upon her. Had he been watching the house and seen her enter? Or seen her leave and followed?

That might be the likelier scenario, because she'd taken great care to ensure no one saw her going in.

Was he connected to the other two men? Somehow, she didn't think so.

Then was he an adversary of theirs?

The Russians were clearly just muscle. The Asian seemed to be something more than that.

She put the bag of ice down, reached over, and plucked her shield off the nightstand.

She knew every facet of the embossed metal. After she'd been awarded it upon graduating from Quantico, she had held it all night, fingering it over and over, like she was reading Braille.

In some ways—no, maybe in the only way—the figure of Justitia represented all there was in the world to Pine. Justice. It wasn't about the greater good. It was about what was right and wrong on an individual basis. Person by person. Because if you neglected the people, the idea of a greater good was a pipe dream created by those whose idea of the "greater good" almost always tended to favor themselves and people like them.

She crossed her arms over her chest. The shield in one, the Glock in the other.

Two critical components not only to her work, but also perhaps to her identity.

Without them, what was she?

The lost, bereaved little girl from Andersonville, Georgia?

She closed her eyes and, as she went to sleep, mouthed the same words she had for nearly thirty years:

I will never forget you, Mercy. Never.

CHAPTER

32

IT WAS STILL STORMING outside when Pine awoke early that evening. She rolled over and let out a groan as soon as all the aches and pains hit her.

She shuffled into the bathroom and took a steaming hot shower, letting the water sink into her soreness. She toweled off, dressed, and walked out into the kitchen, where Blum was sitting with Pine's laptop and a cup of coffee in front of her.

"Your face looks a lot better," noted Blum.

"Looks can be deceiving."

"You want coffee? I just made a fresh pot."

"I'm good."

"Do you want something to eat?"

"I got it."

Pine opened the fridge and grabbed some yogurt. She took a spoon from a drawer, sat down at the table, and started slowly spooning the yogurt into her mouth.

"That's not a lot of nourishment," said Blum.

"For someone who got kicked in the face with a sledgehammer made of flesh and bone, it's just fine. I'm not up to chewing yet. Or hot beverages. The tea you gave me earlier did a number on the inside of my mouth."

"Oh, right."

Pine looked at the laptop screen. "Figured out the password?"

"Not even close. And without Bureau resources, how do we crack it?"

Pine set her yogurt and spoon down.

"Let's put this into some context. I found the flash drive in a basketball. Along with an old football trophy. There were also some gym socks and a basketball jersey." Pine paused and thought back. "On the jersey was printed 'Catholic Church League.'"

"Catholic churches have basketball leagues?" said Blum.

"Apparently so."

"What's your friend's Wi-Fi password?"

Pine said, "*Semper Primus.*" When Blum glanced at her, she explained, "Latin for 'Always First.' It's the Army motto."

Blum went online and typed in a search for Catholic churches near Priest's home.

"There's the Basilica of St. Mary Catholic Church in Old Town Alexandria. It's only a short walk from Priest's house."

Pine rose and grabbed her jacket off the back of the chair.

"Where are you going?"

"To church."

"You want company?"

"No. You better stay here."

"Since you're going to a place of worship, I'll say a prayer for you."

"Can't hurt," said Pine over her shoulder.

* * *

The Basilica of St. Mary was the oldest Catholic church in Virginia. It was located on South Royal Street and its gray stone facade was gothic in appearance. Its stark front was softened somewhat by four sets of wooden double doors with brass kickplates.

The rain had slackened when Pine pulled to a stop across the street and looked around. There were a few people on the side-walks, and a truck slowly drove down the street before its taillights disappeared into the darkness.

The sign in front of the church said it had been established in 1795. A white statue of the eponymous Mary was set in a niche of the building's facade high above the main front door.

Pine got out and walked across the street. She made a searching look all around and then headed up the steps.

The door was fortunately unlocked. She stepped inside and shut it behind her.

She moved through another set of doors and found herself in the worship area proper.

The stained glass windows were immense and colorful. As she looked toward the front of the church she saw Jesus hanging on a cross, which was mounted to the wall behind the marble-floored altar. There were two sets of wooden pews set on either side of the broad nave.

Pine really had no idea why she was even here. Just a reference to a church basketball league? A dubious connection if ever there was one. And yet what other leads did she have?

She took a seat in the front pew and continued to examine the space, looking for anything that might help her.

As she was sitting there, a man walked out from a door behind the altar.

His white collar indicated he was a priest. He was tall, nearly six six, and young, maybe late thirties, with a shock of red hair and sprinkles of freckles.

Maybe a classic Irish priest, mused Pine. She wondered how many of those were still around.

"Hello," he said. "I'm afraid you've missed the last Mass."

"I just stopped in to, I guess, meditate a bit. I hope it's okay."

"It certainly is. We are open for all those seeking a quiet space in which to think and practice their faith."

He drew closer and started when he saw her battered face. "Are you all right?"

"Car accident a few days ago. Still a bit banged up."

He looked at her with a dubious expression. "I've had women come in before and tell me that. If things are not going well at home, I'm here to listen. No one should be abused by another. I can help you with that. We can offer shelter. And maybe you should think about calling the authorities."

In answer, Pine smiled and held up her ringless hand. "I'm not married. And I do MMA. There aren't many guys around who could take me. I really did have an accident."

"Oh, I'm sorry to hear that. But with the way people drive around here. And everyone texting." He extended a hand. "I'm Father Paul."

"I'm Lee," said Pine, shaking his hand.

"Do you live around here?"

"No, I'm actually visiting. I live out west."

"The wide-open spaces, then?"

"A lot wider than here. Father, can I ask you a question?"

"Certainly. Priests are asked lots of questions. But don't hold me to always having the right answer." He grinned.

Pine smiled warmly. "I think a friend of mine is one of your parishioners."

"Oh, yes?"

"Ironically, his name is Ben *Priest*."

"Oh, Ben. Yes, yes he is. Though I haven't seen him in a while."

"He told me he plays in a church basketball league?"

Father Paul smiled. "Yes, it's an informal thing. I actually started it about two years ago. As you can probably tell from my height, I play. But Ben, though he's some years older than me, is an exceptional player. Small forward. We compete against other churches in the area. Nothing official, but it's good sport and fellowship."

"You say you haven't seen him for a while?"

"No. In fact, we had a game last week, but he didn't make it. I called him but didn't get an answer. But he goes off quite often. He'll be back." He paused. "So, you're friends with Ben?"

"Yes. And his brother and his family."

The priest's brow furrowed. "That's funny. He never mentioned a brother."

"Ed Priest. He lives in Maryland with his wife and kids."

"Hmm. Well, come to think, Ben never really talked about himself very much. He just always seemed to be listening to everyone else."

"Yeah, he's like that."

"How do you know him?"

"Through mutual friends. I haven't known him all that long. But I was supposed to see him while I was here visiting. But he's not answering my phone calls either."

"Have you been by his house?"

"I have. And no one was there."

"And he knew you were coming?"

"Yes. We'd made plans."

Father Paul now looked worried. "I hope nothing has happened to him."

"I'm sure he's fine. Like you said, he just goes off sometimes." She paused and added, "I wonder where, though?"

Father Paul sat down in the pew next to her. "You said you met Ben through friends. How well do you actually know him?"

"It's funny. He's always struck me as a person who shows very little of himself. Like you just intimated. What do you know of him?"

"Probably not much more than you do."

"I don't even know what he does for a living. He mentioned something once about politics, government, that sort of thing. I suppose lots of people around here do that."

"They do, yes. Probably half my parishioners work in some capacity that's connected to the federal government."

Pine faked a smile. "I know this will sound silly."

"What?"

"It always struck me that Ben might be some sort of, well, spy."

Her grin broadened as though she thought this was ridiculous, though she hoped the priest would take the bait.

"If you want to know the truth, I thought the very same thing."

Pine feigned surprise. "Really? Why?"

"A million little things, which on their own probably didn't amount to much. But taken together, they just led me to believe that whatever he did was sort of, well, *clandestine*, for want of a better term."

"I wish I could find him. Do you know any of his other friends?"

Father Paul thought for a few moments. "Well, there is one fellow. Simon Russell. He also plays in our league. Ben actually brought him on. We made an exception, since he's not a member of the parish. From what I could tell, I think they worked together. Or at least they once did."

"What does he do for a living?"

Father Paul smiled. "He seems to have the same bug that Ben does. He never reveals much about himself. But he can hit threes with the best of them."

"Description?"

The priest looked surprised. "You sound like a cop."

"No, but if I do run into him I want to make sure it's the right guy."

"Well, he's a bit taller than me and very lean. Not much hair on top. He has a trim beard. He's about Ben's age, I would guess, or a bit older."

"Do you have contact information for him?"

"As a matter of fact, I do. I went to his house for a drink once with Ben and some of the other team members. We won the league championship last year, quite a comeback victory, actually, and Simon, on the spur of the moment, invited us all to celebrate. I thought it was quite nice. I mean, Ben lives nearby but he'd never had us to his place."

"Ben is very private."

"Exceedingly so."

Father Paul wrote down an address and gave it to Pine. As he escorted her out he said, "If you find Ben, tell him to give me a call. I want to know he's okay."

"I'll do that." Pine looked around at the church's interior. "This is a beautiful space."

"It is. But that's just trappings. The real strength of any church, I hope, are its parishioners. Jesus was a poor man. His faith was his pot of gold. Are you Catholic?"

"No. My parents didn't take us to church. And I guess I just never got into the habit of going now that I'm an adult."

"Well, it's never too late."

She gave him a sad look. "You'd think so, wouldn't you?"

33

PINE PULLED THE MUSTANG to a stop at the curb across the street from Simon Russell's large town house near Capitol Hill. Like Old Town Alexandria, the area was definitely high dollar. Pine had worked in DC for two years at the WFO. The only thing she'd been able to afford on her GS-13 salary was a one-bedroom roach motel apartment a ninety-minute commute from downtown.

Whatever Russell did for a living, it paid well. She wondered if his home inside was as Spartan as Priest's. She might not find out tonight. While there were a lot of windows in the place, not a single light was on inside, at least that Pine could see.

She got out of the car, walked across the street, turned left, and then turned right at the next block. She reached an alleyway halfway along the block and walked down it. Another right and a short stroll brought her to the back of Russell's home. There was also a one-car garage back here. This resembled an old-fashioned mews, like they had in England.

The wall around the rear of Russell's home had a high brick wall and a tall wooden gate. She tried the gate, but it was locked.

She checked both directions, gripped the top of the wall, and hoisted herself up enough to where she could see over. This simple movement almost made her cry out in pain, as every injured body part she had screamed in protest.

As she clung to the rim of the wall she observed a small garden, with a stone wall water fountain emblazoned with the figure of a lion, some chairs and a matching wrought iron table, a few flower pots with well-tended plants, and a solid wood back door. Soothing, well-organized, and of no help to her whatsoever.

No lights in the house were visible back here, either.

She dropped back down to the pavement and retraced her steps, deciding along the way to take a direct approach.

She walked up to Russell's front door and knocked.

Nothing.

She knocked again, looking around to see if anyone was paying her the slightest bit of attention. She was also checking for the umbrella-carrying ninja.

She knocked again.

No one came to the door. She peered through the sidelights. It was too dark to see much.

Okay. What was Plan B?

She didn't relish breaking into another home. Her luck had almost run out on the last one.

She walked back to her car and got in. She decided to perform that most tedious and sometimes most valuable of all police work.

The stakeout.

She settled down in her seat and kept her eyes peeled on the house.

At a bit after midnight, her vigilance paid off.

A tall man came walking down the street from the direction of the U.S. Capitol. He had on a trench coat and a felt cap, and he was carrying a leather briefcase.

He walked up the short stack of steps to the front door to his home, fumbled in his pocket, and pulled out his keys.

He was at his door inserting the key when Pine reached him.

"Mr. Russell?"

He whirled and looked down at her. "Who are you? What do you want?"

Okay, normal paranoia or something more?

She slipped out her shield. "I'm with the FBI. I'm here about your friend, Ben Priest."

His features turned even more suspicious. "Ben? What's going on with him? Why is the FBI interested in him?"

"Can we talk about this inside?"

Russell hesitated but finally nodded. "All right."

He let her inside, then turned off the security system and shut and bolted the door. He took off his hat and coat and hung them on a wall rack in the small foyer.

Pine saw that his hair was indeed thinning, and the little he had left had been allowed to grow in any direction it chose. As Father Paul had said, Russell possessed a trim beard and mustache, perhaps to balance out the loss on top. He was quite lean, and she gauged that his feet were about a size fifteen, which made sense for a man nearly six seven. His nose was long and spindly. His eyes were brown and darting. Right above them were a pair of eyebrows that, like the hair, roamed helter-skelter over his compact forehead.

She looked around. Russell's digs were a lot nicer than Priest's. The furniture looked antique, well-worn, and comfy-cozy. There was a fireplace in the room right off the foyer. It had a limestone surround in the design of something one might see in a church. The walls were covered with original-looking oil paintings.

The rug she was standing on looked to be at least a century old. Down the hall she could see colorful and costly wallpaper along with elaborate crown moldings. The ceilings and walls were solid plaster. Outside, she had noted the gutters and downspouts were copper and the roof was slate.

They didn't make them like this anymore. Not unless you had the dollars to pay for it.

His words interrupted her observations.

"Would you like something to drink? Or are you on duty?"

"What are you having?"

"A G and T. Blue bottle Bombay is my preferred choice of weapon."

"I'll just take the T. Thanks."

He led her down the hall to a large oval carved wooden door that looked like it belonged in a castle. He opened it and showed her into a sizable room outfitted as a library or study.

Three walls held shelves that sagged with books. A large partner's desk sat in the middle of the room under which lay a square of faded Oriental carpet. There was a fireplace. Comfortable leather couch and chairs. And a small credenza with bottles and glasses topping it.

"On the rocks?" he asked as he prepared two glasses. "For your T?"

"Why not?"

He opened a paneled door built into a cabinet next to the credenza, revealing an icemaker. He cut up a lime he'd taken from a bowl on top of the credenza, put slices in each glass over the ice, then poured gin and tonic into his tumbler and only tonic into hers, while she watched to make sure.

He stirred the drinks and handed one to Pine, then picked up a remote and pointed it at the fireplace. There was a click, a whoosh of fired gas, and bluish flames popped alive in the hearth. He sat down on the couch and pointed to one of the chairs.

"Nice room," said Pine as she took her seat and looked around the space.

"I do a lot of my work in here, actually."

"And what work would that be?"

He sipped his drink. His features, never inviting to begin with, turned instantly chillier.

" 'None of your business' is the answer that first occurs to me. Unless you have a warrant. And even then, it would still be none of your business. Now tell me about Ben."

"He's missing."

Russell said nothing to this. He slightly turned his head and studied the gas flames.

"You don't seem surprised by that."

He shrugged. "Ben routinely goes missing."

Pine decided to take a chance in order to get the man to open up. "Does he routinely get kidnapped and taken away in a chopper?"

This got Russell's attention. He looked at Pine. "Is this a mere hypothetical or are you being factual?"

"He's in trouble. Big trouble. Let's leave it at that for now."

"I'm prepared to leave it right here."

Pine looked around the room. "If I were to profile you from what I've seen in your home, I'd say you came from money, were well traveled, had an interest in geopolitics, were security conscious, and cared about what happened to your country."

"I won't extend this talk by asking how you came by those deductions."

However, Pine plunged ahead. "The silver set on the table over there is a Tiffany original. The monogram shows it was probably a family heirloom. I'd wager that set is older than your grandparents. That means you inherited it. People who get handed down things like that are usually well cared for in other respects. The rest of my deductions come from your books, the multiple locks and security system, and those detailed maps of China and the Middle East on the walls over there."

"And my caring about my country?"

"The framed letter over there from a past president thanking you for your service."

Russell seemed to appraise her in a new light. He sipped his drink and nodded. "All right. I may be all of those things. What do you want from me tonight?"

"Do you have any idea what Ben was working on that could have led to his being in trouble?"

"We didn't work together."

"That's not what I heard."

"Then you obviously heard wrong."

"You never discussed work matters with him?"

"There was no reason."

"And he never did with you?"

"I thought I just said that."

"He lives in Alexandria and you live here. How did he come to get you to join the church league?"

"Probably some dreary party where we ran into each other and were bored enough to talk about church and basketball."

"So, I guess you have no idea about the other guy then?"

"What other guy?" he said sharply.

"Or about the password-protected message Ben left behind."

Russell was now watching Pine closely as he softly jiggled the ice in his tumbler.

"What happened to your face?" he asked.

"Ran into a door."

"You ran into something. Maybe a fist."

"Comes with the territory."

"How did you come to be involved in this, may I ask?"

"It's my job."

Russell cleared his throat. "Are you in the National Security Branch at the Bureau? Or the Intelligence Branch?" He paused. "But if I can make a deduction, you don't strike me as the type. I mean National Security or Intelligence."

"So you know those types. And you're aware of those branches within the Bureau. At least that's some information you've shared."

When he said nothing to this, she added, "What type do I strike you as?"

"Rogue," he said immediately.

Pine pointed to the bookshelves. "You've got books there written in Russian, Chinese, Korean, and Arabic. Do you speak all of them?"

"As do many people in this town."

"I came to you as a shortcut. I take those when they present themselves."

"Sorry to disappoint."

"So you're just casual b-ball teammates?"

Russell took a long drink before answering. Wiping his mouth with the back of his hand he said, "He's a good small forward. Can pass effectively off the dribble and create his own shots. Mid-range jumper is like clockwork. I'll give him that. With my height, I live in the paint. Turnaround jumpers, hooks, pound the boards, and grab the rebounds. I used to be able to dunk. Now my knees no longer cooperate."

Pine put her drink down and rose. "Well, thanks for the tonic."

Russell looked up at her. "Are you even really with the FBI?"

She took out a piece of paper and wrote something down on it. "Here's where you can reach me if you have a change of heart."

Russell took the paper without looking at it and set it down on a table next to the couch.

"You've actually given me a lot to think about," he said, once more jiggling the ice in his glass while the gas flames threw his sharp-edged features into stark relief.

"I wish I could say the same. I'll see myself out."

She didn't walk back to her car because she knew he would be watching her from the window. Instead, she turned left and walked briskly down the street and turned right at the next corner. Then she took up a position by a tree that allowed a sight line of his front door.

She had gotten nothing from Russell except the weirdest of vibes.

Twenty minutes later the possibility arose that that status might change.

The man came out the door and walked off in the opposite direction.

Pine walked quickly to her car, pulled out onto the street, and followed.

34

Pɪɴᴇ's ᴅᴇᴄɪsɪᴏɴ to follow by car paid off, because Russell had gone only about two blocks when a black SUV pulled up to the curb and he climbed in. They quickly left the Capitol Hill area and proceeded north through the city.

Pine knew DC well because of her time there. They headed west, passing through the business district, and then arced farther north into some of the most affluent areas of the city.

When they entered Cleveland Park in Upper Northwest the SUV slowed. Pine followed suit. Even at this late hour the traffic was brisk, for which Pine was appreciative, because it allowed her to blend in. But she also knew how to tail a suspect, and she was confident no one in the SUV was aware of her surveillance.

When they turned onto International Place, Pine stiffened.

She thought she knew where they were going.

When the SUV slowed and then stopped at a checkpoint, her hunch was confirmed.

Though the famed architect I. M. Pei had consulted on the facility's design, Pine had always thought it looked like a fortress.

But then again, what did you expect from the embassy for the People's Republic of China?

The SUV pulled through the entrance and disappeared from sight.

Pine couldn't follow, so she drove down the street, hit a U-turn, and found a spot on the street to park. She cut her lights, hunkered down, and waited.

The Chinese. Could the guy who had beaten her up have been Chinese?

And what did Simon Russell, and presumably Ben Priest, have to do with the Chinese?

Pine had no jurisdiction to enter the embassy, even if she had been officially working as an FBI agent. That building might as well be in Beijing. It was Chinese land underneath it, as far as international protocols were concerned.

And if the Chinese were involved, how did that tie into the two Russians she had knocked out at Priest's home?

Despite the late hour, she called Blum and told her what had happened.

Blum said, "Why do you think this Simon Russell is there?"

"It can't be a coincidence that he came here right after talking with me. So that means that whatever Ben Priest was involved in, it had to do, at least partly, with the Chinese."

"What are you going to do now?"

"Wait until Russell comes out and follow him."

Pine clicked off and slouched down further in her seat as a car came down the road and its lights cut across her.

Her car clock hit two a.m. when the same black SUV pulled out.

Pine knew it was the same SUV because of the plates. The only problem was she had no way of knowing if Russell was inside.

She had no choice but to follow.

There was hardly any traffic now, so Pine took a chance, shot ahead of the SUV, glancing toward it as she passed. But the windows were tinted and she couldn't see inside.

She drove back to Russell's place, parked, and waited.

Sure enough, he came walking up to his house a few minutes later, the SUV obviously having dropped him off some distance away.

She was deciding whether to approach him again when a quartet of men converged on Russell as he opened his door. They pushed him inside and shut the door behind them.

For an instant Pine sat frozen in her car. Then she burst into action.

She hit a U-turn, turned right, and then right again as she drove into the alley she had visited before.

She stopped at Russell's rear yard and scrambled over the wall, landing softly in the grass on the other side. Keeping low, she glided up to the house and glanced through a window.

She couldn't see anything, but she heard noises. She had no idea who these men were or what they wanted with Russell.

She was certain they weren't cops. If they were cops they would have shown their badges and taken him into custody on the front porch. They would not have forced him inside his house.

If this had been a normal situation, Pine would have immediately called 911. This was not a normal situation.

She checked the lock on the back window and then took out her knife and pried back the bolt. The window opened quietly and she was inside. Keeping low, Pine saw that she was in the home's kitchen.

She slipped out her gun as she moved out of the kitchen and into the hall. She had the advantage of having been in the home before, so she knew some of the layout.

She froze when she heard the raised voices.

"I don't know what you want."

That was clearly Simon Russell.

Pine took out her burner phone and dialed 911.

She gave the address and what was happening.

"Hurry," was her last word before she put the phone away.

She pulled her Beretta from her ankle holster and moved into the hallway with a gun in each hand. Whatever she did or didn't do, she had a feeling this was not going to end well for any of them.

But reverse was not a gear with which she was familiar.

She reached the intersection of the hall and the living room to her right, across from Russell's home office.

The house was dark because no one had bothered to turn on any lights. Not that Pine had expected the home invaders to want to risk illuminating their litany of felonies.

She edged around the corner enough so that she could see what was happening.

In the ambient light coming in from the street she could make out the four men, all standing in a semicircle around Russell, who sat in a chair.

Russell said, "I don't know what you're talking about. I know no one at the Chinese embassy."

"Funny, since you were just there," said one of the men.

"You have me mistaken for someone else."

"What did Ben Priest tell you?"

Russell slowly sat up. "What will that information buy me?"

"What do you propose?" said the same man.

"A free ride out of here."

"I'm not seeing that. You're in too deep."

"I'm not in anything."

The sirens outside made them all turn to look at the window.

"Shit," said one of the men.

"You think?" said another.

"Deal with it," said the first man. "Take the guys with you. You know the drill."

The three men headed to the front. Pine saw them take something out of their pockets.

This left the first man alone with Russell.

Pine took a closer look at him. He was in his fifties, with salt-and-pepper hair and longish sideburns. He had on a suit and tie. His face was weathered, and his nose had been broken at least once. He looked tough and probably was.

Pine flitted to one of the front windows and watched as a squad car pulled up to the curb.

Two DCPD officers climbed out. They were met in the front yard by the three men.

"Shit," breathed Pine.

They were holding up shields and ID cards, just like she had done thousands of times.

They were *Feds of some sort.*

The two officers checked out the creds and started talking to the men.

She stole back over to her original surveillance post and watched the man and Russell.

"You can't do this," said Russell. "It's against the law."

"Nothing's against the law if you *are* the law."

"I want an attorney. Right now."

"We have no arresting authority, Russell. It's not how we do things. So don't expect a Miranda warning. It won't be coming."

"You can't force me to do anything."

"Now there you just went off the rails. National security trumps all."

"Even my damn constitutional rights?"

"The Constitution means protecting all Americans. If we sacrifice a few to do that, so be it. Simple math in my book."

"I want you out of my house."

"Oh, don't worry. We're going to be leaving. But you're coming with us."

"I'm not going anywhere."

"Wrong again. As soon as my men finish with the local yokels, we're going to be taking a trip. We have a plane waiting."

"Where are we going?"

"Classified."

"That's bullshit."

"Okay, I'll give you a hint. We're taking you to a place outside this country that will be more conducive to having a frank discussion with you." He paused and added, "By any means necessary."

"What, you're going to torture me? Give me a break. You can't do that anymore."

"Funny, I didn't get that memo."

"You'll lose your ass if you try that."

"You think you're the only guy we've had to persuade of late? And I've still got my whole ass right where it's always been."

Now Russell paled. "Look, this is ridiculous. I'm an American citizen."

"So am I. Where does that get us? You know things that can get a lot of Americans hurt. If we have to do things to you to prevent that, then that's what we're going to do."

"This is crazy. I'm going out there to talk to the cops."

The man pulled out a gun and pointed it at Russell's head. "Not going to happen."

"What, you're just going to shoot me? Here?"

The man tapped the gun's muzzle. "Suppressor. They'll never hear it out there. Your choice. I'm good either way."

"Look, you don't have to go down that path."

"Yeah, I'm afraid I do."

The man suddenly collapsed to the floor.

Russell looked down at him, incredulous. When he looked up there was Pine holding her pistol, muzzle first. She'd used the butt of the weapon to clock the guy.

She beckoned to Russell. "Move your ass. Now!"

CHAPTER

35

"THANKS."

Pine looked over at the passenger seat of her Mustang.

They had left Russell's neighborhood far behind. She turned onto a side road, pulled to the curb, and cut the engine.

Russell still looked pale and shaken, but some color was returning to his face.

"I didn't save you just for the hell of it," she snapped. "Now, you're going to tell me what's going on."

"Look, I can't, okay? I couldn't tell them, and I can't tell you."

"Those guys were going to kill you. Or at the very least torture you within an inch of your life."

"Maybe."

"There's no maybe about it. Who were they?"

"I don't know."

"Bullshit. They were feds, but the guy said they had no arresting authority in this country. That narrows the list way down. And you know it!"

Russell shook his head stubbornly. "The guy was just bluffing."

"You sure about that?"

"Yeah, I am. This is America, not Moscow."

"Funny you should mention that, since two Russians were at Ben Priest's house in Alexandria and ended up trying to kill me."

Russell glanced sharply at her and sucked in a shallow breath. He shook his head. "Look, no one's going to throw me out a window or stick me with a nerve agent."

Pine started the car up. "Fine, I'll take you back to them, then. No sweat. Have fun wherever they take you. And whatever they stick you with."

Russell placed a hand on the steering wheel. "No, wait, please, don't do that."

"Then I need some quid pro quo and I need it now."

"What do you want?"

"You went to the Chinese Embassy. And don't lie to me. I followed you there, just like the other guys did. Why did you go?"

Russell looked out the window into the darkness. His expression was one of a cornered beast, desperately looking in vain for a path to survival.

"Your visit prompted me to go there."

"Explain."

"Ben Priest."

"What does he have to do with the Chinese? And the Russians?"

"I'm talking geopolitics, so it's not a straight line. How are you at chess?"

"Try me."

"Allies sometimes become enemies. And vice versa. The status can be temporary or long-standing. It can be situational. Transactional. A one-off. Hell, it can be anything, really."

"Ben told me something like that."

"He would know."

"So, you *do* work with him?"

"I know *of* his work. Let's leave it at that."

"I'm not in a position to leave anything anywhere. What was Priest's job?"

"He's very well connected. He got things done that needed doing outside of official channels. That's really all I can say."

"Getting back to the chess. What's the first move? And how did we reach this point?"

"I don't know anything for sure. It's speculation."

"What's your connection to China anyway?"

"I've done work on their behalf."

"Spying against this country?"

Russell furrowed his brow. "Don't be stupid. They have legitimate interests, and I make those interests known in the right places. But I can tell you that the Chinese are concerned that something major is about to happen. They aren't sure what, but they have their suspicions. As do I."

"Speculate away."

"The world is seriously screwed up right now. We've always had hot spots. The Middle East, in particular Iran. Russia. North Korea. But we've never had them all exploding at the same time. Some people, in those situations, look for the fast and easy way out."

"There's an Asian guy involved in this. He could be North Korean or Chinese. He almost killed me."

"That's interesting. I'm sure you know that this country is in peace talks with North Korea aimed at them giving up their nukes?"

"Yeah, I know. And I know the Chinese have a great deal of interest in how it turns out."

"Well, those talks aren't going well. In fact, they may collapse any minute."

"So, what would be the reason why a North Korean would be over here?"

"How about a change in government leadership?"

Pine stared across the width of the Mustang at him. "Where? North Korea?"

"How about right here?"

Pine's eyes widened. "That's nuts."

"One thing I've learned over time, never say never."

"How could anyone possibly manage something like that here?"

He shook his head. "What did I call you when we first met?"

"Rogue. Wait, are you saying that people *within* our government are plotting to overthrow it?"

"It's certainly possible."

Pine sat back against her seat. "And, what, they're teaming up with North Korea to do it? That's crazy."

Russell pulled out a pack of cigarettes and a book of matches. "You mind if I smoke? I'm stressed beyond belief."

"Roll down the window and blow it out that way. And how do you play basketball and smoke?"

"I have maybe one cigarette a month. If that's going to kill me, so be it."

He rolled down the window, lit the Marlboro, took a puff, and blew smoke out the open window.

Pine said, "Okay, since you've opened up to me, I can tell you that Ben exchanged places with a man who rode a mule down to the bottom of the Grand Canyon and then disappeared."

"What man?"

Pine showed him the digital sketch on her phone. "Do you know him?"

Russell studied the image closely, then shook his head. "If I had to speculate, I'd say that this person might have known what was going on and came to Ben for help."

"What would he do?"

"The guy might want to bring that information to the right quarters but was unsure how to do that effectively. You mentioned helicopters and Ben being snatched? How do you know that?"

"Because I was there. And the chopper was one used by the Army."

"Shit, this thing does go high up, then," said Russell anxiously.

"How high is high?" said Pine.

"Maybe higher than we want to believe. If they took Ben, they might be tying up loose ends. Or quarantining everything, like they do with Ebola. That's why they came to me."

"But they let me live," said Pine.

Russell studied her. "Then you're very lucky."

"You really believe that people in our government are planning some sort of coup?"

Russell looked amused by her incredulity. "Didn't you just tell me that Ben got taken away in an Army chopper? And I know that the FBI bleeds red, white, and blue, but your agency has been taking it on the chin, hasn't it? You're all corrupt, so they say."

"But toppling the government?"

"People are fed up with DC. They see it as an impediment. And then they see autocratic governments kicking ass around the world and they want that, too."

"That is not who we are."

"Who we are is dictated by those powerful enough to *say* who we are. If anything, we're a plutocracy and have been for a long time now. And the next logical step in a plutocracy is an oligarchy. I'm not on a soapbox. I'm just stating facts. I've seen it happen in lots of places."

"Is there anything you *can* talk about that might help me find Ben Priest?"

Russell took a long drag on his cigarette and blew the smoke out the window. "Have you ever heard of SFG?"

"No, should I?"

"It's an acronym. Stands for the Society for Good."

"Sounds remarkably cheesy."

"In reality, it's a group of very serious people. They cover a variety of issues of global significance. They've got some heavy-weight members in all sorts of professional disciplines from all over the world. It's like a think tank."

"There are already think tanks on the left and right."

"This one isn't politically oriented. It's been around for about eighty years. They do a lot of TED Talks. Publish papers, give presentations, work with governments and companies all over the world. Trying to do good, as the name implies."

"And what does this have to do with my case?"

"Ben Priest was a member of SFG."

Pine was silent for a few moments as she absorbed this.

"Okay. You think whatever plan he had with the missing guy might have been run through the society?"

"I don't know. But I can tell you that SFG *has* been involved in some whistleblower cases, government malfeasance in some developing countries, things like that."

"But not corruption in this country?"

"Corruption is corruption, right? And from what I know of the membership they won't shirk from what they see as their duty."

"Where can I find them?"

"They have a building in DC on H Street."

Pine leaned back in her seat and gripped the steering wheel. "Can you get me into the place? You're the cloak-and-dagger guy. I'm an investigator with red, white, and blue coming out of her veins."

"I don't know. I'd have to think about it."

"We don't have time to waste."

Russell turned and blew smoke out the open window once more.

An instant later he toppled sideways toward Pine as a foot came through the open window and collided with the side of his head.

Russell hit the steering wheel hard, bounced off, and then limply hung forward, kept in his seat solely by his lap belt.

Pine looked to her right and saw the Asian man. He was not holding an umbrella this time. His hand was reaching for the door handle.

Pine slammed the car into gear and floored it.

The Mustang shot out from the curb like a projectile.

Pine hit seventy before the next intersection, which she blew right through.

"Screw it," she said.

She hit a U-turn at the second intersection and drove back to where she had come from. She took out something from her pocket.

As she raced down the street, she saw him.

He was walking fast down the pavement.

She slowed, as did he.

She had rolled down the window and lifted her hand.

The man braced for an attack as he looked directly at her.

Pine snapped his picture with her phone and then she pulled her gun.

I'm just going to shoot the son of a bitch.

But, in the blink of an eye, he was gone.

Pine floored it.

Five minutes later, after many turns, she slipped into a parking lot at the back of a Starbucks.

She put the car in park and looked at Russell. He had no pulse. His eyes were glassed over, unresponsive. He was dead. She felt the back of his neck.

His vertebrae were like a jigsaw puzzle that had fallen out of a box.

One kick thrown through the small opening of a car window to the head had literally shattered a very large man's spine.

She sat there thinking for a few minutes. When she arrived at her decision, she wasn't happy about it, but she could see no other way. At least no other way that would allow her to remain an FBI agent *and* stay out of prison.

Pine put the car in gear and drove off.

She now had to do something she had never thought she would.

I have to dispose of a body.

CHAPTER

36

Atlee Pine was incredibly strong.

But a corpse was, understandably enough, dead weight, and not so easy to move.

She opened the passenger door of the Mustang, squatted down, clutched the late Simon Russell under the armpits, and hoisted him out of the car. Before he toppled over, she set him against the side of the car, propping him up there by wedging her thigh against his knees, pinning his long legs tight against the Mustang. With her forearm, she kept his torso upright.

Okay, this is just like any other lift.

She counted to three and let go of the body. As he toppled forward, she squatted down and caught him at the waist with her shoulder and then stood. The tall, lean man was hoisted into the air, bent in half over her broad shoulder.

She moved forward slowly.

Pine had debated with great difficulty over what she was about to do. There was nothing "normal" about an FBI agent carrying a corpse and putting it anywhere. She was breaking every crime scene protocol there was, along with more than a few laws.

And sitting in her Mustang, thinking all of this through, tormented by doubt and guilt, and conflicted in a way she never had been before, Pine had decided that this was the only path forward. If she tried to go into the Bureau with a dead body in tow, she figured she would be Blum's age before she ever saw the light of day.

It would have been easier for her to just drop Russell's body in the woods, but she couldn't do that. He would be ravaged by wild animals, which would be not only disrespectful to him, but also disruptive for the forensic investigation to follow. Atlee Pine, criminal investigator, could never be a party to that.

She had picked her location well, far out in rural Virginia. No CCTV cameras, no one else around. One road in and one out. She had driven around until she had found it. She knew this area from having worked a murder scene here years ago while stationed at the WFO. It was typical serial killer land: remote, lots of dirt in which to bury bodies, no police nearby, lonely roads, no witnesses. Same old, same old.

The old house looked like it had been built in the sixties. The chain-link fence had fallen down. The concrete stoop was cracked. The paint was peeling off the siding, and the yard was all weeds.

But it had doors and windows and not a single neighbor. She had no idea who had once owned it, or why someone had built it here.

It smelled of rot and mildew and all the traces the years left on everything.

She pushed open the front door with her boot, carried Russell inside, and set him down on the plank floor. She took a note she had written from her pocket and stuck it in his shirt. It provided details about what had happened to Russell for the police to find and use.

As she hovered over the dead man who stared up at her, Pine said, "I'm sorry, Simon. I... I didn't mean for it to end this way. But I'm going to get the guy who took your life. No matter what."

She left the house, got back into her car, and slowly drove away, her lights out.

Once she reached the main road she clicked on her headlights and picked up speed.

When she was about twenty minutes away she used a new burner phone to call 911, giving them the location and what they would find there.

She got back to the condo in Ballston in the wee hours of the morning.

She found Blum dozing on the couch in her pajamas.

Pine debated whether to wake her or not, then gently nudged the woman's shoulder.

Blum blinked and then sat up as Pine went into the kitchen, opened the fridge, and took out a beer.

"Where have you been?" Blum asked sleepily.

"I'm sorry, I shouldn't have woken you."

"That's okay. I was waiting up for you, but I guess I didn't make it. What happened?"

Pine popped open the beer and took the chair opposite. "I'm not sure I should tell you."

"Why not?"

"I could make you an accessory."

"I'm afraid that ship sailed a long time ago, my dear. And if it makes you feel any better, I was an extremely *willing* participant."

Pine took a sip of her beer and winced. Her mouth still ached from where the Asian had clobbered her. "It's a long story."

"I'm not going anywhere."

Pine methodically set out what had happened.

When she got to the part about Russell's death from one kick, Blum said, "You're lucky that man didn't kill you the other night."

"I'm not feeling too lucky right now, but I see your point. I did manage to get this." She took out her phone and brought the picture of the man up on the screen. She held it up.

"He looks totally innocuous."

"Good cover, because he's totally lethal." Pine chugged her beer. "I need to check out this SFG place, obviously."

"Not to sound like a concerned mom, but how about the next

move being you get some sleep? If you're exhausted you're not going to be much good to anyone."

Pine slowly stood and said in a contrite tone, "I shouldn't have involved you in this, Carol. It wasn't right of me to ask. I can't keep count of the laws I've broken. My career at the FBI is over, no matter how this turns out. Hell, I'm probably going to prison."

"Well, that's one way to look at it."

Pine glanced at her in surprise. "What's the other way?"

"That you solve this case and they give you a big medal. *And* a decent chair to sit in."

Pine gave her a grim smile. "Is that J. Edgar Hoover talking?"

"No, Special Agent Pine, that's pure Carol Blum."

37

W HEN HAD SLEEP ever come easily?

Ever?

Pine rolled over and checked the time on her phone.

Nine a.m.

She could hear people walking down the hall from other condos. The hum of the elevator. And outside, cars driving down the street.

All normal noises. Nothing that should have unduly interrupted her sleep. The drapes were closed tight so no sunlight could get in.

She was exhausted.

And yet here she was. Awake.

She got out of bed, padded over to the dresser, and picked up her cred pack.

Stuck behind her official ID card was her most cherished possession. It meant more to her than her second most prized possession: her FBI shield.

She slid the old photo out and held it in her palm. It was small, just like the subjects captured in it.

It was the last photo of her and Mercy together. In fact, it was the only photo that Pine could remember of them together. It had been taken three days before her sister vanished. It was one of those instant color Polaroids that had once been so popular.

Pine could remember the moment clearly.

She and her sister were out with their mother at the strip mall near where they lived. Their mother had gotten them ice cream and had plunked them down on a scratchy bench, while she smoked and gossiped with two of her friends.

Then one of her mother's friends had pulled out her camera to take a photo of a dress that she liked hanging in the store window. The woman couldn't afford to buy it, Pine had heard her say, but she thought she could get the materials and make one similar to it. After she'd taken the photo, Pine's mother had asked to borrow the camera to take a picture of her girls together. The Pines did not own a camera, which was why Pine didn't know of another picture of the sisters existing.

Despite being often stoned, Pine's mom had her good moments as a mother. Pine had no doubt the woman loved her daughters, in her own somewhat muddled and misguided way. She just had no idea what to do with them most of the time. She had had her girls at nineteen, still more of a child herself than an adult.

She had taken the photo and it had automatically ejected from the Polaroid camera. Their mother's girlfriend had shown the twins how to carefully hold the edges of the photo while their images slowly and, to them, miraculously, appeared on the paper. Their mom had later bought a cheap wooden frame and put it in the girls' room. It was there when the intruder had come in and left with Mercy. It had stood silent witness to a crime of heinous proportion.

With her finger, Pine traced her sister's hair in the photo; it was identical in color and cut to her own. The only way to tell them apart was that Mercy's hair was slightly curly, while Pine's was flagpole straight.

Symbolic, maybe.

She had often wondered what Mercy would be like as a grown woman. She had no doubt that the kindhearted little girl would have grown up to be an adult with an outsized capacity for caring, for empathy for others. And that she would have chosen a career that would have helped people who needed it.

Yes, that surely would have been Mercy's calling.

Atlee had been the helter-skelter hellion.

Mercy had been the angel.

The angel had vanished.

The hellion had become a cop.

Life was funny that way.

She opened the drapes, slid back the patio door, and stepped out onto the balcony that oversaw the plot of green space, rare in the congested area.

The air was crisp, the sky cloudless, the sun well into its ascent, though she couldn't feel its warmth yet because she was currently facing west.

It looked to be the beginning of a pretty day in the capital region.

And she had disposed of a body last night.

With that thought she went back into the bedroom and checked the news app on her phone.

Nothing.

She turned on the TV and sorted through the local news channels.

Simon Russell had been right. The peace talks with North Korea had just now officially collapsed, according to a grim-faced TV anchor. She wondered if Russell had had advance warning of that, perhaps from the Chinese. That story was followed by coverage of a fire at a local school and after that a shooting, and, finally, a teacher having sex with a student. But there was absolutely nothing about the discovery of a body in an old house where the police had been tipped off and the killer's description helpfully left behind. That apparently had not been important enough to make the daily news feed. Or maybe the police were holding all that information back for some reason. Or perhaps they had been ordered to do so by the same forces that had taken the Priest brothers.

She put the photo away, slept fitfully for another few hours, then gave it up and showered for twenty minutes, letting the hot water burn into her skin in a futile attempt to erase the memory of last night.

She came out dressed in fresh clothes, while the ones covered with the smell of Simon Russell's violent death and later disposal went into the washing machine with extra detergent.

"I made lunch and some fresh coffee if you're interested," said Blum, who appeared from the kitchen holding a cup in her hand.

"That would be great, thanks. My mouth feels a lot better."

"Your whole face looks better. The healing power of ice, Advil, and some rest."

They ate sandwiches and drank their coffee in the small dining area off the kitchen. The window here overlooked the street, which was packed with people at this time of day.

Blum observed this and said, "I think there are more people walking down that street than live in all of Shattered Rock."

"There are," said Pine, swallowing her last bite of sandwich and then picking at a few potato chips on her plate.

"I forgot how populated the East Coast is."

"One reason I left. Too many people."

"And maybe too many bureaucrats trying to tell you how to do your job?"

"That too."

Pine cleared the table and put the rinsed dishes in the dishwasher. When she came back into the room, Blum had the laptop out.

"I looked up this Society For Good organization while you were sleeping. It really seems quite interesting. They don't have much of a website, but I listened to some of their TED Talks. I have to say I was impressed."

"Is there a list of members?"

"Not that I could find. But they have offices on H Street."

"That's what Russell said."

"Are you going there now?"

"That's my plan."

"I'd like to go with you."

Pine hesitated.

"Unless you think we're going to be attacked in broad daylight by a bunch of ninjas. And if so, I'll still be going, but I'll have to bring my gun. Your call."

Pine's jaw eased open a bit. "You have a gun?"

In answer, Blum slid out a small, efficient-looking piece from her purse.

Pine took a closer look and said, "That's a Colt Mustang."

"Yes, it is. Chambered in .380 ACP."

"It's okay as a backup piece, but its stopping power is nothing to write home about."

"But it's compact, lightweight, and damn accurate at close range."

"Didn't know you knew about guns."

"I'm from Arizona. It's in our DNA. Rumor has it I came out of the womb with a full head of hair and a jewel-encrusted, nickel-plated derringer clutched in my adorably dimpled fist."

"But the Colt only has a max six-shot mag."

"If I ever need more than six bullets to do the job, I'm in the wrong line of work."

Pine could only smile as they walked out the door together.

38

THEY TOOK THE KIA. The Mustang had been seen several times now, and Pine was worried that it stood out too much. If she hadn't had to use her SUV as a decoy she would have brought that instead. Hindsight held a level of perfection that real-time decision-making could not provide.

The building they found was of an ornate, classical Greek design with Ionic pillars topped by elaborately carved capitals bracketing the front entrance. It was incongruously sandwiched in between two eight-story glass-and-metal-box office buildings. They parked in a nearby underground garage and came back out to street level.

Men and women in suits and carrying knapsacks and briefcases scooted to and fro. All were checking their phones and looking important as they strode along ostensibly doing the people's business in the shadow of the halls of government.

"Quite an energetic town," remarked Blum.

"One way of describing it," replied Pine. "Capital of bullshit is another."

They made their way to the headquarters of SFG. The towering double doors were solid oak and looked strong enough to withstand an RPG round.

There was a buzzer built into the wall with a voice box next to it.

A brass sign said to ring it.

So Pine did.

A voice immediately came on.

"Can I help you?"

"We're with the FBI. We're here to speak to someone about Benjamin Priest."

"Can you hold up your IDs to the camera, please?"

Pine noted the lens staring down at her.

Shit.

She held up her badge, but not her ID.

"Thank you. One moment."

Soon, they could hear footsteps approaching.

The door opened and there stood a large, goateed man in a gray suit with a blue tie.

"Follow me, please."

They followed.

Both women looked around at the spacious rooms off the hall they were traversing. Comfortable furnishings, elegant paintings, a sculpture here and there. And enough chair rail, crown moldings, pilasters, columns, medallions, balustrades, friezes, and frescoes to satisfy any architectural junkie's most outrageous wish list.

They were escorted into a large office, book lined and cluttered. The smell of sweet pipe smoke seemed to rise from every inch of the place.

The goateed man left, closing the door behind him without saying another word.

Pine looked around and said, "Why do I feel like I just stepped into a spy novel from the sixties? Where are you, George Smiley, when I need you?"

Blum noted a stack of books on a side table. "Is that Arabic?"

Pine looked over her shoulder. "Yes. Simon Russell had books in Arabic, too."

"Did he indeed?"

Pine and Blum started and looked over at a high wingback chair that had been turned away from them.

It was now swiveled around, and perched in it was a small man with thick white hair. He wore a three-piece suit with a dash of color at the neck and a kerchief sprouting from the chest pocket.

When he stood it revealed that he was probably barely over five feet tall.

"Please, sit," he said, waving them to two chairs in front of the massive desk, which was heaped with opened books. He took the seat behind the desk and studied them both, his fingers steepled in front of him.

"We didn't know anyone was in the room," said Pine.

"Evidently," said the man. "By the way, I am Oscar Fabrikant."

"Thanks for seeing us, Mr. Fabrikant."

"Oh, please, make it Oscar. Are you both FBI agents?"

Pine held out her shield. "I'm the agent. She's my assistant."

Pine really wanted to get through this without revealing their identities.

Fabrikant nodded. "Now, to business. You mentioned just now Simon Russell?"

"Yes." Pine was annoyed at herself for not adequately scoping out the room before speaking. Now the man knew there was a connection between her and a dead man.

"And how do you know Simon?"

"I don't."

"And yet you know his reading tastes?"

"Ben Priest told me about him," lied Pine.

"I see. And you've come here about something having to do with Ben?"

"Yes." She looked around the office. "Do you run the Society?"

"I'm not sure that anyone 'runs' this place. It's far more democratic, some might say chaotic, than hierarchical." He smiled at his remark.

"And yet they brought us in to see you."

"Well, I have been here longer than most. And it seems that

many of the administrative duties fall into my lap. I don't mind."
He settled farther back in his chair.

"I saw some of the TED talks the Society did," said Blum.
"Very interesting stuff."

"Thank you," replied Fabrikant.

Pine interjected, "Any idea where Ben might be?"

"Why would you think I would know that?"

"Doesn't he work here?"

"No one really works here. We volunteer our time and skills."

"And what sort of work do you do here?"

"We analyze. We read. We discuss. We talk. We listen. We
travel. We write papers. We give lectures. We're advocates on the
policy front. We lobby those in power on important issues." He
motioned to Blum. "And we give TED Talks, which provide us
with a global platform. I think our latest cumulative view count is
north of a billion on various social media sites. Truly remarkable.
What would we do without social media?"

"Well, it certainly has its pros *and* cons," noted Pine.

Fabrikant leaned back in his chair and studied them for a few
moments. "So how can I help you?"

"What can you tell us about Ben Priest?"

"Ben is a friend. A first-rate mind. Traveled the world. Very
interesting person."

"Okay, but what does he do?"

"He does many things. He worked in government for a time."

"What part of government?"

"The State Department, I believe."

"Isn't that what everyone says when they don't want to tell you
what they really do?"

"You take me out of my depth there," said Fabrikant.

"Okay, we understand that Priest helps people who need it. And
that he was helping someone specifically at the moment."

"Who?"

"I don't have a name, but I have a picture."

Pine showed him the digital sketch on her phone. She watched him closely for any hint that Fabrikant recognized the person.

"Can't say that I know him," said Fabrikant tersely.

Either he was an exceptional poker player, or he genuinely did not know the man, concluded Pine.

"Were you aware of anything that Priest was working on recently?"

"Not really, no."

Pine looked around. "This is quite a place."

"I think it's a bit gaudy, actually. It used to be a robber baron's mansion. He wasn't from here, but he built it when he realized having a place close to the people in government he was bribing was smart."

"Some things never change," noted Blum.

Fabrikant nodded his head. "So I believe."

Pine said, "All this talking and traveling and analyzing. It must cost a lot."

"As I mentioned, our members work without compensation. We pay for their travel and other related expenses of course, but no salaries."

"But you still have some form of funding," persisted Pine.

"We have benefactors."

"And who are they?"

"They are private. And will remain so. Are you concerned about Ben's safety?"

"Probably."

"That is unfortunate."

"It certainly is for him." She studied him. "May I be blunt?"

"I thought you *were* being blunt."

"I haven't reached my personal DefCon One yet."

Fabrikant spread his hands. "Please."

"I have come to understand that there may be international implications with this case."

"Such as?"

"Look, I'm going to take a chance that you actually *are* a society for good and tell you something that ordinarily I wouldn't at this stage, because, frankly, I don't know you. But I sense I'm running out of time and I have to get some traction on this sucker."

"I'm listening."

"I'm talking about a clusterfuck of epic proportion that will strike right at the heart of this country and perhaps destroy it."

Fabrikant's amused look faded. "I hope that is your DefCon One. I would not like to think there is another level to be reached." He paused. "What exactly are you talking about?"

Pine glanced at Blum and said, "Maybe a coup directed at our government."

Fabrikant's jaw dropped slightly. "A coup? This is America, not some banana republic."

"This country began with a revolution."

"Yes, well, that was a long time ago."

"So history never repeats itself?"

"Actually, it does, all the time."

"Okay, then."

"You're serious about this?"

"People who know about these things are serious about it."

"You mean like Ben Priest and Simon Russell?"

"And perhaps the Chinese are involved as well."

"Why do you say that?"

Pine took out her phone and held it up.

Fabrikant leaned forward and stared at the photo there. "And who is this?"

"This is a man who has now tried to kill me twice. I would like to know his name and background."

"Let me call someone in who might be of assistance."

He lifted his phone, spoke into it, and replaced the receiver.

After Pine counted off ten clicks in her head, there came a knock at the door.

"Enter," said Fabrikant.

The door opened, and a man dressed in a suit, and nearly as small as Fabrikant, walked in.

"Show Phillip the photo," directed Fabrikant.

Phillip looked at the picture for only a second and then glanced at Fabrikant and nodded.

"You can tell her," said Fabrikant.

"His name is Sung Nam Chung."

"And who is he?"

"Your worst nightmare."

"As bad as he is, he will *never* be my worst nightmare," replied Pine brusquely.

"Is he Chinese?" asked Blum.

Phillip looked at her. "No."

"What is he then?" said Pine.

"Korean."

"Korean? North or South?" asked Pine.

"From what I have learned, he was born in the South. He traveled to the North as a child and was detained there. In a camp. He came out of it alive and now works for whoever pays him. He is quite an accomplished operative. And very lethal when he has to be."

"So Sung is his surname, then?" said Pine.

The man shook his head. "Chung is. He has been in this country for a while now and has Westernized his name. He is very careful, and the authorities can prove nothing against him."

"How does a person like that get into the U.S. in the first place?" said Blum.

"If you have the resources there are ways," said Phillip.

Pine looked at Fabrikant. "The peace talks with North Korea have just gone off the rails. And this guy shows up on American soil. Do you think there's a connection?"

"I can't say definitively that there *isn't* a connection." He turned to Phillip. "Thank you, that will be all."

After the man left, Pine said, "Does Priest have an office here?"

"Yes."

"Can we see it?"

Fabrikant studied her for a long moment.

She said, "I would really appreciate it."

"I can see how you would. Come with me."

39

THERE WAS NO HINT of pipe smoke in Priest's small office, but it was as cluttered and stacked as haphazardly with things as Fabrikant's space. Clearly this coterie of elite, benevolent geniuses were not neat freaks. Pine also noted that there were no personal articles, no photos, no mementos from trips or family events. It was as though Priest had no life outside of his work.

Well, we're not so very different on that score.

Books lined the shelves and were piled on the floor. Binders full of papers formed columns across the floor and tables. The desk was overflowing with more stacks of paper, books, and file folders.

A shiny Apple desktop computer occupied a prominent place on the desk.

Fabrikant watched Pine as she took in the space along with Blum.

"Ben was quite the renaissance man. He had many interests."

"I would imagine that all of you here do," noted Blum.

"Yes, we do, actually. Although some of us also have specialties."

Pine sat down at the desk and stared at the computer. "I need to get on to his computer."

"I'm not sure I can allow that, but, in any case I'm sure he has a password."

"Priest left behind a flash drive that I think has something important on it. But it's also password protected."

"Then getting on Ben's computer won't help you."

"You're wrong, it could."

"How?"

"I'll show you."

Her fingers hovered over the keys even as she eyed the various things on Priest's desk.

"What are you doing?" asked Fabrikant.

"Profiling, for want of a better term."

Her gaze continued to dart to various objects, until it held on one.

It was a coffee mug full of pens. Printed on the side of the cup was a movie poster.

She typed in the name *Keyser Soze*.

Nothing happened.

She added another word to Keyser Soze. Then she added more words and then changed their order.

The computer sparked to life.

"How did you do that?" asked Fabrikant.

"Passwords are a pain in the ass to keep straight. Some people use password vaults that generate passwords for lots of different applications, thus obviating the need for a person to remember any of the passwords other than the vault's. But most people don't use that method. They could base their passwords on things they keep around them. That helps them remember what they are." She looked around the room. "There's absolutely nothing personal in this room. No pictures, or artwork, or memorabilia. Nothing to show the personality of the man who works here. Except for that." She pointed to the mug. "*The Usual Suspects*. Kevin Spacey played the character of Verbal. I tried various combinations that were pretty straightforward, like 'Verbal is Keyser Soze.' But having met Priest, I concluded he's not so straightforward. He marches to a different beat. So, I tried the reverse, 'Soze Keyser is Verbal,' and bingo."

Fabrikant silently clapped his hands together. "Impressive. I like how your mind works."

Pine inserted the flash drive and brought up the screen where the password was asked for.

"Do you think it's the same password?" asked Blum.

"Doubtful, but I'll try. We might get lucky."

She typed in "Soze Keyser is Verbal," and nothing happened.

"Okay, that's a no go."

Fabrikant said, "Do you know for a fact that what's on the flash drive is related to your case?"

"Priest went to great lengths to hide it, so other things being equal, yes, I'm pretty sure it is."

She hit some more keys, and a list of the files on Priest's computer came up. "Is it okay if I print out the list of his files? I can go over them in more detail later."

"Certainly. But just the file list, not the files themselves. I can't allow you to take Ben's work product without his permission."

"Well, I hope he'll make it back one day to give his permission."

"Is it really that serious?"

"With this Sung Nam Chung involved, what do you think?"

Pine printed out the file list and exited out of the computer.

Fabrikant escorted them to the building entrance. Before he closed the door, he handed her his card. "All my contact numbers are on there. If something comes up, or you need some help, don't hesitate."

"Thanks," said Pine, taking the card.

As they walked down the street to the parking garage, Blum said, "Why don't you profile Priest again? That might help us figure out the password."

"I can try," said Pine. "But if it's just in his head, we're not going to get it."

"Glass half full."

"Right."

"What did you think of the people back there?"

"Either they are what they appear to be, or they're a front for some weird shit going on."

"They wouldn't have helped us if they were bad people."

"Depends on your definitions of *help* and *bad*."

"True."

They reached the Kia and climbed in.

Pine pulled out into traffic and turned left. As they drove along, she glanced in her mirror. "Here we go."

"What?"

"We picked up a tail."

"I wonder who."

"Come on, Carol. You don't need three guesses. The Society for Good is on our ass. Jeez, you wouldn't think they'd be so obvious."

"And what are you going to do about it? Lose them?"

"Not quite."

"Why not?"

"I'd like some answers."

Blum sat back in her seat. "Well, you always know just the right way to ask."

40

THE MAN FOLLOWING Pine and Blum turned down another road, keeping them in sight in the traffic.

The Kia made another left, then a right, and the man barely made a traffic light as he continued to follow them.

Then he lost the Kia for about a minute but then picked it back up again.

A few seconds later he watched as the Kia parallel-parked in an open space.

The man looked behind him and found a free spot. He backed up and pulled into it. He put the car in park and waited.

As he watched, Blum got out of the car.

The man checked his watch and settled back into his seat.

This lasted for only a moment before the passenger door was wrenched open and a gun was pointing at him.

Pine climbed into the seat and said, "I thought we'd just cut to the chase."

The man looked from her to Blum, who was looking at him through the driver's side window.

She waved at Pine and then climbed into the rear seat.

The man was the same one who had answered the door at the Society for Good and escorted them back to Fabrikant's office.

"You can't do this," he said. "It's illegal."

Pine held out her badge. "This gives me the right to stop anyone acting suspiciously."

"I wasn't acting suspiciously."

"Then what *were* you doing?" demanded Pine.

"I wanted to talk to you."

"About what?"

"I know Ben."

Pine lowered her gun. "I'm listening. But first, what's your name?"

"Will Candler."

"Okay, Will, let's hear it."

Candler cleared his throat and gripped the steering wheel so tight, his knuckles shook. "He was into something. Something really dangerous."

"Tell me something I don't know," Pine shot back. "And make it quick."

"Ben was at the office one night late a while back. He looked so agitated that I asked him what was wrong."

"And what did he say?" asked Blum.

"At first, he sort of blew me off. Said everything was fine, blah, blah. But I persisted. I told him I might be able to help. I've been in DC a long time. I've worked in a couple of administrations. I've got contacts. Plus, I've served in capacities all over the world."

"So did he open up?"

"Some, yes. You have to understand that Ben kept all things very close to the vest. He has few friends, and his work is his life."

"Yeah, I know, it trumps his family, too."

"Anyway, Ben didn't go into much detail but he said something unbelievable was being planned. And that if it actually came off, there would be global implications. I gather that Ben was trying to stop it from happening."

"But he never told you exactly what it was?" asked Pine.

"No."

Blum said, "But if Ben Priest found out about this, wouldn't those behind the plot know? They wouldn't attempt it now." She looked at Pine. "Would they?"

Candler said, "I don't know. I've found that people in power can be incredibly insulated and therefore unrealistic about what they can accomplish."

"Meaning they're stupid drunk with power," said Blum.

"A more accurate phrase, yeah."

Pine thought back to the Army chopper that had set down in Arizona and lifted off a few minutes later with the injured Priest brothers on board. Then the Russians at Ben Priest's home. The "feds" at Simon Russell's house. And finally, Sung Nam Chung, a Korean turned international killer. If a coup *was* being planned, who was doing what to whom? And who was Chung working for?

Blum said, "There must be something we can do."

Candler shook his head. "I'm a scholar, not Jason Bourne."

Pine said, "Thanks for the information. If you think of anything else, here's a number where I can be reached."

She wrote her phone number down on a slip of paper and handed it to him.

As they were climbing out of the car, Candler said, "Look, there is one more thing."

"What's that?" asked Pine quickly, ducking her head back inside.

"Mr. Fabrikant left right after you did. I heard him mention he was going somewhere."

"Where?"

"I couldn't hear that part. But I checked with his secretary. She makes all his travel arrangements."

"Did she know?"

"Yes, she did. She said it was sudden. He popped into her office right after you left."

"Where is he going? Please don't tell me North Korea."

"No. He's flying to Moscow. Tonight."

41

ALL OF THE FLIGHTS from the DC area to Moscow left out of Dulles International Airport. There were two flights out that night: a Lufthansa flight and a Turkish Airlines flight.

Pine was covering the Lufthansa gate, while Blum was watching the Turkish Airlines departure area. Pine had tried to simply use her badge to get them through the TSA checkpoint. But the personnel there had demanded to see her ID, and Blum's as well.

As they walked through the airport Pine said, "Okay, we might have just blown our cover. Either of us sees anything screwy we text the other, okay?"

"Roger that," said Blum.

The Lufthansa flight left at ten thirty and its Turkish counterpart at eleven on the dot. Pine figured Fabrikant would opt for the Lufthansa flight, because it came with one layover in Munich before a connecting flight took him to Domodedovo Airport outside of Moscow. The Turkish flight overall was hours longer, although it would fly into Vnukovo Airport, which was closer to Moscow than Domodedovo Airport was.

She checked her watch and gazed at the crowd seated in the departing gate area.

For a disguise, she had on a ball cap and a pair of reading glasses she'd bought at one of the airport shops. Blum had gotten a hat and glasses, too. Pine was pretending to read a book that she had also purchased at the shop.

A minute later Pine smiled. She had guessed right, because Oscar Fabrikant was marching down the middle of the concourse carrying a small duffel in one hand and a briefcase in the other.

Pine texted Blum, put her book down, took off her glasses, rose from her chair, and started walking toward Fabrikant. She took out her phone and the card he'd given her and dialed his cell phone.

She watched as he quickly searched through his pockets, pulled out his phone, and looked at the screen.

"How about we do some face time instead," she said, coming to stand in front of him.

He visibly flinched when he looked up and saw her. He put his phone away.

"Well, well, what a coincidence," Pine said. "You're running and I'm hunting."

Fabrikant turned and started walking rapidly away from her, until he saw Blum approaching from the other direction.

He stopped, and his diminutive frame seemed to melt into the airport floor tiles.

Pine reached him, gripped his shoulder, and turned him around to face her.

"Moscow? Really? Care to explain?"

He looked around as Blum arrived.

He said stiffly, "Not now. Maybe when I get back, if I'm so inclined."

Pine pulled out her badge. "You're going nowhere. You're officially detained."

"You have no grounds to detain me. It's not against the law to travel to Russia. So if you will excuse me."

He started to walk past.

She gripped his shoulder and held him in place. "Why are you going to Moscow?"

"For business. *My* business." Fabrikant reached over and tried to remove her hand but couldn't manage it. "Do I need to call the police?" he said angrily.

"If you want to. But I think it would be better if we went somewhere and talked this out."

"I have nothing to say to you. And I have a plane to catch."

"Then maybe you better call the police. And then I can have a chat with them about the Society for Good actually being a place where espionage takes place."

"That's an absolute lie."

"Really? Donations from sources you won't reveal? Your people traveling the world soaking up intelligence? Oh, and one of your members is somehow caught up in a plot to maybe overthrow the government and has now vanished. And as soon as I told you about all that, you're on a plane to Moscow? So let's go get the cops. I'm sure you'll be able to explain all of that in time to catch your flight to see Putin. I mean it's not like the Russians have been doing anything lately to screw with us."

The longer Pine spoke, the smaller Fabrikant seemed to become.

"Where do you want to talk?" he said, after she finished speaking.

"There's a bar right over there. And I could use a drink."

They got a seat as far away from the other patrons as they could. A waitress came over and took their orders. Pine had a beer, Blum a Coke, and Fabrikant a glass of merlot.

"So why Moscow?" said Pine. "I have it on good authority that your trip was sudden and the genesis for it *was* my visit."

"I'm not sure I have to tell you anything."

"Are you really going down that road again? At the very least I have enough to hold you on the suspicion of being stupid."

"I have two PhDs, both from Ivy League schools," retorted Fabrikant.

"Then start *acting* like it," interjected Blum. "I mean, my goodness. We don't have this sort of time to waste."

No one said anything until their drinks came.

After the waitress left, Fabrikant wiped a bit of sweat off his forehead and said, "All right, look, some things you said made me believe that a trip to Moscow was in order."

"What was that?"

"The *Russians* being at Ben's place foremost." He fell silent and tapped his fingers against the table top.

"Oscar, we're waiting," prompted Pine.

"David Roth."

"Who?"

"The man you showed me on your phone. The one who took Ben's place. I *do* know him. His name is David Roth."

"And why didn't you tell me that before?" said Pine.

"Because I wanted to think it through. In fact, that's why I'm on my way to Russia."

"Why? Is Roth Russian?"

"No. But he knows a lot about the country."

"How do you know him?"

"He's very well known in specific circles."

"What circles?"

Fabrikant sat up straight and gazed directly at her. "David Roth is one of the world's foremost WMD inspectors."

Pine and Blum exchanged glances. Pine said, "Roth inspects weapons of mass destruction?"

"He has quite the storied past. You see, his father, Herman Roth, was one of the lead inspectors during the START One inspections that this country did with the Soviet Union commencing back in the nineties. Both sides agreed to reduce their nuclear arsenals, and that involved on-the-ground inspections and verifications. The Soviet Union collapsed during that time, but the inspections continued, and the reductions were completed at the end of 2001. And David grew up to eventually do what his father had done."

"So why would a WMD expert want to ride a mule to the bottom of the Grand Canyon?" asked Pine.

"I have no idea. But it is worrisome."

"I'd say that was the understatement of the year. I told you that an overthrow of our government by insiders might be in the works."

"Are we sure it's only *insiders* involved?"

Pine, who had been about to take a swig of her beer, slowly lowered the bottle. "What are you getting at?"

Fabrikant looked around and then said in a low voice, "The Russians tried to sway the last presidential election using a variety of tools: social media, the planting of false stories, voter suppression efforts, etc."

"That's been well documented."

"Yes, but that may have just been step one."

Pine sat forward. "Meaning their plan contained multiple steps?"

"Everything the Russians do is long-term. In that regard, they're much like the Chinese. Now, Americans are geared to think short-term. Look at American business, for example. It exists only on a fiscal quarterly basis, because the powers-that-be on Wall Street say it has to."

Blum said, "So you're saying that what happened during the last election might be simply the opening salvo?"

"Look at it this way: They attacked our democratic election process, but in the aftermath of that something else has happened."

"What?"

"Many Americans have come to distrust our institutions. They don't trust the Congress or the media." He pointed a finger at Pine. "Or the FBI."

"So where does that leave us?"

"History has shown us that when people stop believing in their institutions, the government often gets toppled."

Blum said, "Surely that could not happen here. Even you said before that we're not a banana republic."

"To which I would respond, every other country always says that, until it *does* happen to them," rejoined Fabrikant.

"What sort of Russian involvement are we talking about?" asked Pine.

Fabrikant shrugged. "I don't know precisely. But there are some Americans in high places who admire the Russians. They think their model of governing is better in some important ways. They think the same about the Chinese, who can make decisions and instantly carry them out. Whereas democracy is messy and inefficient and often comes to a complete standstill. That makes an autocracy quite a tempting template of governance."

"Not for me, because in order to have that, you have to give up your freedom," retorted Pine. "I'll take the mess and inefficiency."

"You give up your freedom *in part*," countered Fabrikant. "For benefits you otherwise would never have. I'm not saying I agree with that concept. I don't, in fact. But it's not so crazy that others don't believe in it. I can tell you, quite explicitly, that many in power do."

"So, you think the Russians have moved on from remote cyber assaults to working with certain parties in America, with the goal of turning our country into something like theirs?" said Blum.

"That's a succinct way to put it, but accurate in all essential respects," replied Fabrikant.

Pine and Blum exchanged another glance.

Pine said, "So, your trip to Moscow?"

"To find out if my theory is right. I've spent considerable time there and have certain contacts in critical places. I should be able to find things out."

"And what if you find out your theory is right?" said Blum.

"Then I come back here and work to stop it."

"But we could be reading about the overthrow of the government in tomorrow's paper for all I know."

"We still have to try," said Fabrikant.

"Oh, I'm not giving up," said Pine. "I just think we need to speed things up."

"How do you propose doing so?" asked Fabrikant. "I can't run over there and start screaming from the heavens about a plot to overthrow the U.S. government with Russian assistance. I'd disappear."

Pine checked her watch. "Okay, you still have time to catch your flight. You have my number and I have yours. Let's keep in touch."

Fabrikant seemed surprised by her acquiescence. He said, "Thank you."

"Don't thank me yet. We don't know what tomorrow holds."

They rose and walked together to the gate, where they ran into two uniformed men.

And then all bets were off.

CHAPTER

42

Washington Metropolitan Airport Authority.

That was what the emblems on their uniforms and their shiny badges said.

There were a pair of them, lean, muscled, veined forearms, each with dead-eye stares, each with one hand on the gun belt buckle and the other close to the butt of the holstered pistol.

The man on the right looked at Pine. "Special Agent Pine?"

Pine inclined her head, her eyes running from the top of the cop's head to his feet. She returned her gaze to his face. "What's up?"

The other cop said, "We've got instructions to take you in and hold you."

"Instructions from whom and hold me for what?"

"We weren't given those details, ma'am, only to take you in and hold you until persons come for you."

"Where do you intend to hold me?"

"We have a facility here." He glanced at Fabrikant and Blum. "And your friends, too."

Fabrikant said, "I have a flight to catch."

The first cop shook his head. He took his cap off, revealing his buzz cut, and wiped his face. He replaced his cap. "No can do. Sorry."

Pine said, "Your instructions said 'friends and acquaintances, too'? 'Take and hold'?"

"We just do what we're told, ma'am. Please come this way."

He pointed to a door to his left. It was a secure door requiring a key card entry.

Pine glanced at it and then looked around the crowded airport. "Okay, let's go."

They escorted them to the door where one of the officers swiped his card and opened it. They passed through into an empty hallway.

"Where to now?" asked Pine. "You have a holding cell down here somewhere?"

"That's right."

"Can I make a phone call?"

"I don't think so."

"Why not?"

"Just following instructions."

"You say that a lot."

"I say it because it's true."

"Can I talk to a superior then?"

"Why? You have a complaint?"

"Yeah, I do, but on second thought, I'll just deliver it directly to you."

Pine landed a roundhouse kick to his head that dropped him on the spot. When he tried to get up, she put him down for good with a brutal elbow jab to the back of his head. He fell heavily to the floor and didn't move.

When his partner reached for his gun, Blum already had hers out and pointed at his head.

"Just keep your hands right where I can see them, and we don't have a problem. You make a grab for that gun, I will shoot you very, very dead."

She had assumed a classic Weaver's shooting stance that demonstrated quite clearly that she could easily execute on her threat.

"You're making a big mistake," growled the man.

"Christ!" exclaimed Fabrikant. "You just attacked a cop."

"That's right, she did, now put the gun down," the man said to Blum.

"That won't be happening," said Blum.

Fabrikant said, "Please do as he says. We could get shot."

"If I put down my gun, we *will* get shot," replied Blum.

Pine pulled her weapon and said to the man, "On your knees, now."

The man exclaimed, "You're in a world of trouble, lady."

Pine flicked her pistol. "On your knees. I won't ask again."

The man got on his knees.

As soon as he did, Pine clipped him on the back of the head with the butt of her pistol. He grunted in pain and fell forward, unconscious.

With Blum's assistance, she pulled the men together and zip-tied them.

"Brings back fond memories of that rest stop in Tennessee," noted Blum. "Men doing stupid things. It never seems to have an end."

"Oh my God," cried out Fabrikant. "You attacked two police officers." He added angrily, "And you made me an accessory. I could go to jail."

"I wouldn't worry about that," said Pine.

"But I saw you do it. You can't deny that."

"That's not her point," said Blum.

Fabrikant snapped, "Then please elucidate the *point*, because it is not obvious to me."

"Her point is that they're not real police officers," said Blum.

Fabrikant retorted. "What are you talking about?" He pointed down at the men. "They're in uniform, for God's sake. They were taking us into custody."

"Doesn't matter," said Pine. "They're fakes."

"How do you know that?"

Blum pointed to the chest of one of the men. "No name tags.

Big mistake number one. No cop forgets their name tag. In fact, you don't get cleared to go on duty without it. Have to have a face with a name for lots of reasons."

"And they've got on the wrong shoes," said Pine, pointing at the men's loafers. "Those are no-no's for active duty time."

She next pointed to one of the holsters where the muzzle of the weapon was sticking out of the bottom. "Not to mention, 'real' police officers do not keep suppressor cans on their pistols."

"Three strikes and you're out," opined Blum.

Fabrikant looked down at the men. "You're saying that these men are imposters?"

Pine nodded. "Seems to be a recurring theme in this case."

Fabrikant looked at her, stunned. "Then...they were going to..."

"Shoot us in the head with suppressed rounds, I imagine," said Blum calmly.

Pine said to Fabrikant, "Okay, go get on your flight. And find out what you can. And let me know ASAP."

"But what about this?" he waved his hand at the men.

"They'll be discovered at some point. And hopefully then their asses are going to be in the fire for impersonating two airport cops. Not my problem—which is good, because my bandwidth is limited."

He nodded, looked once more at the fallen men, and bolted through the door. Pine and Blum followed and then headed in the opposite direction.

Pine said, "Okay, it was just like I was afraid of. Those two guys obviously had access to the TSA log that we were entered into to get through security."

"They acted fast."

"If you have the resources, you can act fast. But when you rush, you miss the small details. Name tags, shoes, and suppressor cans. That last one was actually a biggie."

"Thank God for big mistakes, then. We get to live another day."

"Day's not over yet," said Pine.

43

Pine fieldstripped both the Glock and the Beretta and took her time cleaning every molecule of both weapons.

Blum sat across from her while she did this at the kitchen table.

"Let me guess, your stress-relieving technique?" she said.

Pine didn't look up. She ran a bristle down the muzzle of the Glock.

"Focus enhancer. Which also relieves stress," she conceded. "You screw up on maintaining your weapon, it could cost you your life."

Blum sipped a cup of tea and looked around the confines of the kitchen.

It was early the next morning, not long after dawn had broken, and light had started to seep in through the windows.

Both women looked tired and disheveled. Sleep evidently had not come easily to either.

Blum said, "When I was young, I could have seen myself happily cooking in a kitchen like this with six rug rats running around underfoot."

Now Pine looked up. "But you did that, right?"

"Oh, I had the kids. But I didn't have anything like this. We lived in a trailer that was about as big as this kitchen. Scott, my ex, couldn't even afford a double-wide. He was too busy drinking his paycheck away. When he had a paycheck, that is."

"How did you make it, then?"

"I was a good seamstress. My grandmother taught me. I made dresses for this shop in the town where we lived. I also baked cakes. And I cleaned houses when the kids were in school. I even drove a cab in my free hours. I did whatever I could to make things work and support my kids."

"But you joined the FBI when you were still young."

"I was married at nineteen, Special Agent Pine. I had all my kids by the time I was twenty-eight. For that span, I was considered permanently pregnant." Before Pine could ask how that many children were possible in that period of time, Blum added, "With one set of twins."

When Blum said the word "twins," Pine returned to her weapon cleaning. But Blum was clearly not done.

"Then the time came when my kids were all in school and I answered an ad for an office position with the FBI. I'd never worked in an office before. Or with the government. But I wanted that job so badly."

"Why?"

"It was prestigious. It was the F-B-I. But I didn't know if I would get it. I had taken college courses. I had a two-year associate degree. I read voraciously. I kept up on the news, world affairs. I considered myself bright with a strong work ethic, but just lacking in opportunity."

"Why didn't you think you'd get the job?"

"I was certain there would be lots of women vying for it who were far better qualified than me. And, yes, back then it was all women. Men did the investigating, and women filed the papers and made the coffee." She paused. "And the other problem was Scott was into some stuff. I mean right on the edge of the criminal side. I knew the Bureau would do a background check on me. I'd never done anything that was even close to the edge. But if they looked at Scott's background, well, they could either conclude guilt by association, or just take the path of least resistance and go with one of a hundred other women who had no such issues."

"But you got the job. And they had to have talked to your husband."

"They did. And Scott did the honorable thing. He told them I had nothing to do with whatever he was involved in. And he gave me a great endorsement. As did everyone else they talked to, apparently. You know the usual adjectives: hardworking, honest, patriotic."

"So, your ex came through in the end."

"Not exactly."

Pine put down her cleaning tools and gazed at the woman. "How so?"

"A week after I got the job he filed for divorce. Seems that on the side, he was seeing this rich floozy thirty years his senior. He fed her a load of garbage, and like a lot of women, unfortunately, she fell for him hook, line, and sinker. He was handsome, I'll give him that. And charming. And an asshole, especially when he was hitting the bottle. Anyway, he went off with her and moved into her big house and drove her Jag. But because none of the money was his, I got nothing in alimony. And he could afford pennies for child support, which he was always late with, even when he bothered to pay it. During the divorce, Scott told me that he gave that great recommendation to the Bureau and took responsibility for his actions just so I could get the job and have the money to support the kiddies on my own, because he was out of there."

"How'd you resist the urge to shoot him? Seriously?"

"It was a close call at times," conceded Blum. "But I couldn't leave the kids to be raised by him. They would have been seriously messed up."

"But with all that, you said your kids aren't close to you now. When you sacrificed everything for them."

"The Bureau was a great job that didn't pay very well, though the benefits were solid. So I had to work another job to make ends meet. Sometimes two other jobs. That meant I wasn't home much with the kids. I missed important events. Proms, homecoming, sports, and one graduation. They resented that. I know that for a fact because they often told it to my face. And maybe they blamed me for their dad leaving, not that he ever spent much time with them."

"That must have been tough."

Blum finished her tea. "It *wasn't* easy. But they're my kids, so I love them. Regardless."

"What happened to Scott?"

"He ran through the floozy's money and found another one. Then he got too fat and bald to keep the racket going. Then his health failed. Last that I heard, he was in a state-run nursing home somewhere on the East Coast. He called me a few times from there."

"To say what?"

"He was lonely. Wanted someone to talk to."

"That was ballsy."

"Oh, I talked to him. I mean, what does it matter now? He *is* the father of my kids. And he paid the price for his crappy life. He must have had me on a contacts list because I received a call about six months ago from the facility. They told me he has early onset dementia. Can't remember anything from day to day."

"Maybe that's not such a bad thing," said Pine as she stared off.

"Why's that? He had some happy memories."

"I'm talking about the *unhappy* ones."

Blum sat back and gazed at her. "So I spilled my life story in ten minutes. What about you?"

"You said you read up on me. What's to tell?"

"Always better from the horse's mouth."

Pine shrugged and said nothing.

"That time you came into the office after a run. You had a tank top on. The tats on your delts? Gemini and Mercury. All about *twins*. And you looked down when I said the word." Blum looked at Pine's arms. "And you have the words 'No Mercy' on your forearms."

"Lots of people have tats."

"Lots of people have the usual tats. 'Love you, Mom.' Or a shark or a rose. Not you. Yours have meaning. Real meaning."

"You a shrink?" Pine said quietly, as she applied oil to her trigger coil.

"No, but unlike most people, I'm a good observer. And *listener*."

"I'm just fine, thanks."

Pine started putting her weapons back together.

"Daniel James Tor?"

Pine's hands slightly shook, and the weapon components slightly rattled.

"You want to talk about it?" asked Blum.

"No. Why would I?"

"Because we have jumped over the precipice together. Only we haven't hit the bottom of the canyon yet, no pun intended. I think it gives me certain rights and privileges with my partner in crime. If you disagree, I'll understand. But that's my position, just so you know."

Pine finished rebuilding the Beretta and reholstered both.

Blum waited patiently while she did so.

A light rain had begun to fall outside.

Pine glanced at her watch and said, "I checked, Fabrikant's flight left on time. He'll be landing in Munich soon."

"Let's hope he finds out something helpful."

Pine nodded absently and then fell silent for a bit. "The police thought my father had done it. Taken my sister."

"Not to be too blunt, but are you certain that he didn't?"

"He passed a polygraph. He was a broken man from the minute he found out Mercy was gone. My parents divorced. My father killed himself."

"Did he leave a note?"

"Not that I ever heard. My dad wasn't what you would call the methodical planner type. He acted on impulse."

"He might have killed himself out of guilt," Blum said cautiously.

"Don't think so. I mean he didn't have guilt because he hurt Mercy. He had guilt because he was too drunk to stop it."

"How can you be sure about that?"

"I had memory reconstruction. Via hypnosis. My father never came up, but Daniel James Tor came tumbling out of that session."

"You remembered him abducting your sister?"

Pine said, "Only I don't know if it's because he actually did it, or because I knew he was in the area at the time and I wanted to believe I finally had an answer to what happened to my sister."

"I can see your dilemma."

"You know about Tor?"

"Of course. I *was* at the Bureau when they captured him in Seattle. He'd killed women and young girls in the Southwest, too. One in Flagstaff."

"And one in Phoenix and one in Havasu City. Those three sites formed a triangle."

Blum nodded thoughtfully. "Right. I remember now. He did mathematical patterns. That's how they caught him. What an idiot."

Pine shook her head. "Granted, Tor is missing some key chromosomes, but he's no idiot."

"So you met with him?"

"I did."

"How did it go?"

"Badly," replied Pine.

"Did he admit to taking your sister?"

"No. I didn't expect him to. Certainly not at the first meeting."

"First? So you're going to see him again?"

"That's my plan."

"With what goal?" asked Blum.

"The *truth*. Call me naïve, but it's the only goal I've ever had."

"And if you don't get it? Because I just don't see a creep like Tor giving that up, ever. I *could* see him twisting you in knots while he plays all of this for a game. What else does he have to do up there?"

"That's a chance I'll have to take."

Before Blum could respond, Pine's burn phone buzzed.

She looked at the message. It was from Kurt Ferris.

Roll right now. They know where you are. They'll be there in ten.

"Let's go," barked Pine.

Pine and Blum grabbed their bags, which they'd never unpacked, and raced down to the parking lot.

Sixty seconds later the Mustang blew out of the underground garage and headed south. Pine turned at the next corner and then worked her way back around, to where she was three blocks away from the condo building and sheltered just inside the mouth of an alleyway.

"What are you doing?" asked Blum.

"Just making sure of something."

A minute later, four black SUVs rolled up to the condo building and about twenty soldiers in military gear climbed out and flooded into the lobby.

In the Mustang, Blum looked at Pine. "Is that what you wanted to see?"

Pine nodded and drove away from the condo building.

"Kurt didn't tell me in the text who was coming. I thought it might be the Bureau."

"Well, whatever, that was definitely close. How do you think they found out we were staying there?"

"Military intel has eyes and ears everywhere. And there are cameras all over the place. Luckily, Kurt found out about it somehow and was able to warn us."

"Big Brother lurks," said Blum.

"Big Brother on steroids. And they're going to be coming after us, full bore."

"So which one do you want to be?" asked Blum abruptly.

Pine shot her a glance as she turned onto the highway and punched the gas. "What?"

"Do you want to be Thelma or Louise?"

44

THEY PAID IN CASH at a motel in Stafford County, Virginia, about an hour south of DC.

They settled into the small, drab room, again leaving their bags packed, as they had throughout the trip.

Blum sat on one of the twin beds.

"Do you think Kurt will get into trouble over this? Allowing us to stay at his place?"

"I had told him before to just plead ignorance. As far as he was concerned, I was a friend requesting a place to stay while he was out of town and I was in town. He had no way to know about what I was really doing."

"How do you think he knew they were coming for us?"

"Kurt's with CID. He has lots of friends in the military, of course, and in the intel area. They must have tipped him off, or else he heard some chatter through the vines he listens to."

"What do you believe the FBI thinks about all this?"

Pine sat down on the other bed and took off her shoes and lay back. "Hard to tell. They know I lied about where I was going. They know I'm working this case after I was ordered off it. They probably know about the two guys at Dulles Airport by now."

"Do you think the Bureau has tied in Simon Russell to all this?"

"Anyone's guess. And they may not know about the Army

chopper that took Priest and his brother away. Hell, they may not even be looking into this at all."

"Why not?"

"National security trumps all. They might have gotten called off, like they tried to call me off."

"What would an overthrow of the government look like?" said Blum slowly.

"In other countries, the president or a group of generals takes over the media and says due to—fill in the bullshit reason—martial law is being declared and elections are being suspended because there are enemies of the country all over, and also in high places. That justifies them snubbing their noses at democratic norms. Then the president says he's going to serve for life. I mean look at what happened in China. Or the generals could drive tanks to the capital and tell everyone that they're in charge and will save them. All the citizens have to do is follow orders. Or it could be a group of top-level advisors pulling off a junta. Or a bunch of billionaires tired of simply throwing money at the problem through their super PACs, and opting for a more direct route to get what they want."

Blum stared at her. "What can we do about it? Really?"

"This is new territory for me, Carol. At Quantico, they didn't have a course on countering a coup of the U.S. government. Maybe they need to rethink that."

"What's our next move?"

In answer, Pine took out the pages with Ben Priest's files on them. "We have to crack the password for the flash drive. And the answer may be in Priest's other file names."

Pine opened her laptop on the bed and set the pages with the file lists next to it. She said, "Priest has shown himself to be the sort who bases passwords on personal items."

"What else might he have based the password on?" asked Blum.

"Something in his house, maybe?"

"What was in it besides the basketball and the jersey?"

"Again, not much that seemed personal to the man."

"How about something personal but not connected to his house?"

"What else is there?" asked Pine. "He has a brother who has kids. That makes them Ben Priest's nephews. Wait a minute, you had lunch with his wife. Did you—"

"Of course I did. Billy and Michael are their names." Blum thought for a moment. "Billy is eleven and Michael is nine."

Pine jotted all of this down on a slip of paper. "Any other details?"

"Billy likes to water and snow-ski and is the pitcher on his Little League team. He's terrified of having to date when he becomes a teenager. Michael is the reader in the family, plays lacrosse, and often gets on his mother's last nerve. And he plays bass guitar. They both spend too much time on social media, have their phones glued to their hands, especially Billy, and they think their dad's sole purpose in life is to act as their personal ATM. That may be because he works all the time."

"You learned all of this at lunch with a woman you just met?"

"Moms don't screw around when it comes to information exchange. She knows a lot about my kids, too. We do it very efficiently. And in great detail."

Pine had been writing notes down as Blum was speaking. "Okay, you've given me a lot to use as possible passwords."

She worked away for several hours after using a program on her computer to put together a graph of possible password combos based on what Blum had told her and also using the names from the file list she'd taken from Priest's office.

When she had tried the last possible combination, and nothing had worked, she sat back in frustration.

Blum, who had dozed off on her bed, awoke a minute later. Rain was drumming down on the roof of the one-story motel.

"No luck, I take it?" Blum said groggily.

"Apparently, his brother's family wasn't important enough to warrant being the basis for his all-important password, nor did his list of files have any clues that worked."

"Well, I'm starving. I saw a diner down the street when we were coming here."

They drove over, parked behind the building, and went inside.

They ordered their food and sipped their coffees as the rain continued to pour.

Blum looked out at the gloom. "My God, is it always like this here? I'd get suicidal. I need sun."

"They get rain and then they get sun. And then they get fall and then they get snow."

Blum shivered. "No thank you. Is that why you moved to the Southwest? For the weather?"

"I almost moved to Montana or Wyoming."

"My God, do you know how much snow they get?"

"The weather wasn't the deciding factor."

"What was then?"

"I already told you. The people or lack thereof." She glanced over at Blum, who had her coffee cup halfway to her lips. Pine explained further, "I don't like crowds."

"How would you define a crowd?"

"Pretty much anyone other than myself."

"Well, I'm sorry if I'm *crowding* you then," said Blum, sounding a bit hurt.

"Actually, Carol, I sort of consider us one unit, so when I say me, I include you, and vice versa."

"You know, when I had six kids at home, and several of them still in diapers, I longed to be by myself, for just a few minutes, even. It seemed like every second of my life, someone was calling my name, demanding that I do something for them."

"And now?" asked Pine curiously.

"Now, I live by myself. I wake up alone. I eat alone. I go to bed alone." She glanced at Pine over her coffee cup. "I wouldn't recommend it, I really wouldn't. Crowd or no crowd. Sometimes it's as simple as another human being keeping your feet warm in bed, or fetching you some aspirin because your head is splitting. I mean, really."

Their food arrived and they ate in silence, each lost in her own thoughts.

As they finished up Blum said, "What are you thinking about?"

"The case. My career. Whether either or both are over."

"You ever think about a career outside the Bureau?"

"No."

"I'm a Leo. The lion. We're stubborn control freaks with a streak of kindness. But we adapt. I think you can, too. Are you a Leo? Or are you another sign?"

Pine stared at her without answering.

"I said are you—" began Blum. She froze when Pine jumped up and threw some cash down on the table for their meals.

"Let's go."

"What's up?" said Blum as she and Pine raced back to the motel.

"In answer to your question, I'm a Capricorn."

45

Pieces of paper containing scribbled words were all over Pine's bed. Blum was actively helping her in her task by feeding her words that Pine then inputted to her computer program.

"When did you download this software?" asked Blum.

"As soon as I failed at getting the password manually," Pine replied, her fingers flying over the laptop keys. "I've been crunching passwords all this time, with no result. But it helps a lot if we can narrow the parameters of what the password might be. And maybe we can finally do that."

Blum set down the last piece of paper. "Okay, I think that's everything."

"Let's see if we're going to get lucky."

"Don't say that."

"Why not?"

"Because I haven't been lucky in like twenty years."

Pine hit a key on the laptop. "Here goes."

The program started sorting through possible password combinations.

"What made you think of Capricorn?" asked Blum.

"I was wondering why Priest would have chosen that name for a nonexistent company. I don't know if he's a Capricorn too or not, but it was the only lead I could think of. But until you started talking about being a Leo, I never even considered it. So, if it works, you get the credit." She paused and looked at the screen. "Damn."

A password had just been typed in and the screen started to change.

"We nailed it," said Pine.

"What was the password?" asked Blum.

Pine looked at the password box. "Something unbelievably complex, but everything except the letters *w* and *m* are connected to the sign of Capricorn."

"And what do the letters *w* and *m* refer to?"

"Probably to Billy and Michael. *William* would be Billy's real name. Which goes to show that Priest *did* value his nephews, at least to the extent that he would include them in a password."

"What the hell is that?" said Blum.

A picture had appeared on the screen. Pine scrolled down page after page. They were all very technical drawings. She stopped at one ominous diagram and hit some keys to enlarge it. She read the language on the screen next to the device.

"That's...those are *Korean* characters."

"Can you understand what it says?"

"No, but I can find a translation really fast." She wrote some of the characters down on a piece of paper and then went online to a translation site and input the Korean characters. The translation was almost instantaneous.

"*Fissile* material," said Pine slowly. "Fissile? That has to do with nuclear material."

Blum sat back on the bed. "Dear God. Is North Korea going to...nuke us?"

"If so, that might explain David Roth's involvement. And Sung Nam Chung's. Is this the North Koreans' backup plan in the event the peace talks cratered? Hit us with a nuclear weapon?"

"But if the North Koreans are planning something like that,

how do you explain the military chopper taking the Priest brothers away?"

Pine shrugged. "Maybe they know about the plot and are trying to trace it back to its source."

"So, do we show this to, I don't know, the FBI director?"

"We have no proof that any of this is true. If we go in with this, we might disappear."

"But people don't just disappear in this country."

"Tell that to the Priest brothers." Pine fell silent for a moment. "And even if we get proof, I'm not sure who we should take it to."

"What do you mean?"

"The DD did his best to have me called off this case. And he never would have done that without the approval of his boss and his boss's boss. In fact, this might go all the way to the top, Carol." She stared pointedly at the woman. "And I mean all the way to the very *top*."

Neither woman said anything for a few seconds, as they both seemed to let the enormity of this possibility sink in.

"But we have to do *something*," Blum finally said.

Pine nodded in agreement. "We have to find David Roth, for starters."

"How?"

Pine said, "He was last seen in the Grand Canyon. Wait a minute. There's more to the file." She scrolled down some more pages until she came to something different.

"That looks like a map," she said. "It has latitude and longitude markers."

"Agent Pine, that looks like the Grand Canyon."

She paled. "Shit, it is." Pine turned a shade whiter as she stared at the map. "Do you…do you think the North Koreans somehow planted a nuke in the Grand Canyon?"

"And Priest and Roth found out about it?" said Blum.

Pine nodded. "That must be why Roth wanted to get into the

Canyon. To find the bomb." Her phone buzzed. It was a text. "It's from Oscar Fabrikant. He's in Russia."

"What does it say?"

Pine read the text. "Check out the death of Fred Wormsley. He was very close to both Roth and Roth's father."

Pine went online and found an article on point.

Blum read over her shoulder.

"Okay, it says here that Fred Wormsley's body was found in the Potomac near Three Sisters Island a while back. The police speculated that he fell in somewhere along the GW Parkway, was sucked under by the current, and drowned."

"But obviously Fabrikant thinks there's more to it," said Blum.

"And maybe so does David Roth." Pine pointed to another part of the story. "Wormsley worked at the NSA. He was very high-up there. That's why the police investigation was a little bit more involved than would be normal. They still concluded it was an accident, and now I wonder if they were pressured to say that."

Blum sat back and seemed to process all this. "Okay, Roth is a WMD expert. He found out about this plot by the North Koreans, maybe from Wormsley. Wormsley might have learned about it through his work at the NSA. Then he got killed, maybe by this Sung Nam Chung. After that, Roth hooked up with Priest. They somehow discovered there's a nuke planted in the Canyon. And he impersonated Priest and went down there to find it so no one would know he was involved. So, is he trying to disarm it?"

"I don't know. But why would Roth turn to Ben Priest?" asked Pine.

"Maybe they knew each other before. And Priest was helping him out."

"But if Roth knew there was a nuke in the Canyon, why not just call in the government?"

Blum thought about this for a few moments. "Maybe he's

afraid if the North Koreans know that we're on to them, they'll detonate it. Maybe he's trying to disarm it by stealth. I'm just speculating here. I have no idea how nuclear weapons even work."

Pine said, "Neither do I. I just know what they can do when they go boom."

"Okay, now what do we do?"

"I think it's time to head back west."

"Thank goodness. I can already feel my tan fading." She smiled embarrassedly. "Sorry, bad joke. I do that when my nerves are about to run away with me."

Pine was punching in numbers on the computer. "What if the longitude and latitude lines indicate the spot where the nuke is located? And maybe Roth was trying to give whoever found that dead mule a clue. *J* and *k*? That could point to a hidden cave for those who know about the legend."

"A lot of questions to answer," noted Blum.

"And the answers apparently lie in one of the biggest holes on earth."

46

THE CREDIT CARD purchase was made online at eleven a.m. Two one-way tickets from Reagan Washington National Airport to Flagstaff, Arizona. The fastest flight was on American, which only had one stop in Phoenix before heading on for the short leg to Flagstaff. The flight was scheduled to leave in three days.

Carol Blum's personal credit card number had been flagged and sent along to those parties who had requested the marker. Strike teams were assembled, and a recon unit was dispatched to Reagan to bang out the necessary details for Blum's and Pine's apprehension before they boarded.

The people in charge were wary of the purchase, however, since Blum could be the only one to show up. Or else neither of them might appear for the flight. Thus, the other two airports and the train and bus depots in the DC area were immediately put under watch.

And a secondary team was deployed to the Flagstaff area just in case. Pine and Blum's homes and the office in Shattered Rock were already under surveillance.

Now, all they could do was wait.

* * *

"You want to go *where*?"

The cab driver looked askance at Pine and Blum. He was a

black man in his sixties wearing a felt cap and glasses that dangled on a chain against his broad chest. His checkered shirt was open enough to reveal curling gray chest hair.

"Harpers Ferry, West Virginia," replied Pine.

"Lady, you know this is *Virginia*, right, not *West* Virginia?" said the man.

"I can read a map," said Pine.

"You know how far that is from here?"

"About a hundred miles. You should be able to do it in under two hours."

"The hell you say. Look, ma'am, first thing is, I don't drive to West Virginia."

Pine held up five fifty-dollar bills. She had used her friend's debit card to get the cash.

"Two hours for two hundred and fifty bucks. Do you still not drive to West Virginia?"

The man considered this offer. "Well, I got to drive back."

"Still, over fifty bucks an hour, guaranteed. I doubt that's a hardship for you."

Blum pulled out a hundred dollars from her wallet.

"And this extra amount to cover your gas," she said. "And because you're a nice person."

The man said, "You two must really want to get to Harpers Ferry. Why?"

"I hear it's very historical," said Pine.

"And you got no car?"

Before she'd used her credit card to buy the plane tickets, Blum had driven the Mustang to Reagan National and left it in long-term parking to give credence to their taking a flight from there to Flagstaff.

"We're visiting from out of the area," said Pine.

The man nodded. "Okay, thing is, I got nothing against taking your money, but it'd be a lot cheaper to take a bus, or even the train."

"I don't like crowds. You want the gig or not? Unless you can make more money today somewhere else."

The man eyed their luggage. "Is that all the bags you got?"

"That's it."

He shrugged and slipped on his glasses. "Okay, ladies, let's go."

They made it to the Harpers Ferry train station in a little more than two hours. It was right on the border between the two Virginias. The building was wood sided, stained a dull red, and was Victorian in style. It rested on the buried foundations of old armory buildings.

They paid the promised money, and the cabbie handed out their bags from the trunk.

"Hope you gals enjoy the *history*," he said, patting the cash in his pocket.

"Maybe we'll make some of our own while we're here," said Blum.

The man cracked a grin and knuckle-smacked her. "Now, there you go!"

He drove off, and thirty minutes later Amtrak's Capitol Limited train roared into town.

They had previously purchased their tickets at another train station, paying in cash. When the woman at the ticket window had asked for ID, Pine had pulled her badge and said in a low voice, "FBI, undercover, escorting a valuable witness for the government. Hoping to nail some really bad guys. Do not say anything to anyone about this."

The woman, a matronly type in her sixties, glanced at Blum and smiled. "Good for you, honey. I won't breathe a word to anyone."

Blum smiled. "We all have to do our part."

The train pulled away only a couple of minutes late.

They had reserved a Superliner bedroom compartment with its own bath, which also doubled as a shower. They stowed their bags and sat on the blue couch staring out the window as the West Virginia scenery passed by. Soon they would be looking at Maryland scenery followed by Pennsylvania and Ohio landscapes, with the final destination in Chicago, where they had a layover before boarding the Southwest Chief. They would arrive in Arizona before the flight they'd booked for Flagstaff ever left the ground.

Pine looked around the compartment. "I've never taken the train before. How about you?"

"Once. Along the California coast. I was sixteen. First time I'd been away from home. I went to visit an aunt. I really enjoyed it. Felt free as a bird. Three years later, I was a mom learning to live on a couple hours of sleep a night."

They ate dinner in the dining car. Blum had a glass of wine, while Pine stuck to beer. Both women went to sleep in their clothes, Pine in the top berth and Blum in the bottom. The swaying of the train allowed Pine to fall asleep fast and not wake up until around six.

They reached Pittsburgh at midnight and Chicago at around nine the next morning. They left the train and went to have breakfast at a place in the train station, a cavernous building on the west side of the Chicago River.

Pine and Blum had six hours to kill before they would board the Southwest Chief.

While they were eating, Blum was watching a TV monitor that was bolted to the wall. "Oh my God."

Pine looked at the TV. Oscar Fabrikant's photo filled the screen. The chyron at the bottom read: AMERICAN SCHOLAR FOUND DEAD IN MOSCOW. APPARENT SUICIDE.

Pine and Blum looked at each other.

Pine said softly, "He didn't kill himself."

"How do you think they found him?"

"They must have learned we had met with him. Maybe from the two fake cops." Pine smacked the table. "I should never have let him go. He was a dead man at that point."

"You couldn't have really stopped him," pointed out Blum.

"He could have come with us."

"But we can't collect everyone we run into and try to protect them. We'd all end up dead. But it's so awful." She shivered.

Pine eyed Blum. "I think it would be better if you stayed here, Carol. Get a hotel room and lie low for a few days."

"I use my credit card to get the room and they'll be knocking on my door in an hour." She pointed to the screen. "And I don't want to end up on there with the scroll saying I killed myself."

"But you could find a place that would take cash."

Blum shook her head obstinately. "I'm not leaving you to do this alone, Agent Pine. Like you said, we're a unit, a team. I think we work well together."

Pine eyed her.

"You don't think so?" said Blum, frowning.

"I took an oath, you didn't. I signed up for the danger part, you didn't."

Blum waved this off. "Oh, don't worry about that. I know I'm not a special agent like you, but I did join the FBI, and I promised to do my job the best that I could. And I'm going to live up to my promise. Besides, I shepherded six kids to adulthood without losing any of them. So I can help you, too."

Pine smiled. "You already saved my life once. Back at the airport."

Blum leaned across the table and tapped Pine's hand. "And if the need arises again, I will do so once more. We're two badass women in a man's world. What stronger incentive could we possibly have to stick together?"

Pine's smile deepened. "Actually, I can't think of a stronger one."

47

THE SOUTHWEST CHIEF Train No. 3 headed out from Chicago with its twin P42 locomotives and nine trailing train cars pointed toward the southwest United States. It carried fourteen crew and 130 passengers. It had a max speed of ninety miles per hour, which it would hit on long stretches of the route. However, its average speed over the slightly more than twenty-two-hundred-mile trip to LA would be only about fifty-five miles per hour, when one factored in the thirty-one stops over eight states.

Pine and Blum settled into their seats as the train rocked and rolled out of the downtown Chicago area.

"Do you think anyone else at the Society for Good is in danger?" said Blum.

"I can't rule out anyone," said Pine. "I hope they'll have taken note of what happened and lie low."

"Do you think it makes sense for you to call anyone at the FBI? Anyone you might trust? I mean, if there is a nuke in the Grand Canyon, they would want to know about it."

Pine didn't answer right away. "This whole thing doesn't make sense, Carol. If Roth is a weapons inspector and he found out about a nuke in the Grand Canyon, what would be the first thing he would do? Or Ben Priest, for that matter? I mean, I don't think either of them are traitors."

Blum looked puzzled. "They should have gone right to the authorities."

"Only they didn't. And an Army chopper carries away the Priest brothers. And what looked to me to be feds were going to take Simon Russell somewhere and torture him. Then we were nearly killed by two guys at the airport. And what looked to be our military raided Kurt Ferris's home."

"You'd think our people were the bad guys."

"I don't know if they know about the nuke and are just trying to contain any leaks so as not to panic the public. But right now our government is snatching people right and left and doing some really weird shit. The rule of law has apparently gone out the window."

"My God, we might as well be in North Korea or Iran."

"Or Russia," added Pine. "Because they're involved as well." She paused, looking puzzled. "I didn't think the Russians and the North Koreans were such great allies that they'd maybe work together to place a nuke on American soil. Are they looking to start World War III? If so, they're not going to win. Not that anyone would against us."

"But how in the world could the North Koreans, or the Russians, have gotten a nuke down there with no one aware of it? I mean really?"

"I guess they could have taken it down there in parts, over time. And assembled it in a cave off the beaten path that no one knows about. It's not like you have to go through a security checkpoint and magnetometer to hike down."

"Do you think the latitude and longitude lines mark where this cave is?"

"Yes."

"What are we going to do when we get back to Arizona?"

"I'm not sure. But we have a long train ride to figure it out."

Pine left the compartment and walked down to the train car that sold snacks and drinks. She bought a beer and some chips and sat by herself in the observation car.

She fingered her phone and then decided to make the call.

"Hello?"

"Hey, Sam, it's Atlee."

"Atlee, I didn't recognize the number."

"Yeah, I'm traveling. Using another phone. How are things?"

"Fine. Good. You coming back soon?"

"Yeah, I'm on my way, actually. How was the concert?"

"What?"

"Carlos Santana."

"Oh, right. Hey, it was great. The dude can still bring it, that's for damn sure. I took a buddy. Wasn't as much fun as if you had gone instead."

"Now, that's what I like to hear. Hey, Sam, you hear anything else about Lambert or Rice?"

"No, just that they went to Utah."

"Any replacements for them yet?"

"No, not yet. We're having to pick up the slack for them until the new guys arrive. How's your investigation going?"

"I'm making progress. Turned out to be a little more complicated than I thought."

"Well, I hope you catch whoever killed the mule. I still can't believe someone could be that cruel. I mean, what did that mule ever do to anybody?"

"Yeah, I know. You on duty the next few nights?"

"Yeah, I am. Hey, if you wanted to go out somewhere when you get back, I can see if I can switch with someone. It might not be possible because we're shorthanded."

"No, it's not that. I, uh, I thought I might hike the Canyon one night."

"Okay, let me know when, I'll make sure we hook up down there." He laughed. "I'll bring you a beer."

"Right, sounds good."

"You're not hiking alone, are you?" he said suddenly.

"Well, I'm a big girl. And I've done it solo before."

"Doesn't make it smart."

"I never said I was smart, Sam."

Later, Pine and Blum went to the dining car to eat. They had to sit with two other people and didn't get a chance to talk during their meal.

At half past midnight, the train stopped in Lawrence, Kansas. Two passengers got on and none got off. The train headed out five minutes later.

Barely five minutes after that, the train began to slow.

"Another stop?" mumbled Blum, who had been dozing in her bunk.

Pine sat up and snagged her phone, where she'd downloaded the train schedule.

"Not until Topeka about thirty minutes from now."

"Then why are we slowing down?"

Pine already had her gun out. "Good question."

A minute later there was a screech of brakes, and the train decelerated so swiftly that they were flung against the wall.

That was followed by a jolt.

And then the mighty Southwest Chief came to a dead stop.

48

Wнат нарреnеd?" said Blum, rubbing her shoulder where it had struck the wall.

"I think we hit something," said Pine. She climbed down from her bunk and slipped on her shoes. "You got your gun out?" she whispered to Blum.

"No."

"Then get it out."

"You don't think...?"

"I don't know for sure, so the answer is yes."

Pine pulled the curtain aside and looked out the window. It was too dark to see anything out there.

She heard the sounds of footsteps rushing down the train corridor. She slid open their compartment door and saw a train attendant hustling by.

"What happened?" she asked.

"Not sure, miss. Stay in your compartment. They'll give everyone an update over the PA when they know for sure."

He rushed on and disappeared from her sight.

Pine heard the whoosh of exterior doors opening. A few moments later the train's interior lights blinked twice and then went out, plunging them into darkness.

Pine heard several screams coming from other compartments.

She snagged her Maglite from her duffel, told Blum to stay put, and went back out into the corridor.

While it was true that trains occasionally hit things, she didn't like the odds here. It was too much of a coincidence.

She moved down the corridor slowly, shining her light around and occasionally pointing it out the window into the Kansas night. She could see nothing, however. And no announcement came over the PA. And the lights stayed out and the train did not move.

Other than that, things were great.

Pine stiffened when she heard it.

The sounds of a child crying.

The train suddenly gave a jerk, but then almost immediately stopped once more. The movement nearly knocked Pine off her feet.

The cries picked up again.

Pine ran toward them, reached a door, and hit the open button. The door slid to the side with a hydraulic hiss, and she moved into the next sleeper car.

She shone her Maglite down the corridor. At first, Pine saw nothing.

Then the beam caught and held on a small figure.

It was a little girl, no more than six years old, who was standing in the middle of the aisle holding a tattered doll.

She looked stricken and was crying.

Pine put her gun away, moved the light away from the girl's face, and hustled toward the child.

"Are you okay?" she asked, kneeling down by the child. "Where are your parents?"

The little girl shook her head, snuffled, and wiped her nose with her doll. "I don't know. My mommy went to the bathroom. And...and then it got all dark. I went to find Mommy. But...but I don't know where she is."

"Okay, we'll find her. What's your name?"

"Debbie."

"Okay, Debbie. We'll go find your mom. Do you know which way she went?"

Debbie looked around. "I don't know. It's so dark." She began to cry again.

Pine took her hand. "Okay, I came from this way, and I didn't see anyone. So, I think your mom must be down this way. Let's go see."

They walked down the passage to the end. There was a restroom here.

"What's your mom's name?"

"Nancy."

Pine knocked on the door. "Nancy? Are you in there? I have your daughter, Debbie."

"Mommy! Mommy!" cried out Debbie. She pounded on the door.

Pine opened the door and glanced inside. It was empty.

She looked down at Debbie. "You're sure she went to the bathroom?"

Debbie nodded. "That's what she said. We didn't have one in our room. She told me to stay there and she'd be right back. And then it got dark."

"Let's keep looking, Debbie, I'm sure she's nearby."

They passed through into the next train car, where they saw two elderly couples groping around in the dark.

"Do you know what's happening?" one of the men asked, as he clutched the hand of the woman Pine assumed was his wife.

"The train might have hit something," said Pine. "Have you seen a young woman pass through here? I have her daughter here. They got separated."

One of the women said sympathetically, "Oh, you poor thing. But we've seen no one. We just came out of our compartment."

The other man said, "I did hear someone pass by a bit ago. But I didn't see who it was."

"Thanks. You should go back to your compartment. You don't want to fall down and hurt yourself out here."

Pine and Debbie continued on into the next train car. Now Pine was getting worried. What if the mother had gone the other way and had come back only to find her daughter gone? She would be panicking by now.

There came a sound behind them. Pine whirled around, her hand going to her holster, but then relaxed as Blum stepped out of the darkness.

She tensed a moment later as she realized that Blum was not alone.

Someone was behind her. A short man, because Blum had neatly blocked Pine's view of him.

Now he stepped to the side.

Sung Nam Chung had a hold of Blum's neck.

He tightened his grip when he saw Pine's hand again go toward her gun.

"That would be unwise, for your friend's sake."

"I'm sorry, Agent Pine," said Blum. "He got the drop on me."

"What's…happening?" asked Debbie. "Who is that man?"

"Just somebody I know, Debbie," said Pine.

"Is…is he hurting her?"

Chung reached into his pocket and pulled out a pistol.

Debbie cried out and shrank back. Pine stepped in front of Debbie, putting her body between the little girl and Chung's weapon.

"She's just looking for her mother. She's not part of this. We'll come with you. But she needs to stay here."

Chung did not seem amenable to this.

"She's just a kid," added Pine. "She can't do anything."

Chung looked Pine up and down, then gave a curt nod.

Pine turned and faced Debbie. "Okay, I think your mom is probably just up in the next car. But I want you to wait right here until either your mom comes to get you, or one of the train people do. They'll be in uniform. You know what they look like, right?"

Debbie stared up at Pine and nodded. "You're…you're going to leave me?"

She clutched at Pine's arm.

"Just for a little bit. We need to go somewhere with this man."

"Is he a bad man?"

"Debbie, I just want you to stay right here, okay? Will you be brave and do that for me?"

Debbie finally gave a tearful nod.

Pine glanced down at the doll in Debbie's hand. "What's your doll's name?"

"Hermione."

"Like from Harry Potter?"

Debbie nodded.

Pine knelt down and gave her a hug. "I'll be back to check on you."

"Promise?" said Debbie.

"Promise."

Then Pine stood and faced Chung. "Let's go."

49

THEY WALKED BACK to their compartment without seeing anyone else, though they did hear people talking in their rooms as they passed by.

Pine went in first, followed by Blum and Chung. He closed the door behind him.

"Sit," he said.

Pine and Blum sat on the lower bunk.

"Take your gun out and put it on the floor," ordered Chung as he kept his weapon pointed at Pine's head.

Pine did as he said.

"Kick it over to me," he said.

She did so. He bent down and picked it up, placing it on a small metal desk behind him. Next to it was Blum's pistol, Pine saw.

"Your other pistol too, please," said Chung. "I know that you carry a spare."

Pine took off her ankle holster and slid it across the floor.

Chung pushed it behind him.

"How did you know we were on the train?" asked Pine.

"This is the only train that goes to Arizona. And you two are the only passengers who paid cash for your tickets. And, apparently, you did not provide names to the ticketing person. So, she simply named you Jane and Judy Doe. Quite the red flag."

Pine grimaced at this. "You had the train stop somehow. Did you put a car on the track or something?"

"Completely irrelevant."

"Okay, then what do you want?"

Chung reached into his pocket and held up something. "This man."

He tossed the piece of paper over to Pine, who caught it.

She used her Maglite to look at the object.

It was a photograph.

Of David Roth.

Pine and Blum looked up at Chung.

"I don't know where he is."

Again, the Korean moved so fast, Pine had no time to even try to block his blow. She went heels over ass against the wall.

When Blum stood and tried to lash out at Chung, he merely grabbed her wrist and twisted it until Blum cried out in pain and collapsed to the floor, holding her hand and gasping for breath.

Pine slowly sat up, rubbing blood off her mouth.

"I did not come all this way for you to tell me that you do not know things that you *do* know," Chung said.

"I'm looking for Roth, it's true," said Pine, spitting blood out of her mouth. "But I haven't found him. Yet."

"But you have an idea where he is?" said Chung.

"I think I do."

"Where?"

Pine looked down at Blum. "If I agree to tell you, will you let her go?"

Chung shook his head. "She is not a little girl."

Blum struggled up and plopped down next to Pine.

"Well, good, because I'm not going anywhere." Blum brushed off her clothes, set her hands in her lap, and said pleasantly, "Now tell the nice man where you think Mr. Roth is, Agent Pine."

Pine said nothing.

"Well, then, I guess I'll have to do the honors." She looked at Chung. "We believe that Mr. Roth is in Flagstaff. That's where we're headed. You already know that because you checked on our tickets."

"Why this Flagstaff?"

"There's an FBI office there. It's the largest one near the Grand Canyon. We think he's going to turn himself in there."

"Why turn himself in?" said Chung tightly.

"We think he's afraid," said Blum. "He doesn't want to die. He thinks the FBI can protect him."

"Can they?" Pine finally said, looking at Chung.

"You ask me? It's your employer, not mine."

"Irrelevant to my question," said Pine, mimicking the Korean's earlier statements. "I want to know what you think about that."

Chung mulled this over. "I do not think anyone can protect him. Least of all *your* people."

"Well, then we agree on something. Why do you want him?"

"I think it obvious."

"Not to me, it's not. Unless you want your *nuke* back."

Chung appraised her. "The world is complicated, Agent Pine. Far more complicated than you seem to give it credit to be."

"I think planting a nuke on American soil and killing a bunch of my fellow citizens is pretty simple, actually. Simply insane! You have every reason to work with me."

"Why is that?"

"If that nuke goes off, North Korea will cease to exist. We'll bomb it back into the Stone Age."

"I completely agree with you."

Pine was about to say something else, but then simply gaped at him.

Blum found her voice. "You...you agree with that?"

"Of course I do," said Chung. "Why do you think I'm here?"

Pine said, "Why don't you explain that to me? Because it doesn't make any sense."

"That is not my job to explain things. And if you can't help me, then..." He shrugged.

"Then what, you kill us? What would be the reason?"

"If I let you live, you will make my task much more difficult."

"I guess I see your point," said Pine.

"Your honesty does you justice," conceded Chung.

"You seem far too nice for this sort of work," interjected Blum.

"Your observations deceive you, madam," said Chung. "I am not nice. At all. As, unfortunately, you are about to find out."

At that moment, the train started up again.

It caught them all off-guard, and Chung stumbled backward a bit.

Pine slumped forward, her head between her knees, as though she were about to be sick.

Her fingers closed around the length of pipe. It was the tool the steward had used to lower the top bunk into place. Earlier, she had seen him slide it into a holder under the bunk after he'd finished making up their beds for the night.

She sat up and delivered a blow with the pipe first to Chung's hand, knocking the pistol from it, and then striking his jaw.

He staggered backward against the wall.

Holding his face and his back, he straightened just at the moment that Pine hit him with a roundhouse kick, the force of which lifted him off his feet, and he flew against the window of the train car.

He bounced off the glass and catapulted forward at the same moment that Pine lunged for her gun that had fallen off the desk after Chung's collision with it.

Pine slid along the floor, snatched her gun, hit the wall, turned, and fired.

The shot missed Chung, but smacked into the window and shattered it.

Chung exploded forward and kicked the gun free from Pine's hand. He followed the kick with a hand strike to her side, which seized up her left side and drove all the air out of her lungs.

Shit, here we go again.

Chung straightened and was about to deliver a crushing kick to Pine's head when he reeled backward, grabbing his own head.

Blum had hit him with the pipe.

Blood flowing from a gash on his head, he turned and was about to deliver a blow to Blum that would have killed the woman when Pine hit him from behind with a knee to the base of his spine, propelling him forward into the already cracked glass.

As the train picked up speed, Pine planted her legs firmly around Chung's, pinning them together. At the same time her arms encircled his torso and kept his arms bound to his sides. She levered forward, forcing Chung's face against the glass.

Pine got her delt under Chung's right shoulder blade and pushed upward. She gave a heave, and slowly the shorter Korean was lifted off the floor, the toes of his nicked shoes now the only thing touching there. This was remarkably difficult, since Pine could not spread her legs and plant her feet to give herself the leverage to more efficiently lift Chung. She knew that if she allowed his legs an inch of freedom, he would disable her and then kick both of them to death.

She could have had Blum grab one of the guns, but she wasn't going to make the woman cold-bloodedly shoot the Korean in the head. And she might miss and hit Pine; or since Pine was plastered to the guy, the bullet could pass through Chung and kill her.

But she couldn't just stand here holding the Korean. That was not sustainable. The plan came together in her head in seconds.

"Carol," panted Pine. "The window. The...seal."

Blum looked confused for a moment, but then lurched over, gripped the red lever at the bottom of the window, and pulled it free.

Chung, seeing what they were trying to do, struggled to free himself. He rammed his head backward, catching Pine hard on the chin. Pain rocketed up her face and she winced. But she managed to hold him firmly against the broken glass as Blum pulled the rubber seal free from around the perimeter of the window.

Once that was done, Blum gripped the edge of the glass and tugged hard. It broke free from the wall of the train, slipped sideways, and then fell out of the opening. Air whipped inside the compartment, blowing the curtains straight out.

This was the moment of truth, Pine knew. With the window gone, so was most of her leverage holding him against it. Chung jerked and pulled and bucked, but without his feet being on the floor he couldn't gain the necessary traction, and without that he lacked the ability to strike out.

The interior train lights started to flicker on and then off.

Pine continued to slowly lift the far shorter man, inch by inch, at the same time keeping his limbs pinched to his sides. Her torso, arms, and legs were like a tube, a tube that she was slowly, inexorably forcing Chung through by moving her arms and legs millimeters at a time. The horrific image of a constrictor working its victim down its gullet popped into her head, and it was not far off the mark. Except Pine wanted to cast off Chung, not swallow him.

As she leaned forward, his waist was now resting on the edge of the window.

That meant Chung was halfway out of the train window.

But so was Pine.

The train was only going about twenty-five miles an hour now. But it was accelerating.

The wind whipped into them. They were both facing downward. Aside from her views of Chung's back, Pine could see the landscape sweeping past. The terrain was pancake flat. Lawrence, Kansas, was far behind them now and receding faster and faster.

Pine was reaching the edge of her safety zone. Another few inches and she would not be able to stay in the train compartment. Chung's weight and the angle she was holding him at were straining every muscle she had to its breaking point. Then they would both go flying out the window. And though the train wasn't going that fast yet, the collision with the ground could very well send them bouncing under the train wheels. And that would mean certain death for them both.

Panting for breath, she suddenly felt Blum behind her, gripping her belt and then leaning backward, serving as the extra ballast that she needed.

Pine readied herself. Even as she could feel Chung working his right arm free, her limbs too spent to contain it much longer, she counted to five in her head.

Hold it, Atlee. Hold the lift. Just another few seconds. Another few seconds and you got the gold.

She grunted and then screamed as the Southwest Chief leapt forward with a burst of power from its twin engines. The sudden jolt of acceleration nearly carried all three of them outside, but Blum had quickly leaned back so far that her weight provided enough of a counterbalance to offset the increase in speed.

Three…

Pine had to time this exactly right. She could not afford to allow Chung to cling to her arms or legs. She was so tired that if the Korean managed to remain in the compartment, they were both dead. She wanted Blum and herself to keep their vertebrae right where they were.

She was leaning out so far now that she could barely breathe with the wind hitting her in the face.

Two…

She tensed every fiber, every ligament, in preparation for the release. She could feel the throb of Chung's heart against her chest. She could hear his gasps. She could smell his fear.

As she could her own.

One…

She pushed against Chung's back at the same moment that she let go of the death grip around the man's arms.

She felt his freed limbs flailing in the air. The Korean managed to somehow turn to the side, his hands groping for the now-empty window frame.

They were nearly face-to-face as the lights on the train came on and this time stayed on.

She could see his features, as the wind sliding off the racing train pounded them both. She supposed they mirrored her own:

Terror.

He suddenly reached out and gripped her windswept hair, right as Pine let go of his legs.

His fingers pulled out some of her hair by the roots, even as his feet danced frantically against nothing.

She leapt back as he tried to kick her in the face.

And then the wind caught him, and he was fully out the window, unable to regain any sort of equilibrium.

For a moment, he seemed suspended in the air, and then, like a passenger sucked out of a depressurized plane, Chung was jerked violently to the right and in a flash disappeared from view.

Then Pine was falling backward and into Blum's outstretched arms.

The two women lay there on the floor for several minutes, shaking and gasping.

Finally, they slowly rose as the lights in the train went off once more before again coming back on.

A few seconds later the door slid open and a steward looked in. When he spied the missing window and the curtains being blown around the compartment by the force of the wind, he cried out, "Oh my God!"

Pine dropped into a sitting position in the lower bunk and said, "We need another room." She drew a deep breath. "This one's broken."

CHAPTER

50

W INSLOW, ARIZONA.

Not Flagstaff.

Pine and Blum alighted about an hour behind schedule at the station, which was part of a hotel complex. Pine had figured someone might be waiting for them at Flagstaff, someone whom they really did not want to meet.

Contrary to the song lyrics, they were not here to take it easy.

Yet in keeping with the Eagles' theme, they *did* spy a woman cruising by in a flat-bed Ford.

Pine waved her hand, and Jennifer Yazzie pulled the truck over to the curb.

Pine and Blum put their bags in the truck bed and climbed in, sitting shoulder to shoulder in the cab.

"Thanks for picking us up, Jen," said Pine after introducing her to Blum.

"No problem. What'd you do to your face?" she asked, looking at Pine's swollen chin and cut lip.

"Hit a door."

"Why do I not believe that?"

"How's Joe Jr.?"

"Still giving us fits."

"Sorry to hear that."

"You want to go to your home, or office?"

"Neither one. And I was hoping that Carol here could stay with you and Joe for a while, if that's okay."

Yazzie glanced at Blum quizzically and then back at Pine. "That's fine. I was surprised to hear you were taking the train here. I didn't even know you'd left town. Where were you?"

"Back east. And, if it's all right, I need to borrow some of your hiking and camping gear."

"Heading out again?"

"Going to hike the Canyon."

Yazzie said, "What, solo?"

"That's the plan."

"Why?"

"Got some time off. Haven't been down there in a while. Want to stretch my muscles."

"I could go with you."

"What, in all your free time?"

"Well, Joe could."

"He has even less free time than you."

"It's not smart to hike by yourself, you know that."

"I wanted to go with her," said Blum. "But, well, I'm not sure I'm up to it anymore. My knees and my hip. I'd just hold her back."

Pine said, "I'll take it nice and easy. It's not like I'm going rim-to-rim in one day. I plan to spend a few days down there."

"This have anything to do with the mule that was found butchered down there? And the missing person?"

"You heard about that?"

"This is not exactly New York City. Now, a missing person around here is not so rare, but a cut-up mule is something different."

"Like I said, I'm just going down to chill out."

"When are you planning to leave?" asked Yazzie.

"Tonight."

"You just got back. It's been a long trip. We can grab some dinner tonight and you can relax before heading out."

"I don't think I have time to relax, Jen."

* * *

Later that day, Pine sat on a couch in the basement in the Yazzies' home in Tuba City.

She had seen on the news feed that the Southwest Chief had encountered signal problems, which had necessitated the abrupt stop. There had been some electrical problems and a few bumps and bruises with passengers and crew, but no serious injuries. Freight trains used the same set of tracks, and care had to be taken because the signaling system was critical in making sure one train did not slam into another. There had been no mention of the shattered window.

But a body *had* been discovered near the tracks, the news had reported. No identification had been made.

Pine doubted one ever would be. But at least Sung Nam Chung was certifiably dead.

She had the borrowed gear all together and had gone over her checklist, which was about eighty items long. These included good hiking shoes with support and traction soles, trekking poles, a battery-powered headlamp, a wide-brimmed hat and sunscreen, a first aid kit, salty food, a whistle and signal mirror, something to sleep in, and a lightweight tarp, plus layers of clothing. She would also be taking a refillable hydration bladder with a flow system activated by biting down on the mouthpiece. And all that would weigh less than twenty-five pounds.

And, of course, she had her twin pistols. They were additional weight, but Pine figured they might be the most important items she carried with her.

If she wanted to get back alive.

Blum, who was staying upstairs in the spare bedroom, came

down and joined her on the couch. She looked over the equipment. "What route will you take down?"

"Either Bright Angel or South Kaibab—I haven't decided yet."

"Have you figured out the location from the latitude and longitude?"

"As close as I could. I can't pinpoint it exactly from that."

"Which is even more reason for you not to go alone."

"I can't exactly call in a regiment of FBI agents, Carol. In fact, I can't call anybody in, considering our own government apparently is in this up to their eyeballs somehow."

"I could—" she began.

"No, Carol, you couldn't."

Blum looked away. "What happened on the train," she began.

"You saved my life. No way I'm beating that guy without you there."

"It was only fair, since I endangered your life by letting him capture me."

"I think you can be excused for not taking him out all by yourself."

"At least we were able to find that little girl's mom."

"Yeah, she was really scared. Little kids need their parents."

"Yes, they do," said Blum, looking at Pine, but she kept her gaze on the floor. She cleared her throat. "If there *is* a nuke down there? What are you going to do?"

"Hopefully, I can find David Roth and he can help me disarm it."

"He's been missing for a while now. He might be dead."

"He might be. But I still have to try."

"You realize that there are others out there besides the late Sung Nam Chung who want to find Roth."

"I'm aware of that, Carol."

"And they might have come to the same conclusion as you have. That he might still be in the Canyon."

"Which means I might have some company down there," said Pine.

51

Oᴏʜ Aᴀʜ Pᴏɪɴᴛ.

The remarkable views from here had obviously been the genesis for the name.

Pine had traveled nearly a mile on the South Kaibab Trail and while doing so had descended about six hundred feet below the South Rim, which stood at about 7,200 feet above sea level. The Rim had been cool and pine scented. That would change dramatically the farther down she trekked. The South Rim averaged nearly sixty inches of snow a year, while Phantom Ranch received less than one.

Jennifer Yazzie had dropped her off at the trailhead.

"Joe called before we left," she said as Pine was getting her gear out.

"You didn't tell him—"

"No. But he did tell me something you might want to know."

"What's that?" said Pine as she strapped on her backpack.

"Joe said some feds have been poking around."

"For what?"

"They were asking about you."

"What agency?"

"That's the thing. It wasn't clear."

"How could it not be clear? Didn't they badge Joe and show him their creds?"

"Apparently not. And so he didn't tell them anything." She paused and smiled. "Not that he would have anyway, without checking with you."

"Tell him thanks for me." Pine slid out her trekking poles. "Anything else?"

"A military chopper landed at the Canyon airport earlier today. Joe heard about it from one of the rangers."

"Unusual activity."

"You don't seem surprised," replied Yazzie.

"That's because I'm not."

"If you're in some sort of trouble—"

"Let's just say I'm off the grid right now. And people you thought should be your allies, aren't."

Yazzie looked deeply concerned by this comment. "Look, Atlee, I don't know what's going on, but if you can get cell reception down there, call us if you need help."

"You've done enough, Jen."

"You've been a real friend to the community and, well, we care about you."

Pine had given Yazzie a hug. "I'll see you soon," she had said, hoping that it would indeed be true. Right now, she would not have bet on herself.

As Yazzie's truck lights had disappeared into the dark, Pine had turned around, faced the trailhead, and set off.

Normally, those *not* seeking to go all the way to the Canyon floor would hike down the Kaibab, cross over to the west on the Tonto Trail to Indian Garden, and then head back up the Bright Angel to the South Rim. Because of the rule of thumb that an hour hiking down meant two hours hiking back up, Kaibab was a good choice for the descent phase. It had no shade and no potable water except at the trailhead. After the Tonto Trail and the turn onto Bright Angel, one could take a rest at the shady Indian Garden, drink some water, and continue the steep ascent back to the rim. There were also two additional rest houses on the way up.

Only shade wasn't an issue right now, since it was nearly midnight. And Tonto Trail wasn't an option, because Pine was going all the way down to the floor. She had picked this time of night because there might well be no other hikers. She had passed by no one so far going up or down. This included park rangers. That was good, because for all she knew, they had been instructed to detain her if they encountered her.

It was about seven miles on this trail to Bright Angel Campground near Phantom Ranch. The nearby Bright Angel Trail was more than nine miles down to the same destination. Yet because of the topography and other conditions, hikes down both trails would take between four and five hours.

Setting an ambitious pace, Pine intended to make it down in about three. Under other circumstances, she would not have attempted this sort of pace at night, since, like all trails going down into the Canyon, the Kaibab was full of switchbacks, narrow curves, and turns. And although well maintained, the Kaibab trail was hardly smooth. The last thing she wanted was to make a false step and go hurtling over the edge. But she knew the Kaibab well, and she was keeping to the inside of the trail. Hikers coming up had the right of way and she would have to move to the edge to let them pass, but, so far, it was just her.

Her collapsible trekking poles lightly touching the trail as she went, her headlamp brightly illuminating the area ahead, her long legs smoothly striding, she soon reached Cedar Ridge at the 1.5-mile marker. This was the strongly recommended turn-around point for day hikers, particularly in summer. Because every hike started with the descent first, it drew folks into a false sense of what they could accomplish. The hike out was always harder.

The temperature was under seventy right now, but she could

still feel the sweat trickling down her back as she kept up her pace. She had a buff that she'd soaked in water around her neck. She'd heard rattles as snakes fled the vibration of her footfalls, and hooves striking dirt and rock as large mammals heard her approach and turned in the opposite direction. She accidentally stepped in mule dung once, left over from that day's ride back up. She would meet no mules going down, because she would be off the trail before the mule train headed back up from Phantom in the morning. However, the pack mule train would head down around dawn. That would not be a problem for her, either. She'd be down at the inner gorge by then.

She ate as she went, balancing salty foods with taking small sips on her hydration line only to quench her thirst.

The temperature increased the farther down she ventured.

She passed the ominous-sounding Skeleton Point, having shed fourteen hundred feet of elevation since Ooh Aah. She stiffened a bit and slowed her punishing pace, as she heard footsteps approaching from the other way. The trail would really zig-zag now with a long series of switchbacks as it dropped her into the Tonto Plateau.

She had already passed the "tip-off phone," which was a way to call rangers in case you were in trouble. There would not be another such line of communication on her way down.

Though it was far more prominent in the daylight, it had always intrigued Pine how the trail changed color as one went down. This was because the underlying rock changed. She had gone from red to a light brown.

A moment later twin headlamps appeared out of the darkness. Two men.

Pine's hand instinctively went to her Glock.

But the men, one younger and one older—perhaps father and son—passed by with a wave and matching weary smiles.

Their journey was almost over. Hers was just really beginning.

About three miles later, she reached a short tunnel cut into the stone and entered it. Her hand again went to her gun. This would be an ideal place for an ambush.

She left the tunnel and immediately stepped onto the Kaibab Suspension Bridge, more popularly known as the Black Bridge. This was also the mule bridge, because it was the only one the beasts used. It had high chain-link metal sides and a plank floor. The only other bridge in the canyon was the nearby Bright Angel Suspension Bridge, which one reached coming down that counterpart trail. It was known as the Silver Bridge because of its all-metal configuration. The mules didn't like the open metal floor and thus wouldn't walk on it. It had also been built to carry the water lines between the two rims, and Pine thought it might not be strong enough to support ten fifteen-hundred-pound mules and riders at a time, whereas the Black Bridge could.

Before setting foot on the Black Bridge, Pine could have veered west and taken the River Trail over to the Silver Bridge and crossed the Colorado there, but she liked the Black Bridge crossing. There was another reason she was going this way as well.

As she crossed the bridge, she looked down and saw the muddy Colorado roaring beneath her. Locals called that the true *colorado*, because that was the Spanish word for "reddish." Without the complex dam systems that had been constructed around the Canyon, the mighty Colorado would, in certain parts of a drought-filled summer, be little more than puddles. But the dams had regulated the flow to make it more consistent and also to use it for hydroelectric power generation. It was also the reason that rafters could enjoy the challenging rapids. But without the water controls also provided by the dam system, parts of the Colorado could become so dangerous as to be rendered impassable by raft.

And the dam system had contributed to something else. The

silt tended to accumulate behind the dams, resulting in clearer water downriver. The sunlight penetrating the water resulted in algae thriving. And this contributed to the green color of the Colorado, which was quite evident when viewed from higher altitudes.

She left the bridge and took a few minutes to go down to Boat Beach, lie in the sand, and stare at the star-filled sky. This was the other reason she had crossed at the Black Bridge. Pine made a practice of always coming to the beach and "sky staring," and part of her perhaps thought that sticking to this routine would maybe bring her luck. But, then again, in her line of work, you tended to make your own luck by good preparation and even better execution.

But you've never taken on a nuke before, Pine.

She continued on, and the terrain became far more silty and loose, by-products of the water passing nearby. Pine could feel her feet slipping as she made her way forward. It was like walking on a beach, unreliable footing everywhere. That was the last thing she needed after her swift descent, but it wasn't like she could lift off the ground and fly the rest of the way.

To reach Phantom Ranch she would simply follow the trail that would turn to the north. But she was not going to Phantom, where, no doubt, hikers and riders were now slumbering peacefully before their journey back up; she kept following the riverbank.

Bright Angel Creek was just up ahead. As she reached it, she took off her shoes, rolled up her pants, and waded into the shallow water. She sat down on a rock and let the cool water provide an amazing foot massage. The Creek finished its journey right here as it plunged into the Colorado at a spot roughly equidistant between the two bridges. Bright Angel Creek was the place to plop in the water down here if one was so inclined. The Colorado, even in places where it looked to be slow moving, was actually going more than four miles per hour. Few swimmers could fight that current. It was also deep and cold. Some young people had drowned at Boat Beach a number of years ago when they'd tried to swim across it.

Bright Angel had also been the source of a swimming pool at Phantom. Pine had seen old photos of it. It had been located between the amphitheater and the lodge. She knew it had been hand-excavated some time back during the Depression. She didn't know when it had been done away with or why. It was long before her time here.

Also near the amphitheater was the ranger station. She waded out of the water, walked down a bit farther, and took a small footbridge over the creek. After reaching the other side, she dried her feet and put her socks and shoes back on. Kettler said he would be on duty tonight. That meant she was as close to him as she was likely to be down here. It would be good to have a capable man like Kettler with her on this.

But at the last minute, and after additional deliberation, Pine knew she couldn't do that. This was her job, not his. This was her danger to face, not his. If she didn't make it out of here alive, she wasn't going to take the man down with her.

"Take care, Sam," she said to the darkness. "If I don't make it back, don't forget me. At least for a little while."

Okay, Pine, cut the melodramatic crap. You got a nuke to find. God help me.

CHAPTER

52

SHE PASSED a separate mule corral reserved for Park Service use, though she couldn't see any mules in it now. There was also a sewage treatment plant down here. She headed west, with the campground and Phantom to the north of her. In the darkness Pine could make out the outlines of some tents in the distance, and even hear the echoing of late-night conversation among some of the campers. She walked for a time, her trekking poles methodically tapping the ground as she went. She used them even on level ground. Her knees, back, and hips would thank her later.

After a bit, she slowed her pace and then stopped.

She sat on a rock after checking it for scorpions and snakes. The noise from the river would mask anyone approaching, which she didn't like but could do nothing about. There were many things one could do nothing about down here. In the Canyon, the environment was the master; humans were merely visiting.

She switched off her headlamp, and ate and drank, replenishing her electrolytes and satisfying her belly. She'd brought her filter with her, and she knew sources of water in the area she was headed to. She took off her shoes again and rubbed her socked feet. The pace down had been hard, but she was supremely fit and had come out in good shape. However, climbing out, particularly if she had to match her pace going down, would be a whole other experience.

Hopefully, she would not have to sprint the whole way with a regiment of bad guys chasing her.

She checked her illuminated compass, because being down here at dark was like being on the water at night. Land and sea looked a lot alike. You had to rely on your instruments. And she had now turned away from the river, so she couldn't simply follow its contours.

She checked her hiking watch, which also had a thermometer.

Nearly eighty degrees. That meant the next day would be a scorcher. Certainly not unheard-of for this time of year. She had trekked down Bright Angel once, arriving at Indian Garden, which was roughly the halfway point. Along with potable water, restrooms, and shade, there was a thermometer. That day it had registered 105 degrees. There was a sign next to the thermometer that read, YOUR BRAIN ON SUN. At the bottom of the Canyon, the temperature had climbed to nearly 120. She had arrived drenched in sweat, and dehydrated, though she'd eaten and had water and sports drinks all the way down. She'd lain in the shallow part of the creek for about a half hour before she felt like standing once more.

She looked around into the dark. Out there were many beautiful things. Flowers, trees, animals, rock configurations, things you might not ever see anywhere else, no matter how hard and long you looked. But there were also many things out there that could kill you. And one had to respect that.

As she sat there, Pine felt even warmer. The Canyon sometimes felt like a convection oven. The heat seemed to hit you from all directions. Even from inside. Pine looked up. Though the Canyon was nearly eighteen miles at its widest point, the sky was narrowed by the towering walls.

With her index finger she traced the Milky Way. Constellations always gave her comfort. They were always in the same place when you looked up. They were like a friend keeping watch over you.

If only.

She rested for about an hour and then checked the sky again.

The rule of thumb in the Canyon was that night came fast and the dawn arrived slow.

Both results were caused by the Canyon's massive walls. It was like being surrounded by a sea of five-thousand-foot-high skyscrapers.

She pointed her headlamp on the paper map she had pulled from her coat pocket. It had been on the flash drive. She had already roughly calculated the location of what she hoped would be the cave Roth was looking for down here. She put the paper away, studied her compass, and did some math in her head.

Finished, she sat there and took in the surroundings, steeling herself for what was to come.

Pine had been hiking near the river once when she'd seen something metallic partially submerged in the silt in a shallow part of the Colorado. She'd managed to get it out using one of her trekking poles. It was a long cylinder, and the water had very nearly removed all signs of what it was.

Very nearly.

When she examined it more closely, Pine discovered it was a can of Heineken beer. She had no idea how long it had been in the water after it had no doubt fallen off a passing raft. That day it had been nearly a hundred degrees on the Canyon floor. She'd popped the Heineken open and drunk it. It was the coldest and best-tasting beer she'd ever had.

She resettled on the task at hand. If there was a nuke down here, how had Roth planned to get it out—if that was his plan?

He'd traveled by mule far to the west of either bridge that one needed to cross over the river. And the North Kaibab Trail, which led to the North Rim, was far longer than the trails from the south, nearly fourteen miles from the trailhead to Phantom Ranch.

Pine looked out to the west. The Hermit Trail was in this direction. Not in nearly as good a condition as Kaibab and Bright

Angel, it was actually designated as an unmaintained trail by the Park Service. Yet there you ran into the same problem: Roth was on the north side of the Colorado and the Hermit Trail was on the south side. And there was no way to cross the river, allowing him to access Hermit Trail.

And how heavy was a nuke anyway? Could you carry the damn thing out? Didn't they weigh thousands of pounds?

But maybe that wasn't Roth's plan. Maybe he was just down here to disarm it, where it was. And then alert folks to it.

She looked upward.

Or how about a chopper to take it and him out?

Much farther down the river there was a put-in and take-out helipad spot for tourists called the Whitmore Helipad. It was mostly used for those coming from the Vegas area. But that was the West Rim of the Canyon, near Black Canyon, which was nearly a hundred miles from where Pine currently was. Roth could never have made it that far with a nuke.

So a chopper flying in here after dark would have to come across one of the rims, dip downward, fly between the Canyon walls, and then land at a designated spot, pick up Roth and the bomb, and head back out. If they were spotted, the Park Service might have sent up a chopper of its own or at least contacted local and federal authorities to find out what was going on. But a chopper designed for nighttime excursions over rough, enclosed terrain would certainly be up to the task.

Maybe a military-style chopper? Like the one that had taken away the Priest brothers? Was that why the Army was involved? Were they looking for the nuke, too? Was Roth actually working with them? Should she hike back up and go to them with what she knew?

But Pine knew this really wasn't an option. Her fellow feds had been acting weird on this all the way through. The two guys at the airport, if they were feds—and she strongly suspected that was the case—were planning to murder them.

I can't trust my own people.

It was a gut-wrenching admission.

She hiked to the spot where they had found Sallie Belle. The ground was fairly level here, and there was clearly enough room for a chopper to land. She looked around for evidence of damage or disruption caused by the chopper's skids or its prop wash. The thing was, in the Canyon things settled back down, or critters came out and made marks and moved things around. Plants grew, water trickled, the wind blew, the rains washed away traces.

There was nothing.

She looked due west, and then to the north.

One would think that every inch of the Canyon had been explored by now, but Pine knew that the vast majority of visitors saw the Canyon only from the South Rim. And from that vantage point, only about 4 percent of the Canyon was visible. The folks who ventured down here had permits to camp in certain spots, and they were told to keep to certain well-marked trails. Almost none of them ventured out into the wild. Even the rafters would go only so far up any of the side canyons, because it was damn rugged and snakes and other biting creatures lurked everywhere. Pine had one ranger tell her that while he'd been there thirty years, he'd only set foot on a small portion of the Canyon.

Pine felt her spirits collapse. Was her plan getting chewed up in the face of the reality on the ground? Did she really think she was going to come down here and, in just a few hours, find Roth and the cave and the nuke?

But she shook off these thoughts and regrouped.

Side canyon. It had to be a side canyon where Roth would have gone. That actually would line up with the navigation points on the flash drive.

She checked her watch. Another hour before the light would start coming. She set out.

The Canyon flattened out near the Colorado; the river had seen to that, of course. Yet when one veered away from the water, the land quickly steepened and there were a great many side canyons down here.

Thirty minutes later she reached the first one. After exploring it as best she could by foot, she pulled out a pair of night optics from her pack and surveyed the rest of the area.

The next moment Pine went into a crouch and slipped her Glock from its holster while she trained her optics onto the entrance to the side canyon.

She had heard the clink of boots on rock.

To her experienced ears, they were not the casual footballs of hikers. The footsteps were too stealthy, not that any sensible hikers would be exploring a side canyon in the middle of the night.

She slid to the right and took up position behind a boulder.

Ten seconds later three men appeared from out of the dark.

She saw them clearly through her optics.

She was pretty sure they weren't rangers.

Pine had seen many rangers.

But she had never seen any of them wearing full body armor and combat helmets, and holding M4 assault rifles.

53

PINE DREW FARTHER back against the rock as the men drew closer.

She silently cursed, because as she crouched there, the dawn was beginning to break over the Canyon. Light coming here could be breathtaking. She had hiked over the Canyon at various places and various times simply to see the sunrise. It was a surreal, one-of-a-kind experience.

Now she hated it, for the first time ever.

She could tell the men were real pros simply by the way they moved over the ground. They worked as a team, spread out, one point, two flanks, and communicating efficiently by hand signals, their gazes scanning all points on the compass, methodical, missing nothing.

And, at some point soon, they would not miss her.

They also had night optics, but their models looked far superior to hers. They were dressed in cammies but were not wearing military uniforms. No insignias, no name tags, no indicia of rank.

But they certainly looked military.

As the light began to deepen and then diffuse, they lifted their optics and trained their eyeballs on the terrain ahead.

Her Glock versus three assault rifles. It would be a short fight. She wondered where they would bury her, if they even bothered with that.

They must have come to the same conclusion that she had: namely that Roth was down here, in one of the side canyons.

And that told Pine something else.

They'd gotten the knowledge of Roth's plan...from Ben Priest. After enhanced interrogation? And what about poor Ed Priest, whose only sin was being Ben Priest's concerned sibling?

As Pine focused on the M4s coming her way, she slipped out her phone. One of the major carriers had put a tower in the park, and its customers sometimes could get reception. Well, Pine was a customer.

"No Service" was displayed across the top of her phone screen.

Note to self: If you get out of this alive, cancel your fucking provider contract.

She stiffened as the man on the point reached up and pulled a small communication unit that was Velcroed to his armor. He spoke into it and then listened to the response.

Okay, he's probably got secure satellite communication down here. He would probably have it in Siberia, or Antarctica, too.

If these guys weren't American military or CIA paramilitary, she wasn't sure who they were. The fact that they probably served the same country as she did brought her no comfort. Those had been feds back at Simon Russell's house, too. And they were planning to fly him to a place where torture was considered perfectly legal.

Based on that, Pine believed if she stepped out and flashed her FBI creds they would probably just shoot her in the head. And then shoot her a second time just to be sure.

The point guy put his comm unit away and motioned to the other two men. They turned around and made their way out of the side canyon.

Pine breathed a sigh of relief and then looked to the sky.

The breaking dawn, she knew, had probably just saved her butt. They were as afraid of the coming light as she was. They had probably been searching down here all night.

She wondered where they were camping out. Or was a chopper shipping them in and out? Ordinarily, that was not permitted under the prevailing laws and regulations enforced by the Park Service.

She assumed those laws and regulations had been overruled by a far higher power.

That sent a chill right down her spine.

She waited another thirty minutes before coming out of her hiding place, just to be sure. Then she set up camp behind the cover of a large rock outcrop that also provided some shade.

It was going to get blisteringly hot down here shortly. She had earlier located her water source, then refilled her hydration pack and a second CamelBak bladder after filtering the water. She sat in the shade, and ate and drank until she was satisfied, but no more than that. The heat crept up on you. You simply felt warm one minute, and then sick, dizzy, and disoriented the next. It could take hours or even days to recover, a luxury Pine did not have.

The presence of the three M4 guys here told Pine that they didn't have Roth. And they weren't down here looking for her, because they could have no idea she was even here. Were they looking for the nuke, too? But how did that make sense? Roth was a respected WMD inspector. Why wouldn't he be working *with* the government to get the sucker out of here? This whole thing was as muddied as the Colorado River.

She endured the stifling heat, taking catnaps and keeping her hydration levels up.

Part of her wanted to get up and continue her search for Roth during the daylight. But her good sense made her stay where she was. If the brutal heat didn't get her, the three guys with assault weapons might. Better to do her searching at night.

The day passed and darkness fell swiftly, as it tended to do on the floor of the Canyon.

Pine awoke for the last time around nine. She checked the sky and her brow furrowed.

This time of year, the monsoons would draw on the energy built during the heat of the day, combined with the layers of moisture from the southeast, to create some truly remarkable thunderstorms. Well, it looked to Pine like tonight she would be the recipient of such a meteorological vortex.

She put on a water-resistant poncho and made sure her backpack was zipped tightly. She carried it with her, because to leave it on the ground would invite attacks from squirrels, mice, and other rodent types. And they could chew through steel, given time. At the campsites, the Park Service had metal bars hung up high to hang your gear on for that very reason.

She barely had time to take cover before the first streak of lightning seared across the heated sky. The following thunderclap seemed to shake the very insides of the Canyon.

With the second thunderclap came the rains. Or water bullets, to be more accurate, because the velocity was enough to actually be painful when they struck you.

The boulder above Pine's head provided some cover until the wind picked up and drove the rain horizontally. She turned her face away from the driving water. The temperatures had dropped a bit, but it wasn't like on the rims, where a pop-up storm could drop the mercury by twenty degrees in minutes. She was sweating even though she was drenched.

The storm passed in a half hour and the sky cleared.

Now she could get to work. Checking her compass, she set off.

The second side canyon loomed ahead of her about an hour later.

It was nearing midnight. She used her night optics to make her way over very rough terrain. There were no marked trails or warning signs here. She doubted any hiker had been here in a long time.

She worked her way slowly along, looking for snakes and other dangers. She didn't want to get wedged in somewhere with the result that they found her body weeks, months, or years later.

People had gone missing here only to have their skeletons found a long time later. And if you died out here, the scavengers would move in swiftly. Before you were dead, actually. Why wait on a good meal?

She had been on the alert for the M4 gents all night, but luckily had not run into them.

She had gone over as much of the side canyon as she feasibly could, and it was growing light.

The result: nothing. No cave, no crevice, no David Roth and a neighborhood nuke.

She hiked on and made her camp near the next canyon she would explore. It was shielded from prying eyes, but it was reasonably high ground and gave her a good view of the area. She had some breakfast and water and dozed off for a bit. When she woke a few hours later she again debated whether to commence her search during the daylight.

Then she heard choppers overhead.

She looked up and recognized the tourist birds flying over above the rims. By law they couldn't drop below the rims, but someone could still spot her. That confirmed Pine's decision to confine her searches to the nighttime.

She sat at her camp, munching on some nuts and jerky and sipping her filtered water. She was hot, and she had lost weight, and she felt stiff and sore from basically sleeping on rocks.

She leaned back against an outcrop, closed her eyes, and tried to rest. With her days and nights reversed, her body rhythms had been turned topsy-turvy. It was throwing everything off, but she had no way to correct that.

She had a phone power pack, which did her no good, since she had no bars.

"No Service" on her phone screen had been the most consistent thing about this trip.

In the shade, she decided to take off some layers and looked down at her arms, bare except for the tats. She rubbed her fingers across the name Mercy. She traced each letter with her finger. She remembered quite clearly the day—or rather, night—she had gotten them. She had done her shoulders a few months after her arms.

The tat artist was good and made no objection when she told him what she wanted. He'd also asked no questions about the genesis of the inking she wanted.

"Works for you, works for me," he'd said. "It's your skin, not mine."

His name had been Donny. He'd been tall and far too thin. He later told her he'd been a meth addict for years.

"Kills the appetite, I can tell you that. More than cigarettes. Kicked the habit, but never got my appetite back."

Pine checked her supplies. She had to consider the long hike back to Bright Angel from where she was now. And then it would be a challenging hike out, considering how much ground she'd covered so far. She had the supplies to search one more side canyon tonight. Then she would have to head back.

Well, Pine thought, as she waited for the darkness to fall, the third time was always the charm, wasn't it?

54

For the first time since seeing the M4 guys, her optics fastened on something of interest. She had awoken while it was still light and decided to venture a little into the side canyon. The sun was high in the sky, powerful enough to reach into the depths of the Canyon like a trillion-watt light dumped into the ocean.

And, right now, that sunlight was catching on something farther up the side canyon.

She looked to the left and right to gain some plot points to help her locate it later. She was tempted to try now, only it was brutally hot, there was little wind, and it looked to be quite a hike. And it was still daylight. It seemed to be something metallic. And she assumed it wasn't a beer can. At least she hoped it wasn't.

She kept staring at it through her optics, memorizing every detail of the path she would take. At night, things looked different. She couldn't afford to lose the spot when she made her attempt later. Fortunately, there was a very unusual rock configuration to the immediate right of the reflection.

She returned to her camp, and ate and drank and daydreamed that come nightfall she would find Roth.

And the bomb.

Or maybe I'm wrong about all of this. And I'll find nothing. So, what will my second career be after the FBI cans my ass?

The fact was, this was way out of her league. She was an FBI agent. Give her a bank robbery, a kidnapping, even a serial killer or two, and she would do fine. She would catch her man.

This was not that.

She closed her eyes, then swiftly opened them.

No, this is not a dream. This might be the end of the world if that nuke goes off.

She forced herself to sleep, but set an automatic alarm clock in her head. She awoke at eleven p.m. ready to roll.

Pine was climbing over several large rocks when she heard a rattle that froze her for an instant, but then she kept going.

She reached a plateau and looked around, and then down. She figured she had scaled close to a thousand feet.

The odd rock assemblage she had seen during the day presented itself to her through her night optics. She hurried toward it. Was the Holy Grail lurking just up ahead? Or would it be something totally and completely unconnected to her search?

Please, God, if you can get reception down here, make it the former.

She stiffened and then halted as she drew closer.

The light *had* been reflecting off something metallic.

It was a pole. A long, collapsible pole that was leaning up against a round boulder taller than Pine and more than three times her width.

As she grew closer, Pine noted something truly astonishing. Camouflage netting was hanging off the rock wall. She wouldn't have noticed it except for being this close. It perfectly blended in with the surroundings.

She gripped one edge of the covering and tugged. She peered through the opening this created.

Pine gasped.

A cave. She glanced at her compass. This spot was well within the parameters left on the flash drive. Had she just found Roth? And the bomb?

She let the cover fall back into place, took a step back, and peered around. There was no evidence that anyone had been here. But somebody had to have put up the covering. About thirty seconds went by as she contemplated what to do.

Pine heard nothing, no boot hitting rock. No squawks from a comm pack. No heavy breathing.

She heard nothing until the light hit her and the man said, "Turn around very slowly. Do not let your hand go anywhere near your weapon or we will open fire."

"I'm FBI. I'm going to show you my creds."

His next words hit her like one of Chung's massive kicks.

"Don't bother, Agent Pine. Turn around and keep your hands away from your weapon. Do it!"

She slowly turned, her hands held up near her chest, but no higher. She wasn't preparing to draw down like they were standing in the middle of the OK Corral. But her hands fully up in the air would signal complete surrender. She was an FBI agent. She wasn't surrendering to these guys, whoever the hell they were.

And it indeed did appear to be the same three men from the other night.

"What are you doing down here?" barked Pine.

"I don't see you having the leverage to ask us questions," said the man.

"I've got a federal badge, that leverage enough for you? And you guys are Army."

"Why, just because we have cammies on?"

"More than that. You're outfitted in ACU, Army Combat Uniforms."

He shrugged. "Hell, you can buy those uniforms on eBay."

"But not ones with the Operational Camouflage Pattern. That's very recent. And you're armed with M4s."

The man took a step closer. "What are you doing here?"

"I imagine I'm doing the same thing you're doing. Looking for somebody."

"Who would that be?"

"Do we really have to play this crappy game?"

"Who would that be?" he asked again.

"That would be 'kiss my ass.' Now let me ask you a question. How did you find me?"

"We *found* you the first day you came down. We've been following you."

"Bullshit. I spotted you going up a side canyon. You turned back because it was getting light."

"We turned back before we could stumble right over you. You were behind a boulder, crouching down, your pistol aimed at us. Probably thinking that a Glock against three M4s was not going to end well. For you."

Pine looked up into the sky. "You got sat eyes all the way down here?"

"No, we just know how to track people." He held up his weapon. "You ever been shot with one of these?"

"No, nor do I want to be. So you were following me. Why?"

"Pretty obvious. If you knew where Roth was, you'd lead us to him. After that my orders are to intercept. That's why we're here."

"Okay, you intercepted. What's the rest of the order?"

The man shrugged and attempted a smile, but it got nowhere near the rest of his face and he quickly let it fall.

Pine looked around at the men. They looked to be late twenties, early thirties. Definitely old enough to have been in wars, killed, maybe been wounded. Hardened guys, guys you'd want on your side in a fight.

Only, apparently, they're not on my side.

"Have you been told what's going on here? What's really going on? What this shit is all about?"

"We know enough to do our job. We don't need any more than that."

"That's another way of saying you're burying your head in the sand."

She never once looked at the camouflage netting, hoping beyond hope that they hadn't noticed it.

"You're going to need to come with us, ma'am."

"You got a chopper? Is that your in-and-out method? Saves a lot of time over hiking this sucker."

"Just come with us."

"I'm not going anywhere with you. I'm a federal agent. You can't order me to do anything. So back the hell away before I call in reinforcements."

The man looked around and lightly shook his head, his eyes filled with mirth. "I don't see that you have any backup. And your phone doesn't work down here."

"Back the hell away."

"We have other orders in the event you refused to come with us."

"What's that, shoot me? I'm an FBI agent."

"No, ma'am, right now, you're just an enemy of this country."

"How the hell do you figure that? We *work* for the same country."

"Are you going to come with us? Last call."

The two other soldiers raised their M4s and took aim. One for her head, the other the torso.

Nonsurvivable.

"This is nuts," barked Pine. "I'm a federal agent. Lower your weapons and stand down. Now."

"No can do, ma'am. Last call. Three seconds."

Pine stood there frozen. They were really going to execute her, right on the floor of the Grand Canyon.

She made to reach for her Glock. She might be able to get off one shot.

Good-bye to everybody who cares. I'm coming, Mercy.
Shit.

The round fired. And then a second.

It had happened so fast that Pine thought she had taken both impacts.

The two guys behind the point man flinched, stiffened, and then both fell forward.

Point Man whirled, his weapon aimed on his target.

"No!" screamed Pine, drawing her weapon. "Drop it, drop it or I will fire."

The M4 barked at the same time Pine pulled the Glock's trigger once, her laser sight dead on the back of the guy's neck.

Point Man dropped.

Pine, her hands shaking, slowly lowered her weapon.

Twenty yards away, Sam Kettler stared wildly at her. He was carrying a backpack and there was a pistol in his hand.

Pine looked down at the three dead bodies. Two had been shot by Kettler, one by her.

"Shit," she hissed. "They were our guys. At least I think they were."

Kettler scrambled forward. "Funny way of showing it. They were going to kill you."

She looked up at him. "What are you doing here?"

He pointed at the men. "I've watched a chopper come in the last three nights. I finally decided to do something about it. I grabbed my go pack, picked up their trail, and followed them up here. And saw what they were about to do to you." He looked down at his gun and shook his head. "Why the hell are American soldiers down here in the first place?"

"It's a long story." She reached out and gripped his arm. "Thanks for saving my life."

"Well, you saved mine. The guy had me lined up for the kill. If you hadn't fired and spoiled his aim, I'd have had an M4 round right through me."

She removed her hand from his arm and steadied herself against a rock outcrop.

"You okay?" he asked.

"I'm getting there," she said, taking several deep breaths.

He shot her a glance. "And what are you doing all the way out here? You're not just hiking, that's for sure."

"I'm looking for the missing guy. They were, too."

"You think he's around here? Why?"

"Again, long story." She looked at the bodies. "We have to do something. We can't just leave them here." She looked around. "But this is, well, I guess it's a crime scene. We can't disrupt anything." She rubbed her forehead. "I need to call in a team. I need to secure the area. I...I need...." Her mind was swirling with so many competing thoughts Pine thought she might puke.

Kettler drew closer to her and gripped Pine's arm. "What you need to do is just take a few more deep breaths and give yourself a little time. You were almost killed, Atlee."

"I just shot an Army guy, Sam!"

"Well, I just shot *two* of them."

While Pine was regaining her composure, Kettler spotted the cammie blanket. He moved it aside and saw the cave opening. "Damn, where did that come from?"

"It might be what I was looking for."

"Well, I can put the bodies in there for now."

"I'll help."

"Then we can call in reinforcements."

"No. We have to locate something else first."

"What's that?"

"You'll find out soon enough."

55

THEY CARRIED THE BODIES into the cave and set them down in a corner.

Pine checked them for any ID, but they had none. And no tags on their uniforms.

Kettler said, "Are you sure they're regular Army?"

"I'm not sure of anything right now."

She shone her light around. The cave was large. The ceiling she estimated was about fifteen feet high. A shade darker area near the rear might have been a passageway to another room, but she couldn't be sure.

"Okay, you need to tell me what's going on," said Kettler.

In curt, information-packed sentences, she filled him in on pretty much everything. When she was done, Kettler looked like *he* might throw up.

He looked around. "A nuke? In here? Are you shitting me?"

"I wish I were."

He shone his light around. "Well, it's not in this space."

"But it could be back there," she said, motioning to the rear of the cave. "Hit it with your light. It's stronger than mine."

He did so and the opening to a passageway cut into the rock was revealed.

They entered the passage and moved along it single file, with Pine in the lead.

As they walked along, Pine stumbled over something.

Kettler aimed his light down and she heard him suck in a breath. "Trip wire."

Pine said in a panicked voice, "Like tied to an IED?"

"No."

"How can you be sure?"

"Because we'd already be dead."

They moved forward and were about to step into what looked to be a larger cave when a voice called out.

"One more step and you won't be taking another."

"Mr. Roth?" called out Pine.

There was silence for a few moments. "Who are you?"

"Special Agent Atlee Pine with the FBI. I'm here with a park ranger named Sam Kettler. I was investigating the death of a mule and Ben Priest being missing."

A light beam hit them in the face. "Let me see your badges."

They slowly held up their official metal.

"Look, Mr. Roth, I can understand if you don't trust us. Because I'm not sure I trust my own agency right now."

"I want you to turn around and leave here. Now! Or the consequences will not be good for you."

"Mr. Roth, we're here to help. And I'm pretty damn sure you need help."

"I told you to leave. Now."

Pine glanced at Kettler and then called out, "What about the three bodies we just dragged in?"

Roth said nothing for a long moment. "Three bodies?"

"We just *shot* three soldiers who were looking for you. They were going to kill us, even though I showed them my FBI badge. And I'm pretty damn certain that they were going to kill you next. So we just saved your life."

"This...this is..."

"This is a *situation*, Mr. Roth. And we have to confront it. Ben Priest told me a little about it."

"You know Ben?"

"Yes. And I think it was our military who abducted him."

Another moment of silence passed before Roth blurted out, "They took Ben? How?"

"It's a long story. The point is, everything is screwed up."

Roth kept the light in their faces. "How did you find this cave?"

"Coordinates were on a flash drive I found at Ben's home."

"How did you know about me in the first place?"

"Ben didn't give you up, if that's what you were thinking. Oscar Fabrikant told me. I got on to him because Ben was a member of SFG. Are you familiar with that organization?"

"Yes. What else did Oscar tell you?"

"That he was concerned the Russians were involved."

"They *are* involved. But now you have to leave. I can't trust anyone at this point."

"I can't do that, Mr. Roth. I'm here to do my job. And to track down whoever killed Fabrikant."

There was another long pause. "He's—Oscar's dead?"

"His body was found in Moscow. It was ruled a suicide, but I know it wasn't."

"Oscar, dead? I...I can't believe it."

"Can you point the light out of our faces, please?"

The light vanished.

"Will you trust us, Mr. Roth? Because I think we need each other to finish this."

Roth didn't answer.

"Please, Mr. Roth. What can I do to make you trust me?"

Roth said, "What do you think is going on?"

"I think there's a nuke in here. And since my job is to protect the Grand Canyon at all costs, that's not a good thing."

There was another long moment of silence.

"If you turn out not to be who you say you are, it will be the last thing you ever do," he said threateningly.

"Works for me," said Pine.

"Come fully out of the passageway."

They entered the cave, and suddenly the space was illuminated by a light source that they saw was a battery-powered lantern. Roth must have just turned it on.

And behind the illumination was Roth himself. His face was streaked with grime, and the man looked thoroughly exhausted.

Pine tossed him her badge and creds.

He looked them over and then threw them back.

"Everything I've told you is the truth," she said.

Roth slowly nodded. "I believe you. I'm not sure why, but I've gone with my gut before, and I guess I have to now."

"Was that your trip wire back there?" asked Kettler.

"Yes, just a warning for me in case someone stumbled in here."

"So you're armed, then?" said Kettler, looking around.

Roth replied, "You could say that I'm armed all right."

He shone his light on something beside him.

It was rectangular in shape, had a metallic hide, and was about four feet long and three feet tall.

Both Pine and Kettler instinctively shrank back from the thing.

"That's…that's a nuke?" said Pine.

Roth nodded. "And you've just confirmed for me that you're not involved in this plot."

"How?"

"Because you both just looked ready to run for your lives."

"Who wouldn't in the face of a nuclear bomb?" said Pine.

"This is a very special nuclear device," said Roth.

"It doesn't look big enough to be a nuclear bomb," said Kettler. "Is that what they call a suitcase nuke?"

Roth shook his head. "This is a tactical nuclear device. But, it's plenty big enough. I calculate its yield at about the equivalent of nearly three kilotons of TNT. For comparison's sake, the hydrogen bomb dropped over Nagasaki had a yield of over twenty kilotons.

The largest detonation of all was the Tsar Bomba device that the Soviets set off a long time ago. That had a yield of fifty *megatons*. If the Soviets could have put a depleted uranium tamper on the sucker instead of a lead one, it would have doubled the yield." He patted the device. "But for its size, this is the most powerful tactical nuke I've ever seen. It could have taken a huge chunk out of the Canyon and also left the place radioactive for a few thousand years."

"Is it going to detonate?" asked Pine fearfully, taking another step back.

"I shouldn't think so."

"So you defused it?"

Roth shook his head. "You don't really *defuse* a nuke. It's not like a Hollywood movie with the timer counting down and the hero deciding which color wire to cut. If a nuke is going to detonate, the best you can do is take steps to make sure the nuclear chain reaction does not take place. Then it just becomes a big explosion, but not a nuclear one."

"How did it get here?" asked Pine.

Roth waved them forward and pointed at the front metal panel. "Do you see that engraved writing?"

Both Pine and Kettler peered closer. Pine said, "That's Korean?"

"Yes, it is."

"That makes sense. There were plans for a North Korean nuke on the flash drive Priest had."

"I was the one who gave them to him, along with the coordinates of this cave."

Pine stiffened. "So, the North Koreans *are* trying to nuke the Canyon? The peace talks were just a sham on their part?"

"No, of course they're not trying to nuke the Grand Canyon," was Roth's surprising reply.

Pine looked gobsmacked by his reply. Then she said stubbornly, "But there was a man named Sung Nam Chung looking for you. *He* worked for the North Koreans."

"That may well be, but the North Koreans didn't put this here." Roth paused. "*We* did."

The blood slowly drained from Pine's face. "'We'?"

"Well, certain very powerful elements within the U.S. government did so."

"How the hell do you know that!" snapped Kettler. "Our people putting a nuke here? That's nuts!"

"I agree, it is madness. But nevertheless, that's what happened."

"How can you be so sure?" asked Pine.

"Because I recognize the materials from which it was created. It's Russian made."

"But that's Korean writing on the side there."

"Russia supplied North Korea for years with material for making nuclear devices. Some of those materials were used to make this bomb."

"Again, how can you be sure?" persisted Pine.

In answer Roth took a battery-powered screwdriver from a bag set next to the device and unscrewed the top panel of the device. He lifted it off, and held it up.

"The engraved writing on the inside of this panel, what language does that look like to you?"

"It's the Cyrillic alphabet," said Pine, examining it closely. "Russian."

Roth put the panel aside. "That's right. It states the place of origin and the serial number of the part. It's just recycled."

Pine said, "But if Russia supplied North Korea with nuclear material, it would make sense that it would have a Russian imprint. So how can you be sure that North Korea didn't place it here?"

"Because this weapon was going to be the excuse to destroy North Korea. And I doubt very much that they would want to be a party to their own annihilation."

56

PINE AND KETTLER looked at each other and then stared at the nuke.

Pine finally settled her gaze back on Roth. "You're going to have to explain that."

"It's fairly simple. The Russians supplied us with this tactical nuclear weapon, and our country placed it here."

"Why in the hell would our country want to blow up the Grand Canyon?" said Pine.

"This bomb *can't* detonate. Which is the definitive reason I know that the North Koreans did not place it here."

"But how do you know it can't go off?" asked Pine.

"Because it's lacking vital components."

"What components?" asked Kettler.

"I can give you the layman's thumbnail." He pointed to the device. "This is what is termed a fusion bomb, or a thermonuclear weapon. It actually creates its destructive force in much the same way the sun creates energy. A conventional detonation is called the primary stage. That sends the fissionable uranium into a chain reaction, which results in an explosion producing heat at several million degrees. This heat and power is reflected back into the uranium core, which commences the second stage. This phase initiates fusion, and the explosion resulting from this secondary stage destroys the uranium container. The released neutrons then result in the fusion that makes for the thermonuclear event. Do you follow?"

Kettler scratched his cheek. "Damn, if that's the dumbed-down version, I don't want to hear the complicated one."

Roth added, "The parts that were left out include the lithium-six deuteride, a functional reflector, and an appropriate tamper. Without that, you've basically got a pile of uranium and hydrogen atoms with nowhere to go."

"Then what the hell was the purpose of placing it here?" asked Kettler.

Pine answered. "So we could use it as the reason to attack North Korea. That's what Sung Nam Chung meant when he said he agreed with me that if the nuke went off, North Korea would be destroyed. He was trying to find the bomb and stop the plan."

"Only he couldn't know the *real* plan," said Roth. "The bomb was never going to go off, but it nonetheless would be used against North Korea as though it had."

"But if it lacked the vital components, wouldn't that raise suspicions of it being bogus?"

"Who would know that?" countered Roth. "Journalists weren't going to open it up and check the guts. And when they did get around to having 'experts' examine it, they would just tell them that those parts had been taken out *afterward*, just to make sure no accident happened. I can only imagine the media frenzy when the government announced that they'd found this in a cave in the Canyon. They would have choppered this out of the Canyon for all to see on live TV."

"What would they have done after the device was made public?" asked Kettler.

"I think there would have been a presentation at the UN with graphs and slides, and documentation of exactly how the North Koreans had managed to put a nuke in the Canyon. All fabricated, of course, but seemingly all aboveboard and plausible."

"But would it be *plausible* to argue that the North Koreans would plant a bomb on American soil?" said Pine. "They'd know we would destroy them if the truth came out."

"Well, our side would counter that argument by simply saying if the bomb *had* exploded there would have been no evidence left of where it had come from. But if it came out that North Korea had *tried* to detonate a nuke in the heart of America's greatest natural landmark before we found out and put a stop to it? War would have been inevitable."

"And a lot of people would die in a war like that," said Pine.

"It would be long and bloody with human carnage the likes of which we haven't seen since World War II and the Korean War. Literally millions would die. Hundreds of thousands on the very first day."

"My God," said Kettler. "And I thought the wars in Iraq and Afghanistan were bad."

Roth said, "All wars are horrible when it comes to human casualties. I'm sure some wonks in the government have come up with 'exact' numbers of deaths in all categories along with the justification to sacrifice them in such a conflict." He shook his head. "What a business to be in."

"Why would we need the Russians to help us with this?" asked Pine.

"As I said, the Russians have assisted North Korea with their weapons programs for a long time. They had ready access to 'legitimate' fissile materials that our government needed to go through with this plan. The panel with the North Korean characters and the rest? We wouldn't have to fake it since we could have the real thing. Without Russia we would have had to go out and find similar material, or else try to concoct a bogus weapon made to look like a North Korean weapon using materials we could gather here and there. But the nuclear weapons arena is an elite one. There simply aren't that many players. And the ones in that arena are well known, as are their weapons-building signatures. So if we had gone to third-party sources other than Russia, that would have left a trail that would lead right back to us, making the plan a nonstarter from the get-go."

"Okay, but then why would the Russians help us do this?" asked Pine. "What would they get out of it?"

"It would allow them to partner with the world's only superpower. That elevates them to near our status. And Russia wants to be the lead actor in the Far East, but there is no way they can match Beijing's economic machine. Thus, they're looking for other ways to exert influence and have a voice in the region. I would imagine that Russia would be rewarded in some way. Maybe after we won the war, we would annex part or all of North Korea for Russia."

"Like when they split up Germany after World War II?" said Pine.

"Yes. And North Korea has some natural resources—anthracite coal, for example—that Russia could use to bolster its Far East economy." He paused and looked thoughtful. "Who knows, this might be the beginning of some grand bargain between us and the Russians to divvy up parts of the world. I mean that was what the Cold War was about, although America and Russia were adversaries back then."

"We should *still* be adversaries," said Pine.

"But that does not appear to be how things are shaping up right now."

Pine said, "The North Koreans must know something is up. They sent Chung to find out about it. To find you, in fact."

"They would have every incentive to stop it, since their very existence is on the line."

"How did you become involved in this?"

"Fred Wormsley was a dear friend, both of my father and me. He was a mentor."

"I heard that he drowned."

"He didn't drown, he was *murdered*. And he's the reason I'm down here now."

"What do you mean?" asked Pine.

"Before he died, Fred secretly met with me. With his high position at the NSA, he had actually been recruited for this crazy mission. The thing is, you'd think there would be a thousand leaks with something like this. Well, as far as I know, Fred was the only one who stood up to them. But he pretended to be a willing participant, so he could learn all he could about it. But then, somehow, he was betrayed."

"And you took up the fight he couldn't finish," commented Pine.

"After Fred told me what he knew, I set out to get to this nuke. Fortunately, he knew the location of the cave where it had been placed, and he gave me that information. Otherwise, it really would have been impossible to locate, given the size of the Canyon."

"And Ben Priest? What's the connection?"

"Ben had worked for years at the CIA. Then he joined Defense Intelligence. When I was inspecting WMDs in various countries, Ben was working behind the scenes pushing for greater access for my teams. During that time we became good friends. After that he went out on his own. I've never been exactly sure what he was doing then, but he acquired a reputation for assisting people mired in complex situations that required a first-rate knowledge of geopolitics. When I told him about this conspiracy, he was immediately onboard. Ben instantly saw how incredibly foolhardy this plan was. And that it had to be stopped. At all costs."

"Apparently even if it cost him and his brother their lives," noted Pine.

Kettler said, "And what about the mule?"

Roth said, "Actually, the mule *was* the main reason I approached Ben with this. You see, when I learned where the nuclear device was from Fred Wormsley, I recalled that Ben had previously told me about a mule ride he was going to take to the floor of the Canyon. There was no way I could get a mule of my own. You have to reserve your spot over a year in advance. Thus, Ben and I had hatched the plan where I would take his place on the ride down. It was perfect."

"That all makes sense now," said Pine.

"Also, Ben and I hiked down here before I took the mule ride."

"Why?" asked Kettler.

Roth pointed around to the stacks of equipment and what looked to be protective gear piled next to the nuke, along with food and several water bladders. "You can't open up a nuke with a screwdriver and a pair of swim goggles for protection. And, of course, I needed food, water filters, and other supplies. I couldn't carry it down on the mule ride—there are space and weight limits. On the hikes down, we hid all of it near Phantom Ranch. The night I 'disappeared' I used the mule to transport them as close as I could to my final destination. After that, I carried everything to where I needed it to go."

"But why the hell did you kill the mule?" asked Kettler.

"The mule fell over a rock and either went lame or fractured its foreleg. But to tell the truth, I had intended to kill the animal anyway. I had brought an anesthetic with me to humanely accomplish that."

"But why?" persisted Kettler.

Roth spread his hands. "I couldn't bring it with me here. And we were a long way from Phantom Ranch. And the poor animal had no way to get back there. It would have been attacked and killed by predators. I did not want it to suffer."

"And you carved the letters *j* and *k* on its hide," said Pine. "Why do that?"

"There was no guarantee that I was going to come out of this alive, Agent Pine. Being out here solo in the Grand Canyon isn't smart." He looked at Kettler. "I'm sure you warn all tourists not to do what I've done. Come down without any backup and then go off trail."

"That's true," conceded Kettler.

Roth looked back at Pine. "Ben was the only person who knew I was down here. If something happened to him, like you just said it did, then I would have no cover at all. If I died down here, either due to a snakebite or a fall or dehydration, I wanted someone to know that this had to do with something hidden in a cave."

"So you obviously knew about the alleged expedition by Jordan and Kinkaid and the cave they supposedly found?"

"Yes. I actually heard about it from a local when I was hiking down here with the supplies."

"My secretary is local. That's how she knew about it, too."

"It was the only thing I could think of, really, those two letters pointing to a hidden cave in the Canyon."

"Not much of a clue," said Pine. "I was just lucky my secretary knew about it before and put it together."

Roth said defensively, "Well, I couldn't exactly write, 'Hey, there's a nuke in a cave down here.' For all I knew, it would be the people behind this who found the mule. I didn't want to give them a direct map to me. I just did the best I could with what I had."

"But then you rolled the mule over to hide the carving," said Pine. "Why?"

"Because I knew scavengers would come and tear at its hide. The markings would have been destroyed if I had left them exposed."

Pine looked confused. "But the three soldiers were right outside the cave. I thought they would have already been here to take the nuke, since the peace talks have collapsed. And then the media circus would have started."

"I'm certain they would have, too. Except this is *not* the cave where they originally placed the device."

"What?" exclaimed Pine.

"I couldn't leave it there, Agent Pine. So I moved it here."

"You moved that thing? How?"

In answer, Roth hauled out something from a corner that looked like a high-tech backpack combined with an overlay of exoskeleton technology.

"The weapon is not as heavy as you might think. They did a great job of miniaturizing the nuke, which is both impressive and terrifying. Now this is a lifting pack of my own design. I disassembled it, and Ben carried it down on one of his hikes into the Canyon and hid it in one of the caches. I reassembled the lift pack and used that on multiple treks to carry all my supplies onward from where I left the mule. I also used this to lift the weapon and carry it here."

"How did you even know about this cave?"

"Quite simple. Years ago, when I was in my twenties, I used to hike the Grand Canyon on a fairly regular basis. Once I went off the normal trails and stumbled upon this cave. It wasn't that big a deal; there are caves down here, of course. But when I realized that it was close to where they had placed the nuke originally, I hit upon the plan to move it here. I brought a collapsible pole with me to lever a nearby boulder into place to hide the entrance whenever I left the cave."

"But why would you leave the cave while you were down here?" asked Pine.

This time Kettler answered. "You've been down here for many days. You needed water."

"Yes," said Roth. "There was a source nearby and I had my filters. And some of the battery packs for my power tools were solar. I had to place them outside to let them recharge." He paused. "Unfortunately, I had to leave it open when I was inside. But I used the camouflage blanket that I brought with me to hide the entrance. I used the boulder when I was out of the cave to prevent anyone from sneaking past the blanket and surprising me when I came back."

"So you've been working on this thing all this time?" said Pine.

"Tearing down and then putting back together a nuclear weapon, especially by yourself, is a slow, laborious process."

"I'm surprised they didn't have armed guards around that cave twenty-four/seven," said Pine. "That way neither you nor anyone else could have gotten close to it."

"They couldn't," said Roth. "Suspicions would grow if soldiers were seen *guarding* a cave in the Canyon. Their plan would have been disrupted. Timing was everything."

"It was probably timed with the collapse of the peace talks," said Pine. "Once those fell apart, they could execute their plan."

"And if anyone had spotted armed guards around the cave before then, they would be hard-pressed to argue that they had *suddenly* stumbled on the location of the nuke," said Roth. He smiled broadly. "I would have liked to have seen their faces when they went to their cave and found their nuke gone."

"So you moved the nuke from the place they planted it to here. And those soldiers were searching all around here trying to locate it, and you."

"That is no doubt accurate," said Roth.

"They said they were following me, hoping I would lead them to you. Which I did."

"Fortunately, you were able to stop them before they got to me." Roth paused and shuddered. "Still, we came very close to the precipice."

Pine said, "We're *still* very close to the edge." She looked at the nuclear weapon. "What was your plan?"

"I was going to document everything. Then I was going to leave the nuke here after walling the cave back up and then hike out and make known what I had discovered, *without* disclosing the location of the nuke. I had just finished all that when you showed up."

"But they could just come here and search for the nuke, and

they might eventually find it. And then go on with their plan. And if you protested, or tried to blame them, they'd just say you were crazy, or a traitor. Or you might even disappear."

"But it's not like I could hike out of here by myself with a nuke."

"Maybe we could use a Park Service chopper?" suggested Kettler.

Pine shook her head. "No, I'm sure they're watching all channels like that. And the Park Service has already been called off. Remember what happened to Lambert and Rice."

Kettler said, "Well, we can't just leave it. It might not detonate, but aren't there radioactive elements in there?"

Roth nodded. "In the core, yes. And that *is* problematic, if the device is damaged."

Pine walked over to the nuke and looked it over. "You said the Russians supplied this?"

"Yes."

"The thing is, if I'm them, I'd want something more than a vague promise from us about getting North Korean coal."

Roth came to stand next to her. "What do you mean?"

"Did you find anything on here that you couldn't account for?"

"Account for?"

"You know WMDs, Mr. Roth. Was there something on here you didn't recognize?"

Roth glanced at the weapon. "Well, there were these."

He pointed to rows of small rivets that were punched into the metal panels. "These are on all four sides. I thought maybe they were for structural support. But it really wouldn't be needed."

Pine felt along the inside of the wall and rapped on it with her knuckles. "It's hollow."

Roth glanced at the wall and frowned. "I really hadn't focused on that."

Pine hit each rivet with her Maglite, slowly examining each one as she circled the device. When she was done, she said, "There's one 'rivet' on each side that's a little bit off in appearance." She pointed to one spot. "Can you cut out a section of the metal right here?"

Roth made the cut. Revealed behind the wall was a small electronic device.

Roth said, "What the hell is that?"

"What kind of car do you drive?"

"I have a Mercedes S-class. But what does that have to do with it?"

"You know the round little discs set into the frame all around your car?"

Roth looked at the revealed device in the wall of the bomb. "Those are cameras. Are you saying this is some sort of camera?"

"Yes." She held up the metal piece he had cut out. "And this is the lens disguised as a rivet. It probably has a listening device built in, too."

"But why would that be here?" asked Kettler.

"I worked a case when I was at the WFO. It dealt with a Russian spy ring. I even traveled to Ukraine during the course of the investigation. We were told that our hotel room would be under surveillance and to act accordingly. I slept in my clothes and never used my phone in the room. I never even spoke out loud. The Russians love surveillance stuff. When we were building an embassy over there once, we made the mistake of using Russian subcontractors. The entire embassy turned out to be one big camera and recorder. Luckily, we found out in time."

"But why would the Russians have surveillance devices on this weapon?" asked Roth.

"They used them to record *our* people placing the bomb here, not the North Koreans. The surveillance footage I'm sure has already been uploaded to a Russian database."

"Holy shit," said Kettler. "So you're saying—"

"I'm saying that if we started a war on bogus evidence and killed millions of people—"

Kettler finished for her. "—the Russians would have rock-solid proof that we were guilty of the whole thing and had lied to the world."

Pine added, "It's what they call *kompromat*. How much do you think the Russians could blackmail us for in return for keeping that secret?"

Roth slumped back against the rock wall. "Anything they wanted."

"Right."

Roth suddenly stared in horror at the device. In a whisper he said, "Do you think they're still watching and listening right now?"

"Highly unlikely. You can't get Wi-Fi or even cell service down here. And no satellite signal would reach through this much rock."

"But then how would they have gotten compromising information?" asked Roth.

"They got it long before the nuke ever got to this cave. It had to be delivered to the Americans and then shipped here. They might have audio and video of American officials receiving it, and then our guys, maybe ones in uniform, loading it onto a plane, bringing it to Arizona, and then maybe transporting it by chopper here. Lots of video and audio of our country up to its neck in this thing." She glanced at the nuke. "But to be sure, let's disable the other devices."

Roth took up his saw once more, and with Pine and Kettler's help, he cut the other devices out of the walls of the nuke.

Pine placed them all in her backpack.

"So what do we do now?" asked Roth.

"Contrary to what you said earlier, we're going to hike this nuke out of here," said Pine firmly.

"Why?" said Roth.

"Because now that we know about the surveillance devices, we can use that as leverage."

"How?" asked Roth.

Before she could answer, they all heard the sound.

"What's that?" said Kettler suddenly.

They ran back out into the first cavern. The sounds were much more prominent now.

"That's a chopper," said Roth tensely.

"And I don't think it's coming to rescue us," said Pine.

57

Pɪɴᴇ ᴘᴇᴇʀᴇᴅ ᴀʀᴏᴜɴᴅ the edge of the opening and through the camouflage covering. "There's a light flicking over the rock. They must know this was the last place the search team was."

They waited for a few minutes until the chopper passed over the ridge and was gone.

"Okay, we need to get going," said Kettler, firmly taking charge.

He ran over to the dead men and relieved two of them of their M4s and extra ammo clips. "You got optics?" he asked Pine. She nodded. "Keep a watch on the chopper and the light. They'll make several passes. If they don't see anything, they'll move on to another grid."

"Based on your experience?" said Pine.

"The Army has a way of doing things, the *same* way."

Pine rushed off to do this.

Roth said to Kettler, "But we can't climb out of here with the nuke. It's too heavy to carry all that way. It was hard enough taking it from the other cave to this one."

"We *can* do it if we all take turns," said Kettler. "And use the lifting thing you brought."

"But what about Agent Pine?" said Roth.

"Hell, she's probably stronger than both of us put together. Now come on."

They raced back into the other space, and Kettler helped Roth enclose the nuke in a large camouflage bag Roth had brought down. Kettler took off his go pack and said, "I'll carry it first. Show me how the lift thing works."

Roth helped Kettler into the apparatus and then had Kettler back up to the nuke and squat down. Roth strapped in the nuke to the lifting pack.

"Okay, the pack's pulley and weight redistribution systems and the exoskeleton's battery-powered features will carry about fifty percent of the load. That makes what you're carrying about seventy pounds or so. It's not that bad."

"My ruck in the Army was eighty pounds. So, no problem."

Kettler slowly stood and steadied himself. "Okay."

They moved back out into the main cave area.

"What's the status?" he called out to Pine, who still stood by the opening.

"It's starting to make one more pass," she said. "Hold on." About thirty seconds elapsed after the sounds of the chopper materialized once more. Then, the engine and prop noise started to filter away.

"Okay, it looks like they've moved on."

Kettler explained the plan to Pine.

She glanced at her watch. "It's two in the morning. There's no way we're going to hike out of here before dawn, especially carrying that thing. And they might be waiting at the top of every trail anyway."

"Every corridor trail, but probably not every *threshold* or *primitive* trail," said Kettler, using the Park Service's technical designation terms for trails in the canyon.

"What's that mean?" said Roth.

Pine looked at him. "They're not maintained. So they're a lot more difficult."

"Harder than the trail I came down on the mule?" he said.

Kettler nodded. "Yes, by quite a factor. And the one closest to us is actually a combination of *two* trails. The trailhead lets off on the North Rim. Near a Forest Service Road. It's not a primitive trail, it's a threshold, but, it's still very challenging. At least it's not the Nankoweap Trail. I've done that twice and it's a bitch. A lot of the trail is like inches away from thousand-foot-or-more drops. Definitely not for the fainthearted. But the trail we'll be going on has some of those, too."

Pine said, "Do we have the necessary equipment to do that?"

He held up his go pack. "In here I have climbing ropes and D-links. If we rope all three of us together?"

She looked at Roth. "You good with that?"

"I'm good," he said. "Like I said, I've hiked these trails before."

"Right," said Kettler. "But not like the one we're going up."

Roped together, they hiked east to the trail and started up. Roth was roped in between Pine and Kettler, who knew the trail and was thus in the lead.

"You good with that load?" Pine asked Kettler.

"Yeah."

"Okay, but we'll switch out every two hours."

They followed the contour of the Colorado until they reached a creek flowing directly into the river. Kettler located the first cairn, a stack of stones wired together, marking the entrance to the trail. They had not gone very far before they reached a climb point where the creek was quite high. Pine could see that Roth was struggling with both the pace and the terrain.

She jogged ahead and caught up to Roth.

"Okay, this might get a little dicey, so we're going to do this the smart way."

She called out to Kettler, who quickly joined them. Despite Roth's objections, they used the rope to help him over the ascent and also to make it through part of the creek overflow. Pine grabbed his belt and pulled him over the final hurdle, where he lay wet and breathless at their feet.

"Okay," said Roth. "I might have overestimated my climbing

abilities. I'm not in my twenties anymore. And, to be honest, the hikes I did with Ben kicked my ass."

Pine said, "Don't worry, we're going to get you out of here."

They started climbing a half hour later, after Roth was sufficiently rested and Pine had taken over carrying the nuke pack. The trail was crumbling in some parts and nonexistent in other parts.

Pine noted the growing anxiety in Roth's features as the path became steeper and increasingly twisty. She patted him on the shoulder as they finished a particularly vicious part. "You're doing fine, Mr. Roth."

"I'm David. With the situation we're in, I think we've earned the right to use first names."

"I'm Atlee and he's Sam."

Roth managed a weak smile, but the anxious look remained on his features.

They made good time. Pine checked her watch. Dawn would be coming soon.

"What's that sound?" asked Roth anxiously.

"The falls," replied Kettler. "Coming off the river up here. The river turns south into the creek we crossed, and then it ends at the Colorado. Watch your footing. It gets a little slick up here."

They made their way across a broad valley. After that, some nasty switchbacks appeared, which they had to traverse.

Pine called out, "Sam, I think we need to stop and rest."

Kettler looked back at Roth, who was looking exceedingly unsteady on his feet. "Right."

They made camp, digging into the cliffs as much as they could. They set the nuke pack against the side of the mountain, as far away from the edge as possible.

After they'd eaten and hydrated, Roth fell asleep on a thin sleeping bag that Kettler had laid out for him. They were on the northwestern side of the Canyon, so the dawn would be coming to them more slowly than if they'd been on the eastern end.

The pair sat there with their backs against the rock, the M4s in hand.

"You think he'll be okay?" asked Kettler.

"I don't know. I figure he's about fifteen or maybe even twenty years older than us, and he's not used to this. And he's been down here a long time. It takes it out of you, as you well know. But he did carry that pack all the way to the other cave. That was no mean feat."

"Right."

"You want to get some shut-eye, I can keep watch," offered Pine. Kettler shook his head. "I'm good."

They fell silent.

"So, the fate of the world hangs on, what, us?" said Kettler.

"Apparently so."

"Really not what I signed up for, joining the Park Service."

"Well, it's what *I* signed up for," replied Pine.

He turned to her and smiled. "I'm glad you're here, Atlee. If it were just me and Roth, I might be freaking out."

"No, you'd be doing just what you're doing: what it takes to complete the mission." She paused. "But if you weren't here, I think *I'd* be freaking out."

Kettler stared out at the rock walls surrounding them. "You know there are five ecological life zones in the Canyon? The same number you'd get going from Mexico all the way to Canada."

She glanced at him. "You're just a font of Grand Canyon trivia."

"I go to a place, I find out about it. Just how I'm wired."

"Can we try to hike some more before it gets too hot?" she asked.

"Not much shade on this trail. And the day looks like it's going to get warm really fast. You and I can do it, but I doubt he can. And we go up much farther, there's really no cover. And it gets steep with a lot of switchbacks."

"And if the chopper comes back, we'd be easy targets."

"So, night then? From here, with Roth in tow, we can make it to the top in about six hours. Before the next dawn."

They both looked out into the dark once more.

"Sort of feels like we're sitting in my Jeep," said Kettler.

"Except no beers."

He opened his go pack and pulled out a can.

"You're shitting me," she said in amazement.

He popped the top and handed it to her.

She gripped the can. "It's cold. How'd you manage that?"

"Like I told you before, I have my go pack at the ranger station at all times when I'm on duty, just in case of emergencies, or if I want to hike or climb when I'm off duty. One beer is always in there with a battery-powered 'freeze sleeve.' Kind of my one indulgence. When I was in the Middle East, the platoon always looked forward to beer night." He paused, and his smile faded. "It was really the only thing we looked forward to. Except getting shipped home."

"I'm sure, Sam." She took a long sip and then handed it back to him. "Damn, now I need a cigarette."

He grinned, took a swig, and looked down at the can, his features turning first contemplative, and then grim.

She studied him. "Something on your mind?"

He shrugged. "What the hell. Might as well tell you."

"Tell me what?"

He handed her the beer. "I was leading a foot patrol in this little village, about a hundred clicks outside of Fallujah. Kid, couldn't have been more than ten or eleven, came out of his house, his mud shack, really. I could've knocked it over with a kick. We had some candy. We gave it to him. Had a translator with us. Asked the kid about some Al-Qaeda reported to be in the area. He didn't know anything, so he said. Then this old woman shows up and she's angry as hell. Turns out she's the kid's granny. She grabbed him, told us to get out. She kept screaming and getting angrier and angrier. Some of the young men in the village started to gather. So we headed out. I took the rear flank."

He stopped. Beads of sweat had sprouted on his forehead. Pine didn't think it was from the heat.

She handed him the beer back. "Here, drink this."

He took a swallow of beer and continued. "When I looked back, the kid had an AK-47. I think Granny had it hidden under her clothing. Damndest thing. And Granny, well, she had a grenade." He stopped again, the look on his face one of disbelief. "The damn gun was bigger than he was. But he knew how to handle it. I could tell that right away." He licked his lips. "My guys hadn't even noticed any of this yet."

Sensing where this was going, Pine put a hand on his arm. She could feel the heat there.

"I looked at him and then his granny. I've never..." He licked his lips again and swallowed with some difficulty. "I've never seen hatred like that in my life. Didn't even know me and hated my guts. Both of them."

"They hated what you represented and why you were there, Sam."

"I shot the kid in the leg. I didn't want to kill him. Just stop him from shooting me and my guys. But the round must have clanged off a bone and caught his femoral. It was a geyser. He was dead just like that. Just fell to the dirt and then..."

"You don't have to do this," said Pine, squeezing his arm. "You don't have to say any more."

Kettler shook his head, kept going. "Granny looked down at him and then screamed. She looked back up at me, tears streaming down her face. She was getting ready to pull the pin and throw the grenade at us." He paused but only for a second. "I shot her, too. In the head." He stopped and looked at her. "You want to know why?"

Pine didn't say anything, which he apparently took as assent.

"I figured she wouldn't want to live. So I killed her. I was acting like God, but I wasn't. I'm not. I didn't know shit about shit at that moment."

"You did what you were trained to do. You saved your guys."

"Yeah, trained to kill kids and grannies. Not what I signed up for, Atlee. Really wasn't. No way in hell. It's been over ten years and I still have nightmares about it. I'm pulling the trigger over and over. And they just keep dying."

"You had no other options, Sam. You were caught in an impossible situation."

He glanced over at her. "The night I came by with the beers?"

"Yeah?"

"I had that nightmare. Came out of it soaked in sweat. And then… I thought about calling you and just…seeing you. It…helped."

"I'm glad, Sam."

They sat in silence for about a minute. The only sounds were the wind and the pounding of water from the river below.

She slipped off her jacket and held up one bare arm, showing her tats. "Mercy was my twin."

"*Was?* What happened to her?"

"Somebody came into our bedroom one night and took her when we were six. I never found out what happened to her."

"God, Atlee. I'm so sorry."

"I guess that was the reason I joined the Bureau." She glanced at Kettler. "To make sure other people get justice because…because Mercy never did."

He took her hand and squeezed it. "Can't think of a better way to spend your life."

"I don't really talk about it. Sort of like you." She looked around. "But now I figured, what the hell, right? Tomorrow seems a long way off, if it ever comes."

Kettler nodded and said slowly, "I thought I could beat this on my own. But." He shook his head. "I'm…I'm going to get some counseling. The VA has a place not that far off. I've got to get this figured out. I came out to this place thinking maybe working here would do the trick, but it hasn't."

"Counseling is good, Sam. Really good."

"Well, we'll have to see about that." He sighed and looked away. "You ever think about getting some counseling too? With your sister and all?"

Pine didn't answer him.

58

THE HEAT OF THE DAY passed with no choppers coming for them. And no teams of uniformed soldiers with M4s scaling the trails after them, either. The reason might have been obvious: The daylight revealed everything.

The rains kicked in while Kettler and Pine had taken turns sleeping. When they rose at ten p.m., the weather system had passed, and the skies had cleared a bit. They woke Roth, and the three of them ate and drank enough to fuel themselves for the final assault to the North Rim.

As they roped up, Kettler put his hand on Roth's shoulder. "Okay, Dave, here's the deal. We got some switchbacks coming up and they're steep. But we'll get through them. Then it's long and rough, but doable. Then we get a few miles of fairly flat terrain. After that, we're going to head east where the trail forks. There are more switchbacks, and it's a lot more rugged than the trail to the west, but it's miles shorter. You just watch me and take it slow and easy, and before the light comes, we're going to be on paved surface roads. Sound good?"

"But what about the pack? It's my turn to carry it."

"Atlee and I have decided to divvy up that duty."

"But it's not fair to the two of you."

"You've been down in this Canyon a long time. We haven't. It drains you. Every person has to look at themselves and see what's best for the team and mission. Same thing you and your team probably do when inspecting WMDs."

Roth put a hand on Kettler's shoulder. "It is. And...thanks."

Kettler hoisted the lift pack, and they set off.

Roth struggled at times, and even Pine felt herself having to dig down into extra reserves of strength and endurance. She marveled at Kettler, who just seemed to move like a fluid machine. Even with the lift pack, she could see where he was actually pulling the other two along, making the burden of the climb easier for them, and, correspondingly, harder for himself.

They turned east at the fork and reached the steep switchbacks.

Kettler glanced back at Roth and put up his hand for them to stop.

"I'm...I'm okay," said Roth breathlessly.

Kettler came back down to him. "Yeah, but I need a breather. My calves are spasming a little. And Atlee can take over the pack."

"Okay, if you say so," replied Roth, who collapsed to the ground.

Pine gave Kettler an appreciative look.

Then her features tightened.

Whump-whump-whump.

The sounds of the chopper prop came out of nowhere.

"Headlamps off," snapped Kettler.

They all switched off their lamps.

Kettler grabbed Roth and pulled him under some scrub pines. Pine quickly joined them.

They all squatted there, frozen, as the searchlight started moving across the steep terrain, like a luminous spider gliding over glass.

Pine found herself holding her breath. The only good thing was there was no place here for the chopper to land.

But then she envisioned a cannon opening up on them from the air if the light found them. She gripped the M4 and thought how best to shoot out the chopper's tail prop, if need be.

It seemed like the aircraft hovered over them for an eternity. But Pine's watch showed it was only a couple of minutes. Then it rose, moved to the east, cleared a ridge, and was gone.

They didn't move for a few more minutes, just to make sure.

Finally, when the sounds didn't return, they all came out from hiding.

"You ready to go?" said Kettler calmly.

"I'm ready," said a visibly shaken Roth.

Kettler helped Pine on with the lift pack, and they started climbing once more.

Shortly after, the trail steepened considerably.

And the rain started up again, stinging them in the face. As Roth took a step up on a narrow path that was unnervingly close to the edge of a long fall, the stone gave way and part of the drenched trail crumbled.

With a scream, Roth fell to the side, clawing at the air. And then, with a shriek of terror, he went over the edge.

His plummeting weight immediately pulled hard on Pine, who fell face-first. The full weight of the nuke and the lift pack slammed into her back, smashing her against the dirt and forcing all the air from her lungs.

Down below, Roth dropped lower, dangling from the hitched rope around his waist. He was swinging and trying to grab the rope. This just unsettled things more on the trail as his constantly shifting weight pulled Pine ever closer to the edge. She slid across rock and mud and cacti, as she frantically tried to halt her momentum.

At the other end of the rope line, Kettler was struggling mightily to keep from getting pulled over, too.

As Roth continued to windmill below, Pine's face was now over the edge. She did not want the rest of her to follow. She pressed the palms of her hands into the rocky terrain and pushed hard backward, to keep herself from going over. It was like she was bench-pressing a thousand pounds.

"Shit!" she cried out. She was being stretched to her limit.

The next moment Kettler called out, "Atlee, I'm going to pull back as a counterweight. If I get too close to the edge with you, we're all going over. Once I get stabilized we'll work out a solution. Just hold on."

She gritted her teeth and nodded to show she understood.

Her face peering over the edge, she saw Roth dangling about fifteen feet below her. And after that it was an insanely long drop to certain death.

"David," she screamed. "Stop moving. We're figuring this out up here, but your flailing around is not helping."

Roth, to his credit, instantly became motionless.

Pine tensed every muscle in her body, gripped the jagged rocks embedded into the cliff and tried to lever herself backward some more. But with Roth's dead weight, it was a stalemate. If she hadn't been as strong as she was, Pine would have already gone over the precipice. The added weight of the nuke she was carrying was actually helping her, acting as an additional counterweight to Roth's mass. Yet having the thing pressing down on top of her wasn't exactly pleasant.

Kettler cried out, "Okay, Atlee, I'm going to toss you a rope with a D-link. Snap it into the one around your waist. Do not wrap the rope around you, just snap it into the link."

She nodded again and slowly looked to the side where he was.

Kettler had wrapped the rope connecting him to Roth around a massive rock wedged against the side of the trail. This had stabilized and secured Roth's weight load on his end.

He held up the second rope with the link, so she could see it.

"Here it comes."

The link landed right next to her left hand. She snapped it into the other link that was connected to the stout climbing rope around her waist.

"Okay, good," said Kettler, who'd been watching her.

He took the other end of the rope and, as he had his own line, wrapped it several times around the large rock and then tied it off securely.

Pine understood why he hadn't wanted her to tie the rope around her waist. Roth's dead weight was already exerting enormous pressure on her frame. Wrapping another rope around her could have, if things went wrong, sufficed to squeeze her like a constrictor had a hold of her. Now if she was pulled over by Roth's weight, this rope and the other one Kettler had tied around the large rock would hopefully prevent her and Roth from falling to their deaths. The only dilemma now was that she was literally caught between a rock and a hard place.

Kettler raced over with a fresh loop of rope and a D-link.

He touched Pine's arm. "Are you holding up?"

She nodded, the pain in her features. "But I can't do this forever."

"You won't have to."

He peered over the edge. "Dave, I'm going to feed this rope down. Snap the D-link into the one you already have on, okay?"

Roth nodded and Kettler fed the rope down.

Roth grabbed it on his second try and clicked the link into place.

Kettler took the other end of the rope, ran back to the large rock, and clipped this line into the one he'd already secured around the rock, making sure that it was taut.

He hustled back to the edge and peered over. "You're secured to a large rock up here. Now, I'm going to unlink you and Atlee."

"No!" screamed Roth. "Don't! I'll fall."

"You're *not* going to fall. The rock you're secured to weighs about five thousand pounds. That's the belt. And the line I just fed down to you will serve as the suspenders, just in case. Now, I need to free Atlee, so she can help me pull you up. Now, when I release the line, you might drop a few inches, but you are not going to fall, okay? I've got *two* lines securing you."

"Oh, God, oh please, God," they could hear him moaning.

Pine called out, "David, we are not going to lose you, okay? This is a good plan. And it's the only one we have, okay?"

Roth finally called up, "O-okay."

Kettler looked at Pine. "You ready to be unhitched?"

"My back sure as hell is."

With a mighty struggle, because of Roth's dead weight pulling on Pine, he managed to release the D-link connecting her to Roth.

Roth cried out as he dropped but quieted when he was held in place by the other ropes.

Pine let out a long, tortured breath.

"I need this frigging bomb off me. Now!"

Kettler released the bindings and, with a struggle, managed to get it off her.

She lay there breathing hard.

"Atlee, I need you to help me pull," said Kettler, a bit of anxiety creeping into his voice, as the rain continued to pelt them.

She could understand his nervousness. If the chopper came back now, they were all dead.

"I know you do, just give me a sec." She took several deep breaths. "Okay, I'm ready."

"Great, but we're taking no chances."

In a flash Kettler had linked both of them to the ropes around the large rock.

When he came back over he handed her a pair of gloves he'd had in his pack. He'd already donned a pair.

They stood side by side on the edge of the trail.

Kettler looked at her and grinned encouragingly. "Okay, *almost* Olympian, let's see what you got."

She managed a weak smile in return and then blew on her gloved hands and rubbed them together. "Let's do it."

They squatted down and pulled and grunted and slid and lurched backward. The ground was very slick as the rain kept pouring, and a couple times their feet and fingers slipped, with the result that Roth was pulled up and then dropped down a few feet. But Pine was incredibly strong, and so was Kettler. Their combined efforts lifted Roth inch by inch until the top of his head appeared over the edge of the trail.

Kettler quickly tied the rope off so they would not lose this hard-fought gain.

He and Pine went right to the edge and squatted down again. They both put their hands under Roth's armpits.

"One, two, three, pull," said Kettler.

Roth's upper torso landed on the trail.

"Again," said Kettler.

And the rest of Roth followed. They all collapsed to the dirt and lay there for a few precious minutes, gasping for air, the sweat pouring down their faces, even as the rain drenched them.

They finally stood, undid all the ropes around the rock, linked themselves together once more, and began to set off, with Kettler now carrying the nuke pack.

"Th-thank you," Roth said to them both as they walked along.

"Don't thank us yet," Pine replied. "We're not to the top."

About twenty minutes of climbing later, Kettler looked back.

"It levels out in a bit. And after that is the Rim."

Pine checked the sky and then her watch. "How much longer?" she called ahead to Kettler.

"Couple hours or so."

"Let's push through," she said. At the higher elevations the dawn would not be delayed.

She pulled out her phone and was thrilled to see several bars. She punched in the number, praying the call would go through. The person answered sleepily on the third ring.

"It's Atlee. You said if I needed any help, I just had to ask. Well, I'm asking."

*   *   *

About two and a half hours later, they reached the North Rim. Kettler put his hand up and the others immediately stopped. Roth collapsed to the ground, breathing hard.

Kettler set the lift pack down, came back to them, and undid the ropes holding them together. He squatted down and surveyed the area up ahead with a practiced gaze.

"So what's the plan now?" asked Kettler. "I don't like being exposed up here. That chopper could land anywhere along here."

Pine looked to the sky, watching out for lights cutting through the dark over the Canyon.

If the chopper did come and land, she told herself she would just open fire, aiming for the fuel tanks.

"I've got help coming. They should be here soon."

"Let's hope it's soon *enough*," replied Kettler.

Thirty minutes later, a pair of headlights did cut through the darkness, but they were coming along the road, not through the air. Kettler swung his M4 around and took aim at the approaching vehicle.

"Stand down," said Pine quickly, as the vehicle came close enough for her to see it clearly. "I know them."

The Chevy Suburban stopped in front of them, and Joe and Jennifer Yazzie climbed out.

Joe Yazzie Sr. was a big, burly man. His dark hair, worn long, was shot through with gray. His skin was leathered from living his whole life in a desert environment, and he walked with a bit of a limp.

Pine knew this stemmed from a shot he'd taken to his thigh that was still healing.

He had on his police uniform and held a pump-action shotgun in his right hand, muzzle down.

"Atlee?" called out Jennifer.

"It's us," said Pine as the three of them came out of the shadows.

"Agent Pine? Are you okay?" Carol Blum had climbed out of the rear seat and was hurrying toward them.

"We're all fine."

The group met in the middle of the road. Pine introduced Roth and Kettler to the Yazzies and Blum.

Blum gripped Pine's hand. "I knew you'd find him."

"Well, I wouldn't be here without Sam's help."

Blum put a hand on Kettler's shoulder and mouthed the words, *Thank you.*

Joe Yazzie eyed her severely and said, "You didn't tell us much, Atlee. In fact, you really didn't tell us anything."

"I wish I could tell you everything, and one day I hope to. But right now, I have some things to do. And we don't have much time."

"Where do you want us to take you?"

"Tuba City, as fast as you can."

Joe looked surprised. "Tuba City? Why?"

"Because it's sovereign. And we have to bring something with us."

She and Kettler ran over and grabbed the lift pack. Together they brought it over and set it down next to the SUV.

Joe glanced at it suspiciously. "What the hell is that?"

"That," said Pine, "is our pot of gold at the end of the rainbow."

59

THEY HEADED NORTH to Jacob Lake, then hung a right and traveled east to Marble Canyon, finally dipping south to Tuba City. This was the fastest route, and still the trip took nearly three hours along U.S. Route 89A.

By the time they arrived, the sun was well up.

As they reached the outskirts of Tuba City, Joe Yazzie said to Pine, "What now?" She was in the rear seat directly behind him.

"Drive to the police station," said Pine.

Joe nodded and steered the Suburban in that direction. "Can you tell me anything?" he said as his wife looked on anxiously. "Because I'm not looking to lose my career over crap I don't even know about."

"What I can tell you is that there are some in our government planning some really bad things and I'm trying to stop them."

Joe nodded and then glanced at her in the rearview mirror. "Feds screwing people? Okay, I can understand that. What are you doing about it, considering that you're a fed yourself?"

Pine pointed to Roth. "He found some evidence that is vital to the case."

Joe appraised Roth in the rearview. "Is the evidence what's in that big pack in the back of my truck?"

"Partly, yes."

"And you're dealing with your people, right, not us?"

"Yes."

"That's good to hear," said Joe. "Because we don't enjoy a lot of our interactions with *your* government."

Jennifer quickly glanced at Pine and said, "Present company excluded."

"We're just trying to do the right thing, Joe," said Pine.

"So you people always say." He looked at Kettler. "And what's the Park Service's role in all this?"

"I'm just doing what Agent Pine is telling me to do," replied Kettler.

"Smart man," said Jennifer, with an impish grin aimed at Pine.

Joe did not smile. He said, "While the Navajo reservation *is* sovereign land, we can't grant you some kind of asylum, if that's what you're after. You're a federal employee. So is the park ranger. And this guy—" He indicated Roth. "I don't know what he is, but he's not Navajo."

"I'm not asking for asylum, Joe."

"Then what?"

"Just trust me. You'll see. I swear."

Joe was about to say something when his wife put a hand on his shoulder and nodded.

"We trust you, Atlee," she said.

Joe glanced at his wife for a long moment and then returned his gaze to the windshield.

They drove on.

* * *

The police station was in the middle of flat land. The building was the color of terra cotta, with the round main structure architecturally enhanced by wooden pergola wings.

As they all trooped in, some of the staff and police officers looked at them curiously, and others suspiciously. Joe Yazzie said tersely, "Official business," and kept walking.

Pine, Roth, and Kettler cleaned up in the restrooms of the station.

Jennifer had hot coffee and some vending machine food ready for them when they came out.

Blum helped her pass out the hot coffee and food. She touched Atlee on the arm. "I can't tell you how good it is to see you, Agent Pine."

"We had a few close calls, Carol. But we made it. Now comes the really hard part."

They ate and sipped the coffee in Joe Yazzie's little office, while he and his wife looked on.

"I want to know what's going on," said Joe when they were done. "Right now. You're in my country and it's my rules. So, no more help until you tell me."

Pine looked from Yazzie to his wife. "I never told you this. Anybody ever asks, you don't know anything."

Jennifer glanced nervously at her husband, but Joe kept his gaze resolutely on Pine. "I don't tell anybody anything ever," he replied firmly.

Pine drew a long breath and said, "In the back of your truck is a nuclear weapon."

"Dear God," said Jennifer as the blood drained from her face.

Roth stepped forward. "It's not armed. It can't go off."

"Says you," Joe snapped angrily. He looked furiously at Pine. "You had me drive a fucking nuke to Navajo land? To the police station? With my *wife* in the truck?"

"The weapon can't detonate," said Pine firmly. She pointed at Roth. "He does this shit for a living. And would you have preferred that I left it in the Canyon?"

"What are you going to do with it?" demanded Joe heatedly. "Because it's sure as hell not staying here."

"I'm actually taking it to my office."

"Your office!"

"That's what I said."

Joe shook his head, a disgusted look on his face. "Nukes. When in the hell will you people stop this crap?"

"I wish I had a good answer for you, Joe, but I don't. Now I need a few minutes alone with these folks."

Joe looked at his wife. "All right. Take all the time that you need. I'm going to go out to my truck. Any black chopper that comes near it, I'm going to shoot down. You cool with that?" he added gruffly.

"Knock yourself out, Joe."

After he and Jennifer left, Roth turned to Pine.

"You said you're taking the nuke to your office? Why?"

"Because when you're negotiating, you need some ammo. I'm betting that nuke has all the bullets I need."

Roth blanched. "What are you intending to do?"

Blum said, "You can trust Agent Pine, Mr. Roth. She knows what she's doing."

"But you have to understand, we're dealing with Goliath here."

Blum smiled and said, "Well, then, *David*, you're quite aptly named."

CHAPTER

60

A RE YOU INSANE?"

Clint Dobbs, the head of the FBI in Arizona, sounded like he was about to suffer a stroke, or have an anxiety attack, or both.

"I don't think so, sir, no," replied Pine calmly into the phone.

"Where the hell have you been all this time?" demanded Dobbs.

"On the vacation you told me to take, sir."

"Damn it, you haven't answered any calls or emails."

"There's no service where I was, sir. I'm just back now."

"Do you realize how long you've been gone?"

"Yes, sir, to the day."

"And you want to meet at your office in Shattered Rock?"

"Yes, sir, and bring some reinforcements, like I asked. I'm talking Hostage Rescue Team, long guns, body armor, the works."

"Do not be insubordinate. I'm *not* coming to Shattered Rock. You can come to Phoenix."

"I would, sir, but I have something at my office that I can't really transport."

"What the hell are you talking about?"

"Just trust me, sir."

"I don't see why I should. I've already gotten an earful from the DD about you."

Pine drew a deep breath. "I think the DD might be involved

in what's going on." *Which is the reason I'm calling you and not him*, she said to herself.

"What in the hell are you saying? That sort of talk could cost you your shield, Pine."

"Why else would he have intervened and had you call me off this case, sir? Wasn't that extraordinary on his part? I mean, what does the DD care about a dead mule?"

Dobbs didn't say anything for a long moment. Then: "What the hell are you involved in, Pine?"

"Something bigger than I could have ever imagined, sir. That's why I need your help and support. I can't do it alone. And if the DD won't do it, I need you to have my back, sir."

"And why do I need to bring reinforcements?" asked Dobbs after another few moments of silence.

"Because I expect company here."

"Company? What do you mean, some criminals? A gang?"

"Depends on how you define that, sir, but this company might actually be more dangerous."

"Look, Pine, this is beyond ridiculous. If you think—"

She broke in, "Sir, I would not be asking this if it were not absolutely critical. Once you get here you will understand exactly what is going on. It's a matter of national security. Not just for this country, but for the world." She paused. "I'm trying to do my job, sir, as an FBI agent. I gave an oath. I intend to carry that oath out."

She once more listened to him breathing.

"You're really not joking, are you?"

"I have never been more serious in my life."

"You haven't been on vacation, have you?"

"I would not call it a vacation, no, sir."

"Your career hangs in the balance on this, Pine."

"A lot more than my career hangs in the balance, sir."

There was a short pause. "I'll be there in three and a half hours."

"And don't forget the reinforcements I asked for."

Dobbs already had clicked off.

Pine sighed.

Well, here goes nothing.

* * *

Later, Pine and Blum waited in the Yazzies' Suburban down the street from their office in Shattered Rock. It was important that they arrive at the same moment as Dobbs and his men.

"Did you and Sam get the package into our office okay?" Pine asked.

"No problem. We went in through the garage so no one could see us." Blum paused. "Although, I have to say, it's a little unsettling how easy it was to get a nuclear weapon into a building housing federal agents."

"Nobody stopped you?"

"One ICE agent that I know did. I told him it was a new credenza for the office. He even helped us carry it in."

Pine stiffened as a black SUV drove past at speed down the empty street. It pulled to a stop in front of the office building and the doors opened.

Clint Dobbs, around six feet tall and in his fifties with thinning gray hair, broad shoulders, a thick neck, and the beginnings of a paunch, got out of the truck's rear passenger seat. He was followed by five other agents.

"Shit, he didn't bring enough guys," said Pine. "No HRT. No long guns. Just suits and pistols. Why the hell don't some people listen?"

Pine put the SUV in gear and hit the gas.

They shot forward and pulled to a stop with a screech against the curb.

Pistols came out of holsters and were pointed at the SUV until

Pine and Blum got out and showed themselves. Pine had grabbed a bag and slung it over her shoulder.

Dobbs looked apoplectic. "What the hell are you doing?"

Pine strode over to him. "Waiting for you to show, sir." She looked at the other agents. "I asked for HRT, long guns, armor, sir. Why is this all you brought?"

"I have five armed agents with me. What are you expecting? A war?"

"Pretty much. But it is what it is now. No going back now. Let's go."

Pine strode off toward the building.

Dobbs looked incredulously at Pine and then his gaze shifted to Blum. A spark of recognition came over his features. "I know you, don't I?"

"Carol Blum. I was your secretary back in your Flagstaff days."

"That's right." He looked around. "Well, I'm sorry you ended up here working for what looks to me to be an agent unraveling."

"Oh, don't feel sorry for me, Mr. Dobbs. Agent Pine is the sort of agent the FBI should be proud of. And when you find out what she's done, you'll see that she's far from unraveling."

"Exactly what *is* she doing?"

"Saving the world, more or less."

She hurried on after Pine, leaving Dobbs looking bewildered and a little put out. He motioned to his men. "Well, all right, let's go." He looked warily around but the quiet surroundings seemed to appease him.

"War, my ass," he muttered.

Inside, Pine let them all into the office and turned off the alarm system.

She closed the door behind the last agent and made sure it was secure.

"All right," said Dobbs. "Now you're going to tell me what the hell is going on."

"If you would step into my office."

She led them into the inner space and closed the door.

Pine walked over to the closet door of her office, opened it, and pointed to the bulky object set in the corner with a canvas cover over it.

"What is that?" asked Dobbs.

In answer Pine unzipped the canvas covering the object.

Dobbs said, "What the hell is that?"

"That is what is called a tactical nuclear weapon," said Pine.

Dobbs and his men took a collective step back. Dobbs barked, "What in the hell . . . A nuke!"

"It was hidden in a cave at the bottom of the Grand Canyon."

"Hidden? Hidden by whom?" demanded Dobbs.

"Ah, now that goes right to the heart of the matter, doesn't it?" She closed the door.

"And you *will* tell me right after I call Washington and tell them that we have a nuke in a damn FBI RA office."

"Sir."

He strode over and pointed a finger in her face. "Not another word. My God, Pine, of all the screwups I thought I had seen, this just—"

"Oh, Clint, for God's sake, can you just close your mouth for one minute and let her explain?" said Blum in exasperation. "This is important."

He glared at her. "Clint? You will address me as—"

"I think I'm retiring, so I'll just leave it at Clint." She looked expectantly over at Pine. "Special Agent Pine?"

Pine looked at Dobbs. "I take it that you saw the AED of the National Security Branch was on the email chain about the dead mule and missing person case."

Dobbs's expression turned petulant. "I don't read down the cc list."

Before Pine could respond, the sounds of boots hammered

up the stairs and rolled like a tidal wave down the hall. A few moments later, the sounds of the front door being caved in by a hydraulic ram reached them.

"What the hell is that?" exclaimed Dobbs as he and his men whirled toward the only remaining door between them and whatever was out there.

Pine took out her pistol and pointed it at the door. She looked at the other agents and held up her gun. "Gentlemen?"

They all looked at each other, drew their weapons, and stood next to Pine, their guns pointed at the door. Even Dobbs took out his weapon.

"What the hell is coming, Pine?" hissed Dobbs.

"That would be the war, sir," she replied.

61

THE INNER DOOR was hit so hard, it fell off its hinges. Into the breech charged a dozen heavily armored personnel with combat helmets and carrying either M4s or M16s.

With his free hand Dobbs immediately held up his badge and barked, "Federal agents, weapons down."

Not a single combat weapon was lowered. The armored men formed a wall across the width of the room, shoulder to shoulder, their long guns pointed at the FBI contingent across from them.

"FBI!" barked Dobbs again. "I said weapons down."

Still, not a single weapon was lowered.

"Who are you with?" demanded Dobbs as his men nervously fingered their pistols.

Twelve auto assault rifles wielded by armored shooters against seven semiauto pistols held by agents in suits in a confined space would not be much of a fight.

Suddenly, the middle of their ranks parted and a man in his fifties, dressed in a dark suit, white shirt, striped tie, and scuffed wingtips, stepped through this void.

He appeared to be in charge of the assault team.

Dobbs focused on him and barked, "We are the FBI, so unless you put your weapons down now, you're going to be in a world of trouble."

The man said, "I was about to tell you the very same thing."

There was a commotion in the other room. The next moment, five ICE agents carrying AR-15s burst into the room and pointed their weapons at the armored men and the man in the suit.

Half the armored men pointed their guns at the ICE agents while the other half-dozen kept their guns trained on Dobbs and his agents.

"Federal agents," cried out the ICE point man. "Weapons down. Now!"

The three groups of armed people seemed to be in a standoff.

Dobbs stared triumphantly at the man in the suit. "Okay, we've got you surrounded. So now you're going to put your weapons down."

The man said calmly, "No, we're not. We're here to collect these two women." He pointed at Pine and Blum.

Dobbs said, "For what?"

"Treason against the United States."

One of the ICE agents stepped forward and looked at Pine.

"Bullshit. Atlee Pine is no traitor. Now who the hell are you?"

The man drew out a phone, punched in a number, and spoke into it in a low voice.

He held the phone out to the ICE agent. "Your director wants to speak to you."

The man blinked. "The director?"

"Harold Sykes? Director of DHS? Yes, he's on the line."

The agent took the phone. "Who is this?" He snapped to attention after no doubt recognizing the voice of the head of Homeland Security.

"Yes, sir. What? No. I mean. But she's an FBI agent. I know her. No, I'm not saying…But a traitor. I…no sir…Yes, sir, right away, sir."

Looking thoroughly beaten down, he handed the phone back to the man and looked over at Pine with a helpless expression. "I'm sorry, Atlee."

"It's okay, Doug, we'll get this figured out."

Doug slowly turned to his men. "Okay, let's move out."

"Sir?" said one of them.

"I said let's move out!" barked Doug.

In a few seconds, ICE had vacated the field of battle, leaving the men in armor and the FBI agents.

The man in the suit turned to Dobbs.

Dobbs pulled his phone from his jacket and said, "Okay, I'm calling *my* director right now, asshole."

The man smiled. "Better yet, how about I call *his* boss, the attorney general, and have him order you to turn these women over to us?"

Dobbs glanced at Pine. "There is no way in hell that Pine or Blum are traitors."

"Your opinion on the subject is absolutely irrelevant."

Dobbs gathered his composure and began speaking in a calm tone. "Fine. You show me the appropriately signed off indictments issued by a U.S. attorney, and we'll arrest them right here, read them their rights, take them to a federal holding cell, and then we can move forward through the court system."

The man had started shaking his head halfway through. "This is national security, not a court matter."

Dobbs exploded. "I don't give a shit if it's jaywalking." He pointed to Pine and Blum. "These women are American citizens. Innocent until proven guilty. Right to due process. I'm sure these things are familiar to you, that is, if you *are* an American, which, frankly, I'm beginning to doubt."

"Okay, we're done here. Lower your weapons."

"No!" barked Dobbs. "Go to hell."

"I can call the AG right now and he can order you to do it."

"You can call the fucking president and my answer would be the same."

"You're way out of line," barked the man.

"*I'm* out of line?" exclaimed Dobbs. "We're federal agents!"

"I said we're done here. Lower your weapons or they will open fire. Last chance."

The FBI agents were nervously glancing at each other. They knew, to a man, that this would be a slaughter. Yet they held their line and did not lower their weapons.

"Very well," said the man, shaking his head, as he stepped back behind the wall of armor. "You can't say I didn't give you the opportunity."

Now Pine stepped forward. "Okay, I think this testosterone show has gone on long enough. We need to begin the negotiations."

The man looked incredulous. "Negotiations? You have nothing to negotiate with."

In response, Pine walked over to the closet door and opened it, revealing the nuke. "I have this."

The man snapped, "How the hell did *that* get here?"

"Some people decided to do the right thing."

The man gazed at her with contempt. "Who? David Roth?"

"I won't get into specifics."

"You're all traitors," barked the man.

"Or *patriots*, at least from my point of view."

The man glanced at Dobbs. "Now do you understand why we need to take them? They've got a nuclear bomb."

"How did you know it was a nuclear bomb?" said Pine. "From here it looks like just a metal box."

The man blanched and glanced at Dobbs, who was staring at him grimly.

"Yeah, how did you know it was a bomb? I didn't until Pine told me it was a nuke."

"A *Russian* nuke," said Pine.

"Russian!" exclaimed Dobbs, glancing sharply at her before looking back at the man. "Are they Russians?"

"No, they're Americans working with the Russians. I actually knocked two Russians out who were snooping around Ben Priest's home." Pine gazed at the man in the suit. "And you guys got stung by Moscow. Really badly."

"What the hell are you talking about?" exclaimed the man.

Pine put the bag she'd brought with her on her desk and pulled out the surveillance devices and dropped them on the wood. "Your Russian *friends* included multiple cameras and listening devices inside the nuke."

A few moments of silence so profound passed that Pine thought she could hear every smack of her heart as well as those of the agents on either side of her.

The man said, "How do I know you're not lying?"

Pine tossed him one of the devices. "You must have had blind faith in your Moscow buddies." She also tossed him one of the panel pieces that Roth had cut out. "I bet old Putin is smiling somewhere right now."

The man took the device and the metal piece, walked over to the nuke, and placed the device inside a hole in the enclosure. Then he placed the piece of metal into the hole.

A perfect fit.

He looked at the other sides and noted the same holes in the metal.

Pine thought she heard him say, "Fuck."

The man turned around. "So the Russians have proof we placed a nuclear weapon in the Canyon. Where does that leave us? Isn't it game over?"

"No, because our side hasn't 'discovered' the nuke yet and made the case to go to war with North Korea."

"Why does that matter?" asked the man.

"Not starting a war and killing millions of people on bogus evidence that you trumpeted to the world is a helluva lot better than actually doing so. And that also means the Russians' blackmail scheme just got a lot weaker."

Blum stepped forward. "And it gives you the opportunity to craft a plausible explanation."

The man stared skeptically at her. "Such as?"

"Such as you placed a nonoperating nuclear device in a cave in a canyon because you were exploring alternative methods of storage and were checking environmental factors."

"Come again?" said the man.

Blum continued, "I used to do that with my old pennies when I was a child. In holes I dug in my backyard. Come to think, it's far more plausible than trusting the Russians with the goal of blowing up North Korea. I mean, who would believe we would actually be *that* stupid?"

The man looked at her dully but said nothing.

"Or you can claim all the evidence they had was fake," added Blum. "That seems to be a pretty popular tactic these days."

The man shook his head. "No, that's not going to work." He looked pointedly at the armed men he had brought with him. "All of you are coming with us until we can sort this out. Now!"

"There's something else you need to know," Pine said. "We have *electronic* documentation of everything you've said tonight."

The man flinched and looked around. "What?"

"My office is wired for video and sound."

"And why do you have that feature in your office?" asked the man incredulously.

"I put it in after some goon attacked me. After I kicked his ass, he said I attacked him. So it's to make sure it doesn't ever again come down to she-said-he-said. It's already been uploaded to a secure cloud."

"How do I know you're not bluffing?"

"That's the beauty of it. You don't."

Blum stepped forward. "And just so you know, I've worked closely with Agent Pine for quite a while now. And never, not once, have I known her to bluff."

The man shifted his gaze from Blum to Pine. "And your point?"

"If anything happens to me, Ms. Blum, David Roth, anyone

connected to this case, or anyone else in this room, I'm talking everything from a hangnail to a job demotion to murder, your involvement in all of this *will* come out."

The man stared at her for several long moments. He looked down at the surveillance device he still held in his hand and then over at the bomb. Finally, he glanced up at Pine and his features took on a resigned look.

Reading his expression, she added, "It's the only way any of us get out of this. I think you're plenty smart enough to see that."

Another few seconds of silence passed, while everyone held their collective breaths.

The man said, "All right. Anything else?"

"Ben and Ed Priest?" she said.

The man licked his lips nervously and said quickly, "What do you want?"

"They sure as hell better be alive. Or else all of you are going down."

He hesitated for a moment. "They're alive."

"Then I want them back safe and sound and with appropriate compensation for the shit you put them through. And I'll check on that, so don't screw with me."

"Done. So long as they won't breach any, uh, confidences."

"You're also going to owe a lot of money to Oscar Fabrikant's family. And while you're at it, throw a ton of cash to the Society for Good. I think we need more, not less, good. And we know about Fred Wormsley. So, his family will be receiving substantial financial support for his *patriotic* service to his country."

"All right, anything else?" the man said tightly.

Her features turned somber. "There are three bodies in a cave in the Grand Canyon. Three of *your* guys."

"You killed three of our men?" said the man incredulously.

"Well, I didn't have much choice, considering they were trying to kill me. But I want their bodies retrieved and turned over to their families. And if they *were* military, I want their families to be taken care of. And their service records will not reflect any of this. They go out clean with full honors."

"How magnanimous of you," he said sarcastically.

"They were killed following orders, probably *your* orders. My beef wasn't with them. I would have much preferred to have shot *you*."

"I'll keep that in mind," he said testily. "In case you and I run across each other again."

She looked at him, a smile playing over her lips. "You could have taken me along with the Priest brothers. Or you just could have killed me. But you didn't."

"Well, all I can say is, I don't make the same mistakes twice."

She studied him. "You wanted me to keep working the investigation."

Dobbs said, "But, Pine, why would they want that?"

"Because they needed help to find Roth and the bomb."

"We could have just captured you and made you tell us where Roth was."

"Later on, you made attempts to do just that at the airport and at the apartment where I was staying but failed. What you *did* know was that a nuke was in a cave in the Grand Canyon. Only it was no longer in the cave where your people had originally put it. So, you thought you'd enlist me, however unwittingly, to find it for you. You just expected your men to capture me when I got to the bomb. Only they didn't."

The man's face had lost its sneer and he looked at her with grudging admiration. "Maybe I hope our paths *don't* cross again."

She hooked a finger in the direction of the closet. "And you'll need to take that thing. I don't think the Bureau has a nuclear weapons rider on its liability insurance."

"I already had that on my to-do list," he replied sarcastically. "Anything else?"

"One more thing. Maybe the most important of all."

"What?"

Pine gathered herself and blurted out, "Stop trusting the freaking Russians. They are *not* our friend."

The man looked at her strangely for a moment and then turned to his men, pointed to the closet, and said, "Get that thing and then let's go."

The personnel instantly lowered their weapons. Four of them hustled over to the closet and lifted up the bomb. They all filed out of the room.

The suit was the last to leave.

He looked directly at Pine. "You've done irreparable damage to this country."

"No, I think I actually just saved it. Along with a few million lives. My only regret is that you and every other idiot behind this won't be going to prison for the rest of your lives. Now get out of my office!"

The man stormed out, leaving six FBI agents and one FBI secretary exhaling long, relieved breaths. They all lowered their weapons, their arms collectively shaking from holding their weapons in a firing stance for so long.

A pale-faced Dobbs looked at Pine and barked, "What in the living hell was that, Pine?"

"Basically, Americans behaving really badly, sir."

Blum stepped over to face Dobbs. "While we're asking for things, we'll need the doors replaced. And Agent Pine needs a new chair."

Dobbs snorted but then looked at Pine. "You weren't bluffing that asshole, were you? About your office being wired and all?"

Pine opened her desk drawer, revealing a small metal box inside. She hit a button and a tray slid out. She took out the DVD inside the tray and handed it to Dobbs.

"FBI agents don't bluff, sir. At least not when it really matters."

He looked down at the DVD and then glanced up at her.

She said, "I would respectfully suggest that you use that to full advantage."

Dobbs nodded again, pocketed the DVD, and then glanced around the room before looking at Blum.

"Hell, buy all-new stuff for this place, Carol. Your office included. And send me the bill."

"Thank you, SAIC Dobbs."

Dobbs and his men left.

Now it was just Pine and Blum.

Pine sat in her rickety chair while Blum perched on the edge of the desk.

"Well, thank God that's over," remarked Blum.

"*Is* it over, Carol?"

"Well, for tonight it is."

"I'll take that," said Pine. "And by the way, you can't retire. I need you."

Blum smiled sweetly. "Oh, I'm not retiring, Agent Pine. Unlike you, I was just *bluffing*."

62

HOW'S THE COUNSELING GOING?"

It was around ten at night and Pine and Kettler were once more sitting in his Jeep in her parking lot drinking beer.

"Not bad, actually," he said, taking a swig from his bottle. "The place isn't that far away. And I like the one-on-one sessions. The group ones not so much."

"I can relate. But it'll get easier, Sam."

"You think?"

"It's what I believe." She reached out and gripped his hand. "I'm rooting for you. Any guy that can get us out of the Grand Canyon like you did, can do anything."

"Oh, by the way, Colson and Harry are back at the Grand Canyon."

"Yeah, I thought that might happen," said Pine.

"So, how did things turn out with the nuke and stuff?" he asked.

"For now, good. Down the road, who knows?"

They sat for a few moments in silence, staring at the star-filled sky.

"If I get better—" he began.

"*When* you get better," she corrected.

"Right. When I get better, can we sit and have some more beers like this?"

"In your Jeep? Damn straight. That night was pretty much in my top three of all time."

"What were the other times?"

"Our date at Tony's Pizza." She paused. "And right now."

He smiled and then his grin faded. "Thanks, Atlee. For everything."

"I'm not sure I did all that much."

"You did more than anyone else ever has."

She smiled. "That's nice of you to say, Sam."

"So, are you doing therapy, too?"

"In a way, I am," Pine replied. She finished her beer and said, "I better hit the sack. Tomorrow's going to be a busy day."

She kissed him on the cheek and started to get out of the Jeep.

He blurted out, "I'm not nuts, Atlee, I swear."

Pine leaned over and stroked his cheek with her hand. Smiling tenderly at him, she said, "Didn't you get the memo, Sam? We're all a little crazy. But there's strength in numbers."

* * *

Pine and Blum flew back to the East Coast and retrieved her Mustang from the long-term parking lot at Reagan National. While there, they visited the Priests in Bethesda.

Ben Priest was also convalescing at his brother's home.

When they had arrived at the home, Mary Priest answered the door. Though she had been informed of their visit, she looked in astonishment at Carol Blum.

"I know, dear," said Blum, patting her hand. "I felt awful deceiving you the way I did, but it was necessary to getting your husband back."

In reply, Mary put her arms around both of them and wept.

As they headed up to see Ben, they had seen the boys, Billy and Michael, coming out of their uncle's room. Ed was sitting in a chair next to the bed waiting for them.

Both brothers looked like they had been physically abused, but they appeared to be on the mend. Ben seemed to be in worse shape than his brother. He was pale and thin, and his expression was one of complete exhaustion.

Mary closed the door to give them privacy.

Pine sat on the edge of the bed, while Blum stood next to her.

"You saved our lives, Atlee," said Ed.

"After putting them in danger," she pointed out.

"But everything's good then?" said Ed.

"Until the next time the leaders in this country decide to do something stupid," replied Ben. He turned to look at Pine. "I heard about Simon and Oscar."

Pine nodded slowly. "I think the guys behind this would call that collateral damage. I would just call it murder. At least Simon's killer paid the price. The best I could get for Fabrikant was money for his family and dollars for the Society."

Ben said, "At first, when David Roth came to me, I thought he was nuts. But then I learned that certain parts of our government *had* gone nuts."

"And so you helped him do the right thing," said Pine.

"It was completely fortuitous that I had scheduled that mule ride. But it worked out perfectly."

"Not so much for poor Sallie Belle," said Pine. "But for the rest of humanity it worked out okay."

Ben put out his hand, which Pine took.

He said, "I underestimated you. I thought I was the pro and you were the amateur. Turns out, I got it backward."

"I will never understand the world you live in, Ben. And I never want to."

"I'm coming around to that notion myself. How's David?"

"The last I heard he was off on a long-overdue vacation at a place that only has very flat land."

"I think he more than earned it."

She looked at the brothers. "And this gives you some quality time together as a family. Never take that for granted. A lot of people don't have any family to enjoy."

Blum gazed keenly at Pine as she said this but remained silent.

* * *

Unlike the last time, Pine and Blum had taken a full week to drive cross-country in the Mustang. They had stopped along the way to take in more of America than either ever had.

Now they sat at a little roadside diner in Arkansas eating barbeque and drinking sweet iced tea at a picnic table while some little kids in T-shirts and shorts ran around playing tag. Pine said, "You know, this really is a beautiful country."

"It's actually lots of countries in one, and they each have their own individual beauty, and their own sets of issues." Blum bit off the end of a pickle after dipping it in hot sauce. "But there's a core of humanity and, oh, I don't know, *values* that we all share. Sort of the glue that holds us together." She paused and smiled. "It actually reminds me of my six kids."

"How so?"

"I can't remember one day while they were growing up that they all got along. Not a single day all those years. Someone was calling someone a name. One was hitting another. Two others were in a screaming match. And the two others were playing together and having a wonderful time. Then the next day *they'd* be at each other's throats."

"What do you take away from that?" asked Pine.

"All you can hope is that if one of them gets sick, or gets hurt, or really needs help, that the others will come to their aid. Other than that, I'm afraid all bets are off. Life is messy, and people are just deluding themselves if they think someone will just wave a wand and everyone will suddenly play nice in the sandbox. It's just not how we're wired, apparently." She paused once more to take a sip of her tea. "But I have to say, even with all that yelling and fighting, when there were good times, they were pretty damn great. Wouldn't trade 'em for anything."

They got back into the car, after putting the top down, and drove west.

"I could get used to this," said Blum. "Maybe we should make it an annual thing."

"Thelma," said Pine.

"What?"

"I have to be Thelma. You get to be Louise."

"Well, you and Geena Davis *are* about the same height. And I can't tell you how many people say I resemble Susan Sarandon," she added with a self-satisfied smile.

"So, we're good to go?"

"So good to go I could scream."

And Blum did just that, while waving her hands in the air like she was cheering at some sports competition.

Atlee Pine had never laughed harder in her life.

63

Pine sat in her newly renovated office, adjusting the controls on her state-of-the-art ergonomic office chair that could do just about anything except fly, although there might be a control for that, too, somewhere. She ran her hand over the mahogany wood of her new desk, looked down at the fresh carpet, and then over at the new solid wood door.

But when she glanced at the wall, the indentations were still there.

Blum had been of the opinion that they should remain as a deterrent. And Pine had heartily agreed.

Pine stared down at the news story on her laptop screen. The country was buzzing about some momentous changes that had taken place within the government. Some very-high-up leaders had suddenly announced their resignations. These included top generals at the Pentagon, the head of Homeland Security, and the attorney general, all with differing explanations, but none involving their participation in a foiled plot to blow North Korea off the map. Others had been reassigned in an unexpected shakeup that had caught many off-guard. And certain key advisors within the White House had also resigned, saying they wanted to spend more time with their loved ones. And the president had, out of the blue, announced that he might not seek reelection. Lastly, the peace talks with North Korea had been restarted, but now with South Korea and Japan in the lead roles.

Even by recent standards, it had been an extraordinary news cycle. Dobbs had evidently used the DVD to full advantage. She expected him to be nominated as deputy director any day now. Hell, she thought, maybe *he* should run for president.

Her office phone buzzed.

"Yes, Ms. Blum?"

"Special Agent Pine, there's a gentleman to see you."

"What about?"

"He's from Washington, DC, with a request."

"Okay."

The door opened, and Blum escorted in a short man who looked to be in his early thirties. He carried himself in a very cocksure manner. His features were sharp and his gaze even sharper. He was dressed in a blue suit, stiff white shirt, and solid tie, with a handkerchief carefully aligned in his breast pocket.

Pine stood. "What can I do for you…?"

The man said, "I'm Walter Tillman. I'm with the federal government."

"So many say, and yet it doesn't always turn out to be true. Can I see some ID?"

He took out his wallet and showed her an ID card with his picture on it.

"Okay, what do you want?"

"To formally invite you to DC."

"Why?"

"To talk with some folks there who want to meet you."

"Why?"

He flinched and his look darkened. "They think you're talented and want to recruit you to work on some matters for them directly."

"I already have a job."

He looked around the small office. "Look, no offense, but you're in a crummy office in the middle of nowhere."

"No, I'm in my FBI resident agency office in the middle of beautiful Arizona, within spitting distance of the only natural wonder of the world located in this country."

"Only this position would be far more prestigious, a kick up in the GS level, and a lot more money in your wallet."

"I didn't join the FBI to get rich. And I could give a damn about prestige."

"I'm not sure you understand. They want you in DC. At the highest levels."

"And I decline."

Now Tillman dropped all pretense of civility. "You think you're something, don't you? Because of what you did," he added with a snarl.

Pine looked over at the two indentations in the wall and was sorely tempted to add a third. "I tell you what, Walt. The day your guys get their shit together to *my* satisfaction, I'll think about it. But I won't be stupid enough to hold my breath on that. Anything else?"

"No, that's about it," he said sullenly.

"Good, because I have someplace to go. Ms. Blum will show you out."

As though she had been listening against the wood, the door opened and there was Blum.

Pine took her pistols out of her drawer and slipped them into her twin holsters. She grabbed her dark jacket off the chair, and, passing by Tillman without a word, said to Blum, "I'll be back in a couple of days."

"Safe travels, Special Agent Pine."

Pine left the office.

Down in the garage, Pine put on her sunglasses, took the car cover off, and stowed it in the trunk.

She fired up the Mustang and drove out into the sunshine.

She had a long drive ahead of her, and she was looking forward to every mile and minute of it.

The vintage car roared along, its big block V-8 eating up the highway as she went from Arizona on a diagonal through the southeastern corner of Utah, where she followed the flow of the Colorado River for a bit before cutting east and entering the Rocky Mountain state.

She stopped only once, for a restroom break and some dinner, which she ate in her car, looking at the stars swarming the big sky.

She held up her bottle of water and said, "See you soon, Sam."

Pine drove on, timing it so she arrived at ADX Florence about ten minutes before midnight. She got out of her car, slipped on her jacket, and clipped her FBI badge to her belt.

By the time she cleared security and was being escorted down the corridor to the visiting room, it was one minute to midnight.

She sat in the same seat and looked through the same wall of polycarbonate glass, awaiting his arrival.

Just like last time a half-dozen guards brought Daniel James Tor to her.

They chained him down and left, waiting just outside as before.

Tor popped his neck, placed his manacled hands in front of him, and eyed her curiously. And she figured he *had* to be curious, since he had agreed to see her again.

She reached into her pocket and took out the picture.

She looked at it for a moment.

The image of Mercy gazed back at her.

Pine placed it against the glass so that Tor could see Mercy staring back at him.

"Where's my sister?" she said.

ACKNOWLEDGMENTS

To Michelle, this book has a crackerjack female character who can eye roll with the best, which I know you will appreciate.

To Michael Pietsch, for going above and beyond.

To Lindsey Rose, for never, ever missing a single beat.

To Andy Dodds, Nidhi Pugalia, Ben Sevier, Brian McLendon, Karen Kosztolnyik, Beth deGuzman, Albert Tang, Brigid Pearson, Elizabeth Connor, Brian Lemus, Jarrod Taylor, Bob Castillo, Anthony Goff, Michele McGonigle, Cheryl Smith, Andrew Duncan, Joseph Benincase, Tiffany Sanchez, Morgan Swift, Stephanie Sirabian, Matthew Ballast, Jordan Rubinstein, Dave Epstein, Rachel Hairston, Karen Torres, Christopher Murphy, Ali Cutrone, Tracy Dowd, Martha Bucci, Rena Kornbluh, Lukas Fauset, Thomas Louie, Sean Ford, Laura Eisenhard, Mary Urban, Barbara Slavin, Kirsiah McNamara, and everyone at Grand Central Publishing, for continuing to reach higher and higher.

To Aaron and Arleen Priest, Lucy Childs, Lisa Erbach Vance, Frances Jalet-Miller, John Richmond, and Juliana Nador, for always being by my side.

To Mitch Hoffman, for pushing me on this book to such an extent that it went to ELEVEN (*Spinal Tap* reference!) on the final version.

To Anthony Forbes Watson, Jeremy Trevathan, Trisha Jackson,

Katie James, Alex Saunders, Sara Lloyd, Claire Evans, Sarah Arratoon, Stuart Dwyer, Jonathan Atkins, Anna Bond, Leanne Williams, Natalie McCourt, Stacey Hamilton, Sarah McLean, Charlotte Williams, and Neil Lang at Pan Macmillan, for being the best in the business. Can't wait to see the new digs!

To Praveen Naidoo and the team at Pan Macmillan in Australia, for raising your game with every book.

To Caspian Dennis and Sandy Violette, for being such great advocates and friends. Our tour-end annual dinner is something I always look forward to. Knickerbocker sundaes all around!

To Steven Maat and the entire Bruna team, for leading the way in Holland.

To Bob Schule, for your stellar work on reading through the manuscript.

To Mark Steven Long, for copyediting.

To my good friend Dr. Dana Ericksen, for all the hiking info on the Grand Canyon. The Heineken scene was for you, my friend!

To FBI Special Agent (retired) Bob Ulmer, for providing me with a ton of great information about the Bureau. And to his daughter Wendy Noory, for putting us in touch.

To Dana Schindler, for getting me great research sources, and being a wonderful friend.

To Anne and Paul Buellesbach, for sharing with me all your mule-riding adventures and cool information on the Canyon.

To charity auction winners Carol Blum (Amelia Island Book Festival's Authors in Schools), Sung Nam Chung (Robert F. Kennedy Human Rights), Colson Lambert (Project Kesher), and David Roth (The Mark Twain House & Museum), I hope you were suitably thrilled with your characters. And thanks for supporting such great causes.

To Benjamin Priest, with a belated bar mitzvah gift.

To Michelle Butler, for helping to make Columbus Rose a lean, mean writing machine!

ABOUT THE AUTHOR

David Baldacci is a global number one best-selling author, and one of the world's favorite storytellers. His books are published in over forty-five languages and in more than 80 countries, with over 130 million worldwide sales. His works have been adapted for both feature film and television. David Baldacci is also the cofounder, along with his wife, of the Wish You Well Foundation, a nonprofit organization dedicated to supporting literacy efforts across America. Still a resident of his native Virginia, he invites you to visit him at DavidBaldacci.com and his foundation at WishYouWellFoundation.org.